THE LAST HEIR

To the people who make life worth living

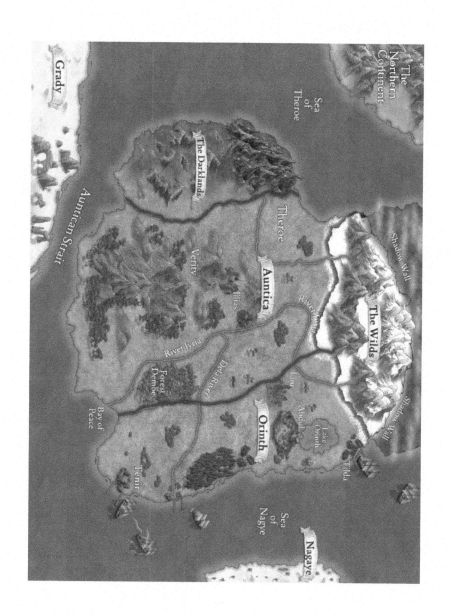

PART I

Chapter 1

Abdul, Orinth

Rider was never a fan of executions. Maybe it made him less of an Orinthian but then he didn't care about that. He never understood why the people of his country enjoyed them so much. They gathered at the gallows as if they were about to watch a sporting event. Their cheers were loud enough to shake the ground and make ears bleed. Money was wagered on so many aspects of the event; would the neck snap? And if not, how long would it take for him to strangle there? Would they cut him down immediately or let him hang there as a warning to others? An execution was a good source of income for brokers around their capital city. They were infrequent, but maybe that was the reason they drew as many people as they did.

Whatever the reason was, Rider found himself at another one.

The gallows of the capital rose above the crowd, high enough for even people in the back to see. It was made of sturdy wood, with the executioner standing on the platform, his hand resting on the lever that would release the trapdoor. There was a line of guards preventing the crowd from getting too close to where the noose was.

As the main advisor to the king, Rider stood next to him on a balcony overlooking the scene, dressed in his typical execution garb, a black suit and a black hat. Today, that garb was suffocating him. The sun beat down upon the gallows and sweat was covering his entire body. He was entirely sure he might pass out. In fact, he desperately hoped it would happen.

He glanced at the King. Tieran was dressed in a light, white robe made of cotton. Contrary to Rider, he didn't look like he was going to faint from heat exhaustion. His grey hair was tied into a knot behind his head, a simple crown adorning it. The wrinkles on his face were apparent in the hot sun. The king was a short man, slightly overweight, but stood in a manner that made it known who the ruler of Orinth was. His mouth was set in a grim line as he observed the crowd that was gathered in the gallows. Rider knew that he didn't like this anymore than he himself did. But there was no other choice, in his mind, no other punishment that could befit the crime that the man had committed.

Rider turned to the princess, who was standing on the other side of him. Alida was dressed in a simple green gown, her long brown hair cascading down her back in waves. She also wore a basic crown. Executions were not the time to be flashy. Alida, unlike her father, was tall and thin. Rider was taller than she, but not by much. Her skin was fair and smooth. When he looked at the 18-year-old, he saw the queen who had died so many years ago. But when her brown eyes met his, he could see her father in her.

"I don't like this," she muttered to Rider. "I don't like this at all."

She was also sweating profusely, despite her gown being sleeveless. Rider knew that she was adamantly against capital punishment, but, like him, required to attend.

"I don't either," He whispered back, barely audible over the cheering crowd. "I tried to talk him out of it, but he wouldn't listen."

"Rider, this is an act of war," she said firmly. "Isn't there something you can do?"

Rider shook his head at her. "Don't put me in this spot, Lida."

Alida rolled her eyes and turned back to the crowd. They stood on the balcony of the castle, the one that had the best view of the hangman and his noose. Directly under them was the castle's dungeon. It was the opposite side of where most of their work occurred. The castle was huge, and this part Rider tried to avoid the most. The dungeon and gallows side. The Death Side, as Alida put it.

Just when the crowd began a borderline riot, the king nodded at the captain of the guard, who in turn nodded at one of the guards down below. The guard shouted an order that was impossible to hear over the scream of the crowd. Rider cringed as he felt the castle shake, as the large gate directly under them was open.

Three guards dragged a young man out and up to the platform. The man could not have been any older than Rider himself, perhaps 35 or 36. He wore rags, most of which were torn and hung off his body at weird angles. Rider felt almost obligated to look away; the man was almost indecent. He hoped that Alida was averting her eyes. Even from the balcony, Rider could see the man's bruises. There was dried blood almost everywhere he looked. The man was malnourished, ribs and bones poking out. It was clear that he had not been treated to the usual standards that the Orinthian dungeon typically maintained. Tieran was not a cruel man. But this was something different.

Alida elbowed him hard in the ribs. Rider coughed, "Your majesty, this is- it seems to be a bit much."

Tieran turned to him, eyes glowing with rage. "Not now, Rider. I can normally deal with your ridiculous high moral standards but not now. So, if you don't want to end up in the gallows right after this man, I suggest you not say another word. And Alida, that goes for you too."

Neither said another word, but Rider felt Alida grab his hand.

Alida was the little sister he had never had. They had met the day Rider had taken a job at the palace. He was twenty-four when he took the job, Alida being a feisty five-year-old who ran around the castle like she owned the place, to the dismay of her mother and the several governesses she had. Rider was a low-level scholar, who had gotten the job because of his connections. He was hired to work in the library, studying and writing and reading. Despite his many other skillsets, Rider loved the job and every second of it.

That all changed a year later, when on a short trip to the dressmakers with her mother, Alida was kidnapped right out of the royal carriage and went missing for hours. The king went into a complete panic, ripping the city apart to try and find the young girl, but to no avail. Rider cursed the day he was born because he knew he was the only one who could locate her. Using some of his skills, he tracked her down to a cave outside the city.

A gang of exiled Wildsmen were holding her captive. Praise the gods, they hadn't touched her. Their plan was to let the king dangle for a few days before hitting him with a ransom so large, it would bankrupt the city. Thankfully, it didn't come to that. Rider walked into the cave and out, with a six-year-old Alida who had been too distracted by a doll they gave her to realize the gravity of the situation. He left behind him seven dead bodies of Wildsmen.

He brought her back to the king, who at first, was mildly suspicious of his newly hired scholar. Rider simply directed him to the caves outside the city, where the seven bodies were found. He wouldn't answer any of their prying questions but just wished for the princess's wellness. He also begged to remain anonymous as the princess's savior. The king granted this as well as promoting him to an advisor. Eleven years later, he was the top advisor.

Only Alida knew how those seven men were killed. She knew his secret, but he knew he could trust her never to say a word to anyone, no matter the temptation to do so.

Since that day in the cave, they had grown closer and closer. Especially after the queen died. It was a cross between a brother-sister relationship and a best friendship. Other times they fought like teenagers, but Rider wouldn't hesitate to kill a single person who threatened his princess, even the king himself. He loved her more than anyone in his life.

Their hands were intertwined as the prisoner was led up to the gallows. The executioner took him from the guards and wrapped the noose around his neck as the screams of the crowd grew louder. The executioner looked up at the king. With a wave of his hand, silence rolled over the crowd.

The prisoner watched with dark eyes as the king began to speak. "Ladies and Gentlemen of the city of Abdul, citizens of Orinth. It is a tragic day. Today is not a day for celebration, but for mourning. Today, we should not hear cheers, but sounds of weeping and crying. For today is the day when the first traitor to my throne is executed before your eyes. He should praise his heathen gods that I don't do worse than a simple hanging. This day is tragic because we know he is the first of many traitors. It isn't tragic that he will die, for he deserves this punishment and worse."

He paused for effect before continuing.

"After our triumphant victory over the people of the Wilds years ago, the relationship between Orinth and Auntica was stronger than ever. I looked to our future with hopeful eyes and open arms."

"Those hopes have been dashed. Months ago, a farmer on the border and his family were slaughtered by Auntican soldiers because a gold mine had been found on his property, property that was rightly his, property he wouldn't sell. Instead of punishing those soldiers, King Grafph praised them and received them with open arms back to Illias, the capital of Auntica."

"From that moment on, Auntica has been our enemy. We hoped for peace, but alas, the man you see before you dashed those hopes once more. For two weeks ago today, this man, Cray Dune, was caught trying to leave the Orinthian border with priceless information about the whereabouts of our armies, our spies, and our secrets. In the hands of King Grafph, this information would be deadly to Orinth. It would result in the deaths of many people, some whom you might hold dear. Yet this information was bound for the hands of our enemy king. It is for that reason today that this man is to meet his gods."

"After a week of attempting to extract information out of him, he would say nothing of what Grafph wanted or if war was imminent. So, we have decided it will be Orinth who makes the first move in this war. I send this message out to you, my loyal subjects. If you are able, fight with us. Fight against traitors like this man. Help us in our fight against Auntica that is surely to come. Protect your husbands, wives, children, those who you hold dear to you. If not you, then who? The glory and triumph of Orinth rests in your hands."

When the king stopped speaking, the crowd exploded into roars, cheers, screams of everything you could imagine. Rider could pick out curses at the man, cheers for Orinth, more curses directed at their neighboring country of Auntica. It was absolute chaos. Rider closed his eyes as Tieran, once again, let the anger of the crowd build up.

This day was the day he had dreaded since he had first heard about the plot in Auntica. It had come out of nowhere. The relationship between the two countries had indeed been strong ever since the War in the Wilds. The threat of the Wild people had been imminent to them both, so they sought an alliance. Together, their two armies had fought for many years in the mountains, suffering equally as many deaths and casualties before finally prevailing as the Wild people retreated further into the mountains, almost to the Shadow Wall, and surrendered. They shared the pain of loss but also the sweetness of triumph. From that point on, the bond between the two countries was stronger than ever. Both economies began to flourish as they started trading. There were several joint projects that resulted in innovation for all.

That was a long time ago. In the last five years, the relationship had crumbled.

Gold had been discovered on the border between their two countries and chaos had followed. Each thought that it was rightfully theirs. Gradually, trade had begun to stop. Travelers stopped crossing the borders. The frequent letters exchanged between the two kings had ceased to be. For the last two years, there had been nothing but silence. Rarely did any Aunticans cross into Orinth, for they were treated with mistrust and contempt. The same went for Orinthians who went into Auntica. Both countries were holding their breath, waiting for something to happen. And then, it did.

Months before, a farmer and his family had been found slaughtered. After investigation by Orinthians, it had been found that they were killed by Auntican nationalists who wanted the gold that was on their land. The gold they had got, leaving behind four rotted corpses.

Rider had waited with anticipation for an apology from Grafph, as he handled most of the diplomatic functions of the kingdom. An explanation for what had happened, a reassurance that the perpetrators had been rightly punished, compensation for the next of kin, compensation for the crown. None had come. Not even a single letter. It was at that time that King Tieran had ordered the army to convene and prepare.

Two weeks ago, an economic handler of the king was caught leaving the castle with detailed notes of all the whereabouts of the army, among other things. He wouldn't say a word, but Rider had a suspicion he had been working for Auntica the entire time and finally had the chance to make it pay. But it didn't. Because Rider watched as that same man stood staring directly at the king, no fear in his eyes, rope wrapped around his neck.

Alida let go of Rider's hand, turned around, and left the balcony. The king didn't even glance at her, continuing to watch the crowd grow angrier and angrier at the man about to be hanged. The guards were pushing people back to stay away from the hangman, as they surged forward trying to get closer.

Rider took a step back and then another and turned to follow her. He wasn't needed there, as a symbol of unity or whatever reason Tieran made him come to those things. The crowd wasn't paying attention to the king. They had only one thing on their mind: death.

Alida had already disappeared, and Rider cursed. She was fast, for someone in a nice dress and shoes. The fact was, he cared about her much more than he did some execution that would most definitely result in a war. A feeling of numb panic had settled into place in his chest. He ignored it as he jogged down the hallway.

He took a deep breath, stepping out of the Death Side and back into the regular castle. There was a certain heaviness that he felt in the Death Side that was never present here. Rider had always been a fighter. He had killed before and he knew most definitely that he would do it again. That didn't stop him from hating death, from hating the idea of death. He often woke up in the middle of the night in a cold sweat, seeing the faces of men he had killed, seeing the faces of their wives and children, or at least illusions of them.

The air of the rest of the castle felt innocent, not reeking of the stench of death. Rider started towards the place he knew Alida would be, the castle kitchens.

Sure enough, Alida sat at the long table that was in the middle of the hustle and bustle of the chefs. They paid her no mind; she had used the kitchen as a sanctuary since she was only a little girl. It was a place she knew the king wouldn't come, making it the perfect place to hide. Plus, the cooks and kitchen attendants would always give her some sort of treat, always had it on hand in case the princess came to her sanctuary.

Surrounding the long table were different stoves and ovens, always in constant use. Beyond the long table was a separate room where dishes were washed and several tables for preparation sat. It was always warm in here from the fires and he could understand what Alida liked about it.

Rider sat down across from her. She wasn't crying but he could see the glazed-over way her eyes got when she was trying hard not to. Alida didn't look at him, but poked and prodded at the pastry sitting in front of her.

"Only you could watch a bloody, broken man about to be hanged and still have an appetite," Rider said, smiling a little.

She didn't say anything or return the smile.

"Lida?"

"Father's going to be upset you left during the execution. You need to remain a united front, remember?"

Rider snorted, "That crowd wasn't looking to see a united front. They were looking for bloodshed and gore and death. I didn't want to see it."

She looked up at him and once again, he was overwhelmed at how much she looked like the late queen, Natasha, who had died ten years ago. "Neither did I. I know he deserves to die, Rider, I really do. He betrayed some of our national secrets to Auntica, who might just be our biggest enemy right now. But it's Cray. Cray with his numbers and his boring talk during meetings about statistics. I just didn't have it in me to watch him die. And if I get in trouble with my father for it later, then so be it."

"I know how you feel. That stupid man helped me open up an account in the royal treasury for my money. It's hard to believe he's not one of us. Even harder to believe he's about to die," Rider said quietly.

"I mean for gods' sake; my father adored the man. But he knows our secrets now. Exiling him wasn't an option. Keeping him locked up forever wasn't an option either. It's a small mercy my father didn't order him publicly flogged. Maybe that was his last gift to the man," Alida sighed.

Rider agreed. "Any other traitor would have been beaten in public. So maybe it was."

They were silent for a moment, as the noises of the kitchen continued. Shouts of cooks, slamming of pots and pans, sizzle of whatever was cooking, but it seemed to be silent for the two of them.

Alida took a small bite into the pastry and swallowed. "Do you really think it's going to come to war, Rider?"

He shook his head. "I don't know. I pray to the gods it doesn't. But this stalemate or whatever you want to call it between us and Auntica, it's been happening for almost five years now. Something must happen to break the ice. And that something might just be war."

"What do you think should happen? If you were my father, what would you do?"

He sighed, "I would exile Cray to the Wilds. He would either die or survive and make his way back to Auntica. By the time he returned, his information would be null so we would be safe. I would send a diplomatic team to the capital of Auntica and settle this petty dispute once and for all. Because that's really all it is. A petty dispute about gold on our borders. We could agree to split it 50/50 or trade it for something else. I don't see any reason to go to war when we could talk and figure it out without all the bloodshed."

Alida didn't say anything but ripped off a piece of her pastry and popped it into her mouth. "But this is about more than the gold, isn't it, Rider?"

Rider stared at her. "I don't know what you mean."

She looked back up at him, her brown eyes gleaming. "I'm not an idiot, Rider. I know you and my father have been keeping something from me. And I know for a fact my father would not call for an entire army to defend Orinth if it were a dispute about gold. It's more than that and if you don't tell me, I'll just figure it out myself."

"Alida." He rarely called her by her full name except when he was deadly serious. He felt the panic coursing through his body, not just a numb feeling in his chest anymore. He was wrong to ever underestimate how observant the princess was. "It's none of your concern."

"Of course, it's my concern, Rider! I'm the one who's going to inherit the throne!" she kept her voice down but he could see the anger in her eyes, directed at him. She threw her hands in the air. "I thought we told each other everything." she muttered.

Rider leaned forward. "Alida, please. You know I would tell you anything. You know almost everything about me. But your father, he told me I wasn't to say a word of this to anyone. He made me swear. On your life and mine."

Swearing on his own life meant very little to him. Swearing on Alida's life was something different.

Her eyes softened a bit but still had her trademark intensity. "If that's your excuse, then so be it but because you swore on my life, you should tell me what this is really all about."

Rider looked around. The entire kitchen staff went about their business without even noticing them, but he knew better. Cray was only the first spy but there could be hundreds more lingering in the castle. He couldn't tell her here. He shook his head. "Not here. Maybe tonight or tomorrow. At some point."

Alida gave him a look. "That doesn't work on me anymore, Rider. You can't say 'maybe tomorrow' and then expect me to forget about it."

Rider cursed under his breath. "Gods help me. Fine. Tonight, let's go for a walk. At eight o'clock. I'll meet you in the gardens. Just please make sure you aren't followed. It's important."

Alida grinned at him and he couldn't help but smile back at her. "Sounds good then. Eight o'clock evening walk with my favorite castle advisor."

He rolled his eyes at her, still smiling. "Sometimes I wish I left you in the caves all those years ago."

She shook her head at him. "You really have to keep bringing that up, don't you?"

"I really do. You still owe me one and until you pay up, I am legally obliged to keep bothering you about it."

They both laughed that time but were interrupted. "Your highness?"

The princess's assistant, Weylin, stood at the head of the table, in a grey dress, dark hair stopping at her shoulders. Weylin acted as everything for Alida and had lived in the castle since she was small. The two of them had grown up together.

"Yes, Weylin?" Alida asked.

"Your father would like to see you and Mr. Grey in his office immediately. I was sent to find you and relay the message."

Rider met Alida's eyes and sighed. "Well, I suppose we were going to be lectured sooner or later." He said, standing up.

Alida followed. "Thank you, Weylin. Have some tea ready for me when this is all over. I suppose I should need it when we're done with my father."

Rider chuckled and offered his arm to the princess. "Your highness?" Alida smiled at him and took it, as they began towards the King's office.

~ ~ ~

The king sat at his desk when they walked in the room, leaning over papers with his glasses on, muttering to himself. There were no traces of the king who had stood at the balcony only minutes ago, overseeing the execution of a traitor. Instead, when Rider saw his king and friend, he saw a tired, old man who wanted a long retirement but wasn't yet ready to say goodbye to his throne. Especially now, when everything was changing.

He didn't look up at them as they moved to stand in front of the desk. He continued shuffling through papers, writing notes here and there, and ignoring them. Alida shot a look at Rider, who shrugged. The king would talk to them when he was ready.

Without even a glance at them, he spoke, "Do you understand that I don't like executions any more than you do?"

Alida took a breath to respond but Tieran held up a hand. "No. Don't say anything, Alida. I'm not upset. I'm not angry. I didn't bring you in here to yell and scream at you about maintaining the united front."

The king took off his glasses and stood up, finally meeting their eyes. "I hated having to do that more than anything in the entire world. But there was no other choice. I know you might be thinking 'oh we could've exiled him to the Wilds' or 'we could've imprisoned him until this war, or whatever might be coming, is over'. Prisoners escape. Exiles find their way home. Cray had too much priceless information to live. He knew who every spy in Auntica is. He knew the exact location of our armies and where we were thinking of sending them. And who is to say that he wouldn't tell someone all of these secrets before he was exiled, or while he was in prison. I know I don't have to justify my actions to you two. Rider, you're my advisor. Alida, you're first and foremost my daughter. But I love you both and if everyone else in this gods-forsaken city sees me as a monster, at least you don't."

There was a heavy silence in the room that lingered for a long time before Alida crossed and wrapped her arms around her father. Her father sighed and returned her embrace, resting his head on her shoulder. They were almost the same height but Alida still tucked herself into her father's chest, like she used to when she was a little girl.

"I love you, father. Nothing is going to change that. I don't think you're a monster. I know you did what you had to," she whispered.

Tieran patted her on the back. "I'm glad to hear it, Alida. I really am."

Alida broke the embrace and tucked her hair back into place. Rider nodded at the king and he returned it, acknowledging that there could be no room for internal conflict in this war. They had just resolved the only possible one. Rider sat down in front of the desk and asked, "So are we going to strategize or what?"

The king nodded. There was still a slight tension in the room but at least they had gotten it out of the way. "If either of you need to take a break, go get a bite to eat or a glass of tea, help yourselves. We're going to be here for a while."

"I might just do that," Alida said with a slight smile on her face. Rider looked at her. "You just ate a pastry, Lida."

The king raised his eyebrows. "So that's where you went."

"Right to the kitchens. As always," Rider confirmed, shooting the king a small grin.

Just like that, the tension between them was gone. The air of seriousness of the events that had happened and the events that were likely to come was still there, but they needed to keep everything in perspective. They had a country to save. They couldn't let themselves be drowned in worry or fear or sadness. If they were able to lighten the mood even a little, it might possibly improve the outcome.

Alida threw her hands in the air. "I will be taking my leave if you two keep teaming up on me."

Rider patted the seat beside him. "Don't be childish, Alida. It's so unbecoming of you."

She smacked his arm hard and sat down next to him. Rider shot her his best smile, and she rolled her eyes, but beamed. They had avoided another lecture on the 'united front'. The day was improving.

The king tugged a map down on the wall behind his desk and pointed at it. It was a large map of their two countries, decoratively done and given as a gift only a decade ago by Grafph himself. Now, they were using it to plan a war.

"Killing Cray Dune will almost definitely be perceived as an act of war," King Tieran began. "If one of my actions happened to be the straw that broke the camel's back, then so be it. We can't sit around hoping and praying there won't be retaliation when there most certainly will be. We need to send out our armies now. We need to get protection immediately to the people on the front, if not evacuate them completely. We need to send out diplomats to establish relationships with surrounding countries, if only to ensure they don't ally with Auntica. If all goes well, maybe they will come to our aid. That's only the beginning."

The next hour, they poured over maps, lists of the number of troops and supplies available, debated about which diplomats should go where, what Auntica's ploy could be. The decisions were made quickly but thoroughly, as they went through every possible option. In the end, it was decided. Orinth's 1st Army would head to Lou, the largest town that was closest to the border of Auntica. They would set up camp there and not move unless given orders by the general. They would serve as protection for most of the border, and the first line of defense if Auntica were to attack.

The King's 2nd army would station where they were, Abdul, the capital of Orinth. It was the largest city in the country, holding the castle, the royal treasury, and the main force of the Orinthian economy. If somehow Auntican forces penetrated the 1st army and made their way into the capital, the 2nd army would be stationed to protect the greatest assets.

Finally, the 3rd army would split into four groups and station between Abdul and the border. This would be their security defense. If Auntica attacked, changes would be made to be the most tactical, and an offensive would need to be developed. Rider and the king had already begun working on one so they would be more than ready.

The king stood up abruptly in the middle of all this and said, "We need to go to a place where we cannot be overheard."

Alida looked up from a list of assassins, as they had been debating sending one into Auntican lands to take out certain military leaders. "Father, it's a little too late for that. If there's a spy that's somehow listening right now, they know all of our military endeavors."

"There are no spies but I'm not taking any risks. Alida, we have to tell you the truth."

Alida raised her eyebrows. "The truth?" She glanced at Rider, who was conveniently studying his shoes. "What truth are you talking about, Father?"

"This war is about more than just gold, Alida," Tieran said with a sigh.

Alida shot Rider a pointed look, but he avoided her eyes. "What do you mean?"

The king stepped towards one of his bookshelves and pulled on the spine of a specific book. Slowly, the bookshelf rotated halfway, opening to a dark corridor. Tieran turned back to them. "Follow me."

Alida glowered at Rider before following the king into the darkness.

Rider ran a hand through his hair and took off after them.

The walk was short before the king opened another door. The room was a lounge, dimly lit and musty, but cozy, nonetheless. It was small, with many couches, pillows on the floor. A table in the corner was covered with books as well as a bottle of what looked to be very old wine. There was an empty firepit that a small draft seemed to be originating from.

"Father, what is this place?" Alida asked as she picked up one of the books, blowing off dust from it.

"My sanctuary. And escape room. In the event the castle was ever attacked, the fireplace is a tunnel that leads very far away from the city of Abdul. I turned the rest of the room into my safe place, after your mother died. I haven't been down here in a while but now is as good of a time as any. If you ever need to hide or need to get out of here, this is how. For now, we talk in here, as there's no way to be overheard. Rider and I can tell you what the real threat of this war is, Alida. Sit down."

Alida sat on one of the dusty couches and crossed her legs, still glaring at Rider, who still observed his shoes.

"We've wanted to tell you for a while, Lida," Rider said, finally meeting her eyes. "We just weren't sure if telling you would put you in anymore danger than not telling you would."

"Continue," she said coldly.

"Yes, this dispute started about gold. It was a petty one, one that should've been resolved with only a few diplomatic missions. Which is what we did, years ago. We sent one of our most experienced diplomats to Auntica, to the capital city of Illias, to decide about the gold. We were right, the dispute about the gold could've been easily solved. But it wasn't."

"Elliot Geller was the name of the diplomat. I don't know if you've ever met him. Once he came back, he left Orinth and moved to Nagaye. We haven't heard of him since. What he discovered in Auntica on his mission left him so afraid, we couldn't convince him to stay."

"King Grafph is-" The king paused, "no longer himself. That much is apparent. I'm not sure who is controlling him. But I know the man. We led side by side during the War against the Wilds. He doesn't have this much evil in him. The man I knew was content with the land he had. There was never talk of expansion or domination. But when Elliott came back, he reported that there had been endless talk of conquest."

"Elliot discovered that the only thing that was on their mind, was indeed, domination. Not just on this continent. Every single one of them. Orinth. Nagaye. Grady. All of them. They planned to even infiltrate the Darklands."

"It's been years. Why haven't they attempted to yet?" Alida asked.

"We weren't sure. After getting the information from Elliot, we waited. For an attack on Orinth. To hear if they had attacked other countries. Any sign of conflict arising. Until the attack on the farm at the border, there was nothing. We've discovered that Auntica, Grafph, they've been biding their time for something. And we believe that time is up. Something big is about to happen." "And this something big. What could that be? Certainly, starting a war is big but the way you're talking makes me think it's something else," Alida said.

Tieran sighed grimly. "We've discovered that the king is going to attempt to destroy the Shadow Wall."

Alida's mouth opened wide and then closed immediately. She glanced at Rider, who nodded grimly.

"But that's not possible!" she exclaimed.

Rider cut in, "But it is. That's what we thought too, but it is."

"The Shadow Wall is what separates this realm from the realm of darkness. If the king destroys the wall, he can't guarantee that he will be able to control whatever emerges."

"Maybe not. But that won't stop him from trying."

Alida gaped, "I don't understand."

Rider began to speak but looked at the king for confirmation. Tieran sat down on the other couch, put his head in his hands, and gestured at him to continue.

"The Shadow Wall was constructed a thousand years ago, to keep darkness out of the human realm. Before it was constructed, however, there was no border, nothing there to separate the two realms. There was constant battle between our side and their side. Our armies were evenly matched, but it is said that some of their soldiers possessed unnatural powers. It is unclear what they were. But the wall went up. And now, the common belief is that the other side contains a demon realm."

"And what do you believe?"

Rider took a deep breath. "I believe it was mostly humans on the other side. Men and women like you and me. But there was magic there as well. Evil magic.

And maybe, since the wall has gone up, that magic has grown stronger. But it's impossible to say."

"How did the wall come to be then?"

"This we know based on the information of scholars. The person who constructed the wall was a demon. He possessed that evil power; a power called the shadow. We don't know exactly what it does or what it was. But it wasn't used for good. Somehow, he fell in love with a human on the other side during the war, or so the story goes. His name was Abdiah. During the war, he stumbled upon a woman named Cassia Messina, a girl who lived close to the border, whose father was a soldier. They fell in love. He recognized that he and his human lover would never ever be safe, while the war continued. The conflict was constant. Abdiah only knew it was a matter of time before it reached the two of them and her life would be in great danger."

"He loved her more than anything in the entire universe. But to do something like close the border between the two worlds? It could only be paid with the price of blood. The price of his life. But it was a sacrifice he was willing to make. He said goodbye to Cassia and went to close the border. With his death, the Shadow Wall was constructed. From that day on, whatever dwelled on the other side was unable to cross into this world and we could not cross into theirs. Of course, it's much safer and better that way."

"That's good then. The wall is up and Abdiah is dead. So how is there a way to reopen the border, to destroy the wall?" Alida asked, wringing her hands together.

"I'm getting there. Abdiah was dead before he could find out that his lover was pregnant with his child. She knew that Abdiah possessed the shadow but assumed it wouldn't affect the child, and that the child would remain human. Sure enough, it was. A baby girl, who she named Arca, which meant Face of her Father. The girl grew up as human and that was it. Peace once again reigned in the human world without the shadow world posing a constant threat. Yet both Arca and Cassia had no idea the girl would always have a part of the shadow within her."

"But without recognizing who she was, and what she was capable of, Arca was just a regular girl. Even though she was partly of the shadow, she grew up to be a wonderful person. It was easy to tell she had inherited the capacity to love like her father had. Long story short, she ended up marrying the then- current prince of what would become Orinth. She had children, one of them partly of the shadow without knowing it. And it spread from there."

Alida took a deep breath. "I don't even know what to say to that."

Rider nodded. "And because the blood of the shadow is what bound the wall, the blood of the shadow reverses this. If a person like this were found, one with enough of the blood of Abdiah, only they could destroy the wall. It would require a blood sacrifice. But if that happened, if the blood were spilled on the Shadow Wall, it would be destroyed."

Alida stood up and started to pace, saying nothing. Rider watched her hesitantly and the king continued to stare at the floor. It had taken them a long time to recover that information, dozens of spies, endless research in the hall of records, consulting renowned historians. But they had come to this conclusion and knew it to be true.

Alida's head popped up. "So there could be many of these half-human, half-shadow people running around right? And almost any of them could have powers? So, couldn't Auntica just find any of them to sacrifice to destroy the wall?"

Rider exchanged glances with Tieran.

"No. It couldn't be just anyone. In fact, even if they tried it with one who had Abdiah's blood, it wouldn't work. It must be the Last Heir of Abdiah, a direct descendent of Arca's line, and only the first born. We looked for a long time to find this information. People who were alive when the war between the worlds was still happening. They were the ones who realized a wall could be constructed in the first place. They were the ones who further realized the wall could be destroyed, using the blood of the shadow by which the wall was constructed. They, of course, wrote this all down. The records were old and hard to reach but we found a man, a researcher in Tenir, who had them. He confirmed that only one person's blood could open the Shadow Wall."

"Do we know who that is?" Alida asked, hesitantly.

Tieran nodded. "Yes. We've checked almost every source we could to find it out, besides the man in Tenir. There is only one person alive who can destroy the wall. The Last Heir of Abdiah."

"Who is it?"

"It's you, Alida."

Chapter 2

Illias, Auntica

"Come in, Mr. Winger," Sawny said politely to the man who was in the waiting room of her establishment. He was an older man, lacking hair and apparently, good hygiene. His clothes were dirty, face covered in grime, and only had a few of his teeth left. She held her breath as she let him into her office, wondering if it was professional to offer him use of her bathtub upstairs in her apartment. Probably not. She didn't think she wanted him dirtying up her space anyways.

Mr. Winger grunted and stepped through the door.

"Please have a seat," Sawny said as she made her way behind her desk, putting on a pair of glasses. She tucked a misplaced strand of her hair back behind her ears and sat down as he did. He looked around the room, horrified. Sawny narrowed her eyes. She wasn't sure why. Perhaps he had never seen a room so clean before. Her office had crisp white walls that were lined with cabinets. Her desk contained nothing on its surface but the file she had left there. Everything else was locked in drawers, away from the wary eye of the public. It was on the smaller side, but undoubtedly professional, in her eyes.

"Now, Mr. Winger, before I disclose this information for you, I must ask for the full payment that is due. I believe I've given you enough time to gather those funds and unfortunately, cannot give you my services without suitable compensation."

He grunted again and pulled out a drawstring bag that clanked as he threw it on the table wearily. "That's all of it. Your information better be good, lady, because this wasn't cheap."

Sawny picked up the bag and deposited it into one of her desk drawers. She would have to count it later.

"Believe me, Mr. Winger, no one has better information than I. So, without further ado-" She opened up the file in front of her. "May I present where your wife went after she ran away from here."

Mr. Winger leaned forward, eyes ablaze. Sawny could see sweat dripping down his forehead and was inclined to offer him a handkerchief, but instead began to read.

"Two years ago, your wife, a Mrs. Sia Winger, ran away from your residence in our capital city of Illias. You had been married for five years, and you, Mr. Rae Winger, describe it as the best five years of your life. Mrs. Winger leaving you was unexpected and brutally painful, in your words. So, you hired me, Sawny Lois, to find out where she went, whether she is dead or alive, and why exactly she left."

Sawny reached into the folder and pulled out a note, sliding it on the table towards him. "This is the note you gave me when you hired me to find your wife. This is the one thing she left, the one thing that made it clear that she ran, not that she was kidnapped or the victim of a crime."

The note was written on top of a page that had been ripped out of a book. It read, in a messy, hastily-written script "I'm sorry, but I can't do this anymore. It's too hard. I love you always. Your Sia". Mr. Winger picked up the note and sighed, holding it close to his chest. The anger in his eyes had now been replaced by sadness, tears starting to form.

Sawny said kindly, "The first thing I did when you gave me this note, however, was look at what book it had been ripped out of. It turned out to be a short story published years ago by a prominent author in Auntica. It was a story about a young woman who had slept with her sister's husband. One of her colleagues secretly found it out and used the information to blackmail the young girl out of everything she had. At the end of the book, the young girl slays her colleague, runs away with her sister's husband, and lives happily ever after. That part isn't important to us, but the blackmail is."

"As I investigated further, I found out that your wife worked with a young man. His name or identity is irrelevant but late one night after work, after a few too many drinks of wine, your wife had an affair with him." Sawny herself had found out this piece of information by seducing the man into telling her about Sia. It had been almost too easy to get him to talk, and she walked away without having to touch him.

Mr. Winger gaped at this and Sawny held up her hand before an angry outburst upon hearing his wife was unfaithful. "Don't panic, Mr. Winger, please. Your wife immediately felt guilty and ashamed for her adultery. She told her coworker this, but he threatened to tell you, if she didn't give him money.

Everything she made from working, was given to this man. I'm not sure if you were aware that she was bringing home nothing from her job. Every single coin went to him."

"She grew weary and finally stood up to him, after three weeks of this. He threatened to kill you if she didn't pay. Sia was scared for your life, that she would accidentally lead him to you, so she left that note and ran away. The man couldn't find her and couldn't find you. She ran away to protect you."

Mr. Winger tried to talk, but Sawny held up a hand. "Hold all questions till the end, Mr. Winger, it will be a lot easier that way. I tracked Mrs. Winger all the way to the river city of Iyria, where she lives now under the name Sarai Lam. She owns a small, yet comfy apartment and works for a trader, running the books."

It had been only weeks ago that Sawny had visited the river city and met the elusive Mrs. Sia Winger herself. When she said her real name, the woman had almost fainted.

"How did you find me?" she had asked in a hoarse, frightened voice.

"Well, you see, Mrs. Winger, that's what I do. I find people. It's my job. And your husband has hired me to find you," Sawny had responded.

In the present, Mr. Winger gasped, "You-you saw Sia? She's still alive?"

Sawny nodded. "Yes indeed, Mr. Winger. She's very alive. She wanted to come back. She did. But she felt guilty. She thought she couldn't be around you after she was unfaithful. She thought she was no longer worthy of being your wife. She wouldn't come back with me, but I have her location if that's what you desire." Sawny pushed the file towards him. "These are the results of my entire search, but they belong to you now."

Mr. Winger sprung up and grabbed the folder. Gone was the dirty, old man who had walked into her building, replaced by a man who had hope again. "I can't tell you how thankful I am to you, Ms. Lois. I-" He grabbed her hand and squeezed it tight. "Thank you. I must go now. But may the gods bless you for the rest of your life." He released her hand and ran out of her office.

She heard the front door slam and she smiled to herself.

Her job and her livelihood meant everything to her now. She had spent almost her entire life savings on this building in downtown Illias, a two-story shop with an apartment on the second floor. She had opened an investigative firm and it had paid off within months. She had underestimated the amount of money people would pay her to find things. She investigated almost anything. Her cases took her all around Auntica, occasionally into Orinth or Theroe, and one time even into the Darklands, a country west of Auntica where there was no government, just tribes of warriors.

She had lost everything when she was fifteen years old, but found her passion and talent: finding people.

Sawny stood up and checked to ensure all her drawers and cabinets were locked. She closed the door to her office, locked the front door to the building, and walked up her stairs. It was about this time of the day, right after she saw her last client, or did her last bit of investigating, that the waves of loneliness would crash upon her.

They would start off small, like tiny waves of the sea. Single thoughts here and there, about the life she had before this. About the family she had lost. About the family that she did not know. About who she was and the deep sense of longing and loss that accompanied wherever she went. The tiny waves would grow larger and larger until she had to curl up into a ball and talk herself out of it.

"I am strong. I am strong. I am strong. I am strong. I am strong. I am strong." Over and over again until she had convinced herself it was true.

Maybe it was. Maybe it wasn't. Most days it was hard to tell. It all felt like pretending, like she was hiding from something. It tortured her, every day. The only escape was working. Improving other people's lives while hers remained incomplete and empty.

Tonight, it was lesser than usual. The love that she saw in Rae Winger's eyes numbed the pain. She had, in some small way, changed his life. She had given him back a piece of himself, given him the location of his wife. She knew that he would find her, would probably leave for Iyria tonight and be reunited with her in the morning. The knowledge that it was accredited to her? That would help her to sleep tonight.

Sawny stepped into her apartment. It used to be a simple one, a kitchen, lounge, and bedroom with not many decorations. Since her firm took off, she had turned the place into somewhat of a luxury. The kitchen had an actual ice box, which was rare in most houses. The living room was stocked with blush couches and chairs, and the bedroom with a soft, fancy mattress that she had gifted herself for her birthday. She was unsure of why she had decorated the apartment so fancily, as no one was ever up here besides herself.

She walked to her bedroom as she let out a sigh of contentment. It had been a long but fulfilling day. She had seen three clients today, more than she usually saw. Two had new cases for her, the last was Rae Winger. In between her clients, she worked on open cases, did paperwork for ones she had closed, paid bills, and planned trips she had to take for investigations. She was worn out and had decided to reward herself with a nice, long bath.

Sawny turned on the water and waited. One of the benefits to living in the city was the running water that came from pipes underground. She would have to heat it up herself, with the small stove in her bathroom, but it was worth it. She began to strip out of her work clothes, which consisted of a clean tunic and black pants. She turned and caught a glance of herself in the mirror. Her blonde hair just touched her shoulders and she fiddled with it, annoyed. It was longer than she liked it and she desperately wanted to chop it back to her ears again. Her skin looked abnormally pale but smooth. She was skinny, probably a little too skinny, but most of the time was too busy with work to remember to properly nourish herself. Sawny quickly looked away.

She hated looking at that reflection in the mirror.

Sawny had found every single person she had ever been hired to find. It had sometimes taken weeks, even months to track them down. In the end, she had happily given locations to clients and put another file into the cabinet labeled 'Closed Cases'. There was never a person who could elude her searching.

Except one.

She was born to an Auntican mother and Orinthian father. That much she knew. Her mother had left her father soon after her birth and moved to the outskirts of Illias. There she had grown up, thinking that the man her mother had remarried was her real father. She had loved him like one. She still did and always would.

The day her parents were killed was the day she found out that her real father was still alive. Her mother's last words to her revealed that much. Why her parents were murdered, she still didn't know.

She had searched the entire continent for anything that could lead her to find out her father's identity and location, for the men who had killed her parents, for the reasons behind it all. She came up with nothing. Of course, it was during this time she realized she could make a living out of this, but it didn't matter.

The truth was that the one thing Sawny desired most in the world would always be out of her reach. She would never find her real father. She would never find out the answers. She would always be haunted by a shadow of the past. When she looked into the mirror, that was what she saw.

After heating the water, she got into the tub and felt her whole body relax as the tension left her. Sawny closed her eyes. Her mind automatically wandered into a maze of cases she had been working on, a desperate attempt to bar her from thinking about anything else. By a blessing of the gods, it worked. Her thoughts were too busy to contemplate anything else, as she wrung her mind for answers about her various cases.

There was a bottle of wine left next to the bath and Sawny chuckled as she remembered herself depositing it there this morning, a promise of a reward after a long day. She grabbed the bottle, uncorked it, and took a long drink. It was Orinthian wine, the best kind in her opinion, even if it made her a traitor to the crown to say it.

The conflict between their two countries had been steadily growing, even when she was fifteen and still living with her parents. Now she was nineteen and living by herself, and the contention remained. She knew within months, maybe weeks, there would most likely be war. But so far, it had only been good for business. She desperately hoped that nothing would drag her into the war, and that it wouldn't get far enough into Auntica to threaten her firm.

She herself was half-Orinthian, according to her mother's last words. And if Orinth ended up taking over the entire country, she would claim to be full-Orinthian. If not, she would be Auntican. That was the benefit to being half and half.

The biggest mystery, in her eyes, was whether her father was good or bad? What was it that made her mother flee? Why had she hidden her birthfather's identity until the moments before her death? What had happened?

After an hour of laziness, Sawny stepped out of the bath. She dried and slipped into a rose silk robe that she had recently bought after solving a case for a rich businessman. He had paid her well, so naturally she used a chunk of it to buy new clothing.

She strolled into the kitchen and opened her ice box. She desperately needed to go shopping for food. There was only a half rotten apple, alcohol, and a breast of raw chicken she knew she would be too lazy to cook. She shrugged to herself. Oh well. She wanted an excuse to go get food in the nicer part of town. The food in Illias was renowned and expensive, but she got paid today. She deserved it.

Sawny turned around and felt her heart stop. She let out a loud scream and felt every bit of herself panic in that exact moment.

There was a man sitting on her couch.

She didn't move, as he had a cross bow pointed directly at her. "I wouldn't move if I were you, Sawny," The man said, in a deep voice.

He was young, probably in his early twenties if she had to guess. And he was large. Not fat, she could tell that every single part of him was firm muscle. He had lighter brown hair, cut short, and a sharp jawline, with piercing blue eyes seemed to stare through her. He was dressed in the garb of a warrior, a black cloak and leather top, not to mention the knives strapped to his belt and a sword that was sheathed on his back. Sawny would have been dumbstruck by how attractive he was had he not been threatening her with a bolt to the chest. "Who are you?" Sawny said, surprised by the own confidence in her voice, "And what are you doing in my apartment?"

The man didn't answer either question but said, "Please sit down." He spoke with an accent she couldn't identify but that didn't seem to matter at the moment.

She didn't move. "No. Tell me who you are."

He raised an eyebrow. "Do you really want to defy the man with the crossbow right now?"

Sawny shrugged. "Well, you know my name. You're in my apartment. For some reason, you've sought me out. So, you're not going to shoot me and kill me just yet. Maybe later but I think I have some time and leverage before I die."

The man didn't smile but his mouth twitched. "Seems risky for the girl who's being threatened with a bolt."

"Tell me who you are," Sawny said firmly. "And then we'll talk." She was inching towards the knife. All of them in her kitchen doubled as throwing knives and her adopted father had taught her how to throw years ago. If she could just get her hands on one, she could have this man dead within an instant.

"Okay but stop moving. I'm not stupid."

Sawny held her hands up. "Fine. Name?"

"You can call me Adriel. It's the closest translation in your language. Now sit." He used the crossbow to gesture at the couch across from him.

Sawny moved slowly and deliberately towards the couch, fists clenched, and sat. Adriel continued to point the weapon and didn't relax, even as she leaned back into the cushions.

"How do you know my name?" Sawny asked him.

Adriel didn't answer, but studied her, his eyes running up and down her body once. Sawny felt heat rush to her cheeks. Who was this person and what was he doing here? What did he want with her?

Finally, he spoke, "You-you're not what I imagined you would be."

Sawny raised an eyebrow. "Oh really? And what did you expect?"

Adriel shrugged. "Someone a lot older. Someone who looked more Auntican. Not what I'm seeing before me."

"How do you know who I am?"

"A year ago, you were hired by a man, named Reno. Do you remember him?"

"Reno? Yes yes. Reno. That was the only case I've ever had to journey into the Wilds for. Reno was a citizen of Auntica who had a brother residing in the Wilds, one who he hadn't seen since the Great War. He gave me a picture and his name, Alec, and sent me to find him. It took me three months, but I did. What does that have to do with you?"

Adriel shifted. "Reno and Alec are both members of my tribe. Older members granted, but we are well acquainted. When I told them I was looking for someone, they told me to find an investigator named Sawny Lois in the capital of Auntica. That if anyone could find who I was looking for, it would be her."

Sawny snorted, "As endearing as that is, most of my customers just set up appointments or come in during my office hours. I don't think a single one of them has broken into my apartment to threaten me. And you can put the crossbow away. Now that I know you need my services."

Adriel gave her a look. "Are you sure you won't do anything stupid or rash if I put it away?"

She held up her hand in a mock salute. "On my honor, sir."

His mouth twitched again, and he put the crossbow down on the couch beside him. "I decided it would be more influential if I were to meet you in this capacity. I couldn't wait for an appointment."

"Well, you've certainly made an impression on me, if that's what you were getting at. Who are you looking for?"

Adriel tapped his feet on her floor. "It's more complicated than that. I'm not some desperate husband coming to you to find out if his wife is seeing another man. Nor am I a desperate businessman attempting to catch a rival doing something illegal. It's more."

Sawny stood up and Adriel moved in a flash, the crossbow pointed at her before she had time to even breathe. She held up her hands again. "Calm down! I'm only going to get a drink!"

Adriel rolled his eyes and set it back down as she moved across the room, back to the ice box. She grabbed the bottle of wine inside and poured a large glass. She turned to her unwanted guest and held up the bottle. He shook his head and she returned it to the ice box.

"You aren't immediately going to ask me who I'm looking for?" Adriel asked, puzzled.

Sawny took a long drink of the wine and let it trickle down her throat. This was not the way she imagined her night would go. She glanced at the clock. It was only eight o'clock, but she knew her favorite restaurant would close at nine. This needed to speed up.

"Tell me," she said.

"I'm looking for a man. I don't know his name. I don't know where he's from. I don't know what he looks like or if he has any family or anything. I only know rumors of an evil power that grows within him. I know only that he is responsible for the death of my brother."

Sawny stared at him. "You aren't giving me a lot to go on."

Adriel spoke impatiently, "I'm not done yet."

Sawny motioned at him with her wine glass to continue.

"I am from the Wilds. I was born there, into what used to be one of the most esteemed tribes, before the War. We're weaker now, but we have adapted to the northernmost mountains, near the Shadow Wall. We are rebuilding, and we plan to stay out of this upcoming war, no matter how much they beg us to participate. In fact, many members of my tribe look forward to watching our enemies destroy each other. I don't share in their excitement, but I admit it will be a welcome feeling to not be in a battle."

"What does all of this have to do with the man responsible for the death of your brother?" Sawny asked.

"My brother was named Zelos. He was much older than me, but we were close. At least until he left our tribe. I was young, but I begged him not to go. He didn't listen. His passion for the Wilds was great, unchecked, and untamed. He left with a group of other exiles, to attack Orinth. The capital Abdul, more specifically."

"There weren't very many of them. But they had enough aggression and vengeance for a hundred men. They planned several attacks and executed them, but they were mere nuisances for King Tieran of Orinth. Things that were solved and fixed within days of them happening. Until they did their final act of vengeance. They kidnapped the princess."

Sawny nodded. "I remember hearing about it, when I was little. The news spread like wildfire across the continent."

"Indeed, it did. Even we, my tribe, in the most remote place on the continent, heard about the kidnapping of Alida Goulding. I knew that it was my brother. I prayed to the gods that they would have mercy on him. The news came only days later that he, along with the six others who had planned the attack, were dead. We didn't know how their deaths had come to pass. We mourned for a long time but had no sense of closure. We didn't have their bodies. We didn't know how they died. We tried to move on, but we couldn't. We had to have answers."

"My tribe sent me to the city of Abdul when I was sixteen, five years ago, to find out how the men died." Adriel's face darkened. "It took a lot of asking around. Orinthians, especially ones in the capital, do not take kindly to my people. But eventually I found out. The men were neither stabbed with a sword nor shot with a bow. They had been killed by something darker, something twisted and malicious."

"A man whom I had met in a tavern told me, the bodies of my seven kinsmen, including my brother, had been found with no wounds. Not a trace of blood on them. There were no weapons, no sign of a fight, nothing. Their bodies had been thrown into a pit outside the city and burned. Yet, the man told me, that the bodies would not catch aflame. Their bodies stayed perfect, even after being doused with fuel, and set ablaze. They finally had to dump their bodies into the sea."

"Something evil and unnatural had killed my brother. A form of evil magic that shouldn't exist in this world anymore but does. Had he been stabbed or killed like a soldier should be, I would be distraught yet accepting. He deserved to die the death of a warrior. But dying at the hands of dark magic, his body still uncorrupt and out in the sea somewhere, is too much for me to bear. I have sworn to my tribe that I would find the man with this ungodly magic and kill him; in the most painful way he could endure. And only then would my tribe find closure."

Adriel stopped speaking then and Sawny could feel her thoughts swarming, both with questions and commentary. The one that was the most prominent in her mind, that she didn't dare to say aloud, was that his brother deserved to die that way, as he had kidnapped a six-year-old girl, held her hostage, and demanded a ransom. She decided against saying that.

"I have been searching for this man for so many years, yet I haven't found a trace. No one seems to know who he is, who could possess that kind of magic.

Most people believe it's just a story, that the men in the cave were killed just like anyone else. But I know in my heart that my brother did not die the way a man should. Yet, I can't avenge him without finding the man who killed them. And that's where you come in."

Sawny nodded. "So you want me to find this man for you?"

"Yes, exactly."

She sighed. "You've searched for him for years. I'm sure you've done as much research as you possibly can. Who's to say I can have any more luck than you do?"

Adriel stared at her. "I've asked myself that several times as I traveled towards Illias. I don't know what you'll be able to do that I haven't already tried myself. But I'm out of options. You're my last hope to finding the man, to keeping my oath to my tribe, to avenging my brother's death. If you can't find them, it's over."

"What happens if you break an oath to your tribe?" Sawny asked.

Adriel shrugged. "I'll be exiled from the Wilds. I won't be able to see my family again. I won't be able to be buried in the place of my birth. I'll have to move to Theroe or the Darklands, as a man of the Wilds will never be able to reside peacefully in Auntica or Orinth. I'll have to start over. That is the penalty for breaking an oath. Not to mention the spiritual consequences. Oaths in the Wilds are not taken lightly."

Sawny cursed under her breath, "You don't leave me much choice then, do you Adriel? I'm not going to condemn a man to a life as an exile."

"I'm glad to meet an Auntican who is compassionate towards a man of the Wilds."

Sawny chuckled. "I don't know if I would say that. I have a price and the price goes higher if the case requires me to travel. This one most certainly will. I also have cases that are currently open that I must take care of before I dive into this one. I have other obligations. I wouldn't be able to start for a few weeks, at least."

Adriel shook his head. "No, we must start right away."

Sawny crossed her arms. "That's not possible. You aren't my only client. I can't just up and leave."

"I am prepared to offer you enough reasons to leave tomorrow."

"What do you mean?"

Adriel reached down into one of his pockets and threw a drawstring bag onto the table in front of him. It was the size of a fist and made a large thump when it hit. Sawny watched as a variety of gems and rubies spilled out, rattling against the hard surface, glittering from the apartment's light.

Her mouth dropped open. "How?"

"The Wilds are full of minerals and resources. I happen to have collected quite a large stock of these minerals, worth a lot in your currency when put together. I have three more bags just like this one. It will all belong to you if you are to find the man. If not, I'll pay you one bag for your troubles, if I believe you've put in as much effort as you could into the search. Do we have a bargain, Ms. Lois?"

Sawny stood up and walked to the window. The lights of the city were sparkling, the torches lighting up the streets and the buildings. It was a beautiful sight. It was part of the reason that she bought this apartment. But the bag of treasure Adriel possessed? Four of them were enough to buy a palace.

With it, she could afford a much bigger office, bigger apartment. She could hire a staff, a secretary to organize her appointments, an assistant to help her with cases. Her workload would lessen immensely. She could afford to take some time off, time to completely dedicate herself to discover what happened to her family. Sawny desperately needed that time. Without having to worry about bills or her business, she could throw herself into her own investigation.

But traveling for a case, most likely into Orinth, during a war? Tracking down a man who, if the story was correct, had possessed some sort of dark magic? Return all her currently open cases to her clients and close the shop for weeks or even months? It was a risk. She could come back to her building destroyed. There were so many dangers with it.

But she ended up with four bags of treasure if she found him. Even if she didn't, the compensation of one bag would still be more than a year's worth of cases. She knew she could probably get more than their worth if she sold them on the black market.

Or you could end up dead. A little voice chimed in from the back of her mind. She ignored it and turned back to Adriel, who was watching her.

"I'll need a few days to get organized before I can leave here."

"How many days?"

"Two at the most."

Adriel nodded. "That should be fine. I'm staying at an inn on the outskirts of the city. I'll come back here tomorrow, and we can finalize the contract, or whatever you want to call it. I know you'll want our bargain in writing. And then I'll come back the next morning and we can leave."

"We can leave?"

Adriel shot her a funny look. "Yes, we can leave. I assume we'll travel to Abdul to start because that's where it happened, but if you have something else in mind, I'm willing to listen. It's your process, not mine."

"My clients normally don't come with me."

He frowned. "You really think that I'm going to promise you that treasure and not go along?"

Sawny scratched her head. "It doesn't work like that. I go and find your person. And then I bring you all the information I gathered. You pay me. I give you the location," she said.

"Well, that's foolish. I'm coming with you. If you find the man I'm looking for, I want to be there to kill him before he runs. Secondly, there is about to be a war. Do you really think it safe for an Auntican girl to be traveling alone to the capital city of her enemy country?"

"Are you implying I can't take care of myself?"

Adriel held is hands up in surrender. "I suggested no such thing. I think it would be safer for two people to travel together, regardless of who the two people are. I think it's even safer if one of them is non-Auntican, so they don't get slaughtered when they enter Orinth. Forgive me if I insulted you."

"I don't like it, but fine. You can travel with me."

Adriel raised his eyebrows at that but said nothing. He stood up, grabbing his crossbow, and walked over to her. Sawny tried not to step back. He was larger up close, towering over her by at least a foot. He stuck out his hand. "I've heard that bargains are confirmed by Aunticans by shaking of hands. So, Sawny Lois, do we have a deal?"

Sawny took his hand. Almost every part of it was calloused, and she wondered what this man had been through. She shook it. "We have a deal. Come back here tomorrow morning and I'll draw up the papers. And then, we leave the next day. I expect you'll bring your own rations and money, as I will bring mine. We will travel quickly, taking as short of breaks as possible. Do you have a horse?" He nodded and she continued, "Then I'll see you tomorrow."

She released his hand and turned back into the kitchen. She heard Adriel begin walking towards the door.

Sawny spoke up, "Oh and Adriel?"

He stopped and turned towards her right as she released one of her knives that buried itself into the door, mere inches above the man's head. He froze.

"Never, ever assume I can't handle myself."

Adriel pried the knife out of the wood and threw it on the ground, eyes not leaving hers. He cocked his head. "Noted."

With that, he opened the door and left her apartment.

Chapter 3

Abdul, Orinth

Alida laid in her bed, eyes staring at the ceiling, unable to sleep. She was very still, every bone and muscle in her body tensed. She didn't know what she was waiting for. Perhaps any second, she was expecting King Grafph to burst into her room, grab her, and haul her with him to the Shadow Wall.

Because, as she had found out mere hours ago, she was the only person whose blood would tear down the boundary.

Alida hadn't been able to speak for minutes afterward, as her father and oldest friend had stared at her, waiting for her reaction.

She had only been able to say, "I don't understand."

With hesitant voices, they explained it to her. The most direct heir, or heiress in this case, of Abdiah would be the youngest descendent of the royal line. The people who had the purest of Abdiah's blood were ones who were born of Arca's line. And that line ended with Alida.

She chewed on that information like a piece of meat that was impossible to swallow. A part of her, some part within her heart, within her very soul, was demon. A part of her belonged in the shadow world. And if she wanted, she could channel the power from that realm and use it to bend other people's minds. That's what Rider had told her, but his eyes screaming something else. *Don't mention anything about the caves.*

Which was why she couldn't get her mind wrapped around it. How was there any possible way that she was Abdiah's Last Heir? Never in her whole life had she ever felt like she had any sort of power, when she knew for a fact that Rider possessed something of the sort.

The memory of the caves was as crystal clear as the day it had happened. She could still see it all. She had been tucked into her mother's side, absolutely giddy because she was on her way to the dress shop. Alida could go twice a year, to design a dress for her own use. She also got to spend quality time with her mother, without silly, stupid governesses floating around, trying to make her learn or practice being a lady. Today was a day for just them. Her favorite part? After buying her brand-new dress, her mother and she always went for special treats downtown, where the best chefs and bakers were.

About halfway to the dressmaker's shop, the carriage roared to a halt. The queen had sat up, shouting at the driver to see what was going on. There were yells of warning as the carriage shook. A body had slumped against the side door and six-year-old Alida, at that point, began screaming. Her mother held on to her tight, yelling at the guards to see what was happening, but it was too late.

The door to the carriage slammed open and a man in a mask held a bow with an arrow drawn back, pointed at Alida's throat. Alida screamed as the queen shielded her daughter's body with her own. "What do you want?" she said, voice not betraying the fear she felt so deeply.

"We'll kill her and you if you don't give her to us," The voice had said, steady and serious.

Her mother had tears running down her cheeks. "Are you going to kill her?"

"Not if you cooperate. Give her to us now or on my honor, we will murder you both."

The queen cried out and turned to Alida, who was wailing. "Darling, you're going to go with these men. Do what they say, alright my darling? I promise mommy will find you."

"I don't want to go with them, mommy!" Alida screamed, clutching her mother's arms.

Her mother looked back up at the men, trembling. "I can't give her up to you."

Without another word, the man took his weapon and struck the queen, knocking her out cold. Alida screamed and clung to her unconscious body but the man had grabbed Alida herself and was hoisting her out of the carriage on his hip. She tried to wriggle out of his grasp, screaming louder but it was no use. He had already begun walking away from the carriage as she cried out for her mother.

She didn't remember much about the journey from the city to the caves, besides being handed off to several different men, speaking a language she couldn't understand. The men were gentle with her, not touching her or harming her. Alida had stopped crying and just wondered who these men were. Were they friends of her mother? Was this a funny prank by her father? He had always loved pulling pranks on her mother. They were normally smaller than this though. Slipping salt for sugar in her morning coffee or scaring her by hiding behind his throne. Alida couldn't remember any pranks like this.

They had reached the caves and one of the men set her down by a rock, towards the outside while the rest of the men went inside. The man had a kind face and was looking at Alida with a sad expression. He ruffled her hair. "I'm sorry we had to drag you into this, Princess Alida. Here, I got something for you to play with while we wait." He pulled out a small doll made of burlap, with clothes sewed on and two buttons for eyes. This doll was not as nice as the rest of her dolls, but Alida grabbed it and hugged it to her chest.

"Are you friends of my father?" she asked the man.

He smiled at her, "Yes, we are. And he asked us to watch you for a couple days while he plans a surprise for you at the castle."

Alida giggled, "I love surprises. But what did you do with my mommy?"

"She's in on the surprise too. Don't worry. By now she's safe back at the castle planning the surprise for you. And if you wait a few days, we'll bring you back and you'll get to see the surprise for yourself. Is that okay?"

Alida nodded enthusiastically. "I can't wait to see what the surprise is!" she exclaimed, as she began to play with the doll.

The man smiled at her once more and made his way to the front of the cave, where he stood watching.

Hours went by and young Alida didn't even realize it. One time, she complained about being hungry and another one of the men had brought her a piece of bread and some cheese. She ate it contently, continuing to play campout with her doll. She was just about to ask to go to the bathroom when some of the men began to shout. The man who had been outside the cave had fallen down, slumped on the rock.

"Zelos?" one of the others shouted, "Zelos!" They ran towards the mouth of the cave when a figure stepped out from behind the shadows.

Alida hid behind the rock. She vaguely recognized the man who had the curly black hair and dark eyes. She knew she had seen him somewhere but couldn't think of when.

"Who are you?" one of the men stammered. "What did you do to Zelos?"

"Where is the princess?" the dark-haired man demanded, his voice calm and quiet.

"What did you do to him?" He repeated again, this time hysterically, staring at the fallen body of his comrade. "Is he alive?"

"No. He's dead. And if you don't give me the princess now, you all will be."

The man screamed, charging at the other one with all his might. He barely took two steps when he suddenly dropped. His scream turned into one of pain. For a brief moment, he shrieked and writhed on the floor, the other man staring at him, his hand slightly outstretched. And then the man stopped moving and, with a final groan, slumped.

The rest of the men backed up, almost to the back of the small cave. "Where is the princess?" The man demanded again, voice rising.

Alida hid still behind the rock. This man was scary. She didn't want to go with him and ruin her parent's surprise. Plus, he had made her friend at the door fall asleep. She liked him because he gave her the doll.

One of the men pointed a shaking finger at where Alida was curled up behind the rock. The man walked over, and she whimpered, hiding her face from him. He crouched down. "Princess Alida?"

She peaked through one of her fingers at the man. He looked at her with a kind face. "What?"

"I'm here to take you back to your mother and father. My name is Rider."

Her face lit up. She did know this man! He worked in the library. A few weeks ago, she remembered, he had helped her find a book she had been looking for.

Alida stood up and jumped into his arms, still clutching the doll to her chest. He shifted her to one hip and turned back to the men, who had observed the whole scenario. "I'll be taking the princess now." He said in a plain voice and turned to walk out the mouth of the cave.

The princess screamed as one of the men grabbed a bow and pulled back the string to shoot at the two of them. Rider kept walking, holding up his hand once more, as the man dropped the bow and, much similarly to his comrade, fell to the ground. Alida watched as he shuddered on the floor, shouting and writhing in pain, before finally going still.

Rider turned back to the remaining four men. "I'm sorry. You've seen too much, and I can't leave you alive." He spoke with genuine concern in his voice.

One of the remaining men stepped forward, hands up in surrender. "Please, sir. We'll leave this place and never come back. I don't know who or what you are, but we know never to come to this place again with someone like you protecting it. Please, have mercy on us."

Rider studied the man, frowning. "I'm sorry," was all he said as his eyes glazed over. Keeping Alida propped up with one hand, he lifted the other just slightly.

Alida watched as the four men repeated the same death as the first ones had, their screams echoing off the walls of the small cave. Before they slumped down on the ground, Rider had run out of the place, leaving the bodies of seven men.

"What about my surprise?" Alida asked him.

"Surprise?"

She pointed her finger at the first man, whose body laid perfectly still at the front of the cave. "He told me they took me here because mommy and daddy were planning a surprise."

Rider set her down on her feet and knelt, so he was at her eye level. "Your surprise got done early, okay? Your mommy and daddy sent me to retrieve you because it's finished."

Alida looked at the man's body again. "Well then why did you kill those men in there?" Her bottom lip began to quiver.

"Those men were bad, Alida. They were going to hurt you and your mommy and daddy. So, I had to kill them, to protect you and to protect the kingdom."

"But you didn't even touch them! You didn't use a sword or a bow or even a trident, like the heroes in my stories."

"I'm not like the heroes in your stories. Alida, I need you to look at me." Alida stared at him. He had really pretty eyes that she liked looking at. "Alida, promise me that you won't say anything, anything, to anyone, even your mom or dad. They aren't allowed to know about my special powers, okay? It can be our secret. Can you promise me that?"

Alida nodded. She liked having special secrets. "I won't say anything to anyone, Rider."

Twelve years later, her promise still remained unbroken. As she grew older, she realized the gravity of the situation she had been in. No, the men had not been working for her parents. They had been a group of exiled Wildsmen who hated the king. No, Rider didn't have special, magical powers. He had something darker and more twisted than that. The one thing she did have right is that Rider wasn't anything like the heroes in her stories.

She never had asked him what he was or where he came from. She wouldn't deny wondering. But Rider had saved her life. She was in his debt and forever grateful. Alida believed, even after seeing him kill the men in the caves, that Rider was inherently good.

After learning what she knew now though, she didn't know what she believed.

As if on cue, there was a knock on her door.

She flew out of bed and opened it slowly. Rider was standing outside with one arm against the wall. One look at him and Alida knew he hadn't gotten anymore sleep than she had. He was still in the dress pants he wore today and a white cotton shirt. His dark curls were tousled and tangled, and his eyes were bloodshot with long shadows beneath them. She studied him. Her oldest friend, basically an elder brother. She knew she could always count on him and thought that she knew everything about him. But who was he? She had never asked about his childhood and he had never brought it up. She knew his father and her father had fought together but who was his mother? For god's sake, she didn't even know his last name!

"We need to talk," he said quietly.

"What's your last name?" Alida asked. He looked taken aback. "What?"

"I said what's your last name. I just realized that I've known you almost forever and I don't know your last name. Isn't that a little strange for people who are supposed to be friends and not keep secrets and tell lies?"

Rider stared at her. "It's Grey. My name is Rider Grey. Let me in, Lida, and I'll explain everything."

She didn't meet his eyes but opened the door enough for him to step inside and shut it quietly. She watched as he strode over to her window and glanced at the balcony, as if someone could be hiding there, waiting to grab the girl who could destroy the world. Alida sat back down on her bed and wrapped her robe around her shoulders. Her fire had died down and the room was still hot, but she felt chills running through her body. Everything she had ever known was a lie.

She had known him for forever. There wasn't a part of her life that she could remember where he wasn't in it. Alida didn't have any siblings. She didn't have friends. The responsibilities of being a princess took up too much of her time. Her father was the king and he could rarely afford to spend time with her, just the two of them. Her mother had been the one there for her and she was dead.

Rider was the one person she could always count on.

And he had lied to her. He had known the information about her being the Last Heir for a long time and had kept it from her. He was supposed to be the person she could count on and yet, she couldn't even count on the truth. It was painful to realize. Did he believe her too naïve to contemplate it? Did he even take her seriously? Or would she always be the little princess to him, the one he had saved in the caves? She didn't know. What she did know was that she was angry at him and would demand an explanation until she got one.

Rider turned back to her. "I know you're upset, Lida, but you have to trust that I would never do anything to hurt you. And I would never let anything happen to you."

Alida looked at him. "I used to believe everything you told me, Rider, but now I'm not so sure. You know, there was a time when I asked you what you were doing for the weekend. I wanted to go riding for a day outside the city. You told me you were overloaded with work and couldn't spare the time. But when I walked into the banquet hall, there was a giant surprise party for me that you had planned. You were there, not overloaded with work, but laughing at me for how you had tricked me. I was okay with you withholding the piece of information about a surprise party for my birthday. But withholding that I'm part of the shadow and that you may be too? I'm not sure I can be okay with that."

He slumped down onto a chair in the corner of her room. "I understand why you feel that way. At least let me try to explain myself. I think it will clear some things up and hopefully you will understand why I did what I had to."

Alida shook her head. "I don't want to hear some excuse about how my father thought it best to put telling me about this off as long as possible. I don't want to hear that you did what you did to protect me. I want to know the truth about who you really are. I was so close to telling my father about what happened in the caves, so many times. But I never did. I swear to the gods if you don't explain yourself, I will leave this room, wake him up, and tell him everything."

Rider didn't respond but she could tell that he was shaken. He was very good at hiding his emotions but after all these years, Alida knew his tells.

Finally, he nodded.

"What I'm about to tell you, I've never told anyone before. And I probably never will again. I haven't forced myself to think about any of it in a long time.

But you're important to me, Alida. If I have to explain all of the dark, messy stuff from my past to make you understand that, then I will."

"My mother died when I was very young. My father by that time was already enlisted in the army and about to be at war with the Wilds. I was given to a shelter in Tenir. My life wasn't uncomfortable. It wasn't an evil orphanage like the ones in stories. But the older boys always found some way to make me miserable. I don't know what it was about a scrawny kid that made them all want to kill me but there it was. It wasn't every day. It wasn't even every week. But it was enough. It started with little things, like pulling my hair or pinching me. As I got older, it got worse. I'll spare you the details. Finally, when I was fourteen, I snapped. And that's when I realized there was something wrong with me."

"They had cornered me into an alley after chasing me throughout the town. I had learned to get back at them in little ways and somehow, they had found out that it was me who had started stealing their money to feed myself. I had stopped living at the shelter and floated from place to place. I occasionally came back to sleep in my old room and when I did, I would take their money for myself. Terrible, I know, but that's what happened. They had me cornered, about six or seven of them, all older and a lot larger than I was. They started beating me, worse than ever before. All at the same time. I was just lying there taking it because I didn't know what to do. And then, all the sudden, something within me snapped."

"I stared up at one of them and he started screaming. I had this feeling of anger like I had never felt before. I wanted him to feel pain. I lifted my hand up, feeling this anger course through me. The more I thought about it, the more he screamed until finally he just died. I wasn't consciously doing anything. The action of thinking it somehow set it off. I had no idea what 'it' was, but it terrified the others. They ran away, abandoning the other boy, as fast as they could, and I never saw them again after that.

"I hid. For a long time. As I, a fourteen-year-old boy, had killed someone who had barely reached seventeen. Worst of all, I didn't know how. But that day, something had awakened in me. It was a part of me that I didn't know existed. I had a power. I didn't know what it was or how to control it or use it, but I knew there was no bottom to it. It was absurdly horrifying and exhilarating all at the same time."

"I learned to use this power in different ways. All it had taken was anger to awaken it. I learned to use my power to manipulate people's minds into giving me food and shelter. I learned to bend their consciousness to make them see and hear and feel what I wanted them to. I possessed knowledge that I had never known before. I could track a person down and find them, just by touching something that belonged to them. That's how I found you all those years ago. And if I wanted, I could kill them. Easily. I didn't know how I had come to acquire this talent, but I had."

"When I was eighteen years old, I had my own apartment, and I was living honestly. I moved to Abdul when I was nineteen. There was a certain temptation to use my power to manipulate people into giving me money. But I knew that was wrong. I worked at a shop instead. I didn't make much, barely enough to live, but I was happy. That's when my father found me, somehow. I was overjoyed to see him. I had only ever met the man maybe five or six times in my lifetime. We talked for a long time in a tavern, and after a few drinks I told him about my power."

"He didn't believe me. He thought I might have gone crazy, growing up on my own. I was lucky though; by the next night he had forgotten. I didn't tell him again. I kept working after he left and for the next six years, I heard nothing of the man until the day your father showed up at my door and told me that my father was dead. He had died protecting Tieran. And for that, he was going to let me come work at the castle. I would have a better place to live and better wages, doing basic scholar work in the library so of course I took it."

"I worked my first year in the castle completely in peace. I was a low- level servant, dealing with low-level problems but I loved that job more than anything else. Until the day you got kidnapped. I was there when the king was talking with his advisors about what to do. I left without them knowing and went down to the site of the carriage. I pulled an arrow out of one of the guards' chest and for the first time in almost seven years, I used my power to find you. To this day, you are the only person who knows. And to this day, I still don't know how I could've come to have these powers. My only guess is that one of my ancestors is descended from Arca. But Lida, the truth is any person of the shadow has the powers I possess, once they are awakened. Anyone who is shadow-born can use their powers if they enter into a situation that is so desperate, they have no other choice but to use it. When those boys almost beat me to death, my power awoke. And if something like that ever happened to you, I'm sure it would awaken. I guarantee it would be much more powerful than mine."

Alida stared at him for a long time, not speaking, but absorbing everything that he had just told her. There was so much to her old friend that she hadn't known, and she almost felt guilty at her level of ignorance.

"Do it to me," Alida said quietly.

Rider's head snapped up from where he had been staring at the floor. "What?"

"Use your power to make me see an illusion. I know you can kill people, but I want you to try and bend my mind."

"Alida, I-"

"Do it, Rider. I would like to see the things that I may be capable of."

Rider sighed but nodded. Slowly, he closed his eyes and took a long breath, hand raising just slightly.

The world around her faded until there was nothing but white. She could no longer see Rider but heard his breaths from across the room. Suddenly, she was in the forest where they rode. She gasped. It was almost as real as if she were standing there herself. The tall trees that seemed to reach the sky, the rich scent of pine, the sounds of birds, and somewhere in the distant, a babbling creek. It was all here, in front of her, within her reach. Yet, by some means, this was all in her head, an elaborate tapestry created by Rider. She knew this as she reached down and touched her bed. But the bed wasn't there. With a blink, her room in the palace returned and the forest was gone.

Rider's deep green eyes were watching to see her reaction. "That's incredible," she managed.

"No, it's not. It's a curse. Lida, these powers come from beyond the Shadow Wall. Somewhere inside me is a part so dark that it doesn't even belong in this realm. And the power, although it feels unlimited, it's not. It takes a toll on me. The more I used it, the more I could feel it eating away at me. It's a curse."

Alida rolled her eyes. "Do you really want to go there? You're talking to the Last Heir here, remember?"

Rider stood up and crossed the room, sitting on the bed next to her. He took a deep breath. "Alida, I won't say what I believe or what I don't believe but you have a right to know. I won't make the mistake of keeping any facts from you about any of this."

He paused, deciding which words to use, before continuing slowly, "There are a portion of scholars who believe that the Last Heir of Abdiah is not someone in the line of Orinthian royals. They believe that somewhere, one of your ancestors dating back to Arca, had a bastard child who was the Last Heir. They hid that child and gave it away to another family, to protect themselves. That was the only child they had. So, the scholars believe that the bastard's line carried the purest blood of Abdiah, but the name of this line is lost to society. There are groups that have dedicated themselves to finding, what they call, the True King."

"Do you believe it's true?"

Rider shrugged. "I don't know. The reason we know any of this is detailed records of your family's genealogy dating all the way back to Arca herself. For the last thousand years since she lived, we know who the heir has been each time. Each time, the heir had a child, and they became the Last Heir. If one of them were to have a bastard child who carried the pure blood, it would not have been put in the records. It's possible. There's no way to know for sure."

"What do you think though?"

"I think the chances of the bloodline continuing for a thousand years in the same family, the firstborn child of Orinth royalty, it's near to impossible." Rider turned to face her. "And it's hard for me to contemplate that there's a part of you from the shadow world, Lida. I don't think you're the Last Heir."

Alida sighed in relief and fell back onto her bed. "I don't think I could be either, Rider," she said quietly. "I've never felt any pull to any sort of dark magic before. I know I've never been angry enough to awaken the power or whatever you just told me, but I can't bear the thought of me being like-" Alida caught herself.

"Being like me," Rider finished for her.

"Rider, I-I didn't mean it like that you know."

"It's alright, Lida. I know what you're saying. Believe me, it's not easy to come to terms with the fact that part of me is demon. It's even harder to realize that at one point in my life I was so angry that I awoke that part of myself. I would be lying if I said I wasn't tempted to use my powers more often. What I did to you just then, that's the first time I've used them in a long time. It would be so easy to get whatever I wanted whenever I wanted but like I said, the more you use the power, the more it begins to consume you. I learned that when I was a teenager and all I had was the shadow."

"I'm sorry, Rider. I can't even imagine what you've gone through. I can't imagine trying to control the power or anything like that. But Rider, you're not a bad person. You're the most selfless person I know."

Rider smiled a little. "Maybe." He laid down next to her, staring at the ceiling, "Alida, I know none of this makes sense. The shadow, the wall, the Last Heir, the True King, any of it. But the important thing is, we believe that Grafph knows about it and he believes it is you who will open the wall."

Alida sighed again, "Right. We're back to that."

"We don't know how long he has known. All of the intel is from spies within Illias, within the castle. They've heard enough mumbling about you and about the Shadow Wall that we can put two and two together. We don't know what his plan is, how it all fits in with the war that is imminent. We're treating it as a war. Regardless of what's happening with the Shadow Wall."

"The war will be happening, and everyone will assume it's about gold. But at the same time, Grafph will be looking for me. Because he wants to open the Shadow Wall, release whatever lies beyond it, somehow control them, and use the army of them to take over Orinth, and well, the rest of the continent." Alida said, a note of sorrow in her voice. She could feel a tightness in her chest, a sense of panic that threatened to choke her out.

"That's about the size of it," Rider replied sadly.

"I'm endangering everyone by staying here," Alida muttered.

Rider sat up. "Alida, no. None of this is your fault. We don't know what Grafph is going to do. When he's going to-well, when he's going to"

"When he's going to come for me," Alida finished.

"None of this makes sense to me. Like your father said, it doesn't seem like Grafph to try and take over the world, to destroy the Shadow Wall and control what emerges.

"How will he do that?"

Rider breathed heavily. "He can't. There is no way to control whatever emerges because we don't know what will emerge. All he can do is open the wall. I have to assume he knows this and is willing to take the chance anyway. Assume they will listen to him because he destroyed the border." He laid back down.

There was a long period of silence as both of them stared at the ceiling. Alida's head was spinning as she thought about everything she had just learned. It swirled around in her brain with no order or sense. She was the Last Heir. But there was a chance that she wasn't and somewhere a True King existed. Regardless, Grafph believed that she was and at some point, during the war that had been coming for a long time, he would attempt to take her. All the way to the Shadow Wall, in the northern most part of the Wilds. Then he would kill her and assume that it would open the wall. Maybe it would and maybe it wouldn't. Either way, she ended up dead.

"I need to leave here," Alida said finally. She sat up and looked at Rider, who looked at her, eyes wide.

"What? No, Lida I-"

"No, Rider," Alida interrupted firmly. "I need to get out of here. Grafph knows that I'm in Abdul. I've never really left. If I stay, he will find me. But if I go and hide somewhere. If I start over, maybe in Nagaye or Grady, I'll protect all of us. I don't know if I'm the Last Heir. But if I am, and Grafph gets to me, he will destroy the wall and try to control what comes out of it. We barely stand a chance against Auntica with just both of our armies. But add Grafph destroying the wall into the mix? We're done. Everyone is done. I don't know much about what's on the other side, but if it's where your power comes from? I can say with certainty we will be outmatched."

"I agree. It's the last thing we want to have to fight against. But we can protect you here. I can protect you here, Lida. I'm not going to let anyone hurt you. If you leave, I can't do that."

Alida covered his hand with hers. "I know you want to protect me. But you have to understand that the reason I leave here would be to protect you."

Rider squeezed her hand in return. "You can't say things like that because it makes me less apt to yell at you until you see things my way."

She smiled at him. "I don't think that has ever worked, Rider."

He laughed. "I know for a fact it hasn't. I don't want to lose you, Lida. I know we've had twelve good years and have made so many memories. Big memories and little memories. I've cherished all of them. I can't bear the thought of not having you here with me, to keep me sane, to lift me up when all of it gets to me."

"I'm not leaving your life forever, Rider, because you know I'll always be with you. Always. And I'll be back. It won't be this easy to get rid of me, I can tell you that much." Alida laughed at him but the tears were starting to form.

"Where will you go?" was all he asked in return. She watched him gnaw at his bottom lip, as he tried to stop himself from crying.

Alida shrugged. "I don't know. Somewhere I won't be recognized, where there won't be any spies. I think I'll go south to the Dela River and try to find a boat to Nagaye. I have a few contacts there I've made over the years from diplomatic missions and whatnot. They can help me settle and then from there, I'll wait and see what happens. If you manage to kill Grafph and win the war, I'll come back. But I need you to promise me one thing."

"What is it?"

"If things start going south and you know we're going to lose the war, come find me. We can run away and start over somewhere. You and me. Brother and sister. Somewhere so far away they'll never be able to find us."

Rider stood up and walked back to the window. Alida watched him, taking deep breaths, and staring out at the front of the castle. When he turned back to her, she could see the tears in his eyes. "I promise. You're tempting me right now. I could go with you and we could both get away from all this. But your father he's my friend. He needs me. Who knows, maybe I can put my powers back into good use again. And if I get ahold of Grafph, well, this will be over pretty quick."

"You mean, you'll use your power against him?"

"Without even thinking about it. I'll kill him. No questions asked."

Alida sighed for probably the thousandth time that night. "Okay."

Rider crossed the room once more and pulled her up, wrapping her in a tight embrace. Alida sighed and buried her face into his shoulder. "I don't want to do this, Rider. I didn't ask for any of it."

He whispered, "I know, Lida, I know."

They stood like that for a long time before Alida finally broke apart. "I suppose I'll have to get packed," she said.

"Yes. You know how to survive in the wild, that much I've taught you. You know how to hunt. You know the basics of self-defense. And we'll send you off with enough money that you can stay in an inn once you reach the Dela. We'll give you enough money for passage to Nagaye and whatever you might need once you get there. Take a few sets of clothes and you can buy more when you get there. Grab any other necessities, and I'll pack it all in a bag for you. This is my first time helping someone else run but I've been on the run enough to know how to prepare for it."

"Maybe you should have let me die in the caves, Rider," Alida said quietly. "Then we wouldn't be in this mess."

He grabbed her by the shoulders. "Look at me," he said. "I haven't done a lot of good in this world. Very little. Gods, a part of me is actually demon. But by far the best thing I've ever done is saving you from the caves."

She looked down at her feet and nodded. "I'm sorry. This is all just-" Alida paused, "-a lot to deal with."

"I know it is. But we're going to get through this together." Rider looked around the room and his eyes widened. He walked over to her desk and picked up a small piece of paper. He held it up. "This. This is a picture they drew of us at your birthday party, remember?"

Alida knew the picture he was talking about. Rider had hired an artist to come to her birthday party, to capture the moment in time. It took forever for the man to draw it, but the picture was the two of them standing over Alida's cake. She had just turned sixteen and was smiling so big her eyes were closed.

Rider was smiling, calmer, but just as happy. Somehow, the drawing managed to capture the utter joy of the moment.

Rider ripped the picture in half.

Alida gawked at him. "Rider! Why did you do that?"

He gave her a sad smile and handed her the half of the picture with his grinning face on it. He held the other half to his chest. "Something to remember me by. And something to remember you by. And the next time we meet, we'll paste it back together."

Alida swallowed back a sob. "Gods, Rider. You're not making this easy."

He slipped the piece of picture into his pocket. "I want you to change your mind more than anything. But you're right. You're safer if you run away. I'll kill Grafph, and then I'll come and bring you home."

Alida stared at the floor. "I'll be safer if I run away," she repeated and then glanced up at him. "I'll miss you. A lot. It feels like you're the only person I have sometimes."

He gave her a sad smile. "Likewise, Lida."

"Keep my father safe," she said. "And yourself. Please keep yourself safe."

"That should be no issue."

"Promise me we'll see each other again, Rider," Alida said. "Promise me."

Rider tucked his half of the picture into one of his pockets and grasped her hand in his own.

"I promise, Alida."

Chapter 4

The sun was just beginning to rise when Sawny and Adriel rode out of Illias. It had been tough to go, to refund and kindly reject all of her open cases. She had met with each of them personally and explained the circumstances. Some were understanding, others were heartbroken. She knew for many of them that she was the last hope of finding whoever they were looking for. But Sawny was Adriel's last hope too. A last hope that would result in an insurmountable amount of money. She was slightly appeased at the fact that she promised each client she turned down to do their cases completely free when she returned, making up for leaving so abruptly.

But as Sawny watched the man from the Wilds sign his name on their new contract, one guaranteeing her either a quarter or the full amount of treasure, she didn't feel as guilty. This was going to change the course of her life, that she knew. She could afford to buy a new, bigger apartment, a new wardrobe, possibly hire a few employees, and definitely spend more on Orinthian wine. Not to mention, the extra money would end up benefiting every single person who came to her for help.

All of yesterday she had spent pouring over her records and her sources she had used over the years to determine what the best course of action was for this case. It was tempting to start right in Abdul, searching for the elusive man who killed seven people without drawing a weapon. But, in all her cases, the first step was always foundation. She couldn't search for a man that she didn't know.

For that reason, their horses were set on a path to Tenir. Sawny had explained to Adriel that one of her most valuable sources was a secret library in the heart of the city that also acted as a records room and an important safehouse for the Orinthian black market. She had no part in the illegal side but was close with the owner of the library, a man called Jare. She had written ahead to alert him she was coming with possibly her hardest case, but she doubted the letter would reach him before she did. Once she established a baseline for this case, then the real search would begin.

Sawny had explained to Adriel as best as she could about her plans for the first leg of her search. She wasn't used to it; having to justify her actions to someone else. And Adriel was impossible to read. His expression always remained the same stony face that she had seen when they had first met, his eyes an impenetrable wall. She couldn't tell whether he approved of her methods or not. But still, he sat on his own horse next to her, staring into the horizon.

She wasn't sure what she thought of the man from the Wilds. Of course, she was undeniably biased against him. She had grown up right after the aftermath of the Great War, when the prejudice against their neighbors to the north was the strongest. The war had only lasted for a few years but the number of Auntican deaths were immense. The people of her country exiled almost every Wildsman, even if they were citizens. Those who managed to stay were treated with hatred. She had always been told that they were monsters who deserved this cruel fate. They married multiple wives. They burned foreigners at the stake. They then ate the bodies. If a woman didn't bear a son, the daughter would be thrown into the river and the wife, off a cliff. She bought into the stories when she was young and realized as she got older that they were dirty rumors to spread hate between the two countries. Any time she encountered a Wildsman, she treated them the same as anyone else. The lies that had been fed to her as a child, however, always remained at the back of her mind.

Adriel was intimidating. He only spoke to her when he had to. He didn't ask a single question about her business, why she lived alone, where her family was, or anything. She was grateful, as she wasn't sure she was ready to explain to him the disaster that was her life. She hadn't attempted to ask him anything either and decided it was probably for the best. They were going to travel with each other for weeks, possibly months. She didn't want any conflict stemming from their drastically different backgrounds.

At the moment, they trotted side by side. The quickest way to Tenir, a coastal city of Orinth, was to follow an old traveler's road that hadn't been used much since the conflict began with Orinth. It also allowed them to stay in Auntica for as long as possible before having to inevitably cross into her enemy country. She had adapted faking an Orinthian accent but there was no telling what might happen once they crossed the border. There would be many small villages that would provide them with constant supply renewals and inns to sleep in. Sawny had brought enough money for several nights in an inn, supplies for many weeks, and an amount left over for emergencies. Most of the money was strapped into a pocket in her underclothes. She wouldn't risk losing it. This way if they happened to run into trouble, she would still have the money on her.

She had dressed in traveling clothes, completed with an old cloak. Her blonde hair was braided back and she had strapped her bow to her back. Her bag of provisions was straddled on the back of her mare. She patted her neck; she had bought Indira two years ago for her journeys. The beautiful, grey horse was fast and not easily tired. The perfect companion for a long trip.

Adriel was dressed almost exactly the same as he had been two nights ago; the clothing of a warrior. His crossbow sat in his hands, always alert. Sawny could also spot two swords crossed on his back and several knives strapped to his belt. She had a feeling there were more weapons out of her line of sight. It was unlikely they would be attacked out in the open in the middle of the road. But she didn't mind. In the event they were attacked, she had a feeling Adriel would be better suited to take it on than she would.

He rode a giant, black horse, who held its head high and proud. Earlier that morning, she had heard Adriel speaking to it in some other language she couldn't understand. If she had to wager, this horse was as important to him as Indira was to her.

They rode all morning, hard, stopping only once to water the horses. The road was mostly empty, as Sawny guessed it would be. At the dawn of a war, people were not concerned with travelling. Occasionally, they would ride past groups of soldiers, clad in the Auntican colors of crimson and black. Adriel would put his head down as Sawny nodded to them. They would nod back and continue riding, shooting a strange glance at the soldier that she rode along with.

She could feel the tension every time they passed the soldiers. The war was coming. But she prayed to the gods that she wouldn't be caught in the crossfire and could work on this case without violence.

The hours flew by so fast that when Adriel spoke, for the first time all morning, she didn't hear him.

"Sawny?"

She broke out of her trance. "Hm?"

"I asked you if you knew where we were going."

Sawny glanced at Adriel, who was studying her closely. That was another part of the man that made her uneasy; every time he looked at her, she felt as if he could read her mind. He was always calculating something, and she could never figure out what it was.

"I do. They call this the Traveler's Road. I've ridden it many times to get to Tenir."

He didn't say anything as they continued but spoke again after a few minutes.

"We'll be riding through the Forest Dembe?"

"Yes. It's the fastest way to Tenir. Is that a problem?"

The Forest Dembe was the subject of much Auntican folklore. The dense forest took up most of the southern part of her country, but few people lived within the trees. It was said to be the home of witches and black magic. The popular saying was that those who went in never returned. Sawny herself knew this to be untrue as she had been in and out more times than she could count. It was the fastest way to get to Tenir, as the Traveler's Road went straight through it.

"No. It's not. I've never been through it is all."

Sawny grinned at him. "Heard about the witches, have you?"

His mouth twitched. "We have our own stories about the forest."

"Oh, do tell."

"I don't think an Auntican would exactly-" he paused thoughtfully, "-appreciate the stories."

"Now I have to hear it."

"It's not a long story. It was spread after the war that Auntican women aren't born. They are spawned in the Forest Dembe as witches and then spread themselves in the land accordingly to torture men for their wicked deeds. After they kill them, they consume their youth and repeat the process."

"Oh."

"Is it accurate? Were you spawned in the forest and now you're going to torture me for my wicked deeds?"

Sawny looked at him. He stared straight ahead but the corners of his mouth were upturned.

"Well, now that you know my secret, I think I have to kill you," she said in response.

"I probably deserve it."

Sawny laughed at this. "Maybe. But I've been through the Forest Dembe many times. I've never encountered any witches or evil magic. But there is a first time for everything."

Adriel shifted in his saddle. "I suppose there is."

"Are all Wilds tales so kind towards Aunticans?"

"We had a set of legends before the war, about Orinth and Auntica. They weren't exactly- flattering you could say. After the war though, they got a lot worse. To sum them all up for you, Auntican women are witches and your men would rather lie with beasts than lie with you."

"Orinth better be just as bad."

"Orinthian women are prostitutes and the men also would prefer to lie with beasts than to lie with them."

Sawny clapped her hands together. "Well then, I would say we're about even."

Adriel shrugged. "Perhaps you are. I didn't make up the stories."

"Do you believe them?"

He shook his head. "I don't think so. Anyways, you don't seem like much of a witch to me."

"Ah but I'm half Auntican, half Orinthian. You don't know which tales are true."

He didn't say anything else but Sawny could sense there was a lighter air between the two of them. She was glad for that. She was also glad of the fact that he was joking about the tension between their countries. She had been uncertain of how safe it would be to travel with a man who she had just met, who also happened to hate her country and her people.

They rode the rest of the day in silence, stopping a few more times to eat or freshen the horses up. It was nearly pitch black when they finally reached a village. It was small but had an inn that was open for guests. Sawny had stayed there once or twice on the route to different towns and cities. It was old and not particularly clean, but a bed and a hot meal beat her usual fondness for fresh sheets.

Sawny stopped her horse in front of the two-story building, entitled 'The Rusty Bucket Inn' according to the wooden sign hanging from the roof. She turned to Adriel. "I'll go fetch a stable boy to feed and water our horses. It's cheap to stay here for the night and the food isn't terrible."

Adriel frowned. "You're welcome to stay here, Sawny. I might have to find other accommodations for the night."

"Why is that?" Sawny asked.

"I just prefer to stay by myself, that's all." His voice held a strong tone of doubt and disappointment.

"Is that really what it is?"

He exhaled. "No."

"Then why?"

Adriel looked down at his feet, as he stroked the neck of his horse. "Auntican inns, they don't accept my people under any circumstances. Even if I'm traveling with one of their own."

"I thought you told me you were staying at an inn on the outskirts of town when we were in Illias."

"I lied. I didn't know how you would judge someone who was camping on the outskirts of town because not a single person in the capital would take him in."

Sawny sighed, "I wouldn't have judged you; I would've judged my people. Are you sure you don't want to at least try to get a room? This is a small inn, and they need all the business that they can get."

He shook his head. "I don't think so. Don't worry though. I've spent most of my life sleeping outside and on the ground. I'll be fine."

"Where will you camp then?"

Adriel looked past the buildings of the town and pointed in the general direction of the outskirts. "I'll find some shelter out that way. But I'll come find you tomorrow morning. As early as possible. Before the sun rises."

Sawny nodded. "Alright. If you're sure."

"I'm sure. Goodnight, Sawny." With that, Adriel turned around and began to lead his horse towards the darkness, away from the Inn. She watched him for a brief moment, patting Indira's neck before turning to the building. "I'll be right back darling," she said, kissing her horse's nose and tying her to a log outside the door.

She stepped into the inn. It was just as she remembered: a small dining room made of old wooden tables and chairs. There was a bar in the corner with a gruff-looking man wiping the counter. She could see a window that led into the kitchen. There wasn't a single person in the dining room besides the bartender.

He glanced up as Sawny strode over to the bar. She had seen his face before, the last time she had stayed.

"Good evening, ma'am," he said politely, eyeing her messy hair and clothes.

"I would like a room for the night and a meal please. My horse is right outside. It would be wonderful if she could be fed and watered and kept in the stables for the night."

The man nodded. "Yes ma'am." He turned into the back and yelled, "Gar! Horse in the front. Feed it, water it, and make sure it's comfortable!" He turned back to her as a little boy who couldn't be more than ten scuttled out of the kitchen and ran out the door. "My son," The bartender explained. "He's a little fellow but he's got a knack for horses. I can barely get him to come out of the stables. He's saving up for one himself. The boy loves to ride."

Sawny felt a pang as she observed the pride in the father's eyes. She had seen that look a long time ago from her own father, the first time she fired a bow. "Your endorsement makes me trust him with my horse then." She smiled.

He smiled back. "Well thank you. Others aren't so...comfortable with my son caring for their beasts. I'm glad you have an open mind."

Sawny spoke, "I'm happy to help. Now, about the room?"

"Ah yes. A room, a meal, and a bath I'm assuming?"

"I'll pass on the bath," Sawny said, wrinkling her nose. No sense in cleaning herself tonight when she was apt to get just as disgusting tomorrow. She paid the man with the money on her and continued, "Keep the change. Put it towards Gar's horse fund."

The bartender took the money and beamed at her. "Thank you kindly then, ma'am." He extended a hand. "You know, I've seen you in here before, but I don't think we've ever been introduced. Kye is the name."

She shook his hand. "I'm Sawny."

Kye turned into the window leading to the kitchen. "Solara! We need one plate of whatever you made tonight for a guest."

An older looking woman who Sawny knew was the wife of Kye stood up from the chair she had been sitting in. "Alright dear. Give me about ten minutes."

He turned back to Sawny. "Well, you heard the woman. Ten minutes but trust me, it'll be worth it. Her cooking is phenomenal."

She wasn't sure. The last time she was here she distinctly remembered an undercooked chicken and a potato that was so burnt it could've been mistaken for coal. But maybe the woman had learned. Sawny nodded.

"What brings you through here?" Kye asked her.

"I'm traveling to see a friend in Tenir," she replied.

He whistled. "You're braver than I am, Sawny. I wouldn't go into Orinth right now if someone paid me to do it."

She shrugged. "It might be the last time I get to see her before this all explodes. I thought I would take my chances."

Kye leaned closer. "It's my understanding that we're real close to exploding."

Sawny cocked her head. "What do you mean?"

"A man came through here a few nights ago. On his way back from Orinth. He was in Abdul for business or something of that sort. He told me he witnessed an execution of an Auntican outside the castle, orchestrated by the king. They had caught one of their servants trying to take information back to Auntica. So, they killed him for it."

Sawny raised her eyebrows. "That's an act of war."

Kye agreed, "I'm sure Grafph will view it as such."

"I did see many soldiers on the way here."

"That doesn't surprise me. He's forming an army. It's only a matter of time before one side attacks the other."

Sawny sighed, "It seems like a lot of trouble to go through for a dispute about gold."

Kye hesitated, and then said softly, "I've heard whispers that it's about something else. Nothing remotely related to gold. The gold was just an excuse to start fighting. The war is something bigger."

"What would that be?"

"If you promise to keep it under your hat?" At her nod, Kye continued, "There are some people who say that this war has to do with the Shadow Wall."

Sawny almost gasped out loud. "The Shadow Wall?"

"That's the one. The wall that is in the Wilds, said to keep evil from this realm."

"I don't understand."

"Neither do I. Neither has anyone I've spoken to about the rumors. But the words that seem to be making their way around Auntica right now; Shadow Wall."

Sawny pressed a hand to her mouth. She had been skeptical that this war was only a dispute about gold. She assumed it had secretly been about the kings gaining more land or more power. Peace between countries only lasted for so long and she never expected the peace to last between her country and Orinth. But the Shadow Wall? Why could the Shadow Wall possibly cause them to go to war?

"It makes no sense," she said.

Kye nodded. "That's what I thought too. The Shadow Wall has stood for a thousand years. What could they possibly want with it when it's been doing its job right; keeping the darkness out?"

Sawny shook her head. "I have no idea."

"They have to know that it's not about politics. The Shadow Wall and everything that lies on the other side of it? That's above disagreements about gold. We shouldn't meddle with it."

"We shouldn't."

"I'm sorry, I just forgot I never asked you if you wanted something to drink," Kye said, smacking himself in the forehead.

"An ale if you have it," Sawny answered but her brain was reeling. The Shadow Wall?

Kye set a mug in front of her. "I'm sorry if I've upset you. That wasn't my intention."

Sawny took a long drink from it. It was cold and surprisingly tasty. "No, it's alright. I'm just a little shocked is all."

Kye went to speak but was interrupted by Solara, who pushed a plate through the window. "Pork loin, grits, and green beans for the young lady," She announced proudly. Kye set the plate down in front of her. Sawny took a whiff of the meal and then smiled at the woman. "Thank you."

Solara beamed back, clearly proud of her work but not waiting to see if her guest liked it. She disappeared from sight. Kye slid a key across the counter. "Here's the key to your room. It's small but cozy and private. Is there a certain time you want your horse prepared?" Sawny told him before dawn and he nodded. "Right. Gar will have her ready to go. Now, I must bid you goodnight."

"Goodnight and thank you for everything." Sawny replied as she watched the man follow the way his wife had gone, back to what she assumed was their residence.

The pork was cooked perfectly, and the grits were done just right. It was more delicious than she remembered. Surprisingly enough, her room was nice too. The bed was clean and there was a small basin in the corner that she washed her hands and face with. When she tucked herself into the covers, she felt content with her first day of travel.

The feeling was almost immediately replaced by guilt as she imagined Adriel sleeping on the ground. He did say he was used to it, she tried to remind herself. And she asked him if he was sure more than once. Sawny could not have imagined Kye kicking Adriel out of his inn. He would have welcomed him with open arms, and he could have eaten some of the delicious meal that was now settling in her stomach. She would make sure to tell him that tomorrow.

And ask him about the Shadow Wall. The news that this war could be about something more than gold was alarming. She didn't know much about the wall or whatever lay beyond it besides what everyone knew; it kept the demons out. Sawny did know for a fact that keeping the demons out was a good thing. Any mention of the wall was not a good thing.

As she felt herself drift off to sleep, she made a mental note to ask Adriel about it in the morning.

She awoke at the crack of dawn and quickly assembled her belongings.

When she went downstairs, she found the young boy waiting with Indira.

"I groomed her and fed her. She's ready to go," he whispered, his voice brimming with excitement.

Sawny smiled at him. "Thank you very much, young man." She took the reins from him and mounted her horse. She quickly made sure all her possessions were still intact and in their place. With a nod at the boy, she nudged Indira in the side, and they were off.

The morning was cold and Sawny instantly regretted the fact she wasn't warm in her bed back at the inn. Or her apartment. The revelations of last night had left her with an unsettling new feeling about the conflict between Auntica and Orinth. She knew whatever happened, she and her business would be alright. Regardless of who sat on the throne, her services would still be needed. But with news of something about the Shadow Wall? That could potentially change a lot.

She wrapped her cloak around her tighter and almost fell off her horse as Adriel suddenly fell in line with her. She remembered telling him that she would wait at the Inn for him to come get her so they would set off together. It was too late now, and he didn't say anything about it, so they rode in silence.

Sawny was undeniably saddle sore. It had been a long time since she had spent an entire day, dawn to dusk, riding, with no long breaks. It was one of the benefits of traveling alone, going at her own pace. Though she tried, most times, to be brisk for her client's sake, she could still settle for a reasonable pace with frequent stops and not having to wake up before the morning's light.

She waited until the sun came up to look at Adriel. He was dressed in the same clothes that he had been in yesterday and his hair was slightly messy. Other than that, he looked fine. No sign that he had had to sleep on the ground the whole night because an entire generation of Aunticans refused to accept his people. She swallowed back her guilt and asked him, "How was your night?"

"Well enough," he responded, patting down some of his hairs that had been sticking straight up.

"I'm sorry," Sawny sighed.

"It's not your fault."

"No, but it is my country's."

"You are not your country."

"I suppose." She took a deep breath. "I heard some things at the inn yesterday that you might be interested in." He didn't respond so she continued, "The innkeeper told me that he has been hearing whispers of the true motive of this war. We've been told it stems from the conflict over gold at the borders. But the man told me that it has to do with the Shadow Wall."

"The Shadow Wall?"

Sawny nodded. "Yes. I didn't understand any of it and that's all he told me."

He didn't reply right away, and they rode for another ten minutes in silence. Finally, he said, "I don't know what kind of conflict there would be about the Shadow Wall, but none of it can be good."

"That's what I said. Have you ever seen the wall before?"

"Yes. We didn't have much of a choice after we retreated northwards. It's only miles away from most of our villages."

"What does it look like?"

He pondered this for a moment before saying, "It's huge. And black. It's made of iron but there's a sort of dark mist that lingers just on the surface, so the iron is almost impossible to see. The dark mist extends all the way to the sky, so there's no way you could climb over it. It's menacing. And even being near it just gives you this feeling. Like there's no good in the world and everything is for nothing. A sense of hopelessness. I've heard of people who have stayed near the wall for too long and ended up hanging themselves because of it. I don't know how true those stories are, but I can see how that would happen. I've only been there a few times because I had to be. I've never enjoyed it. I don't like hearing any whispers regarding the wall."

"It's been standing for over a thousand years. As much as this realm has its problems, we don't need to see what's on the other side of the wall."

Adriel agreed. "Hopefully it's just rumors then."

They rode on but she could tell the subject was running through both of their minds. The Shadow Wall and the impending war between Orinth and Auntica and how it all might be connected.

A few hours later, Sawny spotted a stream and directed Indira towards it. Adriel followed and they both dismounted. She let go of the reins and watched as Indira trotted happily to the running water. Her horse was tired after an already long day's journey. It appeared both of them were out of shape. Adriel let his own horse go and watched as it walked over to the stream.

Sawny sat down on a rock in the meantime.

"How did you learn to throw knives so well?" Adriel asked her. He leaned up against a tree with his arms crossed, watching their horses.

She looked up at him. "What?"

"In your apartment a few days ago. You almost took off my head. That's not a skill a lot of people have."

Sawny chuckled. "I don't imagine so. My-" she stammered a little, "father taught me. When I was eleven. He mostly taught me how to shoot a bow." She patted hers that was strapped to her back along with a quiver. "We worked on it for years. The knife work came after."

"I see. That's strange. I don't hear of many Auntican children learning how to fight so soon. In the Wilds, that's a normal part of adolescence, but not here."

Sawny shrugged. "My father was from the Darklands. The children there are also well versed in how to use certain weapons. He thought I needed to be too."

"I thought you were half-Orinthian."

"I am."

He didn't ask any more questions, but she could feel his curiosity.

"My birth father, I-I don't know who he is. He was Orinthian. My mother fled before he knew I existed. She was Auntican and she married my adopted father, who was a migrant from the Darklands. So, I grew up Auntican but with strong influences from the Darklands."

Adriel nodded. "I see. Have you been to the Darklands before?"

"Yes, once, for a case. It's an interesting place."

The Darklands was the bordering country of Auntica except it wasn't really a country. There was no capital city or ruling leader. There were no diplomatic teams or economic plan in place. The Darklands was a free for all. There were several major clans of people who ruled. The place was in constant battle, each clan wanting all the land for themselves. Sawny's brief trip had been frightening. A man believed his brother, a diplomat sent by Grafph himself to try and make peace, had been kidnapped by one of the tribes. So Sawny had donned some of her father's old clothing, including a valuable bracelet of the Darklands that was on her wrist currently. She brought her bow and journeyed to find the missing diplomat.

She had immediately been questioned by the first tribe she met. They treated her with suspicion but once they saw the bracelet, they relaxed. It was a tribal one with an emblem of her father's, a tribe that had been absorbed into others, made of green dyed fabric. She found a man who knew her adopted father. They talked for a long time before the man agreed to help her look for the diplomat. Within days they knew which tribe had him and where. Still, she had never felt comfortable during the entire time there and wasn't eager to return.

"What was it like?"

"They accepted me once I could prove that my father used to be one of them. It was terrifying but they were impressed with my shooting technique. Mostly because it was their shooting technique."

Adriel's mouth twitched. "I'm sure they appreciated it."

"It didn't hurt. It made them more accepting of me."

"I can imagine. Does your father visit the Darklands often?"

Sawny closed her eyes. Suddenly, her brain was overwhelmed with memories of her adopted father. She had been so distracted with this journey and thoughts of the case; Adriel's brother and the man who could kill in an instant. The pain that so often haunted her had briefly gone away. Until she thought about him once again. His name had been Caleb Ore. He was the gentlest soul she had ever met, despite being from a country of warring clans. He took Sawny, who wasn't even his real daughter, and loved her like she was his own. She saw the way he looked at her mother; like she was anchoring him to this world. Her mother often closed herself off to them. He loved her even through the days where she couldn't bear to look at him.

Sawny had held him in her arms as he died, covered in his blood from the wound in his abdomen. He couldn't manage to get any words out, just stared up at her with something of a smile on his face.

It had been too late to save either of them from the men who had come in the middle of the day and killed them both, but spared Sawny. To this day, she still couldn't understand why.

"My father is dead," was all she said to Adriel, standing up and walking back to her horse.

Chapter 5

South of Abdul

Alida woke up with a start.

She forgot where she was almost immediately. Gone was her soft bed at the palace, with the view of Abdul from her balcony. Gone was Weylin walking in with her breakfast and briefing her on her schedule for the day. Gone was taking an hour to get ready, choosing the perfect dress, getting her hair and makeup done.

Now, she was sprawled within a bed roll, on the cold ground of some forest just south of Abdul.

Her large bag laid a few feet from her. It had been almost a day since Rider had helped her pack it in the dead of the night. She had been crying so much that by the next day, her eyes were still bloodshot, and her face was still puffy. They had walked arm in arm towards the king's office. It had been a convenient day to find out about the tunnel that led directly out of the city. Rider kissed the top of her head and vanished back into the castle, as she started out the dark passage.

She had a vague idea of where she was going but couldn't use the main roads. For one, Alida didn't know if Grafph had agents looking for her. And for another, she was one of the most recognizable faces in all of Orinth. She couldn't have someone spotting her and identifying her. She could be kidnapped again, or the word could travel fast which direction she was headed. Her father could find her within days.

She had left him a hastily written note explaining what she was doing. She knew he wouldn't understand why she would leave the protection of the castle. She didn't completely understand herself. A part of her knew, though, that the best course of action was to flee. She apologized to her father for not saying a proper goodbye and tried to convey to the man that she still loved him and always would, even if they never saw each other again.

It was a depressing thought but one that she had to consider.

Rider had decided it was best for her to go on foot, that it would be easier to stay off the roads without having to care for a horse. She had walked what seemed to be miles in the dark tunnel before coming up stairs and through a trap door into a forest. The sun had just been rising when she emerged from the ground. And from that point on, she walked.

She would find a town on the banks of the Dela. She would get passage to Nagaye. If the town she was in didn't have passage, she would walk along the coast until she found it.

And when she got to Nagaye, she would figure the rest out from there.

She was scared. Actually, scared was an understatement. Alida read a lot of stories about brave princesses. Ones who decided to lead their countries into battle. Ones who pretended to be on diplomatic missions but ended up assassinating enemy kings. Ones who went and slayed dragons or demons or whatever monster they could find. She was not that princess. She wasn't even close to that. She didn't have courage or heart or any of what the characters in stories had. She had something, but it wasn't that.

Running away didn't make her feel strong or brave either. It made her feel weak. The more she thought about her decision, the more she wondered if she was making the right one. Rider told her he understood but she was beginning to wonder if he really meant it. No, he wouldn't let her do something that would lead to her harm.

Alida just prayed to the gods that everything would work out.

All she could think about was being the Last Heir. Or not being the Last Heir. But Grafph thinking she was and killing her anyways. Last night, she had laid on the ground in her bed roll, shivering, but trying to summon the power she saw Rider use. She stared at a small tree just next to her and tried with all her might to destroy it. Nothing happened. She didn't even feel a shred of the power that she might have. There was nothing there but what she had always felt. Now Rider did say his power was awakened when he experienced a near death situation with extreme anger. But still, she thought there should be some sort of sign that she was the Last Heir.

She clung to the idea that it wasn't her who had Abdiah's pure blood. That it wasn't her who would have to be killed to destroy the Shadow Wall. She pondered the idea of the True King. Somewhere, one of her ancestors had a bastard child who received the pure blood. If that was true, she didn't have a trace of demon in her. But someone else unknowingly did, and it was that person who had the capability of destroying the Shadow Wall.

She wondered how many people were partly demon, like Rider, and recognized their powers. It was a terrifying thought. Rider was a good person who was cursed, but that didn't change who he was. The idea of someone who was bad having the abilities that her old friend possessed would keep her up at night.

Alida wished Rider were with her. All this would be so much easier to bear. But she thought of the promise he had made to her. If things went wrong, he would find her, and they would start over.

Alida sat up and glanced around her. It was well into the morning and she cursed herself for it. She was so used to sleeping until Weylin woke her. She didn't know if she was capable of waking up early enough on her own. It technically didn't matter how fast she got to Nagaye but still, she wished to be there as soon as she possibly could. The faster she was out of Orinth, the better. She rolled up her bedroll and put her traveling boots back on. Alida admitted to herself that, yes, she was sorely out of shape. Emphasis on the sorely. After a full day of hiking toward The Dela, she could barely stand. Had she known she was going to do this, she might have taken Rider up on his offer to go running every morning with him.

She slipped the bedroll back into the pack and fished out a package of dried fruit. She sighed as she consumed what she knew would be her breakfast. She tried not to think of what would've been waiting for her if she woke up in her bed at the castle. A steaming hot cup of tea, scrambled eggs so divinely fluffy, crisp bacon, fresh fruit, pastries, and a tall glass of milk. She felt her stomach rumble as she bit into what was probably a dried banana. It was tough to chew and didn't taste like anything.

As she put the remaining fruit back into the sack, her survival knife caught her eye. Suddenly, she had an idea. She grabbed the knife and with one swift motion she cut off her long hair.

Alida gasped at her rash action as her hair fell to the ground. She touched her head. Her hair now just barely touched her shoulders. It had previously reached her lower back. She shook her head wildly. It felt so light and new. She ran a hand through her locks. Hopefully, if she did end up running into other people, they wouldn't recognize her with the different style.

She grabbed her hair off the ground and scattered it to the wind. She put the knife away, strapped the pack to her back, and started walking.

She was in a lighter part of the forest, where the sun still streamed through the trees. The forest wasn't very old, but people had decided not to settle there. She hoped they wouldn't. It was peaceful, with the wind slightly blowing and different birds singing. It reminded her of the place she and Rider went to ride horses. Thinking about that made her sad so she pushed the memory back and kept walking.

She guessed that she was half a day's ride from the castle, which was alarming. A good horseman could catch up to her quickly and they had to realize she was gone. Alida wasn't sure if Rider would tell her father that he helped her to escape. He probably wouldn't confess. Hopefully, he would advise the king to not search for her. But if by chance her father sent his people after her, she hoped they wouldn't search in the forest. Maybe they would assume she would go to Lou. Her father's sister lived there at an estate that was incredibly nice. She knew her aunt would welcome her with open arms but if her father found her, her aunt would undoubtedly send her back. Alida didn't want to endanger her with her presence anyways.

Rider had informed her that the Dela was only a few days ride south of Abdul. She sighed at the prospect of having to walk all of that but continued anyways.

She did what Rider always told her to do. "Look at the positive, Lida." He had said it so many times and it drove her to madness, but now she tried to apply it. She was warmer than she had been, with her white cloak wrapped tightly around her shoulders. She still had an abundance of supplies, not to mention a lot of money. It was a beautiful day out. The forest reminded her of a time and place better than the one she was in. Those were all the positives.

"I think the negatives outweigh them in this circumstance, Rider," she mumbled to herself.

She didn't need to list the negatives because they had been on a constant loop in her brain from the time she stepped foot into the tunnel leading out of Abdul.

She pulled out the drawing of him that she had decided to keep in her front pocket. She closed her eyes and just wished that she could go back in time, to the moment it had captured. She would grab the Alida of the past and shake her and yell in her face, "Appreciate this time, Alida! It's about to turn bad real fast!". She would give her some kind of warning.

She wondered if Rider had looked at the picture of her as much as she had been looking at his. She sighed and put the drawing back in her pocket.

It was around noon when she started getting the feeling that she was being followed. It started off as subtle things. She would hear a twig snap or leaves rustle. Alida couldn't be sure it was just an animal until she heard the distinct sound of a cough. She froze and her hand hovered on her small sword. She turned around but there was no one there, save more trees and forest. But she knew there was someone.

She quickly calculated the situation in her head. If it were one of her father's men, they wouldn't hesitate to grab her and start back towards the kingdom. If it were, gods forbid, an Auntican who was sent to bring her to King Grafph, they probably wouldn't hesitate either. She couldn't think of a reason why someone would tail her through the forest. But she was scared. She had learned the basics of wielding a sword but if this person had any skill, they would probably beat her, if it came to that.

Alida took another few steps and then pulled the sword out. Somehow, it came from its sheath very naturally and she held it in front of her. It almost seemed like she knew what she was doing.

"Whoever is there, I just want to warn you that I have a sword and I know how to use it. So, you can stop following me and we'll go about our business. Or you can keep following me and I'll cut your head off. Probably."

There was no response for a few seconds before Alida heard a chuckle. From behind a tree that was about ten feet from her, a man stepped out. He was very old, with a few strands of wispy white hair on his head and skin that was wrinkled like old paper. He was dressed in clothes she had never seen before, a colorful robe with intricate designs that ran to his toes. He wore a pair of cotton slippers and a small black hat on his head. He was, at least, a foot shorter than her. In a word, quirky but that didn't mean he wasn't dangerous.

"Who are you?" Alida asked, raising her sword. She felt slightly ridiculous threatening a man who was old enough to be her grandfather, but she promised herself to be cautious on this trip.

The man laughed again. "You can put away your sword, dear. I'm not going to hurt you." He had a strong accent that she couldn't identify.

She kept the sword out and repeated, "Who are you?"

He held up his hands in surrender. "If my title is that important to you, you may call me Ledger."

Even with his hands up, she didn't know what to expect. He was an old man, but so was her father, and her father wielded a sword with incredible skill. She gripped her own hilt tightly, knuckles turning white. It could just be an old man, but he could just as very well be a spy or someone who wanted to hurt her. "Why have you been following me?" Alida asked, raising her voice. She hoped to the gods she looked intimidating and not like a small child who was playing with her father's sword.

"It's you who are in my territory, dear. I was just making sure you weren't going to harm anything." He pointed off into the distance. "I live through the woods that way."

She turned to see where he was pointing and sure enough, in the distance, she saw a small hut made of wood. She put the sword back in her sheath and laughed nervously, "I'm sorry. I might have been a little paranoid." Her hand didn't leave the hilt of the sword. She was still unsure of who he was or what he wanted.

"Forgiven. I don't get many visitors through these parts. Who are you?"

She hesitated before saying her name. It would be obvious, if she kept going by Alida, who she was. Best to settle with a fake identity now. "My name is Nova. Nova Grey."

Ledger cocked his head. "No, it's not. You're the princess, aren't you?" There was a wry smile on his face, as if he knew something she didn't. It was unsettling, to say the least.

"The princess of what?" Alida said, swallowing back her surprise. She had been trained never to give anything away with her expression and it was kicking in now that an elderly man in the middle of the woods had guessed her identity in less than a minute of seeing her.

"Princess Alida Goulding of Orinth. I think I would know that face anywhere."

Her mouth dropped open, "How-how?"

Ledger shrugged. "I'm a man of many many years. I am, daresay, wise. And this forest has a way of showing me the truth."

Alida wasn't sure at all what the man meant. "Well, yes. I'm Princess Alida. But right now, I'm trying not to be."

He nodded. "I understand. Often, we try to run from ourselves. And it has led you into this forest. So, might you permit me to feed you lunch? It's just about that time and it's been a while since I've spoken with someone from the outside world. I have a bit of catching up to do."

Alida glanced at the sky. "No. I should be moving on. I'm on my way south and it's time sensitive." She also wasn't about to go follow this man who lived in the woods and whom she had just met. That seemed like a bad idea on her part.

Ledger frowned. "You don't trust me? I suppose I can see why. But I'm not going to poison you. I'm not even from Orinth or Auntica. I don't have any skin in this war. I'm a philosopher. Every person who comes through here I try to talk to and learn about. It helps me to expand my knowledge of the humankind. Plus, I make delicious food."

"I have to go. I don't have time to spare," Alida said again, although she was undeniably hungry. This man didn't seem dangerous, but she knew better than to judge by appearances.

"You underestimate the energy a good meal will give you, Princess. I'm not going to hurt you. Very rarely do people pass through here. At least, permit me to show you my humble abode. Then you can decide whether or not you want to stay for lunch."

Alida looked towards his hut again and as if on cue, her stomach rumbled. She blushed. She didn't think her stomach could handle another meal of dried fruit and water.

Fine, she thought, I'll at least take a look at the place. If something seemed off about it, Alida would leave as fast as she could. But she wouldn't say no to real food, if she decided the place was safe. "Fine, yes. But I can't stay for long," she warned.

Ledger grinned at her and motioned towards the hut. "Yes, ma'am. Follow me."

She took one last glance at the path she was about to take before following the man. She wouldn't mind resting her legs, even for a little while. And a homecooked meal sounded heavenly at the moment. Alida hoped that this man wasn't lying to her and that Auntican soldiers would burst in and take her. But he was old. And according to him, neither Auntican nor Orinthian. She would be safe. Especially with her trusty sword strapped to her waist.

They approached the hut. It was tiny and Alida had to assume it was only one room. It had a large porch attached with a table and chairs. There was a fire pit in the yard of the hut which held a pot over it. Alida took a deep breath and smelled something amazing. Ledger investigated the pot and mumbled to himself as he started to stir it. He looked at her. "What do you think?"

It was small and the table outside was set for a meal. Yes, she could afford to stop. Alida would eat quickly and be off. There was no danger in it.

Finally, she nodded. "I'll stay for a little while."

Ledger smiled and pointed at the table on the porch. "Excellent! Please, make yourself at home. Get the giant pack off your back and relax."

She did as he suggested, her shoulders sagging in relief as she placed her bag on the ground and fell into one of the chairs. It had only been a few hours of hiking, but she was exhausted. She shook her head to herself. She was not great at this whole adventurer thing. But was she supposed to be? Alida had grown up in a castle. There was never a time where she had to hike for days on end to flee the country. Of course, she had been trained in survival for emergencies, but she never thought said emergencies would come to pass. This was a whole new experience.

"So where are you going, Princess Alida?" Ledger called to her, as he worked on whatever was in the pot.

"I'm going to see family in Tenir."

Ledger shot her a look. "Oh really? On the brink of a war?"

Alida narrowed her eyes. "How exactly does a man who lives in the middle of a forest know that a war is going on?"

Ledger shrugged, "I have my ways of finding these things out."

"You're a strange man, Ledger."

"You're not the first to say that and you certainly won't be the last," he chuckled.

"I'm leaving Orinth. It's safer for me that way."

"I see. This isn't the business about the Shadow Wall, is it?"

Alida gaped. "I-how did-no. I don't know what you're talking about."

Ledger laughed at this. "You're a poor liar for a princess. I thought they trained you in this."

"They do and they did. I must be off my game." Seeing the man in the first place had surprised her and now her guard was down. Normally, she could lie to anyone about any number of things and make it seem like it was the gods-given truth.

"It's not your fault. Like I said, this forest has a way of finding the truth. Whether you want it to be known or not."

Alida sighed. "Well then, yes. It is about the Shadow Wall. It's better for everyone if I leave here. If I stayed, I would put the entire continent in danger."

Ledger nodded. "So they think you're the Last Heir."

At this point, she wasn't surprised. "Yes, they do. Me, I'm not so sure. Do you know?"

"I wish I could help but no. I don't know who the Last Heir is. I only know there is one."

"Do you know anything about the True King?"

"I don't know if they exist, if that's what you're asking. But yes, I know about the theory. A bastard child was born of an Orinthian royal who inherited the blood of Abdiah. The Orinthian royal line ceased to hold the Last Heir and another line has the curse now. But no one knows who."

"Do you believe it?"

Ledger shrugged. "I don't know. It's just as possible as you being the Last Heir. But there are many people dedicated to finding the True King. Secret societies who have been looking for him since they found out about the possibility of a bastard."

"I didn't know that," Alida said.

He nodded. "Mainly in cities. Lou, Tenir, and Abdul are the main ones. The groups are very underground. I mean, the fact that there is a Last Heir is already very uncommon knowledge to the average person. But yes, societies have dedicated themselves to finding their True King. It's...interesting I suppose you could say. They, of course, pour themselves over the genealogy of your family, trying to find which member started the new line, if it exists. They look at old diaries and records to see if they can find any mention of a bastard child who was given away. It's an obsession. Very odd, even coming from the reclusive man who lives in the woods."

Alida raised her eyebrows. "I don't know how to feel about that. Why they even call it the True King is beyond me."

Ledger walked into his hut and returned with two bowls. "I don't know why these societies exist in the first place. The True King. It's all a bunch of bogus if you ask me."

Alida was inclined to agree with him as she watched him fill the two bowls with whatever was in the pot. It looked like stew. He set the bowl in front of her, and she could see that she was correct.

"Venison stew," Ledger announced proudly, handing her a spoon. "All of the ingredients, of course, are from this forest. I shot the deer, may his soul rest in peace. The vegetables are from my garden. The spices I created myself. Thank the gods I have someone to share it with. Too much work not to be validated."

Alida took a bite of the soup and sighed in pleasure. It was delicious. The meat in the stew was tender and the vegetables tasted as fresh as the ones at the castle. And the flavors were unlike anything she had tasted before. She nodded to Ledger, appreciatively. "Consider yourself validated."

He clapped his hands together joyfully. "It's been a while since I've had the opportunity to cook for someone. I'm glad you like it."

She finished the bowl of soup within minutes. Ledger refilled her bowl without saying a word and she said a hurried thanks as she was quick to consume the second helping. Alida had no idea how hungry she had been. She was ashamed of herself. One day without the cuisine of the castle and she was already folding like a cheap coat.

Ledger didn't eat much of the soup, which Alida was glad for. She felt less guilty having four bowls of it. He then brought out a cup of tea, which Alida almost cried at the sight of. Wimp, her brain told her, Alida Goulding, you are a wimp.

Over the tea, they talked.

"Where are you from, if not Orinth or Auntica?" Alida asked him.

"I'm from the North. I moved here a long time ago."

"Oh? And why is that?"

Ledger shrugged but Alida noticed a tightness in his shoulders. "There were circumstances in the North that prevented me from staying there. I decided it would be best to leave for good. Take the trouble right out of it. I traveled through the continent but didn't find any place in particular I liked. Until here. This forest, well, it called to me." He looked past his yard and into the trees. "It's not a magical forest by any means but for me, it's home."

Alida studied him. "I'm glad you found a place to call home," she said, unsure of what else she could say. It was apparent there was more to the story than that, but she wouldn't ask him.

Ledger smiled, as if he knew what she was thinking and said, "Have you been to the North?"

She shook her head. "No, I haven't. I've been to Grady once though. I went with my friend, Rider. It was for a diplomatic mission, two weeks at the palace of their king. I loved it there. But you're right. It's hard to get better than here."

"Rider, the king's advisor?"

Alida nodded and smiled. "My closest friend." She pulled the picture out of her pocket and showed it to Ledger. He studied it carefully before handing it back to her.

"I've met him."

Alida cocked her head. "You have?"

"Many years ago. He wandered into this forest and we met."

"I don't recall him ever leaving Abdul," Alida said, perplexed. She couldn't remember a time when Rider hadn't been in the capital, or on a diplomatic mission with her.

"Yes, a young man named Rider. It was years ago, before he was the advisor."

"That makes sense. What was he doing here?"

Ledger shrugged. "He seemed very lost. He was about nineteen years old at the time. Something had happened in the city of Tenir. He was dazed and confused. Of course, I helped him. He ate a meal here and barely spoke a word before leaving. It was indeed very strange."

Alida thought back to everything Rider had told her nights before. She couldn't think of an event that would have caused him to wander through the forest, dazed and confused. Perhaps the reality of who he was hit him too hard on a certain day. She had to remember to ask him the next time she saw him. If she ever saw him again.

"I'll suppose I'll have to find out," Alida said at last.

"He seemed like a nice young man despite the general confusion and sadness."

"He is a nice man. The nicest one I've met."

"Who is he to you?" Ledger asked curiously.

Alida took a breath. "I'm an only child. Rider is the older brother I never had. I've grown up with him. There's not a time I can remember where he wasn't in my life."

Ledger smiled at her. "That's a lovely relationship to have with someone."

"I already miss him. There have been very few days where we were apart from one another."

"The way you talk about him, it seems like you could be family," Ledger said with a small smile on his face.

Alida laughed. "Well, I do consider him family."

Ledger stood up and cleared the table. Alida offered to help but he turned her down. She sat on the porch, staring at the forest and thinking about the past in silence. It was peaceful. She knew that she had only meant to stay here for a few minutes, but it had already been an hour. Yet, she was content with it. This brief rest would fuel her for the rest of the day's journey.

Alida stood as Ledger stepped back onto the porch. She grabbed her bag and strapped it to her back. "I hope I gave you some good conversation," she said to the old man, extending a hand to him.

He grasped it. "Yes, indeed you did my dear. A pleasure." Ledger bowed.

Alida curtsied back to him. "And on the off chance that someone passes here after I do, I would appreciate if you didn't mention I was here."

Ledger put a hand to his heart. "I swear it, Princess. Your presence here shall remain anonymous."

Alida leaned down and kissed the man on the cheek. "Thank you for a lovely afternoon, Ledger. I hope our paths will cross again."

He beamed at her. "I know they will someday, Alida. Remember, you're much stronger than you think you are." He reached into his pocket and pulled out a small bracelet. He held it up. It was a silver band that formed into the shape of a star at the center. "This is from the North. It was supposed to be a gift, for someone important to me. She's gone now and I've been waiting for someone who I think needs it. It's for you."

Alida frowned. "Thank you, but I can't accept something like that, if it was a gift for someone important to you."

Ledger waved her off. "Like I said, she's gone now. I-I don't think I'll see her again."

Alida wanted to ask several questions but she refrained from it. The expression on his face made it known to her that this was something private, something raw and vulnerable.

"In that case, I would be honored to have it."

He smiled at her and handed it over. She placed the bracelet onto her wrist and surprisingly, it was a perfect fit. She admired it. At the castle, she had a plethora of jewelry at her fingertips. But there was something about this bracelet, knowing it was meant for someone important to Ledger, that made it as special as a diamond necklace or a tiara at home.

"It's here for when you need to remember the light. Touch it, use it, feel it when everything seems the darkest." Ledger spoke. There was something in his voice, a certain tightness, that made her all the more curious. What had happened to this man and the person who this bracelet was meant for?

Alida turned back to him. "Thank you," she said softly. "I'll remember that."

Ledger patted her shoulder. "I know you will. Now be off with you! You have a journey ahead of you and not a minute to lose!"

Alida held herself back from telling him that it was he who had invited her for lunch but instead, she began walking back to the forest. She turned back before entering and waved to the old man. He returned her wave, beaming.

As she stepped into the forest, she hoped desperately that she would live long enough to meet him again.

Chapter 6

Abdul, Orinth

Rider watched as the King sat at his desk, head in his hands, staring at nothing.

It had been a day since the princess had fled the castle. Her flight had caused almost as much worry as the time she was kidnapped ten years ago. But this time, the king did not deploy his men to tear the city apart. Rider did not track her using his powers. They both had decided to let her go.

Especially after reading the letter.

He had a hard time holding back tears as he read it, after the king had shoved it into his hands.

Dear Father,

Let me start by saying this: I'm sorry.

Your first instinct will probably be to blame yourself. Don't. This was my decision and I made it for the sake of our kingdom. Grafph knows I'm in Abdul. If he finds me, and sacrifices me to the Shadow Wall, all will be lost. If I leave and he never finds me, you can defeat him. And if that happens, I'll come back. I pray to the gods it will happen.

I wish I could contribute more, be out there fighting for our great kingdom, but this is perhaps the best thing I can do for us right now. Don't worry about me; I know how to take care of myself. Worry about the upcoming war. Worry about Grafph and his armies. But don't waste your time worrying about me.

Trust Rider. He knows what he's talking about (most of the time).

I hope to the gods that I will see you again, Father. But in the case that we never meet again, this is my goodbye. I love you, Father. No matter what. The time I've spent with you has been priceless. Please forgive me for anything I might have done, as

I forgive you. I wish I could convey to you how important you are to me, but alas, I don't have the time or enough paper. So, I'll just leave you with this. I love you. Please take care of yourself and take care of Rider. You both mean the world to me.

Your faithful daughter, Alida Goulding.

Rider read the letter several times, in Alida's neat script, before handing it back to his king. He knew that she had been leaving; he had helped her prepare for her departure. He had talked to her about it, the pros and the cons, the dangers, all of it. But still, the next morning as soon as he opened his eyes, he felt a pang in his chest. She was really gone. And he was shockingly scared for her. He knew Alida was prepared but there was no telling what might happen on the road. He wished he could be there with her; he never had to worry about anything. If anyone attacked him, he could use the shadow and they would die. But Alida? She didn't have the power yet.

If anything happened to her, he would find the person responsible and show them just how demonic he could be.

But, as he stood in front of Tieran, he tried to push everything to the back of his head. He had too much to worry about to be thinking of future revenge.

"I can't believe she's gone," Tieran said finally. "I just can't fathom it."

"I can't either," Rider agreed. It was a lie but at the same time, the truth.

"I'm worried for her, Rider. Alida has never been completely alone outside of the palace."

"She knows enough to risk leaving," Rider corrected. "Alida is too smart to walk into a death trap. She'll take care of herself. But right now, we need to think about the war. Like she said, if we kill the threat of Grafph, she can return to us."

Tieran nodded. "You're right, Rider." He tucked the letter into his pocket and stood, turning to the map behind his desk and observing it. "We have to decide where we are best suited."

"I think you should stay here, Tieran," Rider said quietly.

The king gave him a look. "I knew you would say something like that."

Rider sat down in front of his desk and rested his chin on his hand. "It's safer for you here, among the castle and its many guards. You can give orders from here and have messengers deliver them. There's no reason to risk your life to be near to the front lines. The closer you get to Auntica, the bigger chance there is to be assassinated." The king raised an eyebrow at him. Rider shrugged. "It's true."

"I understand your concern and I acknowledge your opinion. I wanted to get that out of the way before I tell you no. I believe I will be heading to Lou to join the 2nd Army. I am close with the general. I'll know exactly what's happening and won't have to send messengers when I want to make a decision," the king replied

Rider rolled his eyes. "Is it worth asking you to reconsider?" The king smiled a little. "Not at all."

"What about joining the 1st army? They will be here in Abdul and you can still give the orders. It will just be a lot safer."

Tieran shook his head. "I've made up my mind already so there's no sense in trying to change it."

Rider sighed. "I suppose not. And what about me?"

"I want you to track down the general of the 3rd army and march with them. There's no telling where they're at right now. I spread them about the border, so he has to be within one of the four groups. He's brilliant but he's young. I want you to advise him during this war. It will be more beneficial than advising me. I haven't exactly been the best listener."

Rider chuckled at this. The most recent advice he had given the king about Cray Dune had been sorely rejected. And now, he denied Rider's plea for him to stay within the capital. Perhaps it was better for him to go to the 3rd army. Maybe their general would mind his counsel.

"When will we leave?" Rider asked.

"Tomorrow. I'll tell the servants to get us packed tonight. I'll travel with guards, don't worry. And you're welcome to take any you might like with you to the 3rd army," The king responded.

"I'll be faster alone."

"So be it." The king turned from the map and fell into his chair, slouching.

"It's times like these that I wish Natasha was here," he said quietly.

Rider had to agree with him. The queen had always been the loudest voice of reason among them. She was incredibly wise and calm. Every decision she made was after days of calculations, an intricate observance of the pros and cons of a situation. But when decisions were time sensitive, she always made the right calls. Having her here would indeed make the whole situation a lot easier.

If Alida was the Last Heir, it would have been Natasha who passed on the blood of the demon. After all, Tieran had married into the line. Imagining the late queen possessing the same powers he did was incomprehensible. She was one of the kindest people that Rider had ever met. It was another reason he was convinced Alida wasn't the Last Heir.

"She would have this war won pretty quickly," Rider said.

The king laughed. "I'm sure Grafph would have run away with his tail between his legs if she were still here."

"I don't understand what he's doing," Rider confessed. "I've met him only a handful of times and he's never struck me as the continent-dominating type."

"He isn't. Up until a few years ago, we were close. I saw him twice or thrice a year. We exchanged frequent letters. He was a good man, a good father and husband. I was there when Prince Tawn was born. Princess Mae had her tenth birthday party here, with Alida. We were basically family. And then, almost overnight, everything changed. What happened?"

Rider didn't have the slightest clue. "I wish I knew. I don't think it's Grafph doing this, though."

The king replied, "All the reports from the spies say it's Grafph making the decisions. It's Grafph who found out about Alida and decided to come for the Shadow Wall. All signs point to him. But you're right. There must be someone behind him, influencing him."

"Either way, we have to treat him as the enemy. Regardless of our past experiences with the man, he wants to kill Alida. That wipes the slate clean," Rider said, running a hand through his dark curls.

"You're right." Tieran stood up and stretched his arms above his head. "We should go prepare."

Rider followed him.

Tieran turned back towards the office as he was about to step out, glancing at the bookshelf that led to the tunnels. "Perhaps it was a mistake showing her where the escape was."

Rider put a hand on his shoulder. "She would've found another way out of the castle and the city. It's Alida, remember?"

Tieran nodded and sighed before they both exited the room.

He said a goodbye to the king and went back towards his room. He nodded to a few servants as he passed them but for the most part, stared at the floor. He was worried. Days ago, he had told Alida that the two people he cared about most in the world were her and her father. And now, they were both going to be outside of his protection. Alida, fleeing to Nagaye, Tieran, on his way to the front lines of what just may become a battle. He couldn't do anything for them where he was going. And that frightened him. Since he had come to work at the castle, any imminent threats to their safety went through him. He could pretty much deal with all of those threats.

Rider had to learn very quickly that it was a mistake to have people you care about.

There was once someone he cared for so deeply that it almost destroyed him.

Somehow, even after he had learned his lesson, Alida and Tieran had sneaked into his heart. He was grateful for it, but not in times like these.

He entered his room and grabbed his rucksack. It was already completely packed, besides food. Rider had packed it the day he was hired, in case he ever had to make a quick getaway. So far, the opportunity hadn't presented itself. It came in handy now. He opened it and dumped its contents on his bed. A bedroll, several knives, a flint and steel, an extra change of clothes, a drawstring pouch of silver coins, and three canteens of water. He made a mental note to switch out the water that had been in there for twelve years. It would be enough to get him to the 3rd army.

Rider sat down on his bed and began placing things back in the rucksack.

~ ~ ~

The sun had just begun to peak above the horizon when he left the next morning.

He met Tieran for breakfast, where they barely ate anything, mostly sitting in silent anticipation. Afterwards, Rider shook his hand and wished his old friend the best of luck.

"Remember, if you change your mind and want me to join you in Lou, send a messenger. I won't hesitate to leave immediately," Rider told him.

The king nodded. "I will. And if you hear anything from Alida or about Alida or anything of the sort, you must send one too. I just pray to the gods to keep her safe."

Rider prayed that she kept herself safe. Praying to the gods would not minimize the danger of an eighteen-year-old princess on the run.

He put a hand on Tieran's shoulder. "You stay safe. Don't do anything stupid. Please. This kingdom needs you and so does Alida."

"The same goes to you, Rider. Take care of yourself."

They shook hands once more before Tieran embraced him. Rider was surprised, but he hugged his old friend back. The king had always accepted him despite his past. He had almost become like a father to him.

Now, Rider sat on his horse. His rucksack was tied to it, along with a satchel of fresh food from the castle that he would eat today. He carried no weapons with him besides a small sword and hunting knives that were packed away. If he was attacked, he had better ways of defending himself than using weapons.

He nudged his horse in the side, and they were off. There were few people on the streets, mostly shop owners opening their stores and a few people sleeping, probably from last night's bender. He loved the way Abdul looked. Cobblestone roads and wooden houses, a quaint downtown area where you could get the best dessert on the continent. The town square market, where vendors from all over came to sell their products, where live music was always playing. There were street performers who wooed passersby with their magic tricks and sleight of hand. For Rider, this had become home. And he was unfortunately leaving it.

When he reached the outskirts of town, he turned his horse around and stared at the city. The castle in the distance glimmered in the rays of the sun. He felt a pang in his heart. There was always a chance that this could be the last time he saw it, but something about sitting there felt so final. He took a deep breath and tried to take it all in.

Rider exhaled, turned his horse around, and began riding towards the 3rd army.

Chapter 7

After four days of what she considered the most grueling hike she had ever taken, Alida Goulding had reached the Dela.

She saw it from a distance, on top of a hill where she had spent the night.

Alida had to admit, she was getting better at the whole sleeping on the ground thing. Plus, she had learned that if she placed her venison jerky over the fire for a few minutes, it made a delicious dinner. Rider would be proud of her; she was basically a professional adventurer now.

The River Dela sparkled invitingly. It was one of the largest rivers they had in Orinth, large enough for massive sailboats to tread its waters. She didn't see any of those boats as she observed the scene, but luckily enough, there was a town perched on the bank. It looked to be a couple miles from where she stood, clusters of stone buildings and streets. It wasn't nearly as large as Abdul, not even close, but the town looked civilized enough that she was sure she could find transportation to Nagaye.

Alida started forward, gripping her pack to her shoulders. She had to put her cloak away because today the weather was astonishingly beautiful. The sun was out, there was no chill wind, and the cloak just made her sweat. She wore a light tunic with pants on underneath. She had braided her short hair into a ponytail and tied a bandanna around her head. Her small sword was still strapped to her waist but over the last few days, she had grown more confident with it. When Alida stopped to rest, she would pull out the sword and practice some basic steps she knew. It wasn't anything compared to practicing with another person, but it made her feel more comfortable with the hilt in her hand. So far, on this trip, things had gone brilliantly. Eating lunch with

Ledger and talking to him had lifted her spirits. She had lost the foreboding feeling that she had left the castle with. At least on her end, everything was working out. She prayed that Rider and her father were safe and that no attacks had been made yet.

Within minutes, Alida came to the edge of the town. There were quite a few people wandering about, talking, and going about their day. She sighed in relief. Being a princess meant being trained to be a social person. As much as she loved her alone time, the princess side of her always wanted to be talking and communicating with others.

Alida walked into the town, keeping her head down, whilst looking for an inn. She would stay the night here regardless of what happened. Hopefully, there would be an innkeeper who had the information she needed about transportation to Nagaye. According to Rider, they were the most knowledgeable in a town because people took their problems, their news, and just about everything to them.

It took several minutes of searching before spotting a vibrant sign announcing the "Smoky Sunset Inn". It looked clean on the outside and she noticed patrons going into the establishment. Alida decided she would take her business in here and hope for the best.

Upon entering, Alida immediately appreciated the order of the place. Wooden tables and chairs arranged in a geometric fashion. There was a long bar taking up the entire side of the room with a stage taking up the other. Straight forward was a set of stairs she assumed lead to the rooms of the Inn. It was busy for the early afternoon, with many people eating at the tables and just as many at the bar drinking. She sighed. The more people there were, the chance of being recognized was greater. On the bright side, she was a long way from the castle. Hopefully, none of these people had travelled to Abdul. And if they had, hopefully they hadn't seen her. There was faith in her short hair, though. She knew she was renowned, at least within Abdul, for her long and flowing locks. A handful of vendors sold hair products that promised to "get the same beauty and elegance of Princess Alida". Alida had chuckled at it when she heard about it but now, she was appreciative.

The inn was loud and not many people noticed her entrance into the place. She quietly made her way to the bar and sat at the stool at the very end, whilst most of the other customers were on the other side. A man caught her eye and winked but other than that they paid no attention. The bartender was a young woman who looked to be in her thirties, if Alida had to guess. She had bright red hair worn in a high ponytail and a spray of freckles across her face. She was dressed in green pants and a white top. Alida observed her large smile that almost seemed contagious as she talked to some of her clients. It made Alida want to smile. The young woman noticed her at last and walked down to her end of the bar.

"Good afternoon, ma'am!" she exclaimed. "How can I help you?"

Alida lifted her head and made eye contact. The bartender just stared. Internally, she felt relief. No immediate recognition followed by "Oh my gods, the princess!". She was just another person to her.

"Yes, hello. I'd like a room for the night."

The woman nodded. "Of course. Our regular price comes with dinner and drinks. There's a lot of entertainment here in the evening as well."

Alida paid for it. "Wonderful, thank you. Is the room ready now?"

The bartender nodded. "Yes, indeed. If you give me a few minutes, I can lead you up there and help you with your bags." Her eyes landed on the sword strapped to her waist and then back up to her face. "What brings you to these parts?"

"What parts are these exactly?"

The woman laughed. "You're in Rein. It's not big enough to make a map but I love it here nonetheless."

Alida smiled at her. "I'm actually traveling to Nagaye. I was hoping you could recommend some form of transportation to get there. How long would I have to wait for a ship?"

"You're in luck. Sahar Bow just got into town a few days ago. I believe she's leaving for Nagaye tomorrow evening or perhaps the next day."

"Where could I find her?" Alida asked.

The bartender grinned. "Here, of course, tonight. Sahar wouldn't miss watching our very own Sylvester sing and play his fiddle."

"Perfect. I can just go up to her and ask her?"

She shrugged. "Sahar is a little intimidating. I don't know if she takes passengers unless they give her a very good reason. But she has the fastest ship on this side of the continent. If you want to get to Nagaye and fast, she would be the one to ask."

Alida nodded. "Thank you for your help."

Fifteen minutes later, Alida was sprawled on the bed of her room, after ensuring the door was bolted. It was just as clean and well-kept as the rest of the

Smoky Sunset had been. She had let down her hair and changed into a new pair of clothes, a blue dress and a jacket, and washed her face and body as much as she could with the small basin. There was no way she would use a public bathing space. Maybe that made her snotty and arrogant, but she had specific standards when it came to her personal hygiene. Still, she was clean and felt refreshed.

It was at that moment when the exhaustion settled in. Before she knew it, she had fallen into a deep sleep, without any covers.

Hours later she woke up to the sound of a crowd clapping below her. She sat forward and looked out the window. The sun was setting, and darkness was falling over Rein. Alida smacked herself in the forehead. She hadn't meant to sleep for that long of a time. Still, she couldn't complain. She was rejuvenated and some of the soreness had eased out of her back and legs. She stood and glanced in the mirror. Her hair was sticking up all over the place from lying on the bed. She quickly smoothed it out and ran her fingers through it, frowning. Rider had insisted that bringing a hairbrush and a small set of makeup wasn't "essential". They had bickered about it for a minute before he had just thrown his hands in the air and said, "Do what you want, Lida." She ended up deciding to leave it out. Rider knew better than her, at least when it came to traveling.

After she decided her hair could be tamed no longer, Alida left her room. She went back down the stairs and was shocked at the amount of people who now filled the tavern. Almost every table was packed with people, all their attention locked on to the man on stage. He was ridiculously tall and rail thin, playing a fiddle and singing some song in a different language. People were clapping and singing along, some even dancing around their tables. Alida smiled. This was new and different. But she liked it.

She saw one empty seat at the bar and made a beeline for it. No one paid her any mind as she shoved in between two men to take her seat. They shot her a brief grin before returning their concentration to the performer.

The woman who had talked to her hours ago caught her eye and beamed. She walked over to Alida and said, "I believe I owe you a dinner and a drink. Dinner should be ready within a few minutes and our house ale is famous. Can I get you a glass?" Alida nodded and yelled over the crowd, "Yes, please!"

The bartender filled a mug out of a tankard behind her and slid it to Alida. She pointed at the man on stage. "That's Sylvester. He's the son of the man who owns this bar. He plays here once a week and it always gets packed." She then pointed at someone sitting at a table closest to the stage. "That's Sahar."

Alida looked to where she was pointing. A woman who couldn't be much older than she was sat, clapping and singing along with Sylvester. She had long black hair that almost reached her waist and was very muscular, with toned arms that made Alida ashamed of her own. She was dressed in a white tank top and black pants. Alida noticed that she had tattoos scattered all over her body, different designs and words that were impossible to see from where she was sitting. There was a man next to her, also watching the singer, but Alida wasn't able to see his face, just his black cloak.

She turned back to the bartender. "You're right. She does look intimidating."

The woman laughed. "Sahar is tough. But it's easy to earn her respect. No bullshit with her."

Alida sipped on her ale as the man continued to perform. She found herself clapping along with the crowd and enjoying the sound of the fiddle, which perfectly meshed with the man's voice. For once in her life, Alida was blending into the group of people. She didn't have to worry about maintaining her posture or her demeanor. She could, dare she say it, just be Alida Goulding. Or Nova Grey. Or whoever she was. But not a princess anymore. It felt good.

Minutes later, the bartender set a plate of food in front of her. Chicken, rice, and carrots. A classic Orinthian dish. It tasted earthy and natural and was very well done. It was even better along with the music.

She finished the meal in a hurry and turned back to Sylvester, who was now singing a well-known Orinthian folk song. The group of people sitting at the tables had pushed them to either side and had created a floor for dancing. Couples spun around to the music and danced very professionally. Alida was impressed with the intricate movements. She had attended many balls, but never had the dancing been so fast paced. It was an entirely different style than she was used to.

It was at this time when she noticed that Sahar was now alone, leaning up against a wall, watching the dancing. There was a slight smile on her face, but she didn't join in. Without thinking, Alida got up from her seat and approached the young girl.

She leaned up against the wall next to her. Sahar's eyes immediately snapped over to her. She raised an eyebrow at the princess, with an expression that clearly said 'who do you think you are?'. Her hand shifted to the dagger strapped to her waist and Alida watched as her fingers tapped against the hilt slowly. The threat was veiled, but it was there.

"Do I know you?" Sahar shouted over the music. Upon seeing her up close, Alida noticed she had dark brown eyes and her skin was smooth. Her facial features were small but there was no denying her muscles were huge. Still, she managed to look beautiful and remain feminine. Alida was positive this woman could kill her without a second thought. It was slightly terrifying and Alida wondered if coming over here had been a mistake.

Alida shook her head. "No, you don't."

"Then what do you want?" the woman asked, fingers still drumming along the hilt of the dagger.

Alida took a breath, hoping the sudden trembling of her hands wasn't noticeable. "I heard you have a boat?"

"Depends on who's asking."

"Nova Grey. I'm looking to find passage to Nagaye. I need it fast."

Sahar looked her up and down. "Have I seen you before?"

Alida shrugged. "I just have one of those faces."

"Why do you want to go to Nagaye?" she asked.

"I'm getting out of here before Auntica takes over."

Sahar smirked. "Scared, are you?"

"I have family in Nagaye. I'll be safer with them than here."

Sahar turned back to the dancing. "My ship is more than just a transporter."

"I figured. I don't care though. I just need to get out of here."

"It won't be cheap."

"I can afford it," Alida replied.

Sahar looked her up and down. "I don't know if you can."

Alida held herself back from scoffing. She had a feeling that Sahar might punch her if she did. Alida wasn't used to anyone talking to her in that manner. Being a princess made her entitled to the respect of her subjects, but this woman clearly had none of that for her. Alida opened her mouth to respond but Sahar cut her off.

"What can you offer me?"

Alida glanced around. "You want to do this here?"

"Give me one reason I should still stand here and talk to you."

Alida felt like she had been smacked across the face. But she had to get on this ship. It was the fastest one, even if the captain was extremely rude. "Well, I have money. I need transportation. I'll stay out of your way and when we land in Nagaye, you'll never hear from me again. I don't know what's so special about this ship that it'll cost me an arm and a leg to get passage on it, but I'm willing to pay."

There was silence for a moment and Alida thought the woman might stab her with that dagger. Instead, Sahar raised her eyebrows. "What did you say your name was again?"

"Nova Grey."

She nodded, running a hand through her long dark hair. "Well then, Nova Grey. I'll come back tomorrow, and if you offer me something good, it'll pay for passage to Nagaye, landing in the capital city on the coast. You'll get your own cabin and the food our cook makes. No one will bother you if you don't bother them."

Alida nodded. "Tomorrow then."

Sahar extended a hand and Alida shook it. "We leave for Nagaye the morning after tomorrow, should this work out. Be at the docks by sunrise or we leave without you."

"Done," Alida said. "And should this work out, I'll pay you half here and half when we get to Nagaye."

Sahar narrowed her eyes at her. "Fine."

At that moment, the man who Alida assumed Sahar had been sitting with approached them. He looked to be in his early twenties and was, well in a word, beautiful. The first thing she noticed were his eyes, a cool blue color that held a sort of fierceness in them. His brown hair was chopped short on the sides and slightly longer on the top. She noticed a scar that ran along his right eyebrow. His face was unshaven and scruffy and Alida found she rather liked the look. At the moment, there was an expression of mild amusement on his face.

"Who's this?" He asked Sahar, his voice deep and cool. He didn't even glance at Alida herself.

"This is Nova Grey. She just bought passage to Nagaye with us," Sahar replied. She turned back to Alida. "This is Roman, my first mate on the ship."

Alida looked at him, keeping her chin up. "Charmed," she said.

His eyes met hers. "Likewise."

Alida nodded to them both. "I'll see you tomorrow, Sahar." She turned around and started back to the bar. Her stool remained open, and she slid back onto it. "Another ale?" she asked the woman bartender.

She slid another mug in front of her and Alida took a long drink from it. Suddenly, she realized that a huge burden had been lifted off her shoulders. She had almost gotten passage to Nagaye. She knew it would be expensive, when they settled the price, and she had a good suspicion that Sahar was definitely a smuggler, but still. Alida was almost out of Orinth. And once she reached Nagaye, she would disappear. Grafph couldn't possibly find her there, in the deserts that were massive. Alida was so close.

She still had to pay Sahar. She still had to board the boat and the journey by ship to Nagaye was probably three weeks, at the least. She didn't travel by boat very often but the times she had, she had gotten ridiculously seasick. Not even those thoughts could diminish her happiness at the prospect of being out of Orinth.

Someone tapped her shoulder and Alida turned. It was a boy who was probably around her age. He was dressed in a white shirt and green pants, which she was starting to see was the trend in Rein. His face was simply adorable, with messy blonde hair and dimples and big brown puppy eyes. He offered her his arm. "May I have this dance?"

Alida laughed and shook her head. "I'm very honored but I don't know how to dance like this."

The boy scoffed, "Nonsense. You can just follow my lead." She hesitated and the boy batted his eyelashes. He leaned in closer to her. "Do you see the table of guys that are sitting by the door?" Her eyes traveled to where he was referring and she indeed saw a group of about five or six of them, all staring at her and laughing. She blushed and said, "I do."

The boy beamed. "They bet me a couple coins that I could get you to dance with me. If I lose, I owe all of them a round of drinks. Help me out?"

Alida smiled at him and rolled her eyes. "Why me?"

He shrugged. "You are the prettiest girl in here tonight, so I suppose they think you're the biggest challenge?"

She rolled her eyes again but kept grinning. "Fine. One dance only," she said sternly.

He wiggled his eyebrows at her. "One dance. Unless you beg me for more."

She snorted, "One dance. And I should know who I'm dancing with."

"Ellis Larson at your service. And who do I have the absolute pleasure of dancing with?" He extended his arm to her.

Alida took it. "Nova."

He smiled at her. "Well, Nova, I know you said you don't know how to dance like this, but I'll lead for the both of us." Ellis guided her to the middle of the crowded dance floor and placed a hand onto her hip. He guided one of her hands onto his shoulder and held the other one with his own. He grinned at her and said, "Ready?" She nodded excitedly and then everything was a blur.

Ellis was a better dancer than he let on because he danced for the both of them. Alida struggled to remain upright as they spun around the floor, trying to avoid other couples as well as remain on their feet. He made sure her body was in position as they danced. It was incredibly liberating as they whisked around the room. As the music got faster and faster so did they and Alida realized that she was following the rhythm and doing it for herself, dancing.

They remained laughing or smiling the entire time until the song finally came to an end. Ellis held her in a dip until the crowd began applauding. He pulled her upwards and suddenly pressed a kiss hard to her lips.

She wasn't expecting it at all and almost gasped against him. His mouth explored her own and she felt herself melt into his body, letting her hands run up his back and through his hair as he did the same to her. Finally, they broke apart. Alida stared at him. His eyes held a giddiness to them, and he was grinning. No one else on the floor paid them any attention.

"There," he said. "That should get me an extra few coins."

Alida curtsied. "Glad to have been of service."

Ellis laughed again and pressed a kiss to her cheek, before turning around and walking towards the table of his friends. Alida watched as they went wild, slapping him on his back. He glanced back at her and winked before sitting down to the cheers and yelps. They all raised a glass towards her, and she nodded back at them, not bothering to hide her smile.

Alida went back to the bar and flagged the bartender over again for another mug of ale. She felt a little dizzy and lightheaded from the kiss that had been the most unexpected event of this night. It had been a long time since she had kissed someone. When she sixteen years old, she was what Rider called "boy crazy". Every duke's son or steward's son she set her eyes on she would end up kissing later in a random hallway or in the gardens. As she got older, she realized that it was a waste of time when the kingdom needed her. She threw herself into her work and had not kissed anyone since.

Her heart was racing. Yes, she had enjoyed that.

She finished off the last of her ale and started to feel a little sick. Standing up, Alida made her way through the crowd to the stairs. She took one last look at the dancing crowd, the people at the bar, the man on the stage, and the boy who had just stolen a kiss from her, Ellis something or other who she would probably never see again.

Alida suddenly wished she was Nova Grey.

She wished she was just a normal girl who lived in Rein and came to watch everybody's favorite performer, Sylvester, sing and play his fiddle. She wanted to know people here, to sit with a group of friends and dare one of them to go ask someone to dance. She wanted someone to take an interest in her and woo her and court her, without the pressure knowing that whoever she chose would be a fellow leader of Orinth.

Nova Grey was everything she wasn't. She was able to let loose and have fun. She could shirk responsibilities and replace it with just a plain old night on the town. Nova Grey wasn't afraid of Auntican soldiers bursting into a place at any second and grabbing her. She wasn't worried about possibly being partly demon and having the capability to kill by just thinking about it. She wasn't concerned about her death being able to destroy a boundary between her realm and the shadow realm. And she sure wasn't worried about fleeing the country as fast as she possibly could.

But Alida Goulding was. And unfortunately, that's who she was and who she would always be.

That night, after she fell asleep, she dreamed of another life, another world from here, where she was just Nova Grey, and she could be anything she wanted to be.

Chapter 8

Rein, Orinth

She slept in the next morning. Sahar wasn't supposed to be there until the evening, so she had the whole day. Alida wasn't sure what she would do with the time. On the one hand, leaving her room at the Inn would possibly put her at risk of being recognized. On the other hand, this was a chance to explore a place for the first time without pointed fingers, murmurs under breaths, and a security detail on her tail wherever she went. The notion of getting dressed and going out appealed to her greatly and before she knew it, she was climbing out of the bed.

Alida washed herself once again in the basin of the room and tried her best to clean the scent of alcohol out of her mouth. She fished out the last outfit she had brought with her, a pair of soft blue pants and a white shirt. They were intended for travel but also doubled as what she thought to be a cute outfit. She braided her hair again, took one last look at Nova Grey in the mirror, and left the room.

The woman bartender was the only one in the room downstairs, wiping off the tables which were rather dirty due to last night. She smiled at Alida when she saw her.

"I hope you enjoyed last night's performance."

Alida nodded enthusiastically. "That was definitely the most fun I've had in a while. You know, I never caught your name?"

"Milly," she responded. "And you are?"

"Nova."

"Well, pleasure to know you, Nova."

"You as well." Alida slid back onto a stool. "I'm looking for a good place to have breakfast around here."

Milly snorted, "Breakfast? It's almost noon!"

"Lunch then," Alida laughed.

"Just down the road from here is a small little place called Sandi's. They have the best lunch in town. Lucky for them, we're not open for lunch or else they would have the second-best lunch in town."

She chuckled, "Perfect, thank you."

"Enjoy your day, Nova," Milly said with a smile.

Alida nodded at her and exited the tavern. The sun was shining, and it was the perfect temperature out. The streets were crowded with people, walking, talking, laughing. She fell into place with them, walking towards the center of town, looking around for the place Milly had recommended to her. But something caught her eye first.

She stepped out of the crowd and looked up at a building a few blocks down from the Smoky Sunset. It was painted a pastel green color and the sign identified it as the 'Rein Dress Shoppe'. The window of the shop held short and sweet dresses unlike anything she had seen before. Alida didn't think twice before entering the store.

A small bell rang as she walked in and the woman at the counter glanced up. Alida took it in and was reminded of the dress shop she and her mother used to go to. Dresses hung along the walls and on racks in the middle of the room, of all shapes and colors. To the back, curtains surrounding private dressing rooms.

"Welcome to Rein Dress Shoppe. Can I help you?" The woman at the counter asked.

"Hi, uh, no I think I'm just looking for right now," Alida responded, touching one of the dresses thoughtfully.

"Yes, ma'am. If you would like to try any of these on, don't hesitate to ask."

Alida nodded and smiled at her.

She looked at almost every dress and wondered what Rider would think if she spent her emergency money on one of them. He wouldn't be happy. But he also said, "When you're happy, I'm happy" and a new dress would make her more than happy. She had no occasion to wear any of these dresses, as most of them were fancy and meant for only special events. But she was undeniably tempted just to do it anyways.

Alida decided she would at least try one on. She picked it out from the rack. The upper part of the dress was black, but it faded into a white, soft skirt with black lace covering it. She turned back towards the cashier. "I'd like to try this one on."

The woman nodded and led her to one of the curtained dressing rooms. "Would you like any assistance putting it on?" she asked her.

"I think I can do it for now, thank you," Alida replied kindly as the woman closed the curtains, leaving her alone with the dress. She stripped out of her clothes and gently, put the dress over her head. She tugged at the skirt until it was fully on and then she buttoned the back as best as she could.

Alida spun around in the dress as she observed herself in the mirror. She had to say, the dress suited her. It was very elegant and graceful and soft to the touch. She could see herself buying something like this back in Abdul for a ball or small party. It was tempting to do so now. She opened the curtains and spun around for the cashier.

The woman clapped her hands together. "It's lovely!" she exclaimed. "Oh you must get it! No one else will do justice to it like you do, dear."

Alida laughed. "It's quite charming."

"It's affordable too, darling," the woman exclaimed and told her the price.

She almost laughed at it. The price of the dress could buy a horse. Alida opened her mouth and said something that she had never said once in her entire life. "You know? I don't think I can afford it."

She left the shoppe, after taking off the beautiful dress and handing it back to the cashier, who took it with a frown, wishing her a good day.

Afterwards, she strolled the streets of Rein, browsing through a few other shops and eating lunch at the place the bartender had recommended before heading back to the Smoky Sunset. It was the late afternoon when she arrived, and she wasn't sure when Sahar would be there to take her payment. She went upstairs to her room to wash and decided she would sit at the bar until the woman walked in. Already, the Smoky Sunset was filling with people, but, as Milly informed her, there was no performance tonight so it wouldn't be as busy.

Alida ordered an ale and waited for Sahar to get there. She chatted with Milly a little about the war with Auntica and was surprised. The bartender did not seem to be frightened about the potential battles to come. She inquired as to why.

Milly just shrugged. "We have a good king and a good army. I don't doubt that we will win. Tieran has protected us through everything. This will be no exception."

Alida felt her heart swell with pride. That was HER father she was talking about.

At about quarter to eight, Sahar Bow entered the building. She was wearing the exact same thing she had been wearing yesterday with her long black hair tied into a ponytail that swung dramatically every step she took. She caught Alida's eye and made her way over to the bar, sliding onto the stool next to her. "I'll have an ale," Sahar said to Milly, who nodded and walked to get it.

Sahar turned towards Alida. "Let's go upstairs to settle this."

Alida nodded and together, they left the crowded room. Alida led them into her bedroom, picked up the drawstring pouch from her bag and turned back to her. Rider had packed it with gems from the treasury, but Alida had also thrown in some of her better pieces of jewelry, almost worth enough to buy her own ship. She was also aware of the fact that Sahar could mug her and take everything in the pouch, but she had a feeling that wouldn't happen.

Alida took a breath and pulled out a diamond necklace. It was a birthday present from some duke or another who hoped to ask for Alida's hand once she came of age, so she didn't mind parting with it. It was probably worth way more than passage on a ship, but Alida didn't care.

Sahar raised an eyebrow as her eyes fell on the piece of jewelry. "Where did you come across that?"

"Family heirloom," Alida replied, and it wasn't necessarily a lie.

"You'll give me this in exchange for passage?" Sahar asked incredulously.

"This necklace for passage in my own cabin to Nagaye with the promise of being unbothered," Alida corrected her.

Sahar reached out and took the necklace without comment. She studied it intensely before her eyes flitted to the pouch still in Alida's hand. Alida gripped it tighter. There was no doubt in her mind that if Sahar wanted to kill her and rob her right now, she would do it successfully. Alida supposed if she did kill her, none of them would have to worry about Grafph opening the Shadow Wall anymore. That thought didn't stop her from feeling immensely terrified. Her sword was still in the room but that didn't ease the fear.

"Sunrise tomorrow," was all Sahar said instead, tucking the necklace into her jacket pocket before turning around and leaving the room.

Alida immediately let out a sigh of relief. The captain hadn't killed her. She hadn't robbed her. And now, she had passage to Nagaye.

She had done it.

But then, Alida thought about it all. She was leaving because of the war. The Shadow Wall. The Last Heir. It all came rushing back. Alida collapsed onto her bed. Taking a deep breath, she pulled out the picture of Rider.

The edges were beginning to fray from the number of times she had pulled it out. Every night, without fail, she would feel a deep sense of loss. She would try to talk herself out of it; Rider wasn't dead. She knew he was alive, somewhere, working to end this whole thing. Yet she couldn't shake the sense that she would never see him again. And it terrified her. She would stare at the picture, willing him somehow to know, to feel, that she missed him, even if they were hundreds of miles away.

She said a silent prayer for his protection before closing her eyes and falling asleep.

~ ~ ~

By a miracle of the gods, she was up before the sun rose. It was still dark as she packed her things, switching back into a pair of white pants and a jacket. Alida bid one last goodbye to the Smoky Sunset Inn and started towards the docks.

It was chilly and there was almost no one on the streets. She stopped briefly to put on her light blue cloak before continuing. Milly had informed her that the docks were directly straight from the inn, and if you kept walking, eventually you would come upon it. Sahar's boat, The Valley, was the largest one in the port and impossible to miss. Alida took a deep breath. There was an unsettling feeling bearing down on her. She was almost out of Orinth. She had almost accomplished what she had set out to do. So why was the feeling still there?

After about ten minutes of walking, she reached the docks. It was a smaller pier, with only about fifteen or twenty boats perched within, but it was easy to tell which one was Sahar's. Without a doubt, it was the gigantic ship painted a dark green color, with gold writing that read 'The Valley'. She started towards it. A large group of people were loading crates onto the boat, passing each of them from person to person up the plank that led onto it. Alida didn't want to guess what was in the crates but she had a feeling it wasn't legal. She saw Sahar and her first mate overlooking the work going on. She joined them, leaning up against one of the railings, and watching the ship.

Both their heads turned towards her, tense. Sahar relaxed when she saw who it was. "Oh, it's you."

Alida raised an eyebrow. "What's in the crates?"

Sahar returned her expression. "Why do you care?"

Alida shrugged. "I don't. I'm curious."

"It's not technically illegal, just so you know. We transport Orinthian wine to Nagaye and sell it for less than the official import. The crates are filled with the stuff."

Alida nodded but made a mental note. If she got out of this alive, after the war was over, she would tell Rider about this little operation. He had often wondered out loud why their wine market wasn't larger. They had the best quality of anyone on the continent, but not many others bought from them. She now knew why.

Sahar extended her hand towards the boat. "This is the pride of the Sea of Nagaye. The Valley. Don't ever let anyone tell you otherwise. She's the fastest one by far."

Alida replied. "She is beautiful. Not that I know much about ships."

"It doesn't take a lot to see that," Sahar said with a chuckle.

"Where are you from, Nova?" Roman cut in. Alida couldn't be sure, but she thought she heard a trace of suspicion in his voice.

"Tenir," she said, not skipping a beat. Last night, she had thought of a whole backstory for Nova Grey. She was the daughter of a carpenter and had four older brothers. Her parents had been happily married for twenty-five years and it was their idea to send her to Nagaye. Her brothers were all fighting in the war and they wanted to make sure that their one daughter stayed as safe as possible. They lived in a small, but cozy, apartment in downtown Tenir that had belonged to her grandfather and had been in the family for years. There was something so appealing about the world she had created for herself that she almost launched into the whole tale of it.

"What do you do for a living?"

Alida raised an eyebrow. "Why do you ask?"

Roman shrugged. "I'm just curious," he said, repeating what she had spoken only seconds ago.

Alida narrowed her eyes. "I go to school. I'm studying trade and economics."

"Oh, I see. Your school was okay with you dropping out to go to Nagaye?"

"They closed. Most of the students were sent to fight on the front against Auntica. It's a shame but it does allow me to go to Nagaye without worrying about missing any lectures."

Sahar hid a smile as Roman gave Alida a look. "Well. Praise the gods for that then."

Alida tossed her hair. "Praise them indeed."

Within five minutes, all the crates of wine were loaded onto the ship and Sahar led Alida aboard. Alida went back to keeping her head down. These people were sailors and likely traveled frequently. There was no telling who had been to Abdul and who knew what she looked like. It was better to be safe than sorry. She didn't have to worry about it long, though, as Sahar led her down into a cabin.

She opened a door into a small room, even smaller than the one at the inn. It only had a bed and a small table next to it, no basin or mirror to be seen. Luckily enough, there was a tiny window that allowed her to see out the side of the ship.

"This is what you get for the next couple weeks," Sahar stated. Alida dropped her pack onto the bed and looked around. "It'll do."

Sahar chuckled. "It's going to have to. It was the last open one we had so you got lucky. Now, you're allowed to explore the ship all you like but stay out of the captain's quarters, which are my quarters, unless I personally invite you there. And if I were you, I would stay out of the crew's quarters as well. They would eat a dainty thing like you up for breakfast. But all the decks, the mess hall, and the kitchen are free to roam. The toilet is a few doors down from here and-," she leaned in closer, "-there's a bath in my cabin. I never let anyone use it but in a couple of days, come find me and we can make arrangements."

Alida smiled at her. "Thank you, Captain Bow," she said, with a mock salute. Sahar grinned back at her and returned the salute.

"If you need anything at all, you know who to ask," she said, before exiting the cabin and closing her door.

Alida sat down on the bed and took a deep breath. She had made it onto The Valley. She had somewhat befriended the captain, and no one had recognized her yet. It almost seemed too good to be true.

But as she felt the boat began to move, she stood up and glanced out the small window. Sure enough, Rein, Orinth, was beginning to fade into the distance. Alida exhaled as she felt the relief rush upon her. She had done it. She was on her way to Nagaye.

Chapter 9

The Outskirts of Forest Dembe, Auntica

"**A**re you scared yet?" Sawny asked.

They sat on their horses, looking at the entrance to the Forest Dembe, where their path continued towards.

Adriel shook his head. "Not really. After all, it is your kin in there, isn't it?"

Sawny rolled her eyes and his mouth twitched. "I might tell them to eat your youth if you're not careful."

He held up his hands. "Please don't."

Sawny nudged Indira in the side, and they started forwards.

The Forest Dembe was incredibly dense. The only rideable portion of it was the path that they were on, and Sawny knew it wouldn't be bright to stray far from that path. There may not be witches in here, but she had no doubt there were creatures that could threaten their safety. She touched a hand to her bow and arrows. She had never had a problem with this forest before, but as she had told Adriel, there was a first time for everything. It was still the fastest route to Tenir. The legends about this forest weren't bad enough to scare her from the efficiency of the Traveler's Road.

The sun was shining brightly on the warm Auntican day. The weather, luckily enough, had held up during the last two days of their journey. They rode swiftly, stopping infrequently, and never running into any trouble. As the days passed, they saw more and more Auntican soldiers riding north, to Illias. Normally, the Traveler's road wasn't busy. It wasn't a well-known route, but the impending war had it crawling with soldiers. It was disconcerting, but they pushed southwards. At nights, Sawny would find a suitable inn to stay at while

Adriel went outside of the town to camp. Every night she would ask him to reconsider and every night he would dismiss her.

Adriel was....compelling. Since he had asked about her father, there was a sort of unspoken but mutual agreement to stay away from personal topics. When they did talk, it was about arbitrary topics.

Sawny had asked him a lot about the Wilds. "Where's your favorite place?"

He had pondered this for a while before saying, "There's a place in the Wilds. You have to hike quite a ways from the nearest village and then trek to the top of this mountain. It's not hard to climb but it makes you tired. But once you got to the top, there was this grassy sort of flat land, just small enough to sit down on. And the view from it was incredible. You can see for miles. The mountains, the forest, the big wide-open sky. It's all there, right in front of you, close enough for you to touch. It's my favorite place in the whole world."

"It sounds wonderful."

"What about you, Sawny?"

Sawny chuckled. "Me? Hmm. That's a tough one." She thought about it for a moment before continuing, "I've been all over this continent. Your Wilds, the Darklands, Orinth, Auntica, all of it. But my favorite place has to be my old house, on the outskirts of Illias. It was quite far from the city, probably twenty minutes on horseback to get there. It was a little cottage on the edge of this small forest. It faced the east so every morning, you could see the sunrise. It was just stunning. I miss it."

Adriel didn't ask her anything after that, per the agreement. He probably wanted to ask what had happened to that cottage home? She would have told him that she set it on fire after she had to bury her parents. She had grabbed all the money she could find, all of her possessions and most of her parents' before torching the whole thing. And then, Sawny had watched it go up in flames before riding her horse towards Illias.

As they entered into the Forest Dembe, the sun was suddenly cut off. The branches were so thick with leaves it left no room for the rays to get in. It was much darker now, but still a warm temperature. Once her eyes adjusted, Sawny looked around the forest. It was exactly as she remembered. The trunks of the trees were impossibly large, and the tops seemed to reach the sky. Between each giant tree was a plethora of flora. Smaller trees, vines wrapped around them, ferns as tall as she was. She shuddered to think about the bugs that lived within the plants.

The trail was so narrow that the horses were forced to ride single file, with Indira leading and Adriel's following behind. They rode in silence, the sounds of the forest ringing in their ears. The air in Dembe was heavier and harder to breath. It only took an hour or so to ride throughout the whole place, but time seemed to go slower here. Maybe it was cursed. Sawny wanted to say something to lighten the mood, but nothing was suitable. She glanced back at Adriel, who was gripping the reigns so tight that his knuckles were turning white. He had paled significantly and was panting. He never said whether or not he believed the rumors that his people told about this place. Sawny hoped that he didn't and could manage the next few hours without passing out or throwing up.

Indira was skittish as well. She continued to twitch and jerk around, occasionally braying softly. Her horse was normally well adjusted to abrupt changes of their surroundings, but something was off. Sawny started to get nervous. In the times she had been here before, Indira had never acted like this. Sawny herself had never gotten any bad feelings, but today she was sweating and gasping. It had barely been twenty minutes.

Black spots started clouding her vision as slowly her senses begin to shut down. At first, a ringing had begun in her ears, drowning out the noise of the forest. It gradually increased in volume until it was all she could hear. The black spots began to grow larger as well. Her fingers and forearms began to go numb and next thing she knew, she was on the ground.

Sawny tried to scream but couldn't as she heard someone yell her name in the distance. Her body was shutting down. The numbness had spread to her entire upper body and she tried desperately to stand up with her legs, but a sharp pain had replaced the nerves. She couldn't see nor hear anything as she continued to yell before her voice stopped working as well. There was nothing.

She was dying, almost dead, and there were still so many questions unanswered.

She couldn't tell at what point she lost consciousness. She couldn't tell where she was or if she were moving or not. The black still clouded her eyesight but she could see the outline of the forest and figures. The sounds began to return along with one voice, humming. Sawny didn't know whose, but it wasn't Adriel's. She tried wiggling one finger and then the next and then the next. It worked. She moved on to her arms and her shoulders. It was moving again but with great pain. She tried speaking.

"Adriel?" she rasped. "Adriel, are you there?"

There was no response, but the humming continued. She tried to sit up and a sharp pain jolted through her back. She yelled and fell back to the ground.

Slowly, the spots in her vision faded and she was looking at the top of the Forest Dembe, the trees swaying gently. The sun was still gone but this portion of the forest was much brighter than the one she and Adriel had entered.

Adriel. Where was he? She felt the dread grow in her like a disease. "Adriel?" she tried again.

"The boy is fine," a voice responded. Sawny froze. The voice had come from whoever was humming, only feet from her. It was a hoarse voice that was deep, but she could've sworn it sounded like a woman's.

"Where is he?" Sawny asked, her voice sounding foreign to her. Her throat felt dry, and she desperately needed water.

As if on cue, she felt someone press a canteen up to her mouth and pour. The water splashed onto her face and clothes, but she drank hopelessly. After a minute, the canteen was pulled away and a hand supported her back, as it helped her to sit up.

Sawny was looking at her childhood cottage.

She almost screamed when she saw it. It was exactly like the one she had in Illias, the one she had lived in with her parents. It was one story and painted a creamy white color with wooden trim and a wooden roof. She had watched her father fix that roof a million times, patching it up with mismatched pieces of material. Sure enough, the cottage had the same roof, with bits of scrap wood placed in the exact same spot. There were boxes on the window with flowers in them, almost identical to the ones her mom would plant each spring. All of it was the same.

"What-what is this?" Sawny managed, choking back a sob. She hadn't seen the cottage since she had set it aflame. Now it was back, unchanged, and in the Forest Dembe.

"This is your world, Sawny Lois," the same gravelly voice replied.

Sawny tried to turn her head to look at the speaker but her neck wouldn't move. She could only stare straight ahead at her cottage. The same cottage that her parents had been murdered at. She stared at the window where the loft used to be. She had been staring out the same window as she saw the group of riders approaching her house. Her father was a diplomat. She was used to seeing frequent visitors. Normally, she wouldn't bat an eye at people riding towards her house but there was something about this particular set of seven or eight that made her terrified. She had only been fifteen.

She remembered her mother screaming from the kitchen, "Sawny! Go get out of sight now!" Sawny didn't hesitate. She climbed up into their loft and had laid on her stomach within the blankets and pillows until she was out of sight. From the loft, she kept her eyes closed, listening to hear what would happen. She didn't know how long she laid there until she looked out. The men were gone but her parents were still there. On the ground. Everything had gone numb.

Now, sitting up, she couldn't take her eyes off the very same cottage in the middle of the Forest Dembe.

"Where am I?" she asked, voice cracking. She rapidly tried to blind the tears out of her eyes, with no success as they began to stream down her face.

"Your world, Sawny Lois," the voice repeated.

"I don't understand," Sawny whispered.

"Many don't."

"Where's Adriel?"

"The boy is still with you. You're in his arms as we speak."

In a flash, Sawny could see a vision of herself lying limp in Adriel's arms, him yelling and shaking her, checking for a pulse, repeating her name over and over. But she didn't move.

The house reappeared and still, she was unable to move. "It's in my head then. How do I get back?"

"You'll return to your world when I want you to."

"Who are you?"

Suddenly, she regained control of her entire body, movement and nerves flowing back all at once. It made her dizzy, but she stood up and turned around towards the direction of the voice.

The woman was old. Much too old for the world they lived in. Her skin sagged off her body, wrinkled like old pieces of paper. Her hair was so white that it might have been glowing. Her eyes had no pupils but were just solid masses of black. She was smaller than Sawny was, almost a foot shorter, and wore a colorful tunic, a hue that Sawny couldn't find the words to describe. The strangest thing out of all were the tattoos covering every inch of her sagging skin. Images of everything, the trees of the forest Dembe, the streets of Illias, flashes of the Wilds and faces of warriors of the Darklands. So many different pictures that Sawny's head began to spin. The woman just watched her with those empty eyes.

"Who are you?" Sawny repeated, fighting to keep herself upright. She stumbled towards a small tree and grabbed it to lean upon. Too much was going on for her to comprehend. The forest, her old home, this woman. But it was all happening in her head.

"You may call me Matahali. It is one of the many names I've been known as."

"What are you?" Sawny asked, her vision starting to go black again.

Matahali waved her hand and her vision came back, along with her bearings. She yanked the bow off her back, drew an arrow, and pointed it at the witch woman within the blink of an eye. "I'm done waiting for answers."

The old woman smiled, revealing rows of rotting teeth with various ones missing. "Let's not do that." She waved her hand and the bow disappeared along with the arrows and the rest of the weapons she had.

"Before you try anything else, I am not here to hurt you," Matahali spoke, her eyes seeming to stare into Sawny's mind. "I am the soul of this forest. This forest is me. I control all that happens within its borders. I know every single person who has ever stepped foot in here. I am older than Auntica and Orinth and all the little countries you've created. I was here when the Shadow Wall was constructed, and I will be here if it ever is destroyed. I am Matahali and I belong to the world."

Sawny opened her mouth to respond and then closed it. There wasn't a response to a statement such as that one. She knew spirits existed and she knew there was magic in the world but never had she come face to face with it. Until now.

"What do you want with me?" she managed.

Matahali gestured a hand towards her old house. "You've passed through my forest many times before, Sawny Lois, and you've always been an enigma to me. There is so much darkness within you, so much fear and so much sadness. It overwhelms me when you step foot across my border. When you entered in mere hours ago, I knew I needed to know the truth, to talk to you myself. So, I possessed your mind. Don't worry, once I release the hold I have on it, you'll wake up with the man you are with and you will pass through the rest of my Forest Dembe without any obstacles. And believe me, I could create many obstacles. I'm curious about you."

She sat on the ground, facing her cottage, and trying to take in every little detail possible. She wasn't sure whether this was real or not. For all she knew, she could've fallen off the horse and was dreaming this as a result of head trauma. Or it was the spirit of the Forest Dembe wanting to know the truth about her darkness. Either way, she hadn't seen such a clear vision of the cottage since the day she had left. She would try to absorb it as much as she could before this was over.

"What do you want me to tell you?" Sawny asked Matahali.

"Whenever you walk in this forest, Sawny Lois, the first thing I sense is undeniable grief. And somehow, that grief is connected to this cottage. That much I could tell from seizing your mind. Start with why."

Sawny took a deep breath that hurt her lungs. "That's a pretty rough place to start, Matahali."

The old woman shrugged. "My forest, me, we feed upon raw emotion. Every few decades, it's necessary for me to hear stories that are 'rough' as you call it. Everything you say will make this forest stronger. It will protect it. Believe me, the gods will thank you for it. The Forest Dembe is a special place and if it died, the world would suffer insurmountable repercussions."

"So, you've kidnapped me, or should I say my mind, in order to feed yourself and this forest on my tragedies and secrets."

Matahali chuckled. "I don't know if I would put it that way, but yes. It will not hurt you. I am not sucking out your lifeforce or soul. I am feeding off your emotions. It is harmless. Once I have had enough, enough to keep this forest, then I shall release you."

Sawny opened her mouth to speak but the old woman interrupted her, "Sawny, at this point, only I can release you back into the real world. You have no choice."

Sawny looked back to her cottage. She could hear echoes of Adriel screaming her name in her brain over and over again. The quicker she escaped this place, her mind, the quicker they could leave here, leave this witch or woman or whoever she was who had to strengthen her home.

"I lived here with my mother and my father from the time I was just a baby. My adopted father, that is. I don't know who my birth father is. I've been searching for him for a few years, but I don't know where to start. I was born in Tenir but my mother left my father and fled. The thought of my real father, being alive out there, haunts me every day of my life. I keep wondering who he was and what caused my mother to flee. I wonder how my life would be different if I was in Tenir, raised by him and my mother together. But I loved my adopted father, Caleb. I wouldn't change him a bit."

"He was a diplomat. Specifically for the tribes of the Darklands, as that's where he was from. He worked with other higherups and often, King Grafph himself. His job, I would never describe it as dangerous. We never received any threats. He traveled to the Darklands often, which many would perceive as risky, but nothing ever happened. My mother never told him to quit. He was passionate about his job, as was my mother. She worked in Illias, at a shop that sold flowers. She would take me into school and then work until I was done. My mother was beautiful. But also, quite sad. She loved me and my father. But something happened to her, something dark and terrible. Many times, she would become very within herself. She didn't talk to me or my father, she would just stay in her room and lay in bed, staring at something that wasn't there. But she was a good mother, and I was rarely ever unhappy."

"I was used to people coming to our house. My mother and father entertained many guests of the diplomatic world. But on the day they died, I knew it was not diplomats who murdered them. I was fifteen when I saw them approaching. I hid, as my mother told me to. If they would have seen me or found me, I have no doubt that they would have killed me too. I hid in the loft, not watching what was about to happen. I was so frightened, I'm ashamed to admit. I thought maybe if I closed my eyes, when I opened them again the men would be gone and my parents safe. When I finally looked out the window, the men were gone. But the bodies of my parents remained."

Sawny shuddered at the memory of her father and mother's bodies, limp. She had relived this memory a thousand times and each time was more painful than the next. Her eyes were flooded with tears and her heart had a cold, stinging feeling in it. Everything from that day was so clear. The visions had been a constant companion to her for the past four years, plaguing her everywhere she went. She had learned fast that outrunning the past was a fool's mission.

"They didn't search the house. They didn't find the loft or me. I don't know if they knew I was there, if I existed. I ran downstairs to the bodies of my fallen parents. I cradled my father in my lap as I watched the life leave his eyes. He was smiling at me. And then my mother, she was still alive. And with her very last breaths, she told me that Caleb wasn't my real father."

"She told me that my real father had been in Tenir. She had a long-standing affair with him that resulted in a pregnancy. She didn't get to finish, didn't get to tell me who he was or why she ran from him. Her last words were in Orinthian. A prayer to the gods to keep me safe. Then, she died."

"I can't describe how I felt on that day. Words don't begin to come close to the horror, the extent of my grief. As I buried my parents on the edge of our forest, I had become so detached, it was like I was watching myself do it. A darkness had crept into my heart and taken root there, filling me with such agony that I knew, no matter what I did, it would always be a part of who I was. I took everything I could from the house and strapped it to my horse. I took all the money we had, which was quite a lot. Once I was sure, I set my house on fire. I sat on the ground and watched as the flames consumed it, bit by bit. Looking back now, it was incredibly daft as we lived next to a forest. By a miracle of the gods, it didn't catch anything else on fire. Just crumbled into ashes. Because that was all that was left of me, after what I had just witnessed. Ashes."

Sawny sighed, "That's the story of my cottage. It was my haven, my sanctuary, until from that window right there-" she said, pointing a shaking hand at the topmost window, "-I hid while a group of men murdered the two people I loved most in the world. The worst part of it all? I don't know why it happened. I have searched long and hard for the answers, but they escape me. Neither of my parents had any enemies. They were very loved by all who knew them. Why anyone, anywhere, would want to kill them? I don't know. My biggest fear is that I will never find out."

"I have spent many months trying to find my birth father, to no avail. I can't help but think that their murder has something to do with him."

Matahali was silent for what seemed like hours, eyes closed. Sawny wasn't sure she had heard anything of what she had just said but she was not going to repeat it all again. The feeling of grief and anguish that was always with her was now as worse as it had been. It was burning within her, making her feel sick. Abruptly, she threw up everywhere, vomit spraying all over the grass below her feet. She doubled over, hands on her knees, and continued to throw up. Her throat was on fire. Her head throbbed. What was happening to her?

The old woman's eyes opened and in an instant, the pain went away. The vomit disappeared and the physical discomforts with it. The mental torture still plagued her. But Sawny had come to terms with the fact that it always would, some days more than others.

"I am sorry for your loss, Sawny Lois," was all Matahali said in reply. Somehow, after that, her skin seemed to sag less, her back straightening out.

"Is that enough?" Sawny breathed, falling to her knees. "I don't know how much more I can tell you after that."

Matahali ignored her. "You do not know who your real father is?" Sawny nodded, using her hands to wipe large tears away.

"And you do not know who killed your mother and adopted father?"

She nodded again. "As I just told you."

"This is the source of your darkness, then, Sawny Lois. Is it not?"

"It's the source of my pain. It has a hold on me that, unlike yours upon my mind, will never be released. I've learned to live with it, the way a cripple learns to live with their ailment."

Matahali didn't speak for a long time. Sawny held her head in her hands, taking deliberate breaths, trying to stop her racing heartbeat. She had never told anyone out loud what had happened. It was agony, every second of it. She would consider herself lucky if she never had to again.

"Is it enough?" Sawny asked, after the long stretch of silence. "Please," her voice cracked as she spoke, "Please let me go."

"You are a rare individual, Sawny Lois," the old woman said.

Sawny snorted. "Thank you. Now please, release the hold on me."

"There is something within you, something apart from the darkness of your grief. You should not be afraid. You are far more powerful, stronger, than you realize. You are steadfast."

You are steadfast.

The old woman's words echoed in her mind. She wished she could believe them.

The cottage disappeared as did the rest of the forest. Suddenly, she was in the city of Tenir. She recognized its tall brick buildings and brick streets, the sea just on the horizon. There was no one else around and she stood in the center of an alleyway that was surprisingly clean. There were no noises. Every time she had been here before, the city had been loud with shouts of people, hoofbeats on the road, the wind roaring through the buildings, due to the location of the city on the sea. But there was absolute silence.

Matahali appeared next to her, dressed in the same garb, looking less haggard and more upright. Sawny hid her distaste from the witch. She was using her to become more healthy, livelier. She had to get out of her mind and out of this forest. She needed this to become a distant memory.

"Where are we?" Sawny asked.

Matahali pointed towards a door, on the second floor of one of the buildings in the alley. "In thanks for providing me with the stories I needed to keep my forest safe, I'm in turn, providing you with a beginning to the answers you seek."

Sawny tried to walk forward but again, her body wasn't capable of moving. "What is this place?"

"Through that door lies the resolution. You're traveling to Tenir already. Find this alley, find this door, and enter it. That is all I can reveal to you."

She blinked and they were back in Dembe. Her cottage was gone but she had regained all of her movements, along with her weapons. Matahali stood several feet away, glancing up at the trees swaying in the sky. She was singing again, in a language that Sawny couldn't understand. Matahali continued singing as she turned back to look at her.

"I once again extend my gratitude to you, Sawny Lois. I know it was difficult to relive those memories but trust me, you have renewed the life of the forest for many, many decades to come. When you pass through here again, and for the rest of your time on this journey, no harm shall come to you." She nodded her head.

"Wait. Before I go-" Sawny hesitated. She had to ask, had to get confirmation. "The Shadow Wall. Is it in jeopardy? I've heard murmurs of it, more than I've ever heard before."

Matahali stared at her, those black eyes seemingly searching her soul and mind. Sawny shuddered. She was reminded again of how powerful this witch must be, and she grew very frightened.

"Yes, Sawny Lois. There are forces at work that have shoved the existence of the Shadow Wall into danger."

Sawny felt her heart drop. She knew there was a chance, a small possibility, that the rumors were true, but she had denied it. Yet the witch had confirmed her worst fears.

"What-what do we do?"

"I'm afraid there's nothing any singular person can do. Even I cannot see into the cloak of the future that far, to see what it holds. Whether or not the wall will be destroyed, I cannot say."

"I didn't even know there was a way to destroy it," Sawny gasped for breath.

"Yes. Long before you were born, blood was spilled to bind the wall. And the same blood can be spilled to unbind the wall."

"Who's blood?"

Matahali shook her head. "It is not revealed to me. But your king, he believes that he knows who it is. Whether he is right or not, I cannot be sure."

"My father knew Grafph personally; he is a good man. I can't imagine him being behind this."

The old woman sighed. "Nor I. There are strange events in place that I wish I could be able to see, yet I can't. My sole concern is keeping this forest safe from whatever may come." Matahali closed her eyes and Sawny yelped as she felt a burning on her wrist. She grabbed it with her other hand and saw that a sort of blemish had formed, a small symbol of a tree just below her palm. She touched it.

"What is it?"

"It's my mark, Sawny Lois. You have the friendship of the Forest Dembe, all who dwell here, and Matahali, the spirit of the forest. You may find it to be valuable someday. For now, it shall protect you as you continue through this forest. Once again, I extend my gratitude to you. Remember what I spoke to you. You are steadfast. You are stronger than you know. The answers you seek will only appear if you stop being afraid of the truth. Goodbye now, and maybe someday our paths will cross again."

Sawny opened her mouth to respond as she stroked her wrist but before she could, everything in her vision went black. She screamed but no sound came out. It started again, the numbness, the ringing in her ears, until she was in a state of total chaos. Then, almost as quickly as it had begun, it was gone.

She was conscious again. She felt her body leaning up against something solid and she could tell that she was moving. Sawny could once again move, and she opened her eyes.

She was on a horse that was galloping through the Forest Dembe. Matahali was nowhere to be seen and Sawny was almost positive she was back in the real world. She heard the sound of panting and realized she was sitting on the saddle in front of Adriel, her head leaning on his chest, one of his arms holding her against him, the other holding the reigns of the horse. They were moving fast. The burning on her wrist had stopped substantially but the new mark still remained, The Tree of Dembe.

"Adriel?" Sawny managed, her throat dry.

"Sawny?" he choked, bringing the horse to a halt.

"It's me," she said, her voice ragged.

Adriel jumped off the horse and helped her get down. He stared at her dumbfounded. He was pale and sweating and panting, having stripped off into just an undershirt, his armor nowhere to be seen. Without a word, he grabbed Sawny and pulled her into an embrace.

Sawny froze before wrapping her arms around him and burying her face into his shoulder. She hadn't noticed before, but the man smelled good. She had noticed the fact that he was basically all muscle, but this confirmed it as his trimmed body pressed against her own.

"I thought you were dying," Adriel mumbled into her hair.

"I thought I was too," she whispered, thinking back to everything that had just occurred. Reliving her parent's murder had almost felt painful enough to kill her. But here she was.

Adriel released her and looked her over once and then twice. "What happened, Sawny? We were riding for a few minutes and then you fell off your horse. I tried to wake you up, but you wouldn't budge. I've been riding for hours, trying to find someone, anyone to help."

Sawny took a long, deep breath. "It's complicated," she finally said.

He raised an eyebrow. "Complicated?"

"Remember the stories your people have about this forest?"

Adriel nodded.

"Well, they're not completely off."

He looked astonished. "Witches?"

"Something like that." They sat down on the forest floor, as Sawny relayed the story to him, leaning against his shoulder for support. She left out the exact details of the story she had fed Matahali, but the way Adriel's eyes searched hers, she knew that he was well aware of the pain it had caused. She felt entirely exhausted as she spoke, as if something had been drained from her. Every time she moved, she grew dizzy. Adriel listened with intensity, not interrupting a single time until she finished, showing him her wrist.

He held it in his hand and ran a thumb over the tattoo several times. "I don't know what to say," he responded.

Sawny took a drink from a canteen he had offered her. "Me neither. We need to get out of this forest though, please." Her voice cracked as she spoke the last word and Adriel helped her to her feet.

Sawny glanced around, heart beginning to drop. "Where-where's Indira?"

Adriel looked at his feet and then his blue eyes met hers. "Sawny, I'm so sorry. I had to let her go. I couldn't ride fast with you and lead your horse at the same time. I thought if I didn't get you a healer in time, you would die so I left her behind. I-forgive me."

Sawny looked at him, in silence. His eyes never left her own. Finally, she spoke, "You did what you thought you had to do to save me, Adriel. I'm happy you value my life over the life of my horse."

He shook his head. "I know. I should have found some way to bring her." He kicked the dirt and mumbled a few words in a language she couldn't understand.

Sawny stepped forward and touched his cheek. He froze. "Adriel. It's okay. I swear. I love Indira but now she's free. She gets to wander in a beautiful forest for the rest of her days. I wish I was as lucky."

Gently, he reached up and brushed her hand. "When this is over, I'll buy you a new horse. One from the Wilds. They're beautiful up there." He squeezed her fingers and said softly, "Beautiful."

They stood like that for a moment. Sawny found herself wanting it to be longer as he dropped his hand and she dropped hers. Adriel climbed back onto the horse in one smooth stroke.

"Do you want to lead?" he asked her faintly.

She shook her head. "I'm so tired." she said, yawning. "I just want to sleep."

Adriel helped her onto the horse, behind him. "As soon as we get out of the forest, we'll find an inn," he promised. She nodded as he kicked his own horse in the side, and they began at a steady pace.

They rode on for a few minutes before Adriel said, "Sawny?"

"Yes?"

"I-I'm glad you're safe," he hesitated before speaking.

"Are you glad because I'm the only one who can find your brother's killer or are you glad because I'm safe?" she asked him, honestly.

He whispered something softly in his language.

"What does it mean?"

"'My heart rejoices to see you safe.' And it's not because of my brother."

She didn't say anything else but rested her head on his back. As they rode on, Sawny felt a brief moment of peace within her soul and wished it could last forever.

Chapter 10

Somewhere on the Dela

For the first time in her eighteen years of life, Alida had made a new friend who wasn't Rider. Of course, when she was little, her mother would throw other little girls at her, begging her to play with them and bond. She could never find the interest in befriending these people and always preferred playing by herself. Weylin was introduced to her and they grew close, but the girl would never see Alida as a friend; she always saw her as the princess and that distinction divided them. Rider had been her one consistent friend, but there were many things she couldn't talk to him about.

Sahar Bow, captain of the Valley, was her first friend.

She had spent the first few days of the journey not leaving her cabin, spare using the toilet and getting food. She avoided making eye contact with the other crew members of the ship and none tried to approach her. There was almost nothing to do but sleep, eat, and watch what was out the window. It was ridiculously boring, but she was trained for boring. She couldn't count the number of times she had to sit in the throne room while her father conducted business, sitting still and very often, staying silent. She was used to this, to a certain level.

It was on the third day of the journey that Sahar finally sought her out.

It was midday and Alida was just laying down to take another nap when there were three sharp knocks on her door.

She froze. This was it. The Auntican guards were on her ship and they were about to take her away. She rolled her eyes at herself. No. Stop being stupid and paranoid. "Who is it?" she asked.

Sahar opened the door and let herself in without responding. "My ship. I don't even have to knock if I don't want to," she said straight-forwardly.

Alida stared at her. "I paid for this cabin. Knocking would be appreciated."

Sahar raised an eyebrow but there was a slight smile on her face. Today, the captain was dressed in a loose fitting long sleeved white shirt and tight black pants. She wore a bandanna around her head and her black hair was down. Alida half expected her to be wearing an eyepatch or secretly have a hook for a hand.

"Who pissed you off?" Sahar asked abruptly, leaning up against the door and crossing her arms.

"No one," Alida replied quizzically. "What are you talking about?"

"I told you when you boarded, you're allowed to go wherever you want except for my quarters. I've seen you maybe thrice since then. Why don't you leave your room? Do you have some sort of disease?"

"Of course I don't. I just want to stay out of everyone's way until we get to Nagaye," Alida protested.

Sahar rolled her brown eyes. "Bullshit."

"It's true!" Alida insisted. "Why do you care anyways?"

Sahar strode over to the bed and sat down next to Alida, "Very very rarely do other women ever travel with us. Most of my crew are men. The few that are females are too intimidated by me to ever try to form a friendship. You talked to me like you knew me the first time we met. I assumed we would carry on together, but you've been hiding like a scared little mouse."

Alida replied, "It's nothing against you. I don't have many female friends either if it makes you feel any better."

Sahar threw her hands in the air. "This continent and this country. Women are still scared here. Scared to open their mouths and say what they will, afraid no one will listen. I've never given a damn about that in my entire life."

Alida laughed. "I know what you mean."

Sahar turned to her. "Come up onto the decks. Let me show you around. You seem like a halfway decent person. I'll see for myself. If you're not, I'll throw you into the water and steal all your possessions."

Alida stood up. "I'm inclined to prove that I am a halfway decent person." she said.

Sahar grinned. "We'll have to see."

Alida followed the captain through the halls that led to the personal cabins and up the stairs onto the main deck. The day was sunny but cold, and she wrapped her jacket a little tighter around her. The crew was going about their typical business, yelling things to each other that Alida didn't know the meaning of, doing tasks that she assumed were helping. They all stood a little straighter as Sahar passed by, some of them even offering a salute. It was clear that they had the utmost respect for the girl, who Alida imagined couldn't be much older than she was.

Alida looked to see where they were, as being on the deck offered a better view than her tiny window. They were in the direct center of the Dela and she could see the banks of Orinth on either side. There wasn't much to look at, just grassy plains either way with no habitation in sight.

"Are we getting close to the sea of Nagaye?" Alida asked Sahar.

"Well, we aren't going towards Auntica."

Alida shot her a look.

"We're at least three days from reaching the sea. We're stopping at Aram before to get new supplies and throw away old ones," Sahar explained.

Alida had heard of Aram, the city on the mouth of the Dela. She would gladly stay on the ship. It would only present another opportunity for her to be recognized, or gods forbid, taken by Aunticans.

Sahar stopped so abruptly that Alida almost ran into her.

She spread her hands out, gesturing at the main deck. "This is where the magic happens. The whole of the crew works here most of the day. There's nothing too exciting to stay and watch, just a lot of grumpy men who curse at each other and occasionally start fights. They don't report to me, Roman deals with them. But they know if I ever saw them doing anything ridiculously stupid-" she said this last part loud enough to catch the ear of the men nearest to them, whose heads popped up, "-they know I would beat their asses and then fire them."

"You wouldn't make them walk the plank?" Alida joked.

Sahar shrugged. "I've had to before, but we've gone away from that."

Alida couldn't tell whether the girl was kidding or not. Before she could ask, the captain began moving again, at a brisk pace.

They walked up a set of stairs to the top deck, where the ship's wheel was. A larger man was holding onto it and looking to the horizon, back turned to them.

"Nova, this is Lao."

The man turned around and Alida stifled a gasp. She had read many novels when she was younger about pirates and this man is exactly what she had imagined. He had no hair and a red beard that was wild and tangled up. He was indeed wearing an eyepatch and had a long scar that ran from the top of his forehead, across his nose, all the way to the edge of his jaw. He didn't have a hook for a hand but was wearing a black coat that reached his shoes, which were black boots. He wore a triangular hat and had a pipe hanging out of his mouth.

"Lao, let me introduce to you Nova. She's traveling with us to Nagaye. I'm giving her an official tour of the ship."

The large man extended a hand to Alida and she shook it. His hands made hers look like a child's. "It's nice to meet you, Nova," he said in an accent that she couldn't identify.

"And you as well," she responded with a smile. This was her scene. She was good at being introduced to people and socializing.

"What is bringing you to Nagaye?" he asked.

"My parents are sending me away. They don't want me in Orinth when the war hits."

Lao nodded. "So unfortunate, this war. Waste of lives if you asked me." Alida wanted to point out that it wasn't their choice to enter this war, Auntica was forcing them to when they murdered the farmer on the border. But she wasn't about to start debating the man who was currently piloting the ship she was standing on.

"If I may ask, where is your accent from?" Alida inquired.

He smiled. "I'm from Grady. The southern part of it."

Alida whistled. "You're a long way from home, Mr. Lao," she commented.

He shrugged. "You see, Ms. Nova, the sea, the rivers, this ship. They are all my home. And Sahar here, Roman, the rest of the crew, they have become like my family. So, if I may say, I am not far from my home at all."

"That's a lovely sentiment," Sahar said, patting the large man's back.

He smiled down at Sahar before looking back upwards and towards the river, regaining his focus and his concentration. Sahar led Alida back towards the main deck.

"Your crew. They seem to adore you," Alida said.

"I don't know if I would say 'adore'," Sahar laughed. "They hate me sometimes. But like Lao, they're my family. Most of them have been with me for three years or more. And like most real families, you love them, and you hate them. Sometimes at the same time."

Alida asked, "How did you come to have this ship anyways?"

Sahar chuckled. "It's a long story. I'm in a good mood now so I don't feel like telling it. It's not a good story. But I'm here now. I have my ship. I have my family. I love it. Sometimes what we think is the worst thing to happen to us turns out to be something great."

"I get it. I really do." She thought to the caves and how the greatest friendship in her life began because of it.

"I owe it all to Roman," Sahar said quietly.

"You and Roman seem close," Alida said. They stopped walking briefly and leaned against the rail of the ship.

Sahar snorted. "We are. But it's not anything romantic. I love him like a brother. Plus-" She glanced down at her finger and the ring that was on it. Alida noticed it for the first time, a simple gold band with words engraved onto it she couldn't read, "-there's someone else."

Alida didn't ask anything further about who had given her the ring or the identity of this 'someone else'. "How did Roman help you?" she only asked.

"Have you ever heard of the Vacci family?" Sahar asked.

"Yes, of course I have. I would be surprised to hear of anyone on Orinth who hasn't. What does that have to do with anything?"

"Roman Aldin is the youngest son of Damon Vacci."

Alida's mouth fell open. The Vacci family had been a thorn in the side of her kingdom for as long as she had been alive. They were a prominent crime syndicate that operated out of every major city in Orinth. They were smugglers, but also specialized in large scale heists that were so intricate, it was almost impossible to fathom how they pulled it off. Her father had tried time and time again to shut them down, but they could never be caught. Finally, Damon Vacci had met Tieran himself in the castle and struck a deal with him. They wouldn't touch anything of the crown. Tieran agreed to let them continue their operations as long as it was in the private field, where his interests couldn't be hurt. Local authorities still attempted to catch them, but never could. There was somewhat of a battle between the Vacci's and private businesses everywhere. Tieran had always let it run its course.

"Roman Vacci, then?" Alida asked.

Like most people in Orinth, she spoke about the Vacci family with outward distaste, but secretly enjoying hearing about each one of their schemes.

Sahar nodded. "The youngest of five brothers."

"How did he end up here?" Alida asked.

Sahar took a deep breath. "Roman used to be a- client of mine," she mumbled. Alida raised an eyebrow as Sahar spoke again, "Looks like we're getting into this now."

"I used to be a prostitute. In Abdul actually. I grew up with nothing and I had no other choice. I was almost forced into it. Both of my parents died when I was young, and my older sister raised me. She was one too. When I turned fifteen, I became one. It was awful. I won't give you the details but it's a set of memories that only live on in my nightmares. Anyways, we worked at a higher-class brothel that was frequented by the Vacci's. Roman was sixteen years old at the time when his father made him come. It was some sort of sick tradition he had his sons partake in. Losing their virginity at the age of sixteen to one of 'Abdul's finest'. He bought me and we went upstairs, and I took off my clothes and laid on the bed, just waiting. But he wouldn't do it."

"I asked him what he was waiting for and he said nothing. He told me he didn't believe this was okay and he wished he could get me out of this situation. I asked him if he could get me out of Abdul. Get me a new identity and help me start over somewhere else. He said he could, but he needed a few weeks. I asked him to help my sister and he said yes. I couldn't help asking him why he was doing this. He looked at me and said, 'Because the world needs a little more light'."

"He continued to come back to me, pretending like he was just another one of my clients. But each time, we would plan a little bit more. It wasn't easy to get out of a brothel. Especially the one I was at. They basically held you under lock and key. Then, one day, Roman brought someone else. The man who was going to help me with a new identity. I fell in love with him."

"His name was Dax. He was a part of the Vacci family. His specialty was to help their members who got caught to escape and start over somewhere new. Roman brought him to help me but after a few weeks, our plan was to run away together. We were in love. When we told Roman this, he didn't even get mad. He understood. And a couple months later, Dax and myself and my sister, Rochelle, left Abdul. Rochelle and I separated. We loved each other but it was better that way. She went to live in Tenir. Dax and I went to a village on the Dela. Then we got married."

"It all happened so fast. Normally when things happen that fast, it's a disaster. With Dax and me, it was perfect. He was nineteen and I was seventeen. We lived in a tiny hut, only one room, but it was so cozy. I started working at a library and Dax worked at a shipyard. It's when he started falling in love with boats. One day, he decided he wanted to sail. I wasn't going to stop him because I could see the passion in his eyes. We kissed goodbye and Dax left on a boat called the Orderly. It was supposed to be a short trip, to Nagaye and back, carrying passengers. Only he never came back. I waited for months and heard nothing. I never heard that he died. Some of the others with family on the ship heard nothing either. I panicked. I got in touch with the only person I knew could help me find him. Roman Vacci."

"Roman came immediately. He contacted his people in Nagaye, but they couldn't find him either. So, he bought me a ship. I called it the Valley. I hired a crew. And Roman and I started sailing to find what happened to Dax. After a few months of searching, we started doing work for the Vacci family, so I had a source of income. Roman fell in love with sailing almost as much as I did. In time, it turned into our own smuggling trade. Now we only do Orinthian wine, and it brings in quite a lot of money. But that's why I have this ship. It's why I never stop sailing. The smuggling, it's just for the money. I sail because I know that somewhere, Dax is out there. Waiting for me. I know I'll see him again. I hold onto that hope and until the gods themselves come down to stop me, I will never cease looking for him."

She finished talking and exhaled. Alida put her hand over Sahar's. "I know saying I'm sorry could not do anything to change what has already come to pass. So, I'll say this; that story that you told is an inspiration to me. The way you changed your life like that gives hope to all of us. So instead of an apology, let me say thank you."

Sahar blinked a few times, trying to keep the tears in and set her other hand on top of Alida's. "That's very kind of you to say, Nova. But it wasn't me. It was all Roman."

Alida shook her head. "No, it wasn't. Roman isn't the captain of this ship, is he? You had the courage to do all of this. You should be proud."

Sahar looked down at the water and then back up into Alida's eyes. "Thank you," she whispered.

Alida chose her next words very carefully. "I have a friend. He's very very good at tracking people down, as long as he has one of their possessions. When this war is over, if you still haven't found Dax, then I'll have to introduce you to him." She also would speak to Rider about ensuring that every brothel like the one Sahar had just described was shut down. There was no excuse that operations such as those were still in existence. By the time Alida was queen, they would be dead and gone.

Sahar straightened up. "I'll hold you to that, Nova Grey. I don't know what he could do that I haven't already done to find him, but I'll hold you to it." If Alida knew Rider, she knew, without a doubt, that he would help Sahar track down her husband. He had told her that he didn't like to use his powers at all. But this was for good. She was sure he would do it, if it were for good.

Sahar led Alida onto the front of the ship, up a set of stairs, to where a sort of observation deck was. There was no one on this deck, spare one man mopping. He saluted to Sahar, who returned the salute. Alida was amazed. This girl, who could only be twenty or twenty-one at the most, a former prostitute, who had lost her husband, was the captain of a smuggling ship. She had earned the respect of every person who worked for her. And she made money in order to find her lost husband. It made Alida feel a little ashamed? Yes, ashamed. She had been born into money, had a childhood that was easy. Yes, she had lost her mother at a young age, but there was never a time she would've had to turn to prostitution to survive. Her life was painless, up until a few days ago, after learning she was (or maybe wasn't) the Last Heir. Sahar was strong. Alida was well, not.

"Do you stay in touch with your sister?" Alida asked, trying not to think about it anymore.

Sahar nodded eagerly. "Oh yes. She lives in Tenir still, and I see her once or twice a year. She's married and she has two children. A boy and a girl. Somehow, I've adopted the role of the doting aunt," she laughed.

Alida laughed with her. "That's the best role. You get to hold them and cuddle them and then when they start to cry, give them back to their mother."

"Do your brothers have children?" Sahar asked.

Alida had a brief moment of panicked confusion before responding confidently. "Yes, they do. My two oldest ones."

Sahar opened her mouth to speak but before she could ask any more questions, Alida said, "Does Roman still have contacts within the Vacci family?"

"He does. This technically isn't a Vacci operation anymore, but he is still a part of the family. A very messed-up, dysfunctional, manipulative, psychotic set of assholes, but still a family. The name Vacci comes in handy often. He goes by his middle name, Roman Aldin, just because they have a lot of enemies."

"And Damon Vacci doesn't care that he doesn't work their operations anymore?"

"No, he doesn't. Roman was never the favorite son. I think Damon is glad to keep him at an arm's length."

Roman snorted from behind them. "Alright then."

They both whirled around. Roman was standing there, dressed in a black shirt. His hair was messy in the wind and for some reason, the scar on his eyebrow was more distinct than usual.

Sahar grinned at him. "Am I wrong though?"

"No. My father has never liked me. I see you've been telling our guest from the north my family history." He glanced at Alida. "Just so you know, I'm Vacci in name only. Most of my brothers are assholes."

"Told you," Sahar said, the grin not leaving her face.

"And you're not?" Alida asked.

Roman scoffed, "Me? Never."

Sahar and Alida exchanged a look. "Vacci's are notorious liars," Sahar said pointedly.

Roman smiled. "Notorious," he repeated.

"Is there anything in particular you need, Roman, or did you just come up here to be a general bother?"

Roman shrugged. "Well, at first it was to give you a report. But now it's definitely to be a general bother. I have to protect my darling family name, you know? Can't have people disrespecting the Vacci's."

Alida snorted at this and Roman shot her a look. "Can I help you, Miss Grey?"

Alida shook her head, innocently. "Oh no. I think I'm fine. Actually, is there any way you could introduce me to your older brother? What's his name again? Cathan Vacci?"

Roman was confused. "Yes, my older brother Cathan. Why do you want to meet him?"

"Oh, you know. I just want to meet a member of the Vacci family who's actually important."

Sahar started laughing and Roman smirked at her. "Hurtful, but understandable. I'll see what I can do, Miss Gray."

She smiled. "You can call me Nova, Mr. Vacci."

He rolled her eyes at her and turned back to Sahar. "I came to let you know that we're about three days out from Aram, if the winds hold up."

Sahar nodded at him. "Is that all?"

He raised an eyebrow at her. "That is all. You in a hurry?"

She shrugged. "I've known you for so long, Roman. And this ship has so many men on it, it's time I spend a little more of my life with women. They're smarter and more polite and less gross and—"

"Alright, alright," Roman said, holding his hands up, a slight grin on his face. "I get it." He retreated a few steps back. "I'll leave you both alone. Sahar." He glanced at Alida. "See you soon, Nova," he breathed before walking away.

Alida had met two Vacci's in her lifetime. One of them was Damon and ironically enough, Cathan Vacci. The few times they had come to the castle to do business with her father, she had been asked to attend dinner. Damon Vacci was an overly charming man who looked much too young for his age, but his looks didn't deceive her at all. He was corrupt and destructive. She constantly asked her father why he allied with the man instead of destroying his operation. Her father explained that yes, the Vacci's were bad. They stole and they pillaged but they also kept other gangs from taking over in the cities of Orinth. Other gangs were capable of more evil, human trafficking and worse. Tieran chose the lesser devil to prevent from greater evil. Alida couldn't comprehend it. But she did trust her father.

The rest of the day, they talked on the observation deck. Sahar spoke little about her previous life and tended to focus more on her sister, her nephew, her niece, and her brother-in-law. She talked of certain journeys she had made, all over the world. The people she had met. The experiences she had. With every word she spoke, Alida was filled for a sense of longing. There was so much she hadn't seen or accomplished. Her whole life had been spent doing the most trivial of all things. Balls, charity dinners, dress fittings. She rarely was allowed to travel and when she did, it was under heavy guard. She wasn't complaining about her lot. She had a sheltered childhood. But her heart yearned for something she never had even thought about before. She wanted to see it all, to start living.

But there was so much else going on. It wasn't that simple. She wasn't just a person who could give up everything. She was the princess. She was heiress to a throne. She was the Last Heir. Her death, the spilling of her blood, could bring about the destruction of the border between their two realms. She would spend the rest of her life looking over her shoulder, no matter where she was. Alida Goulding would never find the true freedom that Sahar had somehow managed to find.

Nova Grey was another story.

Sahar finally had to leave her side and go attend to her duties as the captain. She left Alida standing against the side of the ship with her face to the wind, overlooking the Dela.

Freedom was a word she would never truly grasp. But as she stood by the side of the ship, a part of her felt free.

That night, instead of hiding in her cabin for dinner, she joined the rest of the crew in the mess hall, along with Sahar, who normally ate alone in her quarters. There was about fifty or so, spread about six different tables. She ended up at the table with the apparent leaders. Sahar sat on her left side and Roman was across from her. There were a handful of other men who were natural leaders of the crew, ones who weren't officially recognized but highly respected and listened to by the rest. They were briefly introduced to her and she tried hard to keep track of each.

It was the most rambunctious dinner she had ever been exposed to.

She had never in her life heard more cursing in one conversation from almost every person at the table, including both Sahar and Roman. They transformed into different people when they were around the crew. Alida remembered what Lao had said about these people becoming his family. She understood it now. They were one, big, crazy family. Sometimes they spoke so fast she couldn't catch it all, besides swears and constant talk about women. Sahar was the only person managing to keep it at bay by yelling at them when things got too vulgar. Alida didn't say a word, just ate the food and blushed furiously at some of the comments they made. They barely seemed to notice her. Sahar shot her apologetic looks occasionally but Alida could tell she found this almost as amusing as everyone else.

They didn't ignore her for long. After the meal had been cleared away, between their third and fourth round, one of the men pointed at her.

"Now, honey, tell me. Is there a man who calls you his own?"

Alida took a long gulp of her beer before responding. The drinks they had on the boat were phenomenal and very very strong. "No. And even if there was, he would never call me his own." Alida thrust her mug into the air and clinked it against Sahar's. "No one will ever own me!" she yelled. It was at that moment she realized that she was perhaps dangerously drunk. It was getting harder to remember her cover name and her cover story. Nora? Nota?

The men laughed at her, but good-naturedly. "Are you sure you're Orinthian?"

Alida snorted. "Believe me. I know I'm Orinthian."

The same man who asked her leaned forward and shot her an almost toothless grin. "Are you looking for a man?"

She grinned at him. He was probably five or six years older than her but at this point she couldn't care less. "No. I'm not."

All of the men began shouting and the guy slumped down onto the table, chugging the rest of his beer. Sahar filled her mug again.

After they went for a sixth round, Alida realized she had to get out of there or she would say something ridiculously stupid. She nodded at Sahar and slipped out of the room, unnoticed by the rest of the crew.

She walked back up to the main deck, her vision hazy, her heart light. She stopped abruptly when she saw the sky.

The stars looked like they had erupted into the night. They were everywhere, clusters of them in different shapes, of all different sizes. It was like nothing she had ever seen before. In Abdul, few stars ever dotted the sky. The light from the city always blocked out any other light. This was incredible. She laid down on the deck and couldn't remove her eyes from it.

She was good at being a princess. She had been trained to be good at it. She didn't have any other choice, being the only daughter of Tieran and Natasha.

But laying on the deck, looking at the stars above, she felt as if she had finally found where she belonged.

Chapter 11

Sawny was exhausted. They had flown out of the Forest Dembe and didn't stop at an inn like Adriel had told her they would. He started towards a village but Sawny had shaken her head. She wanted, needed, to get as far away as she possibly could from that place. It had been two days since then but the image of her cottage, Matahali, and the memory of her parents were as fresh in her mind as if it had been seconds ago. They kept riding, trading places leading the horse, until finally, they stopped. Adriel had offered to take the first shift of watch and Sawny didn't argue with him. She fell onto the ground and went to sleep immediately, not caring what could be there. She had never been the most outdoorsy girl in the world. She hated bugs and spiders especially. But her exhaustion trumped her fear.

She woke up and it was in the early evening. Adriel had made a fire, organized their stuff, tied his horse to the tree, and was cooking something that smelled amazing. Sawny noticed that she had been moved onto his bed roll sometime during the night, which was surprisingly comfortable.

"Do you want to sleep?" Sawny asked him.

He was holding some sort of meat over the fire as his mouth twitched. "I figured that the person who endured the most emotional trauma in the last few days deserved to sleep more. And on something other than the ground. You won that one."

Despite herself, Sawny laughed. "You didn't have to do that," she said. Adriel responded, "Yes, I did. I was happy too."

Besides vague mentions, they hadn't talked about what she had seen in the Forest Dembe. They had barely talked at all. The experience had drained them, and they decided that for a day, before crossing into Orinth, they would rest and recharge at the edge of a small, wooded area. They spent most of the day sleeping and as the sun set, they sat on the ground, chewing on some nuts Sawny had in her bag.

"How good at shooting are you?" Adriel asked, glancing over at her. They were both leaning up against trees, a few feet apart.

She shrugged. "The Darklands shooting technique is considered the most proficient in the world. My father trained me since I was little up until I was fifteen. Once I moved to Illias, I tried to practice once or twice a week. I'd say I'm still pretty good."

Adriel stood and strode over to their bags. He dug through his before retrieving an apple. It was rotten and turning brown, but he held it up to her. Sawny wrinkled her eyes. He walked towards the clearing at the edge of where they were camped, about sixty feet from her, and said, "Hit this when I throw it up."

Sawny snorted. "What are you talking about?"

Adriel shrugged. "I'm from the Wilds. The tribes of the Darklands are sometimes considered our rivals. I believe the Wilds have the best shooting technique, not the Darklands like you say. So, show me how good you are, and I can judge for myself."

Sawny raised an eyebrow. "You do know I'm an Auntican, right? This won't be very accurate."

"You seem a little scared."

"I'm not scared!" Sawny protested. "I just don't want you to judge the entirety of the Darklands shooting skill on my own."

"That's something a scared person would say."

She glared at him as she stood up and seized her bow from the pile of their stuff. It was the same bow she had had since she was thirteen years old, made of wood that was carved with markings. Her father had brought back the bow as a present from a diplomatic mission in the Darklands. She fell in love with it. After he died, she considered selling the thing but decided against it. Although, she now knew that it was almost worth as much as her own horse, because of its intricate craftmanship. She grabbed her quiver and strapped it to her back. The feeling was so familiar that she almost felt like she could close her eyes and when she opened them, be back at the cottage, her father standing beside her as she shot arrows at a target far away, him critiquing every shot.

Sawny locked an arrow into the bow and stood ready. "You're going to regret this," she shouted towards him.

He held up the apple and, for the first time ever since Sawny had met him, smiled. She had a hard time not smiling back because something about it that was so authentic. His face lit up and it was genuine and gods, did he look attractive when he smiled.

"I know I will. There isn't a question in my mind."

She hoped he couldn't see from sixty feet away that a slight pink had risen to her cheeks. Sawny was suddenly very aware of him, this man from the Wilds who had spent probably every day of his life working out. That had to be the only explanation. She wondered for the first time whether he had someone back home in the Wilds. Was there some girl as beautiful as he was expecting Adriel to return to her? She tried to push down the tiny bit of jealousy that arose when she thought about that. She shoved those thoughts away.

"Are you holding it up or-" she didn't get to finish because at that moment he threw the apple high into the air.

Everything turned into slow motion as she tracked it through the air. Her eyes locked onto the piece of fruit as it hit its peak height and began to fall. She didn't bat an eye as she released the arrow. Time resumed and the arrow struck the apple through the center before it fell to the ground, right next to Adriel's feet.

He whistled and picked up the apple, observing the arrow before, fast as the streaming rain, chucked the apple as hard as he could directly at her.

Her instincts kicked in and she had pulled another arrow, shot the incoming one, and locked another one into place within a matter of moments.

Adriel clapped his hands and leaned his arm against a tree. "I mean, it's kind of impressive. I could do better using my own technique but-"

He was interrupted as Sawny drew one more arrow and let it fly, going directly towards the tree he was leaning against. It buried into the bark, only inches above his arm.

"Oops," Sawny said, shooting him an innocent look.

He stared at her. "You could've killed me."

Sawny shook her head. "I don't miss."

"You could've."

"No."

"What is with you and always trying to almost kill me all the time? First in your apartment and now here?"

"Keeping you on your toes."

He smiled at her and again, she tried to ignore her rising heart rate. Adriel yanked the arrow out of the tree. "Fine, Sawny Lois. Very impressive." He started back towards her. "If we get attacked by anyone, we're in better hands with you than with me."

Sawny laughed. "Oh yes, says the warrior from the Wilds who trains every single day."

"I can shoot a bow but not like that. We trained more in hand-to-hand combat. Swords and spears. Axes. I spent a year learning how to shoot but I'm not even close to that."

"I would offer to teach you but I'm sure a Wildsman would never consent to learning the techniques of the Darklands."

Adriel snorted. "You are correct."

"Your loss."

"Maybe."

Sawny took the quiver off her back and returned it as well as the bow to their pile. "My father taught me combat with the sword. I learned a lot about throwing knives. But the bow was the main one. I'm glad it was."

"How are you with hand-to-hand?" Adriel asked, in a tone she couldn't identify.

She looked at him. "What do you mean?"

"Hand-to-hand. No weapons. Just fighting."

"A little bit."

"Do you want to learn?" He was looking at her, his eyes light.

Sawny shook her head. "No. I already just proved what a badass I am. I'm not going to embarrass myself in front of you."

"Oh, why do you care though? I'm just a warrior from the Wilds. You Aunticans don't care," he said in a mocking tone.

She rolled her eyes. "Go back to being the quiet and brooding man from the Wilds and then I won't care. This new Adriel though, I won't be embarrassing for."

"Attack me," he said.

"No."

"Do it."

"No."

Adriel threw his hands up in the air, exasperated. "Sawny, we're going into Orinth, your enemy country. If we get attacked, and it's close contact, you'll have to know."

Sawny shook her head. "No man is going to get close to me. I have my bow. And if they do, I have my sword and knives. And a scary man from the Wilds."

"Fine. But the offer still stands, Ms. Lois. Anytime you want to fight."

Sawny smiled at him. "What is with you lately?"

"What do you mean?"

"Ever since we've left the Forest Dembe, you've been in good spirits, compared to the stone-face man who broke into my apartment."

Adriel sat down against the tree once again. "The Forest Dembe was terrible, Sawny. As soon as we got in there, there was something about it so dark. It felt like all the good was being sucked out of me replaced by such hopelessness. I thought I was never going to get out of there. And then you collapsed off the horse and you were out for hours. I thought you were going to die, and I thought it was my fault. It is my fault that you had to be in the forest to begin with. I've already seen so many people die, in the Wilds. I wasn't ready to watch another. I know we've only known each other for a week or so but I couldn't let you die. Then you woke up, and although it was painful, you were alright. And we got out of there and now we're here. We're getting closer to Tenir, to the answers that I'm looking for, for the answers you're looking for. So, I guess I'm in good spirits because the alternative is you being dead and me being alone."

Sawny didn't respond for a while as she sat back down. It was still quite light out and the small fire they had built was providing some warmth. She turned to him and their eyes met, "The witch, Matahali," Sawny took a deep breath. "she made me tell her about how my parents were killed, when I was fifteen. It gave her enough emotion or whatever to keep her forest healthy." She glanced down at the tattoo on her wrist. "I don't know what it means. I didn't know any sort of magic was real. She said some things to me that I-I don't understand. But I'm here now. That's got to count for something."

"You said Matahali showed you where in Tenir to find your answers. Do you think you'll find out the reason behind your parents' death?" Adriel asked.

"I'm not sure. She told me it was the answers I sought out that I would find behind the door." Sawny closed her eyes. She could see exactly what the door looked like but still. Tenir was a larger city of Orinth. How she would be able to find one, specific door there was beyond her. But she would try. This was the first time she ever had a true lead. She wasn't sure on what, but it was a lead.

"We'll find it," Adriel said.

Sawny opened one eye. He was leaning forward stoking the fire. "It might take time away from me investigating your case," she told him.

"I don't care. This is just as important," was all he said in response. The sound of the gentle breeze and crickets replaced their voices.

Sawny felt something that she had not felt in a long time within herself. Caring. She cared about Adriel. She wasn't exactly sure how she cared for him but for the first time since her parents died, she had something to lose.

She chose her next words carefully. "What will you do if we find Zelos' killer? Will you really kill him?"

His face darkened. "I have to. I made an oath to my tribe."

"And then after that?"

"I guess I go back. I haven't been back in so many years. I'm not even sure if they're still there. But yes, I go back. I rejoin my people, oath fulfilled." He sighed. "I miss it. The Wilds."

"Do you have any other family in the tribe?" Sawny asked.

"I have a little sister. But that's it. My parents are gone. My father died in the war. My mother grew sick after we had to move further north and died. My sister is named Masha." He shook his head. "She is an absolute madwoman."

Sawny laughed. "And why is that?"

"She has a temper. And she is so senselessly stubborn about even the smallest of things. I once told her she needed to eat healthier and then she didn't touch a vegetable for three weeks just to prove a point. We'll be hunting and I'll say 'Masha, we need to run faster' and then she'll walk slower until I have to beg her. But I love her. I miss her. She's probably seventeen by now. I'm guessing she's already married."

Sawny whistled. "That seems young."

He shrugged. "Maybe for an Auntican. For us in the Wilds, that's right around the age where you get married. Masha has been betrothed since she was thirteen or fourteen to the same boy."

"Is it an arranged marriage sort of thing?"

Adriel shook his head. "No, not at all. They chose each other. You choose someone, and either gender can choose. If that person accepts, you go in front of the tribal council. If they approve, once you turn sixteen, you can marry that person. It's a much different idea from those in Auntica and Orinth. Marriage here is-" he struggled to find the words, "-civil. You're married in the eyes of the law. Of course, there's a ceremony and a celebration. But in the Wilds, it's more than that. You're bound to that person, for life. They become your world. It's not just the law that recognizes it. It's the world. The continent. The gods. Everything. They all know that you're with this person until the end of time."

"That is so lovely," Sawny said softly.

Adriel looked at her. "I like that word. Lovely. We don't have a word for that in the Wilds. Lovely is a lovely word, Sawny Lois."

She beamed at him. "It is, isn't it? Lovely."

"I hope one day you meet Masha. You two would get along, I think."

"And what about you? You're what? Twenty-one, twenty-two? You must be married now according to the Wilds." She despised the fact she was holding her breath waiting for him to answer.

"No. Since Zelos died, things have been different for me. My life's goal has been to find the killer and find out what happened to him. There's been no time for courting someone, asking permission, getting married, all of that."

"You're a free man then?" Sawny chuckled.

Adriel shot her a strange look. "Free man?"

"When people here don't have a-well a woman I suppose, they call themselves free men. And then when they do get married, their freedom is gone."

He scoffed at this. "That seems a bit self-important, doesn't it? You're not free if you love someone?"

"I'm starting to learn just how different the Wilds really are from Auntica. People here see any sort of relationship as a burden. There, you see it as something wonderful."

"What about you, Sawny? Do you have someone? Are you a free man, or I suppose, free woman?" Adriel asked, a hint of laughter in his voice.

She smiled but shook her head. "No. I'm working so much. It's cliché, but I have no time for anyone right now. I've also had no desire to tie myself down to anyone."

"I'm not so sure there is a man from Auntica would deserve you anyways," he said in a low tone.

She raised an eyebrow at him. "Oh?"

Adriel shrugged. "It would hurt their egos if you shot better than they could."

Sawny snorted. "I suppose it would. It hurt yours, didn't it?"

His eyes met hers. "I'm not from Auntica, am I?" The tone in his voice changed and Sawny felt heat rising to her cheeks again. She ripped her gaze from his and settled it onto a nearby rock.

"Well, I guess you'll have to-" she didn't get to finish when they suddenly heard a loud yell come from the open field.

They both sprang to their feet and were armed within seconds. Adriel with his sword and Sawny with her bow. Adriel stomped out the few flames that were remaining. Then, he glanced at her.

"Hide," Adriel ordered, all traces of fun gone, replaced by the warrior she had met weeks ago.

"No," Sawny replied back. "You just saw I can defend myself."

"It's not that, Sawny," he said back, something like desperation entering his voice. "I don't know who is coming but if they see it's only me, they may pass me by. If they see you.." his voice trailed off as the people came into view.

It was a group of soldiers, but they did not wear the crimson of Auntica. They wore navy blue uniforms and Sawny realized they had to be Orinthian. There were about six or seven of them, with no horses, talking and laughing loudly, walking right towards where their camp was. The way they were moving was sluggish and all over the place. They had to be drunk, Sawny thought as she watched one man stumble and burst into high-pitched laughter. They were deserters. She didn't know they were that close to the Orinthian border, but this confirmed it.

Her hand rested on her bow and she slowly drew an arrow from the quiver. Drunk Orinthians, soldiers nonetheless. Nothing good could come from this, especially considering her companion was from the Wilds. Orinthians were almost as prejudiced as Aunticans were towards Adriel's people. She glanced at the man, who seemed relaxed and calmed, as if his instincts had kicked in. But she saw the way his jaw was tightened. Even Adriel was uneasy when they could possibly be outnumbered three to one.

They were within about a hundred feet from the camp when one soldier spotted them and pointed. The men stopped to look. Sawny exhaled. Wonderful. Simply wonderful. The men started laughing and continued towards them.

"Adriel, get out of here," Sawny muttered.

"No."

"Orinthians hate people from the Wilds. They will hurt you."

"Oh, and they're keen on Aunticans at the moment?" he said ironically. "I'm not leaving."

She cursed under her breath.

He didn't reply as one of the men shouted something at them. She couldn't hear it through his slurred tone.

She replied in Orinthian. "It would be suitable for everyone, gentlemen, if you moved along." She was surprised at the confidence in her voice as she spoke. Adriel stiffened and the soldiers stopped where they were, about twenty feet away.

"Auntican eh?" the man in the front said. "Your accent gives you away, darling." He looked her up and down, slowly dragging his eyes over every part of her.

"Don't make me repeat myself," she said, tightening the grip on her bow.

The men started laughing, speaking to each other in Orinthian. "Who is this with you, sweetheart?" the main one spoke again, gesturing to Adriel. "Is he your husband? You can do better, sweetheart. Any of us could do better than that." His eyes fell upon Adriel for the first time, "Wait a minute. No. It can't be. Someone from the Wilds?"

The whole group exploded into more laughter, shouting again. Among Orinthians and Aunticans, warriors were typically feared, especially those from the Wilds. Yes, they hated the people, but they still realized that the warriors from the Wilds were extremely dangerous and deadly. She had to assume because they were drunk that their judgment was completely gone.

"Get out of here-" Sawny said calmly, and the men stopped laughing, "-or I swear to your Orinthian heathen gods that I will put an arrow in each of your hearts before you can touch me."

The leader held his hands up in surrender. "Honey, we're not trying to hurt you. We're trying to help you. Clearly, an Auntican woman would not be with a piece of crap from the Wilds. Blink twice if you're being held hostage."

Adriel made a sound in his throat and Sawny cursed in her mind. She hoped that he didn't understand Orinthian and the insults these men would fling at them. She said nothing.

The man took a step forward and at once, Sawny had an arrow locked into place, the tip pointing at his heart.

He froze and then all at once, they burst into another round of guffaws and yells.

"Women in Orinth, they know how to shoot," the leader began. He had to be in his thirties, at least. He was unshaven, dirt all over his face and his rumpled uniform. His hair was messy and unkempt, and she could almost smell the alcohol from where she was standing. "Women in Orinth know how to do almost anything, you know? But we've always been told that women in Auntica? Different story. They know how to cook, clean, and pleasure men. Care to demonstrate?"

Everything happened at once. The man lunged at her, jumping from his feet, and attempting to tackle her to the ground. He never made contact, as an arrow found itself in his chest and his body fell to the ground. He screamed in pain as two more found its mark, in his neck. The other soldiers fell silent as the leader gave one last pained scream before slumping onto the ground.

No noises could be heard besides Sawny's breathing and the wind through the trees. The men stared at her.

"You killed him?" another choked out, his accent thicker than that of his leader. "You killed him!" he screamed again.

There was already an arrow drawn back and pointed at him. "I did. I hate to be the one to tell you this, but Auntican women know how to do more than just pleasure Orinthians. We can kill them too."

The man gave a strangled cry and unsheathed his sword, charging this time at Adriel. Within seconds, he disarmed the Orinthian and had his blade pressed up against his throat.

Sawny switched to Auntican. "If any of them move, kill him." Adriel nodded and she turned back to the remaining soldiers, who had looks of numb shock on their faces.

"Now, you have ten seconds to get out of here and back to the shithole of a country that you came from. Or else I will kill every single one of you. Ten-" The men turned around and began to run while the one man whimpered against Adriel's sword. Adriel watched her with an expression she couldn't read. Sawny returned her bow to her back and the arrow to the quiver.

She knelt down in front of the man, who refused to meet her gaze. "Look at me," she ordered.

He whimpered softly and still, stared at the ground.

"LOOK AT ME," she said louder, and the man's eyes met hers, nothing but fear in them. He too had to be in his thirties, the same dirty appearance as his leader, who now laid slain on the ground feet from them.

"What are you doing here?" she asked calmly.

"I-we-I we deserted some of the Orinthian forces more than two weeks ago stationed on the border," he cried softly, his whole body beginning to shake.

"Why are you coming into Auntica, if you're Orinthian?"

"We're trying to escape from being punished by our superiors."

Something in the way he said it, as if he was unsure of the answer, alerted Sawny to the fact that he was lying.

"Lies," she said softly.

"No! I swear it's true, I swear it!" he moaned.

Adriel pressed the sword tighter into his throat. "Tell her the truth," he said.

The man wept. "I'm not supposed to tell," he sobbed, tears streaming down his face and snot clogging his nose as he continued to sniffle.

Sawny shrugged. "I'll kill you if you don't tell, it's just that simple. I suppose it's up to you to decide who exactly it is you fear more. These mysterious people or I, whose companion has a sword pressed to your throat."

The man sniveled. "If I tell you, you'll let me go?"

Sawny nodded. "I am a woman of my word."

"We did desert the army. That much is true. But we were met by a man. He was Auntican like yourself. He said he worked for the king. Your king, that is, Grafph. The man has been sent out to recruit anyone he can find to look for a certain person."

"Who is this person my king is looking for?" Sawny asked.

"If your friend releases the sword from my throat, I'll pull the paper out of my pocket with her name and her picture. Please," the man said. He had stopped crying and had gained a calmer tone.

Sawny locked an arrow into place and drew it back, pointing it at the man's head. She nodded at Adriel, who released the sword from the Orinthian and took three steps back. The man, with shaking hands, reached into the pocket of his navy coat and drew a wrinkled-up paper. He held it out to Sawny who shook her head and gestured to Adriel. "Give it to him," she said.

Adriel took the paper from the man's hands after he put his sword away. He unwrinkled it and observed. He looked up at Sawny. "Alida Goulding," he said softly.

Sawny was taken aback. "The Orinthian princess?" She let her bow drop, but the man didn't move under the threat of Adriel's sword.

Adriel nodded. "That's what it says. I don't know if this is what she looks like but-" He turned the paper around and showed her. Sure enough, in scribbled writing was the name 'Alida Goulding'. Above it was a sketch of the princess, that was detailed enough to give an exact picture of what she looked like. Round eyes and long hair, she had never seen the princess before but guessed, from the picture, she had to be around the same age as Sawny herself.

"What does the king want with Alida Goulding?"

The Orinthian spoke, "All I know is that the man had hundreds of these pamphlets in a bag. He stopped us and told us that we were to go to the Darklands to look for her, but on the way pass out as many of them as we can. The king is offering an immense ransom for her capture, enough gold that a man could buy a palace."

Sawny and Adriel exchanged a look. This made no sense. In the scope of the war, Alida meant nothing compared to the generals and masterminds of the Orinthian armies, not to mention King Tieran himself. But an enormous reward? There had to be something else at play.

"So, this man paid you to take the pamphlets and pass them out as well as search for Princess Alida Goulding?" Sawny confirmed.

The Orinthian nodded.

"So, you're a traitor to your country?"

The man sputtered, "You're Auntican! Why do you care?"

Sawny wasn't sure exactly. She trusted her king. But something about going through these lengths to get the young princess of their enemy country made her feel sickened. "I don't. It disgusts me to see the lack of loyalty you have to your country, though. And what would you do if you found Alida Goulding?"

"Give her to your king," The man admitted. "And claim the reward."

Sawny shook her head. "If you were an Auntican, I wouldn't hesitate to kill you for that kind of treachery." She didn't have to look to know the man had peed himself out of fear. He was genuinely afraid she might kill him. Sawny didn't even know herself what she would do.

"Sawny," Adriel said, a warning in his voice.

"I would be so ashamed to see such unfaithfulness within my fellow countrymen. I would consider it my duty to the king to kill them and make sure they don't do any more harm." The Orinthian started to quake again as he watched Sawny. She had drawn the arrow back again, the tip of it pointed directly at his heart.

"Sawny, let him go," Adriel said quietly.

Out of nowhere, the anger rose within her. She was angry at this man, for deserting the people who he had pledged his loyalty to. For deciding to track down an eighteen-year-old girl, who for some reason, had a part to play in all of this. But the fact of the matter was she was eighteen. Barely an adult. And this man was going to hand her over to his enemy king. Not to mention the fact that if Sawny would have been defenseless, these men would have assaulted her, without a question. And now, she held his life in her hands.

Just like the men who had galloped to her house all those years ago. They had given themselves the right to hold her parents' lives in their hands. And they had made the decision to take the life. If they would have seen her, they would have killed her too. Now, she had the same power. She took a deep breath. There was something hideously exhilarating about the feeling. This man was a bad man. She could tell from the last few minutes in his presence. But how many other terrible things had he done in his lifetime? What sins had he committed?

She had become the judge, jury, and executioner.

Her hands were trembling as she held her bow, staring at him. His eyes were dark but not like Matahali's black eyes. There was no fear in the witch's eyes days ago, but the Orinthian's held intense despair. He was truly afraid for his life. He didn't know what she was going to do. She could kill him right now. Did he have a family? She wondered that as she continued to watch him. Was there a wife somewhere, praying that her husband would come back safely? Did he have children who wondered where their father was? And instead of fighting for that family, he was selling out an eighteen-year-old.

She was paralyzed with these thoughts and didn't see Adriel move to stand behind her. He gently set his hand upon her own and helped her to lower the arrow and the bow. She shuddered and dropped it completely and watched as the Orinthian sprinted the other direction as fast as he could go. She fell to her knees and put her face in between them.

She didn't see but felt as Adriel knelt before her and grasped her hands in his own.

"I wanted to kill him," she whispered.

"I know," he replied softly.

"I would have."

"But you didn't."

"Only because you were here. If you hadn't stopped me, Adriel, I would have buried the arrow into his heart or throat. I would have ended his life. I wanted to do it," Sawny said quietly. There were no tears. "I wouldn't have even regretted it."

He said nothing in return but stood up and reached a hand down to her. She took it and he pulled her to her feet. Sawny took deep breaths as her heart felt like it was about to beat out of her chest. The adrenaline she felt from pointing the arrow at the man was sickening. She shouldn't feel that after nearly killing him. Was there something seriously wrong with her?

"Let's go, Sawny," Adriel said. He didn't let go of her hands but stared down at her. "Let's leave this place."

"Why aren't you trying to convince me otherwise?" Sawny asked, looking into his icy blue eyes. She was back to being unable to read the expression on his face. The stony mask had returned.

"I've killed before, Sawny. Many, many people. I've killed to save my country, to save my people, to save my family. Some say after you kill you can't be forgiven by the gods. But I would do it all again. And if he would have tried to hurt you, I would have killed him. I'm not going to judge you for almost killing the Orinthian. Or-" He glanced to the corpse of the leader of the group of soldiers, who had three arrows sticking out of him, "-killing him. You did what you had to do."

Sawny shook her head. "It's not the first time I've killed, Adriel," she spoke softly.

Gently, he pressed a kiss to her forehead, so delicately she wasn't even sure if his lips touched her skin. "Let's go."

Without speaking, they packed the gear onto the horse. Sawny tried not to watch as Adriel dragged the body of the other Orinthian into the forest and covered it with leaves and sticks. But she couldn't take her eyes off it. Adriel climbed up onto the horse and helped her get behind him and they were back onto the road, under the cover of night.

The guilt caught up with her within minutes. It wasn't the shame of ending a life, it was the shame at her lack of emotions to ending that life. She had killed a man. Yes, he had been attacking her, but still. She had ended his life and she felt nothing. Just emptiness, where her conscience should have been. She had killed before. Once. While traveling for a case, she had been attacked by an unknown assailant. She was unsure whether they wanted her or anyone. It was a man whose face she had never seen. He had attacked her from behind as she walked back to an inn she had been staying at. She had grabbed her knife, after minutes of struggling, and plunged it through his heart. Panicked, she left the city without even finishing her work there. She did not feel the slightest semblance of guilt afterwards, just fear. She had almost lost her life, hands attempting to choke the life out of her. She wasn't sure how she had survived. By luck or by the blessings of the gods, she had walked away.

Her father had told her stories of his times in the Darklands. He, like Adriel, was a warrior who had to kill many times. Sawny remembered asking him how he managed to feel normal afterwards. She remembered what he said to her as if it were yesterday.

"You never feel normal after killing someone, Sawny. Whether it was justified, self-defense, protecting people, what have you. But you can't let yourself fall to darkness. I always have to tell myself: find your humanity."

Find your humanity.

She felt like she was falling into a pit of darkness but then, without thinking, she wrapped her arms around Adriel's waist and sighed into him. She felt him tighten in surprise before relaxing into her.

Adriel was her humanity right now. And she would not be letting go for a while.

Chapter 12

The Outskirts of Orinth

The morning of a battle was always too tense for Rider to handle. He had been an advisor to the king for twelve years and, of course, had encountered brief skirmishes here and there. The moment his eyes opened on the day he knew he would be fighting, he would throw up. Out of any other man, Rider was the most equipped to handle anything their enemies could throw at him. But there was something about the feeling in his gut, the fact that today might be his last, that made him sick.

Rider had been put in the tent that sheltered the general. He was young, as Tieran had said, only twenty-five. They had hit it off as soon as he had galloped into their camp, days ago. His name was Gael, originally from their northernmost city of Tilda, but moved to Abdul and grew up there. He went to the capital's most prestigious military school. From there, he rose through the ranks faster than anyone had before, due to his natural leadership skills combined with his talent for fighting. He also was a military genius when it came to strategy and approach to the upcoming battles.

Intel from Gael's spies had told him that an Auntican army was moving towards their position and looking to come into Orinth, on their way to sack Tenir. Rider had to admit that the plan was sound. Aunticans probably assumed that all Orinthian forces would be sent to protect Abdul, the capital. Tenir was almost as valuable. It was the main trading center between Orinth and the rest of the world. Every import had to go through there and almost half of their income was from the coastal city. It was smart but what they didn't anticipate was the wide dispersing of Orinthian forces. The 3rd army was spread along the entire border, their spies reporting on movement anywhere. The Aunticans would be destroyed, or at least severely battered, before they ever reached Tenir. And even then, Tenir had its own militia who could easily protect its people.

Besides discussing and debating the fight that was about to happen, Rider had mostly talked to the general about trivial things.

Rider laid under a thin blanket and took slow deep breaths. He could already feel the vomit rising in his throat and he fought to keep it down. He tried to think of something, anything else. Alida. Tieran. Orinth. The Shadow. Grafph. True King. Last Heir. Nothing stuck. The sun had not yet come up, but it was getting lighter out. In mere minutes, the horn would ring throughout their camp, awakening the soldiers. It was Gael's goal to be marching at dawn's light. The Auntican army, they assumed, knew that they were near, but they had no idea just how close they were. He hoped this would add in a certain element of surprise. They had chosen a flat, grassy plain to attack them at, similar to the ones they trained on as soldiers. It would feel familiar to the men and hopefully improve their fighting.

According to the intel they had received from spies about the opposing army, they were evenly matched, almost man to man. From the outside, it was impossible to say who had the advantage.

But what both sides didn't know, is that Orinthians had the upper hand. They had a man who possessed demonic powers on their side.

He closed his eyes and felt it within him. There it was. The endless depth of power somewhere in his soul, where he couldn't feel the bottom, couldn't feel the limit. It would be ridiculously easy to throw himself into it, let his power control him and devour him, give in to the shadow. But he wouldn't. Today, he would use it for the sake of his kingdom. He would have to be cautious, though. He remembered how it used to feel when he was a teenager and pushed the limits. It grew harder and harder to stop using it. He would grow so exhausted, so drained that he often felt he might die from it. It was the one restraint the shadow had; too much use had drastic effects.

He wouldn't allow that to happen today, though. He would be careful. Gently, he dipped into the shadow.

It ran through his body and responded. It was ready. It was always ready. Waiting to be used, waiting to feed on someone else, waiting to feed on Rider himself. Simultaneously, Rider was in awe of the power as well as extremely terrified. He didn't want to leave this tent and go face the battle, using those powers.

He wasn't aware that he had fallen back asleep until he was awoken by the sharp and loud sounds of the horn. It rang through the air and hit his ear hard. Rider groaned and tucked his head further into his pillow. It barely dulled the sound. He heard Gael let out a loud yawn and his bed creaked as he stood up. He took several deep breaths and Rider decided he should probably wake up to be there for the young man.

He sat up and stretched out his back. Gael was still in his nightclothes, a white shirt and shorts, and was staring out the flap of their tent at his soldiers, who were all beginning to rouse. He was sweating, Rider noticed, and wringing his hands.

Gently, Rider tapped into his power and just barely influenced the man's emotions. He gently eased the fear, the anticipation, and the nervousness away and replaced it with something of confidence. He watched as Gael stood up straighter and turned to Rider.

"Good morning," he said, his face bright. He walked towards his cot and grabbed his uniform out of his rucksack.

"Good morning," Rider said, standing up and letting go of his emotions. The small shift would last him at least until the battle started, where the adrenaline would kick in and the fear would disappear.

"Sleep okay?" Gael asked.

"Not a wink," Rider chuckled.

Gael nodded. "Me neither, Rider. I've been thinking all night about whether this is the right move. Strategically speaking. I know we've gone over it time and time again but what if we're walking into a trap?"

"We're not, Gael. Like you said, we've been over it again and again. You've trained these men well. The captains and the sergeants know what they're doing. These men are loyal soldiers, and they won't let you down."

Gael frowned. "What about those who deserted days ago?"

Rider replied, "There's always some exceptions. There's never going to be a perfect army. But you yourself know that the majority of your men are good."

Gael bit his lip and without responding, turned around to get ready. Rider didn't take it personally. He would never understand the pressure that the young man was currently facing. To have the life of every man in your hands, dependent on your strategies and decision-making? He didn't think he could ever take something like that.

He had to be conspicuous today. Gael had told him that he was to stay back in the general's tent during the battle, but Rider had other plans. He had brought a uniform and planned to don it as soon as the general's back was turn. He would weave his way into the fight and then he would begin. He couldn't use waves of mass destruction; the power would consume him. But he could take out major threats. He could give the men more energy, more gusto. Maybe he wasn't the weapon of mass destruction, but he would shift the balance in their favor.

Rider began to get ready. He slipped into the uniform that the captains normally wore and smoothed down his hair. It was sticking straight up from sleeping on a burlap pillowcase. Alida would have teased him relentlessly for it. He exhaled when he thought of his young friend. Alida. Where was she? How was she doing? He reached into his pocket and pulled out the picture of her, grasping it by the fingertips. Closing his eyes, Rider tapped into the shadow and used it to locate her.

When he used this power, he never received a clear picture of her or her location. Instead, it was a whisper inside of his head. The Dela.

Sighing in relief, Rider returned the picture to his pocket. He had been checking on her once every few days. She was still safe. He had to keep telling himself that. If she wasn't, she would be in Auntica or the Wilds, not on the Dela.

Whenever he thought of her, the panic rose in him like bile. He had to remind himself. Alida was strong. She was the strongest person he had ever met. She was fearless and hopefully, she would reach Nagaye soon. But he couldn't focus on his own fears; today was about winning the battle.

Within minutes, Gael and Rider were both dressed to go. A lower-level soldier entered the tent and saluted to the general, who returned it.

"Sir, we will be ready to move out within the hour," he said, stone-faced.

Gael nodded. "Good. Get some men to tear down this tent and pack it up. Send some men ahead to set up our strategy tent and my tent but ensure they stay hidden. Have our morning spies returned yet?"

"Yes sir. They arrived back only minutes ago and reported to Captain Daniels. He was waiting for you to finish preparing."

"Well, I'm prepared. I'll go find him," Gael said. He turned back to Rider. "I'll meet you by our horses in twenty minutes."

Rider nodded and started packing his gear into his bag. He took several deep breaths once again, trying to slow his heart rate. He gently touched his power once again and let it soothe him. Gradually, his chest stopped thudding.

It was strange, to even be just barely using the shadow. He had grown so used to blocking that part of him out with all that he was. Over the years, he had built a mental barrier between the human side of him and the part that came from beyond the wall. He never used his powers. Ever. He sometimes denied he even had them, to himself. He pretended to be normal always.

It was somewhat of a relief to be able to let the barrier fall. It was terrifying, but in a way, he felt complete again. He felt like he did back when he was a kid in the streets of Tenir, just living his life and doing what he had to do. When he was angry back then, he used the shadow. Scared, shadow. Sad, the shadow. Anything he could possibly think of, he could use the shadow. Even he didn't know just how much it was capable of. So far, he had figured out that he could kill people. Easily. He could control their minds, make them see what he wanted them to, gently persuade their emotions. He couldn't read minds; he knew because he had tried thousands of times to no avail. He could track people down using an item that belonged to them, by tracing their mental scent, as he had just done with Alida. Those he knew for sure. Others, he had a suspicion. He believed that he could plant ideas in people's heads if he wanted to. He had tried it once or twice and it had somehow worked, but he didn't want to try it again. Most of this he discovered when he was a teenager, testing the limits of this strength, this curse.

Of course, it was safer now. He knew the threat of using too much of the shadow. His years in Tenir had showed him that. He shuddered at the thought of it. There was a memory he had blocked off since the day it happened. If he let himself think about that day, it would shatter him.

There was no one he had told about that. Not even Alida. He wasn't sure he was physically capable of talking about it. That day. The girl. The death. Rider shook his head, shook the memories away, and walked out of the tent.

There was a large number of men in their camp. At the moment, every man was disassembling their tent and packing gear. Some had horses, others didn't. Gael had explained yesterday that the frontline was made up of soldiers armed with long pole arms. Then, their massive infantry and flanks upon flanks of deadly archers. The cavalry would come after the first charge, the archers paying special mind to cover them as they attacked. It was a technique, Gael explained, used for hundreds of years in the Orinthian military. Given their number of conquests, Rider assumed it was successful.

Rider strode through the camp, mostly unnoticed. The majority of the men did not take kindly to outsiders, especially one who posed a threat to their normal routine. Rider had tried to stay out of their way and make no major changes, spare light suggestions to Gael. Some of the men gave him a curt nod, which he returned.

He reached where the general's and his horses were kept. A young man who couldn't be older than sixteen was still grooming Rider's mount. His eyes widened as Rider approached and he immediately stood up straighter as he went about his work.

"Hello," Rider said, trying for cheerfulness. The lump in his throat made him sound more scared than cheerful.

"Good morning, sir," the boy said. He was extremely tall and lanky, wearing a uniform that was a few sizes too small for him. He wore no weapon and Rider had to guess he was one of the staff for the healers. Tieran would never allow boys as young as him to fight, especially on the front lines.

"How is he looking?" Rider asked, nodding at his horse.

The boy glanced at the large, black stallion and patted his back. "Good as he can be sir. Fed and almost done being groomed. Battle ready, if I do say so myself."

Rider stroked his horse's mane. "I'm glad to hear it."

"Sir, if I may ask, what is the horse's name?"

"Starlight," Rider replied, trying to keep a straight face. The boy snorted and then immediately stopped.

Rider waved him off. "You can laugh. I lost a bet with a friend of mine and that's the name she chose." Alida had been fourteen when Tieran gave the horse as a 32nd birthday gift. Alida challenged him to a game of chess right away for naming rights and, never being able to say no to a high stakes game of chess, Rider agreed. He had been badly beaten and of course, the young girl chose a name like 'Starlight' for his beautiful creature.

The boy continued chuckling. "That's unfortunate."

Rider shrugged. "Maybe. What is your name, soldier?"

The boy straightened up once again. "Bentley, sir. Bentley Williams. Healing division."

Rider extended a hand. "Nice to meet you then, Williams."

Bentley hesitated, not used to superiors even acknowledging him, before returning the handshake. "Thank you, sir. You as well. I'm embarrassed to ask, sir, but I don't know your name or who you even are."

"Rider Grey. I'm the advisor to the king."

The boy's eyes widened with shock. "You're what?"

Rider laughed. "It's not that big of a deal. He rarely listens to me anyways."

Bentley looked confused. "He doesn't?" He quickly forgot what he was talking about and asked, "So, you've met the princess then?"

He nodded and tried to ignore the lull of panic in his chest again. "She's a good friend of mine."

Bentley looked down at his shoes and smiled a little. "I've always fancied her."

Rider laughed. "Oh?"

"I mean, she's gorgeous." His head snapped up. "Just like all princesses are," he stammered. "I'm sorry, sir. I shouldn't say anything like that to offend you if the princess is your friend."

Rider held his hands up. "None taken. I'll tell you what, Williams, if we get through this, I'll introduce you to the princess myself." She would probably kill him for it but hey, maybe it was what this young boy needed to get through the war.

He raised both eyebrows. "Do you mean it?"

"On my honor."

Bentley finished brushing the horse and said, "Gods, if my mother could see me now. Talking to the king's advisor, grooming his horse, and preparing to meet the princess. She'd be proud."

He slapped the young boy on the back. "Indeed. Now, if you don't mind, I'll be taking my horse and getting ready to go."

Bentley took a few steps back and gestured at Starlight. Rider climbed onto his back and looked down at the boy. "Don't get yourself killed, Bentley Williams. Stay strong." With that, he kicked his horse in the side and began to ride back towards the middle of camp.

All the tents were gone, replaced by groups of men beginning to sort into their various sections for the upcoming battle. Rider could tell without even having to use his powers that each one of them were anxious. He didn't blame them. This would be the first major battle since the War in the Wilds. It was very possible that any one of them may die today. Most of the men didn't even know the true reason behind the war. They assumed it was about the gold at the border. Rider wished he could tell each of them that this was about something so much bigger. They weren't protecting Orinth; they were protecting the entire world from the threat of the Shadow Realm.

They were protecting the world from more people like Rider.

He shook that thought out of his head. He wasn't a demon. He was still human. Just a little bit of shadow in him. He almost laughed at that notion. 'Just a little bit of the shadow in him.' Yes, he was a demon but just a little bit.

Within a few minutes, the general joined him on horseback as the final groups assembled. They were in order and ready to march in, yet they were facing the opposite direction of where the battlefield would soon be. Instead, they looked upon the general, who sat straight in his saddle, a grim look upon his face. It was tradition for the general to give a speech before the fight, one to motivate the men and attempt to replace their fear with passion for their country.

"Soldiers of Orinth. I'm going to make this short. We have somewhere to be and there's no use delaying the inevitable loss the Aunticans are about to face," Gael began.

A low chuckle rippled throughout the group as Rider could sense the tension ease just a bit. Strategically, it was a good move by Gael. Start it off with a joke to get people a little more relaxed.

"Today, we're not just fighting for Orinth. We're not just fighting for our king. We aren't just fighting for the crest on our armor. Today, we fight for the men beside us. We fight for our brothers in the uniform. We fight for the friendships we've made while we've been here. For the long nights drinking by the fire, telling stories, laughing, singing, all of it. We fight for the nights we've cried, missing our loved ones and wondering whether we were going to see them again. We fight for the big things: our families, our country, our people. But today, we fight for the small things as well. The taste of beer. The sound of the wind. The sunrise in the morning. All of it. Today, we fight for each other." There was a brief moment of silence followed by a momentous cheer.

Rider felt the chills on his arms and let out the breath he didn't know he had been holding. The delivery, the content, all of it, had been perfect for this moment and the men felt it too. Gone was the fear Rider had felt in the morning, replaced by exactly what Gael had intended it to be replaced by: passion. Yes, he understood now why the general had risen in the ranks as fast as he did. He was a genius.

With a shout of commands, the men started to ride. Gael shot Rider a small smile before joining the group that he had planned to fight with. Rider had advised him to stay in the general's tent and strategize but, like Tieran, he completely rejected the suggestion. Gael had decided to fight with one of the sets of archers. Apparently, the man was one of the most skilled in their army and was too good to not fight. Rider respected his decision and hoped that Gael would respect his to also fight.

Rider watched as the first group of men began to march. Gael was the only one on horseback but would join them on the ground as soon as they reached the Aunticans. Rider trotted his horse away, towards the set of tents where the healers were, over to the side where young Bentley was waiting for him.

Yes, he had asked the young boy to look after his horse when he spoke with him earlier, after he had mounted. Bentley agreed. He would take the horse while Rider slipped into one of the ranks of infantry. The bulk of the army acted as swordsmen so it was where he could blend in the most. He would move throughout the groups so no single person could tie down where he was or figure out that he wasn't just an ordinary soldier. He was killing without any weapons. It wasn't something he wanted other people to know.

Today, he fought for two people. Alida, of course. But for another person from his past, a person so distant he sometimes wondered if he ever really knew her. The person whose memory could destroy him with a thought. He fought for her.

Bentley didn't say anything but nodded at Rider as he took Starlight from him. Rider quickly grabbed his bag from the horse and slipped into his soldier's clothes. The men were still marching, and none had noticed the exchange. Rider gave a mock salute to Bentley before running to join the assembly.

He slipped into the rows rather easily. A man next to him cast a confused look and Rider shrugged. "I overslept," he explained to the man, who just rolled his eyes and looked away.

Rider gave a sigh of relief as he continued to march. He hoped the man wouldn't raise alarm, but then again, why would he? He was just posing as a man whose platoon had left without him. Rider hadn't been out and about the camp enough for people to directly recognize him as the king's advisor, who was currently advising the general. Or at least trying to. Rider frowned when he thought of it. The last few bits of insight he had given to Tieran or Gael had been ignored, with the king leaving to fight with the 2nd army and the general going to join the ranks. So, not just ignored, but both decided to do the exact opposite. Maybe he needed to start thinking of alternative employment options if they lived through this.

They marched for an hour, the sun fully risen and casting long beams of light upon them. It was hot and the air felt so muggy. Already, Rider had sweat through his soldier's uniform and was so tempted to strip. He could tell some of the men surrounding him felt the same. Even with the heat and what already seemed like forever walking, the passion called on by the general was still there. Some of the men were talking, laughing with the people beside them. Others said nothing, but the expressions on their faces said it all. These men were ready. Rider was happy to see it.

Suddenly, the captain of their platoon yelled for a halt. Rider glanced ahead of them and tried to see what was going on but there were so many men before him. He heard a large cry and felt the ground shake beneath him. The frontline was charging. They had arrived in Auntica, just on the border, to the camp of their enemy. The men around him began shouting too so Rider joined in as they all began running forward, towards the Auntican camp.

Finally, in a large clearing, he saw their enemy. Their camp was entirely assembled, the small tents of their soldiers to the larger strategical tents. The surprise factor had worked, as there were only several hundred crimson uniforms who had gotten their bearings and were trying to defend themselves from the onslaught by Orinthian men on horseback. The rest of the men were running around, looking for weapons, trying to avoid the arrows flying and the swords of the cavalry.

The Orinthians came upon them in waves. Rider drew his sword as he charged into their camp and began to slice and swing at any red uniform he saw. It became a blur of men as he went. Over and over again, he cut them down, the Aunticans. Some of them were attempting to fight back, still in their night clothes but holding weapons. Others were running for shelter and safety away from the assault. There was barely even a challenge as they fought.

Rider put his sword away and looked across the battlefield. The Aunticans around him lay dead and wounded from his sword. Only feet away, the fighting continued. As the time went on, more Aunticans had joined the fight, these ones equipped with weapons. Now was his time to use the shadow.

He ran throughout the fight looking. He stopped as he saw his first target. A large man, probably standing around 6'7, was wearing full armor and swung an axe with all his might. He slayed several Orinthians with it as he swung, no match for a sword and a shield. He was a moving machine, screaming words in Auntican as he killed man after man. How he prepared so quickly after the surprise attack was incredible but there was no time to wonder about it.

Rider focused in on him and took a deep breath as he felt the shadow swirl around him and in him. He closed his eyes, letting the power simmer beneath the surface before opening them and letting it release. He felt the rush of adrenaline as the shadow left his body and surged forward towards the man with the axe. The man stopped suddenly as it reached him and immediately began to scream and convulse as the shadow devoured his soul. Rider felt the power surge through his body as the man dropped to the ground and continued shaking. The soldiers around him stopped fighting and stared, utterly confused. An Auntican soldier nearby screamed and ran towards his friend as the man with the axe finally laid still.

Rider exhaled as the shadow returned to him, satisfied with the man's demise. He suddenly felt more energized than he ever had been in the past twelve years. He felt like he used to when he was twenty-one and in the best shape of his life. It was making him stronger, both physically and mentally. He could see and hear everything so clearly and his reflexes moved at a new speed as he took off running from the scene, before anyone connected him to the man with the axe.

The battle continued raging around him, flashes of crimson and navy, shouts of war, the sound of metal hitting metal, men wounded on the ground groaning and yelling for help. Rider tried not to faint at the smell of it all; his sense of smell was keen, and he could almost pick up the scent of every death.

He continued weaving through the grounds of the Auntican camp, spotting the best soldiers and taking them out, but fleeing before someone saw him. On the tenth man he killed, he realized he needed to stop. His heart was pounding in his chest so loud he could hear it. He was sweating like crazy, not from the heat, but from the use of his power. And he was utterly exhausted, eyelids starting to droop close, but the shadow remained an unlimited power that was ready for action, almost begging to be used again. No, he couldn't. It would overcome him if he used it much more. Every time he used it, he lost a tiny bit of his humanity, the part of him that still belonged to the mortal world.

Rider fell onto the ground among wounded Orinthian soldiers who were groaning. He had to get out of here, find a place where he could fall asleep before the shadow consumed him, without the threat of Auntican soldiers around him. As he watched the fighting, he wasn't sure now who was winning the battle. He prayed to the gods that Orinth was. They needed this fight.

His thoughts were interrupted by a piercing scream that rose above the rest of fighting.

Rider sat up slowly and tried to identify the source of the noise and quickly did so. There was an Orinthian soldier, a boy almost, who had been pierced by an Auntican sword only yards away from where Rider sat. The boy's face was painted in agony as the soldier above him laughed as he shoved the sword in any further.

Time seemed to freeze for a moment because as he looked at the boy's face, he suddenly saw Alida's there instead. Alida being stabbed by an Auntican, her blood being spilled in order to open the Shadow Wall. Grafph standing above her laughing at her pain, her suffering.

He stood up and his power exploded within him. He raised a shaking hand.

The Auntican didn't even scream but just dropped dead as the shadow reached him, twisting around his body and taking his soul without even a thought. The sword remained in the boy's body as he began to wail, calling in Orinthian for a healer or the gods to save him. But Rider only heard Alida calling for him.

Rider ran over to the boy and gagged at the sight of the wound. The sword had penetrated through his entire body and was sticking out the back. It was a miracle he was breathing in the first place. Without a thought, Rider pulled the sword out of his stomach as the boy screamed again, sobbing. He knelt down beside the boy and cradled him to his chest. He had to be a teenager, with his youthful face and brown, childlike curls that were messy. His grey eyes looked up at Rider but were filled with tears.

Rider held him and said, "I'm sorry."

The boy croaked. "Home. I want to go home," he whimpered, wincing in pain once again.

Rider asked, "Where is home for you?"

"Lou," the boy managed to say.

Rider closed his eyes and tapped into the shadow again. In his mind, he pictured the city. Its buildings made of stone and clean cement streets. It's town square, where vendors lined on the weekends to sell all sorts of stuff. The smells that came from the bakeries, the sound of street performers trying to earn their keep, the beginning of the northern mountains. Lou. Gently, he transferred it to the boy's mind.

The boy suddenly stopped crying as his eyes glazed over with the vision. He tried to smile but it ended up as more of a grimace in pain, as the blood continued to rush out of his side. Rider ripped off his coat and tried to tie it around the wound, but it was no use. Already, he was covered in blood as was the entire ground around them. The boy was fading and fast. But in his mind, he was home. Hopefully, that would be a painless ending.

"Home," the boy whispered once again before slumping into his arms with one last breath.

He was dead. Rider pressed his coat harder into the wound to stop the blood, but it was for nothing. The boy was dead and gone. He was holding a corpse in his arms.

But when Rider looked, it wasn't the young soldier, but Alida. Wearing her green dress that she always wore but it was covered in blood from the wound. Her long brown hair was matted with it and her heart was no longer beating.

Rider broke into tears as he cradled the young boy into his chest.

There was so much more at stake here than anyone could have ever imagined. This was just a boy for gods sake. A boy who couldn't be older than twenty who was stabbed by an Auntican because Grafph was going to open the Shadow Wall. He had forced them into this fight and now, so many men, fathers, brothers, husbands, friends, all of them would die because of it. Alida might die. Tieran might die. Any of them could and it was inevitable. All because one single man had decided he wanted world domination and would do anything to get it. Including breaking an alliance and starting a war.

Because of it, this boy was dead. Rider didn't even know his name.

He didn't know how long he sat there, holding onto the boy, drifting in and out of an illusion that it was Alida instead. The use of the shadow had taken a toll.

Before he knew it, a blackness had settled in front of his eyes and he slumped down onto the ground beside the boy. The last thing he remembered before he lost consciousness was the shadow, trying to find another person to take.

Chapter 13

Somewhere in Orinth

Sawny wrapped Adriel's blanket tighter around her and shivered into the night. For some reason, the Orinth air was chill. It was getting closer to the summer season so nights like these were rare. But she wasn't surprised by it. Of course, there would be a freezing cold night. The last few days of their journey since entering her neighboring and enemy country had been a nightmare. It started off with their encounter with the soldiers. The scene haunted her every time she closed her eyes, killing one man and almost killing another. If not for Adriel, the other man would be dead. From then on, they had stumbled along, with barely any sleep or energy. After getting a day's journey away from the spot where it had gone down, neither of them had the strength to stay awake on watch. When they awoke the next morning, half of their food had been ravaged by vermin of some sort.

Adriel had cursed himself. Sawny said nothing.

By the mercy of the gods, most of their supplies were on Adriel's horse. With no other choice but to keep going with less supplies, they began the long road towards Tenir. She was just glad that she still had the pouch with her money in it. Once they reached Tenir, she could afford to buy herself another horse for the rest of their journey.

As if things couldn't get any worse, the whole day was a downpour of rain that never seemed to cease. At first, they tried to wait it out in a small cave. Upon realizing that it wasn't about to stop, they put up their hoods and braved it on top of the horse. Both ended up soaked to the bone, Adriel with a loud cough that had begun to worry Sawny. That night, they had slept on muddy, wet ground.

The next day hadn't been quite so awful. It drizzled a little in the morning but seemed to stop at noon. Alas, after the rain, a chill set on the land that not even the warmth of her wool cloak could keep out. She couldn't stop her teeth from chattering and Adriel continued to look worriedly at her, as she sat behind him on the horse. She shook him off, citing that his cough was something to be much more concerned with.

Orinth was just bad luck to her, she supposed.

It was almost dark when they stopped. If it weren't so cold out, she might have been enjoying the evening. The night sky was full of stars and they were camped out by a spring of freshwater that would probably feel good if it were the right temperature out. The moon shone bright, illuminating all that was around them.

Adriel had insisted on her having his soft, cotton blanket, despite her multiple protests. She had to give up her cloak, it was soaked and was actually making her colder. Somehow, his blanket had stayed dry and warm from the past two days and now, she snuggled into it, wrapping it tight around her shoulders as Adriel tried, and failed, to build a fire for them.

"It's not going to work, Adriel," Sawny said. She had offered to help him several times, but he had waved her off.

She leaned against a tree and watched him. He had taken off his wet armor and was only in a long-sleeved shirt and a pair of pants. His weapons laid next to his armor, also soaked. Sawny tried not to notice the way his clothes clung to him.

Adriel turned back around to her. His dark hair stuck to his forehead and surprisingly enough, sweat dripped down his face. "You're being too negative for the person who's wrapped in my blanket right now," he replied with a straight face, but she could sense his amusement.

"Are you even cold?" she asked, glaring at him.

"Not at all. I haven't been this whole time. This is like a hot summer's day in the Wilds, Sawny. You Aunticans are weak." She made a face at him and he shrugged. "I'm building this fire for your sake."

"I won't stop you from trying, but the wood is wet. I thought a smart outdoorsman like yourself would know that that stops the fire from lighting."

This was how they had gotten on since the Orinthian soldiers. Sawny was afraid he would look at her different, now that he had seen a part of the darkness that she was always trying to keep at bay. No, she wouldn't have regretted killing the other man, just as she didn't regret defending herself and shooting the other. She was numbed to it now and that part of her sometimes terrified her. Adriel acted like nothing had changed. Besides a few hours of silence the morning after, they had talked for the entire time. Sometimes about their lives, other times just joking and laughing at things. A few times, Adriel had started singing what he called "Wild Traveling Songs" and Sawny had almost cried with laughter, his voice was the most out of tune she had ever heard in her life. He had scowled at her but couldn't hide the smile on his face.

They had gotten each other through the past couple days and Sawny was glad for him. Her humanity.

Somehow, he had eased the pain of the burden she had been carrying on her back for four years. When she was with him, she didn't feel guilty for her parent's death, or that she should have been the one to die instead of them. She didn't feel the panic and confusion at the manner of their deaths or her real father. All of that seemed to fade into the background and it was just Adriel.

She knew the scar of it all would always be there and never disappear. Most of the time, the wound of it was still fresh. But not with him

"Again, I'm from the Wilds. It's almost always snowing there, in the mountains. We had to learn how to adapt. I can do it."

"I don't think you can. It's your ego talking."

He looked down at her. "Okay, fine. I'll make a deal with you, Miss Lois," he said, his accent very thick as he spoke her name. "If I light this fire, you have to jump into that spring right there." He pointed at the spring that was twenty feet or so away from where they had camped out, looking cold as ever in the waning light of day.

Sawny snorted. "Unlikely. What's in it for me?"

"If I can't light the fire, you can keep that blanket.

Sawny opened her mouth and looked at the blanket bunched in her hands. It was so incredibly soft, unlike anything she had touched before. She assumed it had to be from the Wilds; if they sold something like this in Auntica, she would've bought it by now. Adriel observed her and muttered under his breath, "If you're wondering, that was homemade by one of the men in my tribe. Real cotton and everything. It took him months to gather the material and even longer to make it. He gave it to my family as a grieving gift, as we call it. There are only a few of its kind on the entire continent. I'm sure it would go for a large amount of money, at least back in Illias."

Sawny raised an eyebrow. "I don't care about the money. I just want the blanket."

Adriel grinned at her, "So we have a deal?" He extended a hand down to her.

Sawny felt the heavy cotton at her shoulders and before she knew what she was doing, she reached up and shook it. "It's a deal."

Adriel winked at her and she felt her heart beat a little louder in her chest. He couldn't do it. She had spent a good part of her life outdoors and one thing she knew for certain; wet wood doesn't make a fire. But something about his cocky grin was making her nervous. She eyed the spring and shivered. It was already so cold. Going into that spring might just kill her. But he wouldn't do it. He turned back to his wood and started whistling a tune as he worked.

She couldn't see what he was doing, but she could feel his full confidence. She watched as he beat a flint and steel together repeatedly. After a few minutes of it, she felt slightly better. He had been going at it for a while and there hadn't been so much as a spark.

She started to doze off after a while, him whistling in the background. It was still light out, but the sun had hidden behind the cloud's hours ago. The air was chill but wrapped in the blanket listening to Adriel whistle some tune, she found her eyes beginning to droop. The last couple of days had been exhausting. There was a weariness in her bones that never accompanied her when she came on these journeys alone. The Forest Dembe, losing her horse, the Orinthians, all of it had drained her. But she was still here, and with a man whom she, well, felt something for. She didn't know what the feeling was, but when she was with him, she felt like she was starting to heal somewhere deep within her soul. Maybe she was tired, but in another sense, she was starting to wake up to life again.

She fell asleep rather quickly after thinking that thought, one that seemed to comfort her to the depths of her spirit. She didn't see or notice Adriel turn around and look at her, a slight smile on his face, before continuing working on the wet wood.

Minutes later, he knelt down before her. "Sawny?" he whispered.

She opened her eyes, briefly forgetting about where she was at for the moment, instead focusing on his face. When she saw it, she smiled at him, at his icy blue eyes and messy, wet hair and his lips. Familiar. This face was familiar and when she looked at it, she felt safe. He froze from what he was about to say and stared into her eyes. She hoped that he could see within them that she was healing. She was trying. She was a person who was broken but striving to be wholly together all on her own, without the help of anyone.

"Yes?" she whispered in a reply, not losing her smile.

He was staring at her. There was something in his eyes she didn't recognize, had never seen. It was impossible to put into words what it was, but there was something there that had not been before. She wished she could freeze time at that very moment and stay there with him forever. She wished the rest of the world would disappear, that their pasts and futures would fade to darkness. He would be just a man and she would be just a woman and there would be nothing in the way of that. What would happen if it were like that?

And then the moment was gone as suddenly as it had come. The look disappeared from his eyes and was replaced by a goofy grin. "Look behind me."

She searched for the look again, but it was truly gone. She tried to snap herself out of it and looked around his shoulders. There, where only moments ago a pile of wet sticks and logs had sat, was a roaring fire. Sawny could feel the heat from where she was sitting, still under the blanket.

"Oh my gods. How did you manage that?"

Adriel sat down next to her, his shoulder just brushing her own. "I hate to say I told you so, but I told you so. You see, the key is with wet wood you must increase the amount of kindle you use by threefold at least, maybe even four or fivefold. Then you have to create a teepee formation around it all, like a little house, the kind you would see in a village. Once that's all set up, light the kindle and woosh, it all catches on fire. The kindle burns long enough to catch the wet wood on fire and there you have it."

He was rambling, talking fast and nervously and she suddenly knew that he had felt the moment too. Adriel knew something had just happened between them and neither knew what it was or what it would become.

"I guess I'll know how to light the fire next time we have wet wood," Sawny breathed.

They didn't speak for a minute before Adriel stood up and turned to look down at her. She could tell he was trying to put up his stone face that he wore whenever they were around other people, the one he wore when they had first met but she never saw anymore. He was failing, the smile leaking through the cracks. "Well?" he said.

Sawny's head fell towards her chest as she stood up next to him. "My word is the only thing I have. A deal is a deal." She let the white blanket drop to her feet.

Adriel shook his head and began to laugh. "I was kidding, Sawny. I'm not going to make you jump into that spring. I'm sure it's freezing and you're already so cold, I won't do that to you."

Sawny started walking towards the spring, to the dismay of the man. "No, I'm doing it. I told you I would and I'm going too."

Adriel made a grab for her arm and she dodged out of his grasp and snickered as she continued towards the spring. "Sawny!" he said, exasperated. Sawny grinned at him. "This is what you wanted," she said, eyes twinkling as she lifted her light blue shirt up, over her shoulders, and threw it onto the ground.

She only had a brassiere on and Adriel raised an eyebrow. She shrugged at him. "I'm not going to get my clothes wet or dirty. I only have a few more clean sets." She unbuttoned the latch on her black skirt and let it drop to the ground as well. She strode and stood at the edge of the spring. It was deeper than it looked, the ledge sitting at least ten feet above the water. And even then, she couldn't see the bottom of the clear, blue water. She turned back to Adriel, who was slightly flushed at the half-naked girl in front of him. Still, he wore an expression of amusement and, dare she say, cockiness. He crossed his arms and shook his head at her.

"Just remember, if I drown or die from cold, it's on you," Sawny said, tossing her hair back.

He raised another eyebrow at her. "I gave you an out."

She shot him a look. "If I don't jump in this water, you will never ever let me live it down."

He gave a tiny smirk. "Well, maybe. But I don't want you to freeze to death either."

Without thinking about it, she whirled around and jumped off the ledge. Time slowed as she hit the water and sank below the surface. She gasped at just how cold it was but closed her mouth as the water rushed in. Yes, it was freezing, but in a way, refreshing. She felt as if layers of grime and dirt were falling off her skin, years of it almost. It was cleansing everything she had been carrying with her subconsciously.

She opened her eyes underwater and saw it was so clear, she could see an outline of Adriel, standing above the spring and looking down. The bottom of the spring was still a good twenty feet below. She moved her arms and swam back to the top.

She coughed when her head emerged from the water and treaded to stay afloat. Sawny glanced back up at Adriel, who was kneeling next to the edge of the water and observing her.

"How is it?" he asked, the laughter in his voice apparent.

She threw her head back, so it was just her hair in the water. "It's actually not too bad."

"Oh?"

"It's cold. But I haven't had a bath in so long, it feels good." She dipped under the water and came up again, shaking her hair back and forth.

Sawny watched as Adriel in one smooth stroke took off his shirt. "What are you doing?" she asked him.

He wrinkled his brow at her. "What do you think I'm doing?"

"Oh, no," she began as he took off his pants, standing in just a pair of some sort of undershorts.

"Oh, yes," he said, grinning as he took a few steps back and started at a dead sprint towards the edge of the spring. Sawny shrieked and tried to move out of the way as the man dove into the center of the spring, just missing hitting her body with his own. He barely made a splash as he dove in, body cutting right through the surface. She laughed as he emerged from the water. His dark hair, which had gotten longer since they had left Illias, was matted in front of his eyes.

He grinned at her, wiping the hair off his face, and pushing it back so it stood up, spikey. Without a word, he dove back into the water and started swimming towards the bottom. Sawny followed him, taking a deep breath and going under. He moved fast in the water, which didn't surprise her in the least. His arms created smooth and fluid strokes while his legs kicked in rhythm propelling him forward faster than she could keep up. She had been taught to swim by her father, who probably wasn't the best choice of teachers. He rarely swam in the Darklands, so   she ended up moving very awkwardly when she learned. Since then, she had attempted a few times to learn how to move better, but always gave up. She was meant to be on land, not a fish in the sea. Which apparently, Adriel was. She watched him reach the bottom and look back up at her as he laid on his back, body stretched out, with his arms behind his head.

Sawny tried not to blush as she could now see almost everything. She had to consciously not stare at him, but for some reason, in the water right now, she was having a hard time not looking. He is a client, she repeated over and over again in her head, but she couldn't help but wondering. Something had happened only minutes ago, and she was sure he felt it too.

She stuck her tongue out at him as she drifted to the surface to get some air. Sawny could barely hold her breath for even a few seconds and her lung capacity was lacking. She took long deep breaths as she broke the surface. She shook her head at herself. That was it. When she got back to Illias, she would find somewhere to start practicing her swimming.

Sawny shrieked as she felt something grab her ankle and she kicked as hard as she possibly could. Her foot made contact with something solid, and she heard a shout. She looked down and saw Adriel, floating to the surface, hand gripping his chest where she had just kicked him.

He broke the surface and said breathlessly, "Gods, woman!" and cursed in his language. "What did you think I was?"

Sawny started laughing. "I'm so sorry!" she exclaimed, the sarcasm apparent in her voice. "I thought you were a fish or something trying to bite me!"

"That had no teeth and five fingers?" he shouted. "Gods, I think you might have stopped my heart. There will definitely be a bruise. Possibly worse."

"Oh my gods, Adriel, I didn't even kick you very hard!" she said, shoulders shaking with laughter as she treaded to stay afloat.

"Tell that to my bleeding heart, Sawny!" he said, but she could hear he was laughing too. His head snapped up at her and he suddenly splashed the cold water all over her. She gasped at the coolness of it on her face and coughed.

"Serves you right," Adriel announced, a smug smile on his face.

Sawny dove at him, swinging a hand to hit him in the face, but he dodged it and went under the water. She followed him this time, trying to catch him but he moved like the wind. She cursed angrily, making bubbles in the water as she went back to the surface, this time watching what was under her. Adriel swam a little ways away and popped back up.

"I guess I found another thing I'm better than you at, Sawny Lois," he said, laughing. Sawny splashed more water at him but it didn't even come close. He raised both eyebrows. "Okay, make that two."

She couldn't help smiling this time. "You're an idiot. You know that, right?"

Adriel shrugged. "I do. I really do." He disappeared back under the water and reappeared, only a foot away from her. "Are you going to splash me? Please, have mercy on a poor man from the Wilds. All your Auntican brethren have already splashed me."

Sawny shook her head at him. "We're playing the 'poor me from the Wilds' card, are we?"

He tried to make a sad expression but continued smiling. "Yes, we are."

She rolled her eyes but continued beaming at him. "Fine, fine. I'll let you off easy this time."

He gave a yelp of victory and then stopped, narrowing his eyes at her face. "Hold on." He reached out and with one finger, touched the skin just below her eye. She felt every muscle in her body tense as he held up that finger and showed it to her. "You had an eyelash," he announced.

"Am I supposed to make a wish now?"

Adriel gave her a quizzical look. "What does that mean?"

"It's an Auntican thing. An eyelash represents a wish. If I blow on it, and make a wish in my head, then it will come true."

He snorted. "Oh, that's how it works, does it? I would have been pulling my eyelashes off by now to get a damn wish." He looked down at his finger and then held it out to her. "Well, fair is fair. Make your wish."

She closed her eyes and saw very very clearly what it was she wanted. She thought about it for a moment and then opened them. Adriel studied her as she tried to blow the eyelash off his finger but there it stayed, stuck because it was wet. She tried again, harder this time, but it didn't move.

Adriel snorted loudly.

Sawny glared at him and tried again, to no avail. Finally, she grabbed his finger and stuck it into the water, so that the eyelash was washed away.

"Will it not come true now?" Adriel asked, his finger still in her grip.

She shrugged. "Probably not. Either way." She grinned at him.

He smiled back at her. "Isn't this funny, Sawny Lois?"

"What's funny?"

"Here we are, in some freezing cold Orinthian spring, while the whole world is falling apart around us."

She laughed. "Not really. I mean, my life has already fallen apart to the fullest extent. I'm sure yours has too. Maybe it's time for the whole world to follow our example."

He stared at her. "Maybe it is," he said, all traces of laughter gone. She looked at him, still smiling. "What?"

"I don't think your world has fallen apart, Sawny."

She huffed. "Maybe or maybe not. Regardless, I won't be a part of the whole world falling apart."

"Look at you."

"Look at me, what?"

"I mean, four years ago, you lost everything. But now you have your own business, one that has quite a lot of fame. You're significantly wealthier than a good majority of people. Regardless of how this war ends, you won't lose anything. You're young, you're beautiful, and you're the most alive person I've ever met. You don't let your pain define you. You feel deeper than most people. And yes, there is a side of you that's dark, that's been created by loss and grief and hopelessness, but it doesn't control you. I think that you're doing rather well, actually."

She blinked and opened her mouth to speak and then closed it. "I-I-"

"You don't have to say anything back to me. I just thought you should know."

Sawny stared up into his eyes, battling to stay afloat. It was back again, the look that had been there by the tree. She tried to breathe, but it was becoming increasingly harder, between the words he had just spoken and the swimming.

He raised an eyebrow at her. "Do you need help?"

"No—Adriel-I-" Suddenly his arms looped around her waist, his hands holding her steady and up. He pulled her closer to him, their faces only inches away now. She stopped struggling as he held her, keeping her adrift.

"Thank you," she whispered. "Thank you."

He nodded. "Anytime," he responded, still looking into her eyes.

"I've always felt like my life was in pieces around me," Sawny began, "until we left Illias. In the Forest Dembe, I realized that I've been clinging so tightly to all of it, with good reason. My pain is a part of me. Maybe it's a dark part and it's something I'll always carry. Just like how you will always carry the Wilds and your past. But our pain doesn't control us And when I'm with you—" her voice trailed off, "-I don't know. There's something here."

"Something here?"

"There's something here," Sawny repeated.

"What is that something, Sawny?" he asked, moving her a touch closer to him.

"I don't know," she said breathlessly. "I was hoping you could tell me."

His forehead just barely touched her own. "I think you'll have to figure it out and let me know."

With one hand, she reached up and pushed his wet hair out of his face. "I guess we'll have to figure it out together, then."

He smiled a little. "I would like that."

She let her fingers fall from his face down onto his cheek. His skin, despite the bitter cold of the water, was warm to the touch. She traced a circle around once and rested her hand on the back of his neck, wrapping her legs around his body so he was completely holding her up, one hand around her back, the other treading water.

She let her forehead fully rest against his own as he tucked a piece of hair behind her ear. He leaned in, just a little, and she looked up into his eyes once more. He was going to kiss her. She was almost sure of it and she hoped to the gods that he did. Just looking at his lips made her desperate for them to meet her own. She took a deep breath as he angled his head again and leaned in a little more.

He almost dropped her when they suddenly heard a roaring sound of a horse.

Their heads both snapped upwards. Standing on the ledge, where both of them had just been, was Indira.

Sawny almost shrieked as she pushed herself away from Adriel and shouted, "Indira!" She swam over to the closest piece of shore and shivered as she came out of the water and onto the banks. The cold air met her like a slap in the face, but she didn't care as she ran up towards the ledge where Indira was waiting. Her grey horse stood, proud and fair, head thrown in the wind, like a proud soldier returning to his country. Sawny flung herself towards the horse and wrapped her arms around the mare's neck. Her heart was racing so fast, and she was breathing so heavily. So many things had just happened at once and she wasn't exactly sure what. Had her horse, whom she had lost so many days ago, in Auntica no less, really returned? And did she really return at the precise moment when she and Adriel were about to…kiss?

It was too much but right now she was just overwhelmed with gratefulness that her horse had found its way back to her.

Indira still wore her saddle, but she was cleaner than before and had been groomed by someone. Sawny noticed that tucked beneath her saddle was a piece of paper, folded. She opened it up.

I found her in my forest. She belongs to you, although a beautiful creature such as this one can never truly belong to anyone. She was looking for you. I hope your journey is proving to be a success, Sawny Lois. Remember you are steadfast and have the friendship of my forest. If you need to remember, just look at my mark. -Your friend, Matahali

She read it almost three times as Adriel came up behind the both of them. He stroked Indira's nose and Sawny could hear him breathing deeply. She could feel where his hands had been on her skin, his breath on her lips, the sense that something big was about to happen, but the moment was gone now. Adriel said something to the horse in his language.

Sawny turned to him and handed him the note shivering. "Indira doesn't speak your language, Adriel," she said, trying for humor. He laughed, in mercy or in amusement, as he read the note.

"Watch her please. I'm about to freeze in place."

Adriel nodded once, continuing to read, as Sawny hustled back to the camp. She grabbed her cloak, which was now completely dry, and used it to dry herself. She slipped back into her shirt and skirt and grabbed Adriel's blanket again, wrapping it around herself as her teeth chattered once more. Gone was the refreshing feeling of the water, replaced by pure cold. She jogged back to where Indira and Adriel were standing.

Adriel handed her back the note. "I suppose your friendship with the forest witch came in handy after all," he said. She couldn't sense what his tone was, but if she had to guess, it was something akin to disappointment. Not about the horse or the witch, but the fact that it had interrupted something. Their something.

"I'll watch her and take her back to camp. You go get some clothes on," Sawny chuckled. "Or you may just freeze in place as well."

Adriel shook his head. "I'm telling you; I am used to this. Like I said, hot summer day in the Wilds." Still, he began walking back towards their camp.

Sawny grabbed Indira's reigns after kissing her once on the nose and began guiding her back towards the camp. "I trust you with my whole heart, Indira, but I'm going to have to tie you to a tree today. I know, I know but we can't afford to have another horse run off. Also, what was that timing about, Indira? We were close to figuring it out and you had to show yourself then? Always one for dramatic timing, Indira. Always," she whispered to her and Indira brayed happily. Sawny had a feeling the horse could understand what she was saying, and she smiled at the thought.

She left Indira anchored to a tree, happily munching on some grass, a short distance from their camp. Adriel was dressed again in his same pants and shirt, stoking the fire. When she approached, he looked up. "How is she?"

Sawny sat down with a sigh. "She's wonderful. I'm grateful for Matahali, somehow sending her back to me."

"It's scary how she could find us like that."

Sawny held up her wrist. "I think she used this. I don't know what it means but we have two horses now."

Adriel nodded. "Indeed we do." He stood up. "I think this fire begs for fresh meat. Do you want to go hunt something or should I?"

Sawny stood up and eyed her bow, sitting by the pile of their gear. "I will. I'll let you do the gross part of skinning it and stuff." She strode over to it and picked it up, enjoying the familiar sensation of the weapon in her hand.

When she turned, Adriel was watching her. "Sawny, I meant everything I said earlier. About your world."

She took a step towards him. "I know you did. And I meant everything I said about...us."

He raised an eyebrow and his mouth twitched. "Us?"

She could feel the red beginning to creep up into her face, "I mean-no. Yes. I mean us. Our-" she searched for the right word but couldn't find one, "-something."

He laughed, his beautiful smile coming across his face like always. "Alright, Sawny Lois. Alright."

Sawny tied back her hair into a knot and strode over to where he was standing. She reached up and pressed her lips against his cheek, which, despite the chill air, was hot. "I'll be back," she whispered into his ear, enjoying the way he tightened when she did.

"I'm counting on it," he shouted after her as she started walking. "I want to figure out this something pretty damn fast."

From the chill that went down her spine when he said it, she knew she did too.

Chapter 14

Aram, Orinth

There was a puppy on the boat, and it had made Alida's life increasingly happy. His name was Louie, apparently after one of the men's favorite bartenders in Abdul. They had picked him up when they set sail, a mutt who had been on the side of the road within a litter that no one had wanted. They could only take one, because puppy upkeep was apparently too much for a whole group of sailors. Over the course of their days on the water, however, it had become Alida's job and responsibility, despite the fact she didn't technically have to work for her position on the boat. But she loved it. Louie was so tiny she could pick him up in her arms easily. He was black with white patches all over his body and he loved playing fetch. He would run around as fast as he could and then lay down and fall asleep wherever he was standing. The past couple nights, Louie had found his way into her room and snuggled into her bed, under her covers.

Alida let the dog follow her around the ship, a companion even more faithful than Rider. The men often poked fun at her about how much she loved her furry pal, but she didn't care. When she held the dog or played with him, all of her troubles melted away.

Her plan had been to stay on the ship and play with the puppy while the Valley made its last stop in Aram before setting sail to Nagaye. Alida felt the anxiety creep back into her brain. Another stop in Orinth was another chance for Grafph to catch her, and take her, and cause the end of the world. She had felt so good about leaving Rein, felt so free, and now they were stopping again. She couldn't even protest without giving them a reason for it and blowing her cover. She had become Nova Grey so perfectly, had embraced her alias with all that she was. Sometimes, she forgot there was another life for her waiting in Abdul when this was over. There was a temptation to let go of Alida Goulding and become

Nova Grey. She could get a job working for Sahar; they had become as thick as thieves during the journey. She could help her with the books for her smuggling, keep track of her accounts, or even help wash dishes. Anything to continue living the life she had been living for the past few weeks.

She dreaded the moment when she felt the boat slow and pull into the harbor at Aram. Alida was laying on her bed, head on her pillow, Louie on her lap, napping. It was very comfortable, in her cotton white pajamas Sahar had lent her, hair in two braids, also done by Sahar. She wondered if her friendship with the young captain was what having a sister was like. She guessed it was. They shared clothes, gossiped about people on the ship, laughed, talked, complained, all of it.

Except the fact that sisters knew their real identities. Sahar still believed she was Nova Grey.

Which was undoubtedly a good thing. Alida wasn't sure what the captain would do if she discovered her true identity. No one, she hoped, knew that Grafph was looking for her. It was impossible to tell what would happen. But for now, she was Nova Grey.

A knock on the door interrupted her thoughts about her identity. "Who is it?"

The door open and Roman poked his head in. "It's me," he said.

"What do you want?"

He scoffed, "That's such a nice greeting, Nova. Good morning to you too." His eyes softened when he saw Louie on her. "That dog loves you."

She smiled and reached down to stroke his soft ears. Louie twitched a little but didn't wake up. "I know he does."

Roman opened the door and leaned against the frame. "He barely even acknowledges the rest of us anymore. You've stolen all of his affection."

Alida shrugged. "I've been known to do that before."

Roman rolled his eyes but smiled at her. "I'm here because Sahar sent me. She's already on shore, meeting some smuggler or another. She'll be done at noon, and then I have to go meet with some people until the evening. She wanted me to ask you if you want to come out on the town with her."

Alida hesitated. Her first instinct was to say yes. She wanted to see as much as she possibly could on this journey, even in her home country. Sahar probably knew the best places to see and visit. But, once again, it presented every opportunity for her to be recognized. She was confident none of the people on the ship knew she was the princess. She had been sailing with them for almost two weeks and no one had said a word. She hadn't noticed any strange glances or quizzical expressions. She was just another passenger to them. But the people in Aram? Who knew who she might run across? Aram was much bigger than Rein had been.

"I don't know," Alida sighed, glancing down at the puppy on her lap. She sat up and placed the dog onto the floor. He ran over to Roman and rubbed up against his legs. Roman, in turn, picked Louie up and kissed the top of his head as the dog licked his face in return. The man chuckled.

"What do you mean you don't know? Do you want to or not? I don't think she'll be mad if you don't want to," Roman replied.

Alida shrugged. "It's nice on the boat. I'm not sure if I want to go into the city. There will be so many people. I could just stay in here and cuddle with Louie all day."

"Well, that is tempting. I mean, look at him." Roman held up the dog to her, his little tail wagging as he panted for breath. Alida smiled and stood, striding over to the pair of them. She took the dog in her arms and stroked its little cheek.

"I wonder how much I'll have to pay Sahar to take him with me when we get to Nagaye," Alida said aloud. That, she was completely serious about. Alida or Nova, both wanted to keep Louie.

"Don't worry; she fully plans on letting you keep him for free," Roman said, before clapping a hand over his mouth. "Shit. I don't think I was supposed to tell you."

Alida shrieked with glee, "Really? Oh, thank the gods! Did you hear that, Louie? Your mommy gets to keep you!"

Roman snorted. "Don't make me try to reconvince her. So, is it a yes or a no now? Knowing that you'll get to keep this precious little ball of fur."

Alida set him down again and looked up at Roman, smiling. "A definite yes."

Roman returned the smile. "I'll come get you in a few hours," he said, turning around and closing the door behind him.

No one would recognize her, with her short hair. Plus, whenever she went out in public back in Abdul, she was always heavily made up. Fancy dresses, hair done, makeup on, back straight and perfect. She hadn't worn makeup since she had left the castle and her hair had been slept on. No one would be expecting to see the princess, so no one would be looking for her. It would all be okay. She had a good feeling about it.

After a few minutes more, she exited her cabin and started towards Sahar's quarters. Rider had made it clear to her before she left that her old life, one of luxury, would have to be sacrificed. She would be sleeping on the ground, with no assistant to bring her tea or draw her bath or anything. She would just be a normal person who did everything for herself. Which, she was fine with, but clearly, Rider was not anticipating the captain to share her bathroom, with its many many luxuries, with Alida.

On her way towards the bathroom, a few crew members said good morning or gave her a small, curt nod. She always returned with a smile. Every night, since Sahar had made her, she had eaten dinner with the crew. Some nights, Sahar and she ate by themselves, but she was never alone. The crew had begun to include her in some of their activities. She had been invited multiple times to participate in drinking games, but she declined. Often, they pushed her and pushed her until she sang them a song, an Orinthian one of course. Sometimes, a few of the men would break out instruments and she would sing along with them. They played cards and rolled dice and gambled their life fortunes.

Alida was having the most fun she had ever had before in her life.

She reached the bathroom and slipped inside. It was as large as Alida's entire cabin, with a huge tub in the corner, a basin, and a vanity all managing to fit inside. Alida strode over to the basin and began to wash her face and her hands, being careful not to use too much. Sahar had several barrels of freshwater for herself, but it was still limited. Alida checked her reflection in the mirror. She noticed that somehow, she looked happier than she usually did. This ship and its people had become a sanctuary for her, away from the madness of the present. Maybe she wasn't meant to be a princess.

The more time she spent here, the less she believed that she was the Last Heir.

After redoing her hair, leaving it down and curly, she returned to her room and changed into a sundress that Sahar had lent her. That was another thing about the captain; she had a wide variety of styles. Most of the time, she dressed like a badass, with leather pants that had knives strapped to them. But just as easily, she could wear a cute dress and a hat almost perfectly. Alida was stunned by it.

She patted Louie on the top of the head and tucked him into her bed, leaving the little dog sleeping. She kept the door to her cabin open so he could roam if he wished. Then, she headed towards the upper deck.

It was a sunny and beautiful day in Aram. She felt a small pang of homesickness as she stepped onto the main deck. If she were back at home, what would she be doing right now? When days were this gorgeous, sometimes she and Rider would take the day off to go to ride their horses. Other times, her father and she took a picnic to the forest, just the two of them, and talked about old times. On the best and luckiest days, the three of them would go to one of the natural springs around Abdul and swim.

She missed them both desperately and thought about them constantly. If it weren't for the happiness that the ship and its crew brought her, Alida was positive she would've returned to find them by now. She was unsure of both of their whereabouts but had heard no news concerning them. Of course, they had been on the water for weeks on end so there had been no opportunity to. She guessed they both had to be with an army by now, at least based upon the plans that they had made before she left. Rider could take care of himself, easily. But her father? Yes, he had an extensive security detail but that didn't stop her from worrying about him.

But at least, for now, an Orinthian flag still flew in Aram as she saw it, with its clay buildings and red tiled roofs. She had been one time, as a child, and didn't remember much about it. The ship was in the harbor, anchored to the dock, with no other ships near it. There were a few crew members unloading boxes off the ship, others just lounging on the dock. She eyed Roman, standing near the wheel of the ship and made her way towards him.

Roman had been a surprisingly positive part to her trip. Sahar's first mate possessed many qualities that made him a good addition to the ship's crew; he was a natural leader, problem-solver, and just overall brilliant. She wasn't sure if it was from his past, being a part of a crime syndicate family, but it was clear he was a major part of the brains behind the operation. One could see he respected Sahar and her authority and would never try to challenge it. They worked extremely well together, both as mates and friends. Roman treated Alida with just as much respect. When he saw her, he always said hello, and often asked her to join him in whatever duty he was performing at that moment. He made time for her and she appreciated it. He also was ridiculously attractive, but she didn't let herself go there. Most of the time.

When she approached him, he was leaning against the side of the ship and looking down at a paper.

"Whatcha lookin at?" Alida asked him, standing beside him and trying to get a look.

Roman wrinkled his nose at her. "So nosy." At her glare, he laughed. "I'm just looking at this order form Sahar gave me, for when we get back from Nagaye.

I'm meeting with the client today at one of the taverns in Aram. He's a restaurant owner from Illias and man, is he ordering a lot of wine."

Alida froze. "Illias?"

He looked up. "Yes, Illias. Why, is there something wrong with Illias?"

"Well, the fact that it's in Auntica," Alida said.

He chuckled. "You're really buying into the whole war with Auntica thing, aren't you?"

"Are you not?"

Roman shook his head. "They've been saying that we're going to war with Auntica for almost five years. If it was meant to be, it would've happened by now."

"What about the farmer they just slaughtered on the border?"

He gave her a funny look, "It matters this much to you?"

Alida stammered, "No. I care about my country though. Right now, Auntica is not our friend. The sooner we win this war, the sooner I can go home."

Roman held his hands up. "Okay, okay. I'm Orinthian too, you know. You see, Nova, with our business, smuggling that is, we don't care about Orinth or Auntica or the Wilds or Nagaye or any of them. We're here for profit and we'll do almost anything to get it."

"Isn't that a little too much?"

"I don't mean it like that!" Roman protested. "I'm not like my father. We do things for a profit without caring who they benefit. For example, I'm about to sell a shit ton of Orinthian wine to an Auntican business owner. It will create a profit for him and probably improve the Auntican economy, undoubtedly. That won't stop me from selling it."

Alida rolled her eyes at him. "Aren't you a model citizen?" He snorted, "I'm a Vacci, remember?"

"I don't often forget it."

"Yeah, yeah." He grinned at her and slipped the paper into his pocket. "Well, Sahar has a few more hours of meetings left, but we can go to shore anyways, if you want."

Alida nodded. "I suppose so. Will anyone recognize you?" she asked him.

He laughed. "Maybe. My father has people in every city so someone will probably tell him I'm here. No one's going to approach me or anything. I'm not high enough in the Vacci line to attract that much attention." Roman held out his arm to her. "Shall we?"

She took his arm, and they began towards the exit of the ship; a wooden plank that led onto the docks. "It must be a lot of pressure then," Alida said to him, rather enjoying the feeling of her arm in his.

He shrugged. "Sometimes. But again, I'm not a fulltime family member. I sometimes take breaks to go work with my father and brothers, but not often. They don't expect too much out of me."

They stepped onto the plank, single file, Roman keeping one hand on her back. They stepped onto the dock and he took her arm again.

"What do you do for him?" Alida asked as they began walking towards the city.

Roman raised an eyebrow. "What, are you some sort of spy for a rival family?"

Alida laughed. "No. Just a boring, normal Orinthian who doesn't often meet someone who's part of a crime syndicate."

He smiled at her. "Well then. I suppose I can divulge some secrets. It's not very exciting. Most of the time I help organize their books. I help them plan heists at times, or coordinate consultants."

"So, you're the brains?"

"I guess so."

Alida coughed the word 'failure' very audibly under her breath.

Roman elbowed her. "Now hold on there! I've been a part of a few robberies! Don't count me out completely, I can hold my own!"

Alida chuckled. "Yeah, yeah," she copied his phrase from only minutes ago.

He sighed, "I never thought a sweet, Orinthian girl like yourself would say I'm not criminal enough."

"I never said that!"

He laughed and she joined in. "What about you, Nova?"

"What about me?"

"We've been talking about me this whole time. Tell me about you."

Alida shrugged. "There's not much to tell," she said.

He scoffed, "Well of course there is! Tell me about your life back home in Tenir! Don't you have like four older brothers or something? And you go to school and are smart and educated?"

"I don't know if I would say smart or educated. But yes, I go to school. And yes, I have four brothers."

"What's it like being the only girl?" he asked.

"It can get lonely," she said, realizing it wasn't a total lie anymore. "Especially when my parents are working. Luckily, one of my brothers is pretty great. We're very close."

"What's his name?"

"It's-Erik. Erik Grey."

"Ah, Erik. Now are your brothers the type that bully you or are they overly protective?"

Alida smiled. "Definitely the overprotective type. They tease me now and again, but I know they have my back. I miss him-them. A lot."

"You'll see them soon. Like I said, I think this war is a bust."

"I don't think so, Roman."

She was interrupted as they walked immediately into the commerce part of Aram, with seemingly hundreds of street vendors, all shouting at once towards the pedestrians on the street. They fell into a large crowd of people surging forward, Alida holding onto Roman's arm for dear life. Slowly, they moved, squeezing between and dodging others around them. Strangely enough, it felt nice to be around a crowd of people again. Yes, it was a group of sweaty Orinthians at the peak shopping period, but still.

"Where are we going?" Alida shouted to Roman above the noise. "We're almost there!" he yelled back.

"Where!?" she asked.

He broke through the crowd and towards a booth, a little bit away from the rest but surrounded by people. The booth was pressed against a building, made of wood and covered in canvas. Unlike the other booths, there were no vendors shouting out in front of it. It seemed to speak for itself, with the long line leading up to the counter.

"What is it?" she asked him.

"The best dessert in Aram is what it is," Roman told her, smiling.

"Which is what?"

"You'll have to wait and see," he replied with a wink. "Oh, and-" he reached into his pocket and pulled out a piece of jewelry, "-I believe this belongs to you."

She took it from his hands and gaped at him. "This was just on my wrist!" It was her bracelet she had received from Ledger weeks ago, with the star charm. She hadn't taken it off since getting it. It reminded her of the man in the forest who had somehow managed to instill a confidence and calm within her.

Roman laughed. "It wasn't me, I swear. A pickpocket nicked it off you a couple minutes ago and I got it back."

"How?" she demanded. "How did he do it and how did you do it?"

"This is a huge sea of people, in other words a pickpocket's paradise. They just float throughout the people and let their hands travel to whatever they will. One got your bracelet, I noticed, so I stole it back."

Alida shook her head. "How do you know how to do that?"

He grinned at her. "Does this at least prove I'm a Vacci?"

"No, it proves you are a cheap crook," she said smiling. "But thank you for getting it back for me." She handed it back to him. "I think it's safer with you for now though."

Roman tucked it into one of his shirt pockets. "Good choice. It's very beautiful. Where did you get it?"

"It was a gift."

"From whom?"

"A friend of mine."

"What sort of friend?"

"An old friend." It wasn't technically a lie. Ledger was quite old.

"What's their name?"

She narrowed her eyes at him. "We're curious, aren't we?"

He shrugged. "You're awfully mysterious sometimes, Nova. You know that right?"

"I have to keep you on your toes, Mr. Vacci."

"Fair enough."

Alida looked at him. "The truth is I'm not mysterious. My life is just pretty boring compared to yours and Sahar's and the crews'. So, I don't talk much about my own life because it would pale in comparison."

He snorted, "I'm sure that's not true. Maybe you're not a swashbuckling, sword fighting, wine-smuggling pirate, but I bet your life is far from boring."

She wished she could tell him. No, her life was not boring. She was a damned princess, for gods sake. Her best friend in the world could end lives with seemingly just a thought. Her father was the ruler of Orinth and had actually met Roman's father. Alida, being the last Orinthian royal, was possibly the Last Heir, whose blood was able to destroy the Shadow Wall and release the demons from their realm. But there was a chance it wasn't her, so she had run away from her kingdom and her country so she could protect all that she loved. She had paid to be a on a ship smuggling wine and selling it to Aunticans, all while taking on a new identity. Not very boring.

"You're wrong. It is boring. But the last few weeks have been exciting, with you all at least. I love being a part of it all."

"They all love you, you know? The crew, Sahar, all of us. Having you on board has been a breath of fresh air."

Alida laughed. "I don't know why."

"Because you're crazy. You sing and laugh and you throw yourself into everything that you do. You smile at everyone, but you don't take any of their bullshit. And you and that damn puppy. All of us have this shit in our past and maybe you do and maybe you don't but every day, we watch you treat life as if it's a gift," Roman finished.

Alida looked down at her shoes and blushed. "Well, thank you. I don't know how true all of that is, but I'm glad I'm helping in some way. Besides just letting Louie sleep in my bed all the time."

Before he could respond, they reached the front of the line. A small and elderly Orinthian woman stood at the small counter, the delectable smell of chocolate originating from a pot behind her. "Good morning, dears!" she said brightly. "What can I get you?"

Roman held up two fingers. "We will have two of your chocolate puddings please and thank you," he said with a smile.

The old lady returned the grin and whirled around to her pot, adding two scoops of its contents into two separate cups. She handed them both to Roman and he paid her with a few coins. "Keep the change," he added.

The old woman bowed. "Thank you very much, Mr. Vacci." She glanced at Alida and nodded at her. "You're a lucky girl to nab this one."

Alida began to protest, but Roman thanked the lady once more and led her away from the stand, carrying their two puddings. Without saying a word, he guided her through the entire commerce section of Aram before they finally came out the other side, to a street full of shoppes, these ones indoors. Roman selected a bench on one of the streets that was in the shade of a small tree and sat down. Alida followed.

"How did she know you?" she asked the man.

Roman handed her one of the puddings along with a spoon. "Be careful, it's hot."

"Roman?"

He chuckled. "I may have frequented her stand a few times. Word travels fast around here."

"I guess I'm with someone sort of famous," Alida said, taking a bite of her pudding and sighing in delight. It was absolutely delicious. It was rich, warm, and somehow flavorful, while managing to still taste like pure chocolate. Alida quickly shoved another few bites into her mouth.

"I wouldn't say famous. I'm not royalty but like I said earlier, some people just know me. Slow down! I paid for that, at least stop to breathe and enjoy it!"

Alida almost choked when he said he wasn't royalty. It ended in a fit of coughing in which Roman looked over at her concerned, patting her on the back a few times.

"You good?"

"Fine, sorry. It just went down the wrong tube."

"It's because you're trying to inhale it instead of eat it!"

Alida laughed. "Maybe. It's just that good."

Roman took a bite of his. "Oh, I know. I've been coming to this stand since I was a kid. They only serve this pudding and it's lasted for this long."

It was quite pleasant sitting on the bench, in the shade, eating their puddings. They were only a little way from the streets but far enough back it seemed private. Benches like these lined the road the shoppes were on, bustling with activity, so much so that Alida completely forgot her fear of being discovered. None of these people were paying attention to them. They were so absorbed in their own lives and business that no one gave her a second thought. Orinthians were notoriously ambitious. Most of the time, they went about their lives without noticing there were other people in the world. It was part of what made Orinth so successful, a driven bunch of citizens.

Roman took her pudding once the container was empty and put it inside of his. He stepped away and returned after disposing them. He checked a small watch in his pocket. "Well, I suppose we should start towards Sahar now. She still has an hour or so to go but we can surprise her by being early."

"Are you sure she'll like that?"

Roman shrugged. "Probably not. But her meeting is at a tavern and I want a drink."

Slowly, through the large mass of people in Aram, they made their way towards Sahar. Alida decided, when all of this was over, she would come back to this city. It was very beautiful, and she saw a handful of shoppes that she wished she could look into. She was sure that Roman would have let them stop if she had only asked, but she decided against it. After all, she was supposed to be a lower-middle-class girl from Tenir with four older brothers who lived in an apartment with her family. It may be suspicious to display her taste for fine material items in front of Roman.

She had come to the conclusion that he was ridiculously observant. From the moment she met him, he had questioned almost everything about her and about her story. He always noticed her expressions and mannerisms whenever they were together and always knew when she was upset or happy or any emotion. She was almost surprised he hadn't yet figured out who she was. Or at least figured out that she wasn't who she said she was. But, then again, maybe he had. Maybe taking her to get pudding and walking through the streets of Aram and asking about her life was an attempt to start figuring it out. She wasn't sure. But he looked to be enjoying himself as they went, and she was too. If he was faking it all to get answers, he was doing a good job of it.

"Here we are," Roman said, stopping in front of one of the clay buildings. It had no sign or title and was squeezed in between two people's townhouses, also made of clay.

"Where is here?" Alida asked as he guided her into the door.

"You'll see," he said with a grin.

It was pitch black as they walked in but gradually, as they continued through what seemed to be a hallway, it grew lighter. Alida could hear the sounds of talking, laughing, glass clinking together, and music. Finally, they entered a large room, filled to the brim with people. There were no tables and chairs, but a large bar that took up the entire room, in the formation of a circle.

Three bartenders worked in the center of the counter, getting drinks from underneath and almost every seat was taken. One of the bartenders, a small man with dark hair, caught Roman's eye and smiled. His eyes briefly rested on Alida before he said something to the other bartender, another man who was taller.

"What is this place?" Alida asked as Roman led her towards the last two empty stools around the giant bar.

"Alfie's," Roman explained as they sat down. "The best secret bar in all of Orinth."

Alida looked at him as she put her elbows on the counter. "Alcohol isn't illegal here, so why would there need to be a secret bar?"

Roman laughed. "You don't get it! Yes, alcohol isn't illegal anymore, but this place was built when it still was. Alfie never got rid of it, and now, it's sort of a secret spot. You're technically not supposed to tell anyone about it, but it's easy to find. Alfie doesn't mind, of course. It's good for business."

He stopped talking as the small bartender came up to them and extended a hand to Roman. "Well, if it isn't Roman Vacci," he said with a smile. He was dressed in a blue shirt and an apron and had a long black beard. Alida doubted he was even over five feet tall. He was overall a small person, from his shoes to the small pair of glasses he wore on the edge of his nose.

Roman shook his hand, grinning. "Good to see you, Alfie. This is my friend, Nova Grey."

Alfie took Alida's hand and kissed it, much to her surprise. "It is my absolute pleasure, Ms. Grey." Alida beamed at him as he froze for a moment, eyes on her. "Nova, was it?" he asked, the tone in his voice suddenly changing.

Alida felt a pang of panic in her chest. "Yes, it is. Pleasure."

Alfie looked at Roman and then back to Alida. "Where are you from, Ms. Grey?" he asked her.

"Tenir," Alida replied confidently.

"What are you doing in Aram?" Alfie drummed his fingernails on the counter of the bar, his eyes narrowed. Somehow, this bartender in a secret tavern was suspicious of the lies she was telling. Alida swallowed back her fear and responded.

"I'm sailing with Roman and the crew. We stopped here for the day." He seemed satisfied by this answer and stopped with his questioning.

"Well, what can I get you both?"

Roman pondered this before saying, "I will have a whiskey."

"I'll take an ale," Alida said.

Alfie nodded at them with a grin. "It's on the house, for Roman Vacci. Always," he said, turning around to start their drinks.

Roman looked at her. "He doesn't normally question people like that," he said slowly.

Alida shrugged, trying to look relaxed despite her hammering heartbeat. "He's probably wondering how someone so beautiful is accompanying you."

Roman snorted, "Probably." He pointed directly across the bar. "There's our girl."

Sure enough, Sahar sat across from them, deep in conversation with another woman, a wine glass in her hand. The other woman also was drinking wine. She was dressed fancily, with her long blonde hair cascading down her back and lipstick that was so red Alida could see it from where she was sitting.

"She looks so intense. What are they discussing?" Alida asked him.

"That right there is Eria Elliot. She controls the entire black market in Aram. Not just for wine but for everything. Anything you want, you can get at a better price on the black market. Sahar has been thinking of expanding which goods we sell to countries outside this continent. They pay a lot for wine, so we're thinking we can start incorporating other items into our sales, make even more of a profit."

Alida tried to ignore the inner princess inside of her that fumed at all of this illegal trading that was probably destroying their economy little by little. Gods, when she got back to Abdul, there were going to be some major changes revolving around smuggling and the blessed black market. But then again, after being involved in it for weeks on the Valley, watching her new friends work, coming to realize that they weren't bad people in the slightest, she might have a difficult time fighting against them. Maybe she could find a way to work alongside them once she became the queen.

It didn't matter anyways. She didn't know when she would ever get back to Abdul.

"Oh, I see. Do you do all the meetings here?"

"Yes, always. For the most part, we can trust everyone in here. Most of them are either affiliated with the Vacci's already, Sahar, or Eria. Alfie and I have a little agreement. It works out for everyone."

Suddenly, Sahar's head snapped up and saw where Roman and Alida were sitting. Her eyes met Alida's and she appeared to be confused. She excused herself from Eria and made her way over to where they were.

"What are you guys doing here?" she asked in way of greeting. Alida noticed that she appeared nervous and was breathing faster than normal.

Roman was just as confused as Alida. "I came to get drinks with Nova while we waited for you. Is something wrong?"

She glanced at the blonde, who still sat at the counter, sipping her drink with perfectly manicured fingernails. "It's Eria. There are problems in the black market right now. Apparently only days ago there was a huge battle between Auntican and Orinthian forces on the border."

Alida felt her heart drop in her chest. "What?"

Sahar nodded. "It's true. Eria had a shipment of silk coming from Auntica that was supposed to be in weeks ago but was held up by the battle."

"Well, what happened?" Alida demanded. "Who won?"

"The Orinthians did. Auntican forces surrendered and fled back into Auntica."

Alida let out a long sigh of relief. "Thank the gods," she muttered.

"Anyways, this meeting is going to run long." She shot an apologetic look to Alida. "I'm sorry, Nova. I really wanted to go shopping and hit the town, but it appears that duty is calling. For Roman as well."

Alida shrugged. "That's okay. Another time, maybe."

Sahar nodded enthusiastically. "Of course." She turned around and called out, "Jak?"

A man sitting at the bar looked towards them. Alida recognized him as one of the crew, with his bright red hair and face sprayed with freckles. He was one of the quieter ones but always at the dinners and activities. She had never talked to him directly, but he always greeted her when he saw her.

"That's one of my men," Sahar explained as Jak approached them, mug in hand.

"What's up?" he said quietly.

"Can you take Nova back to the ship, please? Roman and I have some business to take care of that will probably take until the evening."

"Of course," Jak said, finishing his drink and setting it back on the counter. "Cover my tab?"

"I got it," Roman said, smiling at Alida. "I'll see you later, Nova," he said, sliding off the stool and walking towards where Eria was sitting.

Sahar put a hand on Alida's shoulder. "I'm sorry, I really am."

Alida shook her head. "Don't be. I completely understand."

Sahar pulled her into a quick embrace. "Thank you, Nova, you're a darling. I'll see you tonight at dinner then." With that, she headed towards where Roman had just gone.

Jak offered Alida his arm and she took it as they exited Alfie's. Slowly, they made their way back towards the harbor and the Valley. Her companion didn't talk much but was kind. After a few minutes, they arrived back to the ship.

Jak helped her up the plank and then said goodbye as he went back to his quarters. Alida decided to do the same and started towards her cabin. She walked in and smiled at the sight of Louie, sleeping right where she left him. She sat down next to him and petted his furry head. He sighed contently but didn't wake up. Alida laid her head on her pillow and stretched out next to him, feeling very happy with her day. She didn't know she had fallen asleep until she felt the boat lurch.

She sat up and stared out the window. Aram was a tiny speck in the distance, a few blinking lights. It was nighttime, way past when they were supposed to have dinner. Alida furrowed her brow. Sahar normally woke her up to go eat, but the captain hadn't tonight. She was probably busy dealing with whatever she had been dealing with at the bar. Louie was gone from her bed too, asleep in the corner of her room.

Alida sat up and went to look for her friends. When she stepped out onto the outer deck, there was no one there. That was also strange. Normally, a few of the crew lounged around outside and smoked something. The lights in the mess hall were dim too, and there was barely any noise coming from it. She decided to go to the captain's quarters and see if Sahar was there.

She knocked twice loudly and said, "Sahar?"

There was no response. There was light creeping out from below the crack in the door so Alida assumed that she was in there. She knocked again.

"Nova?" The voice came from behind her.

She whirled around to see Roman standing there, dressed in the same clothes he had been wearing when they went out in the morning. "Oh, it's you. Where is Sahar?"

Roman shifted, almost uncomfortably. "She didn't feel well when she returned from her meeting. I believe she is resting."

"Oh. What's wrong with her?"

He shrugged. "I'm not exactly sure but she asked to be left alone."

Alida sighed, "Alright, I suppose. I missed dinner so I'm going to go to the mess hall and see if Cook has any leftovers." She started to walk, but Roman grabbed her arm and pulled her back.

She tore her arm out of his grip. "Roman! What was that for?"

He looked down at her. "I'm sorry, but I don't think you should go to Cook right now either. I think someone may have picked up a bug when we were in Aram. There was no dinner tonight because he was taken ill as well. If you go back to your cabin, I'll get one of the crew to bring you something."

Alida took a step back from him. "Oh-okay. Is everything okay, Roman? You seem a little off."

He shook his head and tried to smile, but it came out tight and strange. "Yes. It's fine, Nova. I'm just worried about Sahar and the crew. Listen, you should probably just stick to your cabin until Sahar gives the okay. We don't want you getting sick now, do we?"

"Of course not. Sure, yes. I'll stay in my cabin."

Roman nodded. "Thank you. It's for the best. Just give it a couple days and I'm sure everything will be back to normal."

Alida said, "Okay, Roman. Goodnight."

"Nova? Wait a second." He rummaged through his pockets before taking out her charm bracelet that he had carried for her.

She took it from him, mumbled a thank you, and turned the other direction and began back towards her cabin. There was a feeling of disappointment as well as confusion starting to grow in her. The past couple of weeks with the crew and Sahar had been paradise. She didn't want to have to stay in her cabin again. There was something about Roman's explanation of the illness that seemed strange as well. She had met the Cook before; he was a gruff, old man who could barely walk but always managed to feed a crew of fifty every single day, three times. She had a hard time believing that he would be taken out by an illness.

She returned to her room and waited for the tray, which came thirty minutes later, and consisted of a turkey leg, mashed carrots, and rice. Alida wrinkled her nose. Cook had definitely made this. It was incredibly delicious and had his signature medley of spices. He was not sick, so why had Roman lied to her? She left the tray outside her door and decided not to push it. Sahar had been talking to the black-market woman, Eria, with an intensity and determination that Alida had not seen before. Something was going on and it had to do with that. Roman was probably keeping her out of the way to protect her. After all, as much as it felt like it sometimes, Alida was not a part of this crew. In all reality, she was a guest who had paid to get passage to Nagaye. What she did not pay for was to become a member of this family.

Yet the past few weeks, it had felt like she had.

She shook her thoughts away and laid down on her bed. Alida didn't want to go to sleep. She had been sleeping for most of the day. She wanted to go out and sing for the crew or play cards with a half-drunk Sahar.

She forced herself to close her eyes and eventually fell into slumber.

The next few days remained much the same. Alida was confined to her cabin, as suggested by Roman. She didn't see Sahar a single time and three times a day, food was placed in her door. Louie was her only companion. When she went to the bathroom, the crew gave her a wide berth, and she didn't see Roman out and about anymore. She was starting to grow seriously concerned.

Was Sahar actually sick or did something happen in Aram that made her scared? Could it possibly have something to do with her past, or with her husband, who had been lost to the sea? Perhaps she had found out what really happened to him. Could he be dead? She prayed to the gods that he wasn't. Sahar deserved to find him and get to live out the rest of her days with him. Alida saw the look in her eyes when she spoke about Dax. Losing him would break her.

But maybe not. It was hard to see a woman like Sahar and imagine her ever breaking.

It was about the fourth day of being confined that she snapped. She awoke with an anger she hadn't felt in a long time, the anger she had first felt when she found out about Grafph's plot to begin with. Alida rolled out of her bed, pulled on some clothes, and marched out the door to find out what was going on.

Once again, the crew gave her a wide berth. Sahar was nowhere in sight but Roman was standing next to the ship's wheel. When he saw her, his face darkened. She didn't care. She didn't care if she got sick, she was done being forced to stay inside.

"Nova, what are you doing? I thought I told you not to come out," he said, his tone something she had never heard from the man before.

Alida crossed her arms. "See, that is the thing, Roman. I paid for passage on this damned ship. I don't have to do anything you say, or frankly what anyone says. I can't stay in my cabin for another minute, or I might kill someone."

Roman's mouth pressed into a firm line. "Nova." It was the way he said her name, with some sort of desperation, that made her hold back the rest of the comments she was about to unleash on him.

"What?" she asked, taking a deep breath through the nose.

"I promise you; it'll be safer if you just stay in the cabin. Please. Sahar is really sick, as are most of the men on the crew. I don't want you to get it either. I know it's terrible but please, just trust me. It'll be easier for everyone."

She opened her mouth to snap a reply and then hesitated. Princess Alida would snap and demand that she be allowed to go wherever she want, because she had indeed paid for it. Princess Alida would stomp her feet until she got what she wanted. Princess Alida would slap Roman across the face for even suggesting that she follow his orders.

But she wasn't supposed to be Princess Alida anymore. She was Nova Grey, the youngest of four older brothers, who would probably indeed listen to what Roman was saying. She was so close to Nagaye, but she couldn't let Nova Grey go yet. Without saying a word, she whirled back around and stomped back to her cabin.

It was the last time she had attempted to leave the place.

She began to sink back into a sadness and homesickness without the company of the crew. She spent hours staring at the picture of Rider with tears in her eyes. She missed him so much and wished he were here with her. She felt more alone than she ever had before. There was always a certain element of loneliness with her after her mother died. But without Rider or her father, it had multiplied. She didn't even care about getting to Nagaye anymore; she wanted to go home, to Abdul. She wanted to be with her people, helping them in the war, advising her father, discussing battle plans with Rider. She wanted to start organizing the hospitals for wounded soldiers and food drives to send up to the front. She wanted to get her hands dirty, not run away like some scared little girl. As she racked her mind, she couldn't even remember why she decided to leave anyways. Yes, she was the Last Heir, or at least believed to be and yes, Grafph was after her. But who would she be safer with than Rider? In the midst of the Orinthian army.

The days continued in a lull, as Alida stopped eating the food that was set in front of her door. She wasn't hungry anymore, only tired.

It was about the seventh day of isolation when she heard a shout from the deck above her.

"Land ho!"

Alida jumped out of her bed faster than she believed possible. She shoved the picture into her pocket and quickly jammed her feet into her traveling boots. Sickness be damned, they had arrived. It all rushed back to her, the thrill of her journey and the confidence of being independent. She had made it to Nagaye and was finally safe from Grafph's reach. Once in Nagaye, she had enough money to afford passage to their capital city of Triad, where an Orinthian embassy stood proudly. And then, all she had to do was wait. Weeks after leaving Abdul, her castle, her family, and her life; she had done it. She had reached Nagaye.

It was her second time in the country, but she tried to dress for the occasion. Nagaye was a desert country, and almost always blistering hot. She changed into a white, cotton skirt and green blouse. She tied her hair behind her head and made sure her picture was tucked into her pocket. She quickly shoved all of her clothes and belongings into her sack, which was difficult considering how messy her cabin already was. In a matter of minutes, she was ready to go. She looked around for little Louie, but he was nowhere to be seen. He was probably on the upper deck. After a few days of being isolated with her, the dog had grown tired of being cooped up and abandoned her for the freedom of the decks. Since then, she had only seen him a few times, which only added to the sadness.

Alida looked at the cabin one more time with a sigh of contentment. Although it had felt like a jail cell for the past few days, she would probably end up missing her little wooden room. Strangely, she had a feeling that she would be back on the ship, after everything was over.

Straightening up, she closed the door to her room and began walking towards the upper deck.

The wind hit her as soon as she stepped up onto the main deck. There were, again, very few crew members out and about, especially considering they were about to sail into the harbor. Normally, everyone leaned against the rails and cheered as they made it to land, a silly tradition about celebrating not dying by the sea. However, only a few essential crew members worked the sails. Alida could see Lao steering the ship but no one noticed her, as she walked to lean against the side where most of them usually stayed.

There it was: Nagaye.

When she had come here before, they sailed out of a port only a few miles east of Abdul. She couldn't remember where they had landed in Nagaye, but from the sea, she could tell it was a desert. Where they were landing, however, it wasn't so obvious. There was a city, she saw, perched on the sea, but in the distance, was a forest, with lush trees and flora. Alida wrinkled her brow. They were coming into a different part of Nagaye, then. She wasn't even aware that there was anything but desert in their neighboring continent, but then again, she wasn't familiar with the terrain.

As they sailed closer, she began to observe the buildings that were in the city. They were all made of stone. That was also strange. Most of the cities in Nagaye were made of the clay and sand, buildings that ensured cool air would stay in and the hot air would stay out. The way these buildings were designed would not focus on insulation at all. It was strange, for Nagaye. Unless…

"I don't think we're sailing into Nagaye," Alida whispered to herself.

She whirled around looking for a crewmember. "Hey!"

Sahar and Roman stood about fifteen feet behind her. She hadn't even heard them approach her, but she saw them now, a crossbow in Sahar's hands, pointed directly at her heart.

"Sahar, what are you doing? Where are we? This isn't Nagaye!" Alida demanded, starting to walk towards her.

"Don't move unless you want me to shoot you," Sahar said, sternly and sadly. There was a mix of anger and regret within her expression.

Alida froze. "Sahar, Roman. What is going on here?" She pointed towards the shore. "Where are we?"

Roman spoke up, "Tilda, Orinth." His mouth was set in a straight line, his face holding a seriousness she had never seen before, the tone of his voice low and threatening.

Tilda. A city north of Abdul and on the coast. The closest major Orinthian city to the-the Wilds.

Alida took a step back. "I think you've made a mistake," she whispered, holding her hands up.

Sahar shook her head, eyes stone-cold and unreadable. "No mistake," she said quietly. "I'm sorry, Princess."

Chapter 15

Tenir, Orinth

It was nighttime when they reached Tenir at last. Since the night by the spring, it was like fate had given them a break. Every day of travel had been easy, the weather perfect. They hadn't run into a single other person in Orinth, which was incredibly lucky. In Auntica, it was only Adriel who was in substantial danger. In Orinth, they both were unwelcome. Indira had new spring in her step since being in the Forest Dembe and they had reached the coastal city in almost four days. Sawny was grateful for the ease of their journey. She was also grateful for the way things had been. There had finally started to be some light in her life, some hope. She was traveling with a man whom she was beginning to consider a friend. She had a lead on the mysteries of her past, courtesy of Matahali. She was working a case that would give her more money than she had ever had, even if she didn't solve it. And, since she had jumped in that gods-damned spring, the darkness had stopped following her, because she knew what Adriel said was true. It would always be there, a part of her, but it would never ever control her. She had come to terms with the fact that she had a scar and that was what freed her from it.

It was never truly nighttime in Tenir. The times she had been there, the city had always been a glow, buzzing with life, even when the sky was dark. Even on the brink of war, it hadn't changed. Tenir was surrounded by a large, stone wall, to protect itself from outside forces. It was the hub of trade and the economy in Orinth and was well protected. As they rode in towards the iron gate of that wall, they could hear the lull of the crowds in the street. Sawny felt her breath catch when she saw that there were guards at the gate, checking each group that came in. She glanced at Adriel on his horse.

"Get on the other side of me," she ordered him.

He didn't ask but led his horse to the other side of Indira, still about 100 yards or so away from the guards at the gate, who were too busy talking to each other to notice.

She nudged Indira in the side, but not hard enough to make her run or even trot. She needed her horse to look relaxed and be walking as they went towards the city walls.

"What's going on?" Adriel asked softly.

"They're checking people. It's not surprising because there is a war about to happen, but they won't let us in if they know I'm Auntican. Just be quiet and go along with whatever happens."

"That is not reassuring," Adriel mumbled.

"Trust me?" Sawny responded through clenched teeth.

"I do," was all he said in response.

"Then don't make eye contact with them. Keep your head down and don't say a word."

"Done."

As they approached the guards, Sawny could tell they weren't officials from the Orinthian army. No, these men were clad in black cloaks with long bows strapped to their backs. They were protecting the city, but not under official orders from the king or anyone affiliated with the royals. They were vigilantes and could be so much more dangerous than a typical soldier.

"Woah," Sawny commanded Indira, who stopped as the guards finally noticed them.

There were two of them, both somewhat young and fresh looking. One leaned against the entrance to the gate while the other stood directly in front of their path, hands on his hips. She had come through the gate before but there had never been guards outside of it. Tenir had taken it upon themselves to keep their own city safe, which Sawny respected. But now, it was causing them another pointless risk between them and their mission.

"What's your business?" the man standing in front asked them.

Sawny took a deep breath and put on her best Orinthian accent. "We come from the south to get away from the potential fighting. We're staying with a family member."

The man narrowed his eyes. "What's your name, ma'am?"

"Anya Deloris," she said, maintaining her thick Orinthian.

"And who is the man?"

"My lover," Sawny said, without hesitation. "And he prefers to keep his identity to himself." She hoped to the gods Adriel was keeping his head down.

The two guards exchanged glances before one nodded at the other, and he began to open the gate, "Be safe, now," the first guard said, stepping out of their way.

"Thank you. You as well," Sawny said, moving her horse forward and into the city.

They walked a few yards beyond the gate before both consecutively breathing a sigh of relief.

"That was fantastic," Adriel whispered. "Where did you learn to fake Orinthian that well?"

Sawny chuckled, "I am Orinthian, remember? My mother taught me the language when I was small, and I learned the accent when I was here, always just in case I ever needed it. It's worked out several times."

"I'll say. What was that about a lover, by the way?"

Even though she wasn't facing him, Sawny felt the heat rush to her cheeks. "Orinthians are less likely to get married than Aunticans but almost all of them have a lover. It was the most believable story I could come up with. Anonymous lovers are very common here so I knew they wouldn't ask questions."

"I see," Adriel said. Sawny could sense he was smiling without even having to look at him. "So, where are we going then?"

"Jare's. He's always there so I figured I could get started on my investigation right away." She felt a slight thrill when she said the words. For the last few weeks, she had just been a traveler but now, she was back where she belonged, investigating and putting the pieces of the puzzle together. "We're going to have to find somewhere to stay tonight because I don't want to face the guards again."

Adriel agreed. "I'll find one while you're working. I'll have to stay inconspicuous and keep my head down, but I'll manage."

Sawny knew the streets of Tenir well, with its brick buildings and smooth stone roads. Almost every block they passed was crowded with people, drinking, talking, laughing, singing. Forget the war, forget Auntica, forget all of it, the people in Tenir always knew how to have a good time. Already, Sawny could smell the salt of the sea and she breathed it in deeply. She had always loved the smell, had always been tempted to take to the water, just to see what was out there. She never did, but always enjoyed going to seaside cities, especially Tenir.

They were still far away from where the water would be, but she would make it a point to at least visit it before they left, even if it could only be briefly.

This stay might last longer than the rest of hers, as she remembered vividly the picture Matahali had shown her, the door that led to the answers. Adriel had promised her that they could search for it, and she would tear apart the whole city if she had to. How credible the vision was, she couldn't know. But for the first time ever, she had a lead, and she'd be damned if she didn't see where it led to. But, for now, her focus was on the man who killed Adriel's brother.

"Where is this mysterious Jare?" he asked her.

"We're getting closer," Sawny told him, steering Indira through the crowd, who were starting to pile onto the streets instead of staying on the sidewalks. Adriel followed closely behind her. After a few minutes of riding through the town, she turned her horse down an abandoned alley. It was different from the one that had been in the vision, and familiar to her, as she had been there multiple times. There was not another soul in the alley, nor was there any light, but Sawny knew where she was headed. She stopped Indira and jumped off, looking up at her companion.

She began to tie Indira to one of the hitching posts on the wall. The many times she had been at Jare's, Indira had been safe and unbothered in the alley, so she never worried about anyone stealing her horse. "I don't know how long I'll be, and I don't want to leave you," she said to Adriel.

He patted his horse on the side. "I'll be fine, Sawny. I'll go look for an inn somewhere and hopefully, get us a room. At this time of night, maybe the innkeeper will be so drunk, he won't fight a man from the Wilds. And if not, well, I'll be fine. Don't worry about me and just focus on your work. I'll be back in an hour, okay?"

Sawny sighed. "Okay. Just please be careful."

He smiled at her. "I will. I promise."

She returned his smile and then turned around to the door that was behind her. She knocked once and paused, and then knocked another four times. There was silence behind the door, but she heard Adriel turn back and head out towards the streets again. After a minute of standing in the dark, hand on her knife, the door flew open.

She could only see the silhouette of a figure in the doorway but heard his familiar voice loud and clear, "Sawny Lois. Is that you?"

Sawny put her hand to her forehead in mock salute. "In the flesh."

Jare Micheals grabbed her hand and pressed a sloppy kiss to it as he pulled her into the building. "Come on, let's get out of the dark so I can see the most beautiful woman in all of Auntica."

Sawny laughed breathlessly. "I'm Orinthian right now, Jare," she said as he pulled her along through a dark hallway, "I'm not exactly bragging about the fact I'm Auntican." A newcomer would not have noticed that the hallway was not going straight, but at a slight angle downwards.

"Orinthian Sawny it is. And good call. The news came about a week ago that my Orinthian brethren just defeated an Auntican army at the border."

Sawny wasn't exactly sure how to feel about this. She hadn't yet decided about her position in this war. Professionally, it would be best if Auntica won, for her business and her home in Illias. But politically, she was starting to lean towards Tieran in Orinth, after her encounter with the soldiers in the woods. Grafph had something to do with the apparently widespread search for the Orinthian princess and that fact made her uneasy about her king. So, upon hearing the news about the battle, she remained unfeeling and neutral.

"I trust you to keep my secret?" Sawny asked him.

Jare chuckled. "Of course. There are not many people here right now anyways. All of my smugglers are out and about somewhere. I think there are two other scholars wandering around, doing research. But of course, they don't compare to the best investigator on the entire continent."

Sawny rolled her eyes at him as she started to finally see some light at the end of the hall. Together, they walked into the secret library of Orinth.

She had been there multiple times, but it still amazed her. A gigantic room filled to the brim with books and records and scrolls and manuscripts and maps and everything you could possibly imagine. It was significantly larger than the building that housed it because it was all underground. In the center of the room was one long table, also stacked with books, where two others sat, pouring over books. They stood on a balcony above all of it, with a spiral staircase that led down to the main floor. From where Sawny was standing, she couldn't see where the shelves ended.

She looked over at Jare, who was looking proudly at his place. He had inherited the library from his father who was a former royal scholar and used his own underground connections to help it gain its notoriety. He was older than her by a few years, tall but very scrawny, with small limbs and lengthy legs. Jare always took pride in his brown beard and long tangled brown hair that reached his shoulders, almost longer than Sawny's. He had made it a pattern to dress in whimsical clothing and tonight was no exception; he wore a pink and white striped shirt with white pants and pink shoes.

"Never gets old," Sawny said as they started down the stairs. "How did you hear me knock?"

"There's always one of my people watching who walks down our alleyway. As soon as you stepped foot in the alley, I knew. Speaking of which, who's the tall, scary-looking warrior you rode in with?"

Sawny laughed. "My client."

Jare turned back and raised an eyebrow at her. "Client?"

She nodded. "I'm not telling you his name or who he is or anything."

"Oh, I know. I'm just surprised you brought a client."

"Money," Sawny said and Jare laughed at that.

They reached the floor of the library, the shelves of books towering over them, making Sawny feel like a tiny bug on the floor.

"What is it you're looking for today, Sawny?" Jare asked her.

The library was unique in the fact that yes, it held books of all kinds, but it also held records of almost everything that had ever happened in Orinth, as well as many other places. Jare had hired a team of advanced scholars to write detailed accounts of any major events, events of interest, anything. If something had happened, chances were it had made it into the records. Considering Jare's connection with the black market, even underground activities were recorded.

"I don't have much to go on. Do you remember twelve years ago when a group of exiled Wilds kidnapped the princess and tried to ransom her for a giant portion of the Orinthian treasury?"

Jare nodded. "Everyone remembers that."

"Exactly. But the one thing no one can seem to figure out is who killed the men holding the princess. And how."

Jare stroked his beard like an old philosopher. "You're not the first person to come in and ask that, you know."

Sawny nodded. "I assumed as much."

"Why don't you come into my office and we can talk about it before we start the research."

"You're going to help me?" Sawny asked him as they started walking towards a small room under the balcony that acted as Jare's headquarters.

"Of course, I will. Normally I let you go off and use whatever you need all on your own, but I'm interested in this one. For my own purposes but I'll always help a friend in need." He grinned at her.

They entered his office, which was a large space with an oak desk in the center of it. Jare slid across it and sat in his chair while Sawny took a seat in front of it. The office also had its own ice box, a set of leather furniture in the corner, as well as his own personal shelves, with what Sawny was sure were invaluable books and scrolls.

"Do you want a drink?" Jare asked her, pulling out a bottle of something from the ice box and grabbing two glasses from under his desk.

"What is it?" Sawny asked.

"Orinthian wine."

"Then that's a yes."

Jare smiled and poured the red liquids into both glasses, sliding hers across the desk. She took a long drink of it and sighed. She hadn't had any since she had left her apartment in Illias and had forgotten how much she loved the stuff. This bottle especially tasted fresh and cold, better than what they sold in Auntica, probably because it was closer to the source.

"So, Sawny, tell me everything you know about the case so far," Jare said, grabbing a piece of paper and a pen. Whenever Jare agreed to help her with cases, he always took his own scribbled notes that Sawny could never read. He claimed it helped him to stay organized, but she couldn't tell.

"None of what I know is confirmed with evidence, besides the fact that the men took the princess. That she was saved by an unknown person. That someone killed the seven men in the caves who took her to begin with. I don't know if the person who saved her is the same person who killed the men. My sole purpose is to find out the identity, and ideally the location, of this man."

Jare wrote as she was speaking. "You've told me what you have so far backed up by hard evidence. Now what are some of your conjectures, that you don't have proof for."

Sawny took a breath. "Well, it is said the men in the caves were killed with some sort of dark magic. They had no wounds when their bodies were discovered and apparently, the bodies couldn't be burned or disposed of in any normal way. They had to throw them to the sea just to get rid of them."

Jare didn't say anything but his hand moved ferociously across the paper. After a few minutes, he looked up. "I have heard that as well. Over the years since that has happened, many souls have wandered into my library, seeking the answers. They want the identity of the man, but for a much different purpose than what I believe you're seeking it for."

"And what is that purpose?" Sawny asked, cocking her head.

Jare leaned forward. "How much do you know about the Last Heir, Sawny?"

"The Last Heir?"

"So, nothing, I'm guessing," he said. "Not many people do, especially Aunticans."

"What is it?"

"You have undoubtedly heard of the Shadow Wall, right?"

Sawny opened her mouth and closed it. "Yes. A little too much lately for my comfort level."

Jare nodded grimly. "Me as well. It's all connected, I believe, with what's happening right now. There's so much to dive into, so I'll start at the beginning. All of what I'm about to tell you is backed up by the records we hold in this library and you are more than welcome to fact check any of it. I can help you find them if need be."

Sawny held her hand up and reached into her jacket pocket and pulled out her small notebook. She had decided to leave her case file with Adriel and their gear and just take notes and transfer it over later. She got out her pencil and motioned for him to begin.

"The Shadow Wall is the barrier between our world and the Shadow Realm. However, it is believed that there are some people who still have the blood of demons within them, which gives them access to the power of the shadow. What that means exactly, I'm not sure, but it's not an amicable power. The reason the Shadow Wall came to be in the first place was a demon blood sacrifice that created it. It works the same way to reverse it. The blood of a demon destroys the wall, essentially removing the barrier and giving the shadow world access to our world once again."

Sawny couldn't make her pencil move and stared at Jare. "You're joking, right? There are demons among us?"

Jare shrugged. "Some believe that there are. However, how many and who and all those questions cannot be answered. There is only one line of half-demons that is important when it comes to the Shadow Wall. You see, it can't just be any one person's demon-blood. It must be from the original line of the demon who sacrificed himself to create the wall. We call it Arca's line, as Arca was his daughter, and the first half-blood to exist. If someone would have spilled her blood on the wall, it would have been destroyed. Arca ended up marrying into the Orinthian royal line."

"So that means-" Sawny began.

"-that every Orinthian royal born from the same line is part-demon," Jare finished.

"And capable of destroying the wall," Sawny said, her heart beginning to race. It all began to make sense, why the Shadow Wall was being talked about and why Grafph was looking for the princess. Her king was planning to open up the Shadow Realm. Unleash it on the world. And for what? Did he honestly believe he had the power to control it? She could feel her heart beating faster and faster as it started to make more sense.

"We ran into some soldiers a few nights ago," Sawny told him. "And they had these pamphlets with a drawing of the princess on them. Grafph is tearing the continent apart looking for her. He's going to try and destroy the wall."

"I believe so. If all the records of the Orinthian line are correct, then it would be Princess Alida's blood that could destroy the Shadow Wall."

"So, it's the princess herself who killed the men then? With her shadow power or whatever?"

Jare shook his head. "You see, that's the thing. It may have been Alida with her powers, it's a possibility. But there is another hypothesis for who the Last Heir is. It is highly unlikely that the purest demon blood would stay in the same family for a thousand years. There are some who believe that a bastard child was born, carrying on the line, and hid from the world. Through that person, Arca's line continued, while the Orinthian line went back to being human. You see, for some reason, it is only the firstborn who inherits the blood. The second born and so on are always human."

"So, there's a possibility that it's not Princess Alida who's blood is required."

"Correct."

"But Grafph, he thinks that it is?"

"Also correct. Which would explain why he is tearing the continent apart trying to find her. The word is she left Abdul and fled towards the sea. No one has seen her in weeks."

"But if it's not her, then who is it?"

"That's the thing, we wouldn't know who it is. But if you consider that it isn't Alida, the obvious answer is whoever was in the caves with her is the Last Heir."

"And it's that person who used their powers to kill the exiles then."

"It appears so."

Sawny let it all sink in as her pencil began scribbling across her paper, writing detailed notes of all she had just heard. Her head was spinning, both with questions and with fear. Grafph believed that it was Alida who would destroy the wall and was prepared to kill her for it, though there was a chance that it was the other person in the caves that day. She prayed that the princess was as far away from Auntica as she possibly could be. Preferably, far from the continent.

"So, our question now is, who was the person in the caves? And also, how does Grafph plan to control whatever comes out of the wall?"

"The second one I can give somewhat an answer to. The person who spills the blood of the Last Heir will have the favor of whatever emerges. More or less, will have them under their control. It's not a guarantee, but that's the myth."

"And the person in the caves?"

Jare shrugged. "That's up in the air. Have you ever heard the term 'True King'?"

"It's safe to assume I know nothing at this point."

He chuckled. "Fair enough. The True King is a term used to describe the real 'Last Heir', if it isn't Alida Goulding. Since all of this was discovered, shortly after the wall was constructed, there have been detailed records of who was believed to be the True King. It was part of the underground, groups of people who were dedicated to tracking whose blood could destroy the realm. They still exist today. Some believe that the line never broke, and it is Alida Goulding. Other believe the line split early on into the family of a wealthy noble. Others believe it happened much later. All of these groups have banned together to form, what they call, the Society of the True King. They meet and discuss, and research and they've been doing it for centuries. Obviously different members, but the passion for the truth remains."

"And you know all of this how?"

"A few of their members have come here for research. I let in some but reject others. Some of them are a little too passionate bordering crazy."

"So, have any of them found the right person?" Sawny asked.

"There's no way to really tell, unless of course, you spilled their blood on the wall and it worked. But I've seen a few hypotheses that make some sort of sense, you could say. They are all in one specific manuscript within this library and you can start there. I can have someone go get it if you would like," Jare suggested.

Sawny nodded her head absent-mindedly.

Jare left her sitting in the room, clutching her pencil, her mind moving a thousand miles a minute. There was so much new information she was receiving, she tried to focus on one part of it at a time. The Last Heir. Alida Goulding. Shadow Wall. Grafph. True King. Blood sacrifice. Arca's line. Orinthian royal firstborn. None of it made sense. But she needed to only look at what affected her case for the moment. Right now, all she had to figure out was who the possible other person in the caves was, the one who killed Adriel's brother. But it connected so easily because whoever killed Zelos would also no doubt be the Last Heir and the True King. Adriel was set on avenging his brother's death but at what cost? The person would kill Adriel before he even got close to them.

It was still possible that the Last Heir could be Alida Goulding but how? Did she use the power when she was six years old to kill seven men who kidnapped her? It did not seem likely, but Sawny had no clue how the power worked. It was too much for her, without even considering the fact that the king of her country was trying to unleash the Shadow Realm on them. She didn't care that she was Auntican; that was a terrible, evil idea for everyone. She had always trusted her king and he had always ruled fairly. There was something else going on, there had to be.

She tried to take more notes, but she couldn't transfer her thoughts onto paper at the moment.

Luckily, Jare came back in, carrying a giant manuscript, bound together with twine and almost falling apart. He set it on the table, where it landed with a loud boom.

"This is it," he announced to her, patting the front cover. "This is the many, many theories of the Society of the True King. My people have compiled almost every single hypothesis that they have heard. It's yours to go through. And while you do that, I'm going to go find something that I've been keeping around for you."

"What?" Sawny asked.

Jare just winked at her. "Trust me." He strode out of the room, leaving her speechless and very, very confused.

She decided just to dive right in. She opened the front cover and blew the dust off the pages. In messy handwriting was a synopsis of what Jare had just told her, the creation of the Shadow Wall, the blood of Arca that had to be spilled, the Last Heir and the True King. She skimmed it once again, just so it was in her head completely. Still, she couldn't wrap her brain around it. This would not be easy to explain to Adriel and the more she read, the more she realized how much pressure was on her.

He had made an oath to his tribe to kill his brother's killer, which left the risk of exile and never being able to enter his homeland again. She had grown attached to him and would refuse to let that happen. But, regardless of who it was, the person who killed Zelos had the power of the shadow. A power that they probably would use in self-defense should some large man from the Wilds try to kill them to fulfill an oath. Then, the last person she cared about in this world would be gone.

The next hour she spent reading the manuscript, pages upon pages of various theories of who had the power, whose line was Arca's, and which person of the Orinthian royal line had the bastard child. Each theory ended with a selected person whom the writer believed to be the True King. Never did the writer plan to seek the person out and ask, but only hold the knowledge of who could bring about the Shadow Realm. They didn't want the wall to be destroyed.

Some of the theories were outrageous, stating the True King was actually Graph himself because of this or that reason. Some stated there was no True King, there wasn't even a Shadow Wall, that the Shadow Realm was just something made up by their rulers to scare them into submission. Sawny was positive that one wasn't true, due to the fact that Adriel had seen the Shadow Wall. Every time she came across a logical theory, she took note of it, writing down the most important details and the final guess at who the True King was. The compiled manuscript was thorough, as was all of Jare's research whenever she used it.

Jare checked in on her a few times, but was clearly busy doing something else, until he walked in and threw an envelope down in front of her. She was in the middle of leaning over the manuscript when she jumped back.

It was a smaller envelope, a bit faded, but in black ink on the front of it was her name. Sawny Lois.

She looked up at Jare. "Where did you get this?" she asked him, her voice cracking. The handwriting on the card was undeniably her mother's.

"A few weeks ago, a woman died who lived in an apartment across town. She frequented this library and had a large number of rare books. She was old.

We had an agreement that when she died, I would take her cats into my library and take care of them in exchange for her collection of books. We were good friends, and it was more of a joke than anything, but her cats live here now. As I was going through her collection, I found this."

With shaking hands, she picked up the envelope. "The woman. Did she live on the second floor in an alley, kind of like the one outside of here?"

Jare raised his eyebrows. "Yes, she did. How did you know that?"

Sawny shook her head. "I-my mother used to live in Tenir. I have no idea how this woman came to have this letter, but I suppose I should open it." The scar had opened, and the fresh pain of loss rolled over her in waves. Her mother and father were dead. The fact she could never escape.

Jare seemed to realize this and took a few steps back. "I'll leave you alone to read it then. If you need anything, just yell for me, okay?"

Sawny nodded and tried to say thank you, but her throat was dry. She heard him walk away and close the door and she took a long drink of her wine, before tearing the envelope open. There were a few sheets of paper in it, and she immediately began to read.

My darling Sawny,

I hope you never have to read this letter. If you're reading this, that means I'm gone. Please know that I'll always be with you, my darling daughter. At the time I'm writing this, you're out in the yard right now, playing with your father, of course. You've always been your father's girl. You're only eleven years old but already tremendously skilled with a bow. I'm taking a trip to Tenir tomorrow while you and your father journey to the Darklands. I'm leaving this letter with my dearest Sienna Courtright. I'm leaving it because if anything ever happens to me, you deserve to know the truth.

My loving husband, your father, is not your real father. Of course, he is real in the sense that every father is, you just don't share the same blood. Your father, your real father, is a man whom I've never been able to stop loving. Don't take this the wrong way, Sawny, I love your father so much. But there's always a piece of me that will stay with your real father for the rest of my days.

I'll start off by saying my real name isn't even Ali Lois. It's Marvolene Pere, but I always went by Marvie. I was born in Auntica but I grew up in Tenir my whole life, because my parents died when I was very young. I was raised by my uncle and his wife, Sienna, who now has this letter. They were so good to me. My uncle has since passed, but I do hope you get the chance to meet my aunt.

When I was seventeen, I fell in love with a boy here, so ridiculously in love as only seventeen-year-olds can be. Luckily for me, he felt the same way and just like that, he became my life. His name was Auden Frae and he was my entire world. He had no family either and worked all the time just to get by. My aunt and uncle always invited him to stay with us, but he declined, politely of course. He was everything I dreamed of having in a man. He was kind and sweet and gentle. He understood me better than I understood myself. We spoke in our own different language and became one whole person together.

Auden was broken. Something had happened in his past that he would never tell me about. He never took this out on me, and he hid it well, but I could tell. There was always a faraway look in his eyes, a sadness when he smiled that he could never fully rid himself of. Of course, being the young girl I was, I thought I could fix him and heal him and make him unbroken. I couldn't. But whatever it was didn't change his feelings about me. We were together for an entire year, the happiest year of my life, when something terrible happened.

We were walking home from a dinner after dark, holding hands and being silly when three men whose faces I will never forget attacked Auden. They grabbed me first and threw me to the ground, I was seeing double and I still don't know what I saw and heard. They said that Auden was dangerous and what they were doing was to protect Orinth. They tried to kill him, but I watched Auden kill all three of them, on his own. I don't even remember how he did it, I just remember him carrying me back to my uncle and aunt's. They were terrified and so was I. I remember he kissed me on the forehead and told me he loved me and then walked out the door. I never saw him after that.

It took me awhile to recover from that night, I stayed in my bed for almost a month, mostly from the shock of it all. Auden didn't come to visit me once. Then, I searched for him, for a long time. I wanted to find him for two reasons. One, I was in love with him, and I would never not be in love with him. Two, I was carrying his child. I had found out shortly after he left, and I didn't get the chance to tell him. I know without a doubt in my mind that he would've stayed had he known. I never found him. So, I did the only other thing I could think of. I ran.

I said goodbye to my aunt and uncle in a letter and I ran away, back to my home country of Auntica. I took all the money I had and bounced from inn to inn, so depressed and despaired. All I could think about was the man who I loved, who had left me. I didn't know why, and I didn't believe he would leave me with nothing, no answers. All he had left me with was a child. I am ashamed to say it, Sawny, but for the first nine months of your life, I despised you. I saw you as the bane of my existence, the reason why my lover was gone. And then, in some shabby little medicine house in Iyria, Auntica, you were born. The moment I saw your face, I fell in love again. I named you Sawny, which means Defender of Men. I chose this name because I knew you would be strong. And you were. Even as a baby, you were. I stopped running and settled in Auntica, working for a baker while trying to raise you at the same time. I met your adopted father, Caleb Ore, in Illias. He came to the bakery every day and was so shy sometimes, but it was adorable. He always talked to me and finally got the courage to ask me out to dinner. We married only three months after that.

Like I wrote earlier, I love Caleb. He is a wonderful husband and a wonderful father to you, the daughter who isn't his own blood. Even on days when I get so sad thinking about Auden and the life I once had, he is wonderful. I don't deserve him, and I believe that it is the gods themselves who blessed me with him, to give you a good childhood.

If you're reading this, it's because I didn't get to tell you this in person. When you were about eight years old, Sawny, I started getting threats. They came in the form of letters, at my place of work, at Caleb's, sometimes delivered to our cottage on the edge of the forest. It continued for years. We tried to investigate, to discover who they were from, but we never could. Each letter said the same thing 'I know who you really are.' Not even Caleb knew that I was Marvie Pere. The letters began to get more detailed. 'Where is he?' 'You're dead' 'The secrets of the past will come to destroy your future'. I was terrified and so was Caleb, but we kept it from you. He continued to ask me why they were being sent but even I didn't know. I assumed it had something to do with Auden. I didn't know how they found me or knew I had a connection to him or anything. My first priority was protecting you because they would hurt you if they found you, I knew.

At the time I'm writing this letter, I still am unaware of the identity of these men. I've never stopped looking for Auden, and now if you're reading this, I hope you look for him too. I've had time to forgive him. He truly is a beautiful soul, with so much darkness that he didn't deserve. Find him, tell him who you are, and get to know him.

If I'm dead, Sawny, and I was killed by someone, it was the people sending the letters. I don't know who they are, but you can find out. I'm not asking you to avenge me, please don't take this that way. You're probably tortured by the not knowing and this is how you know. But the first step of this is finding your father, Auden Frae. Once you find him, tell him what happened to me. Let him read this letter even. Then together, you can find out the truth.

Sawny Onica Lois, my beautiful baby girl. I'm sorry for not being a better mother. I'm sorry for not being able to tell you the truth, being so afraid I had to write it in a letter. Please know that I love you more than anyone in the entire universe. You are strong and you are powerful, and you can be anything you want to be. You are steadfast, my Sawny. I love you. Your father loves you. And I have no doubt that when you find your real father, he will love you just as much. Remember me, but move on from the pain and go live life to the fullest it can be.

All the love in my heart, Ali Lois/Marvie Pere

She wasn't sure how long she sat there, tears streaming down her cheeks, holding the papers with trembling hands. She read it one more time and then again and again until the words blurred together in one long black line. She couldn't contemplate it all at once. Auden Frae. The name of her real father. How he had left her mother because he thought it would protect her, not knowing she was carrying his child. And somehow, the men who were after him had found her mother and father and murdered them in cold blood. What was so bad about her father to make him enemies that severe? And was the only way to find their killers was to find her father.

Auden Frae.

She tried to say the name out loud, but the words wouldn't come out of her mouth.

Auden Frae. Her father.

Who was he? Where was he now? How could she go about finding him and what happened if she did? Her mother wrote in the letter her father wouldn't have left but would he even believe she was his daughter.

Sawny closed her eyes. Everything she had known was a lie. She thought she knew her mother. Of course, there were the days where she didn't come out of her bedroom, barely spoke or moved, but Sawny always assumed they were just bad days. Everyone had them. She had no idea how deep the pain ran within her. She didn't even know her mother's real name. That thought shook her to her core. Her last name was one that Marvie Pere had made up when she ran away. Sawny Lois should actually be Sawny Pere or Sawny Frae. Who even was Sawny?

She let her head fall onto the wood of Jare's desk as it began to pound with pain. What Matahali had told her would be answers had created even more anxiety within her than before. No, she thought, no, it didn't. It gave her answers to some of the questions she had been asking herself since the day her parents had been murdered. She knew the name of her real father and could use that to start seeking him. That answer would hopefully lead to more. And then what? Sawny asked herself. What happened after she knew all of the answers? The answers wouldn't bring them back. It wouldn't ease any of the pain of losing them to begin with.

But maybe, just maybe, there was a man out there named Auden Frae who she would find. Her own flesh and blood. Her father. She could meet him. Tell him her story, listen to his. Maybe there was a future there.

Her head was on the table when she heard Jare come back into the room and stop.

"Sawny?" he said, hesitantly. She could hear him taking heavy breaths, as if he had sprinted back to the room.

She lifted her eyes and turned around, hoping the crying wasn't as obvious as it felt. She pushed back her hair and shrugged her shoulders a few times to loosen up. It was pretty obvious and if Jare commented on her appearance, she might start crying again. "Hey," was all she managed to say.

Jare walked towards her. "Sawny, you have to come quick. Your companion, the man. He came back to the alley, with his horse. He stood next to it, waiting for you and these men, they came and grabbed him. He tried to fight; he managed to kill three of them, but he was outnumbered. They knocked him unconscious and dragged him. It just happened; we have to go now."

Sawny grabbed the paper and shoved it into her pocket. Jare ran out the door and she jumped to her feet, following him. Adriel. The terror that consumed her borderlined on hysteria, and then fell into a quiet, deadly calm. Adriel. Her mind switched, calculating. A group of men had grabbed him, but who? He had no enemies, but he was a man from the Wilds. It was always dangerous for him. He was an incredible fighter but even he would stand no chance against a mob of people. Did they take Indira? Indira had her bow and her arrow and all of their weapons and if she had run away, Sawny was left with the small knife she was carrying. It didn't leave her many options. She could throw the knives but against a group, that wouldn't help.

They ran back through the hallway towards the exit, two of Jare's men suddenly joining them. They burst out the door into an empty alley, where thankfully, Indira still stood, looking skittish, her ears pressed flat against her head. Sawny ran up to her and stroked her neck. Adriel's horse stood, also skittish in the alley, braying softly. She didn't hesitate before grabbing her bow and quiver from her saddle.

She ran towards the street, where the sound of the crowd was distant enough. She looked both ways but there were only people walking in and out of bars, no group of men with Adriel. Jare stood next to her, his eyes narrowed, scanning for him. "They took the corpses of the men they killed with them. They were just here a moment ago." Sure enough, Sawny noticed pools of blood on the cobble stones, beginning to ooze through the cracks towards the street. She didn't have time to be disgusted by it or wonder what had happened.

Without a word, she turned around and ran back to Indira. In one swift jump, she mounted the horse and prepared to start riding.

"Wait, Sawny!" Jare yelled, catching up to her. "I'm not letting you go alone."

"That man, the one I'm traveling with. He's from the Wilds. I don't know who they are but they're going to kill him."

Jare's face turned white, "The Wilds?"

"I don't have time to debate with you about people from the Wilds, Jare. I have to go NOW," Sawny said, kicking Indira in the side.

Jare held his hands up, trying to stop the horse, who reared up with a loud neigh. "SAWNY! I don't care he's from the Wilds. If you trust him, I trust him. Let me send some men with you, to protect you. Please, let me do that. You don't know who they are or where they've taken him. You don't know how dangerous they are! You could be killed!"

"I would rather die than watch anything happen to him, Jare. Move aside. If you send men, then fine, but I'm not waiting another second."

Jare glared at her. "Sawny-"

"Take care of his horse until I come back," she said firmly.

"Just wait a moment-" he began but it was too late. She steered Indira around the man and towards the street. She heard him call after her as she turned the corner and started riding towards the outskirts of town. She didn't know where she was going or how she would find the men who had him. She didn't even know where to steer her horse as she wove through the crowd as fast as she could go.

But she had her bow and her arrows and a drive in her heart that she would do anything in her power to keep anything from happening to Adriel. Even if it meant killing again.

Chapter 16

The Outskirts of Orinth

He could hear people talking around him, but Rider didn't know where he was. He was laying on something soft and covered in blankets. His muscles were all relaxed and he was warm but not too much. For a second, he wondered if he was back in his room in Abdul, in the castle where he felt the safest. Was he waking up before the sun rose to get an early morning run in, a habit he had since he was just a teen? Would Alida and Tieran meet him for breakfast on one of the balconies and discuss everything from politics to petty castle gossip? The thought of being home filled him with so much joy, he felt utter disappointment when he woke up and saw the top of a canvas tent.

He observed the room around him while still laying back. He was clearly in an infirmary somewhere, laying on a cot in a long row of them. There was another man in the cot next to him, sitting up and eating something, while chatting in fast Orinthian to another man. The tent had to be large, as Rider couldn't see the entrance flap. There were several people walking around and kneeling besides beds, talking to patients, giving orders to others. It was just generally busy, and Rider had to wonder why he was here.

The battle came rushing back to him. They were fighting against Aunticans. They had surprised a camp of them that were going to attack Tenir. The battle had started off as a landslide victory but as more Aunticans got their bearings, the tides had begun to turn. Rider had been using the shadow to take out major threats when the boy-

The boy.

The Orinthian who had been stabbed in the chest and didn't stand a chance. The boy who, for some reason, had reminded him so much of Alida that he had lost it.

Rider sat up abruptly, causing the soldier next to him to jump.

"Easy there, mate," he said to Rider, with wide eyes. "You almost gave me a heart attack."

Rider glanced at the man, who was middle-aged and very large. He had blonde hair that was almost white and pale, pasty skin. There was a nasty cut that ran down his face and his right arm sat in a sling.

"Where am I?" Rider asked, his voice raspy.

"We're in Auntica, right on the border of Orinth. The infirmary tent to be more exact. The lesser of the two. This tent is supposed to be for those with cuts and bruises. Major wounds and inflictions are somewhere else. You've been out for a few days. You won't get much time though; we're supposed to be moving out tonight," the man explained.

Rider looked around. Almost every cot was occupied with men, most of whom were awake. He looked down at his hands. He had been out for days? What had happened? He remembered specifically trying to limit his use of the shadow. He had only used it against people who were a direct threat to Orinthians at that exact moment. But then, he had used it to show the boy his home and that had driven it over the edge. That, and the illusion of Alida that had almost immobilized him. The combination had tanked him completely, apparently for days.

"Do you know where we're going?" Rider asked.

"A messenger from the king arrived this morning. There are no more armies from Auntica on the way to Tenir so it's safe for us to leave where we are. The king wants our entire army to come to Lou. Apparently, the brunt of Auntican forces are gathering and planning an attack on the city soon. We don't know why but we've been called to come join them."

"So, we won the battle with Auntica then?" Rider asked.

The man nodded happily. "Yes, with very few casualties. They fled away further into Auntica. We dismantled their entire platoon, killing or capturing a good half of them."

Rider sighed in relief. Well, at least they had won. But the victory did not taste as sweet as it normally did. He couldn't seem to rid himself of the vision of the boy on the ground, impaled by the sword. Was the victory worth losing that one boy, who probably had a family and a future somewhere? Rider shook those thoughts out of his head. This was a war, and he was an advisor to the king. Harsh as it might sound, he couldn't become emotionally attached to the thought of one boy's life. Or perhaps he should. He had always been told to look at the bigger picture, what's best for Orinth as a whole but wasn't that boy an Orinthian? Didn't he deserve to live as much as any one of them?

He desperately needed a drink.

He swung his legs over the side of the bed and stood up, before immediately falling back. His head was still spinning, and he couldn't even hold himself up. A nurse spotted his attempt and rushed over to him.

"Don't try to stand again," she ordered him. She was a younger looking woman but looked like years of being a nurse for soldiers had hardened her. There were wrinkles around her eyes and her mouth and her bright red hair had streaks of grey in it. Regardless, she was beautiful, and Rider couldn't tell how old she was. Anywhere between thirty and fifty.

"You don't understand," Rider said to her. "I need to see the general immediately."

She eyed him. "You must be delirious." She grabbed a pitcher of water from one of the tables and poured him a large glass. Despite her calling him crazy only seconds ago, Rider took the glass from her hands and gulped it down. She filled it up again and he drank the second glass just as quickly.

"I'm not," Rider said, though the stars in his eyes said otherwise. This sensation was familiar. It used to happen all the time as a teen when he used his power too much. It was almost like a shadow 'hangover'. "I'm the advisor for the general. My name is Rider Grey. I was supposed to stay back at the general's tent during the battle, but I went and fought instead. I need to see him, he knows who I am." Rider was aware of the fact that he was beginning to babble incoherently, and it probably wasn't good for his case of being a not crazy person, but he couldn't stop himself.

The man on the bunk next to him snorted, "Yeah, alright. Not delirious."

The nurse agreed. "I'm sorry, sir. I'll try and get a message to the general that you're here, but I can't let you leave. You've been out for several days and we couldn't even figure out why. There were no injuries besides a few scrapes and bruises and no serious trauma to your head. Why don't you just lay back and rest."

"But I've been resting for days!" Rider protested, also realizing he sounded like a child.

The nurse helped him to lay back into his pillows and tucked his blanket in. "I'll bring you some food and something to do."

Rider shook his head, biting back some choice words he had for the nurse, and closed his eyes. Don't do it. He thought to himself. Now is not a good time to do it.

But it was too late. The shadow reached out and latched onto the nurse's mind. Her eyes glazed over, and her body swayed a little as she spoke softly, "Actually, I'll take you to the general now." She reached towards him and helped him to stand up.

Rider tried not to think about what he just did as he leaned on her for support. The shadow, even after being out for days, was just as powerful and ready for action. He hated using it on innocent people, but he had to see the general. He needed to plan and strategize and see where they were at. It was his job.

The nurse led him through the rest of the tent where he observed a number of people with different afflictions. None, however, were very serious. He knew this was the tent for minor injuries but still, it was optimistic to see the men, sitting up, talking with other soldiers, drinking and eating. Most of them were happy with the results of the battle and looked ready to keep moving, keep defending their country.

They walked outside to where the camp, once again, was assembled. The whole place, like the infirmary, was bustling. Some men were training, practicing fighting with swords, doing push-ups, running back and forth between tents. Others stood in groups socializing with one another. It boosted Rider's spirits to see it all, almost exactly as it had been before they fought the first battle against Auntica. Clearly, everyone was continuing to celebrate their victory. Rider thanked the gods for it. Winning the first battle in a war often determined the final outcome. Winning that battle instilled confidence into their men, made them proud and ready to fight again for their country. It was important to have a skilled army, but it was almost just as important to have a mentally sound one.

After a few minutes of walking, Rider managed to take steps by himself. He thanked the nurse for her help, swallowing a lump of guilt in his throat, and continued towards the general's tent. He found it a few minutes later, with several more higher-up soldiers talking and laughing outside of it. They barely even noticed Rider slip past them and into the tent flaps.

Gael sat at his desk, hunched over a map of the continent, studying it thoughtfully. His head snapped up as Rider entered.

"Rider!" he exclaimed, jumping to his feet. "Thank the gods! I didn't know what happened to you!"

Rider shook the man's outstretched hand and smiled. "You didn't think you would be the only one to sneak into the fighting, did you?"

Gael laughed. "I hoped so, but I knew you wouldn't be able to sit out. It's hard for anyone. I'm just glad you're okay. I had some of my men look for you among the sick, but they couldn't find you. I thought something might have happened."

"Well, here I am," Rider said, spreading his hands apart. "Apparently I was out for a couple days. I don't even remember what happened to me," he lied.

"Are you hurt?" Gael asked, concern creeping into his voice as he looked Rider over.

Rider shook his head. "Not at all. I must have been knocked out or something. But I'm fine now. How are you?" He tried to change the subject as fast as he could.

Gael looked concerned, but he answered, "I'm very happy, at the moment. We won the battle with very few casualties. What more could I ask for? The remaining soldiers of the Auntican army retreated far back into Auntica. We let them go. The entire tactic worked perfectly. I couldn't have imagined it going any better."

"Congratulations," Rider said, clapping him on the back, "We really did it then. Won the first battle in this whole mess of a war."

Gael shrugged. "I shouldn't get any credit. It really was the men who did everything. They're great soldiers."

"You got them here. Your speech was incredible. A good leader makes men want to fight for them and you did. So, I think you get a little credit for that."

Gael shook his head but still smiled. "Maybe. Do you want a drink? You look like you could use one. And some new clothes."

Rider noticed for the first time he was in a pair of white cotton pajamas, probably provided by the infirmary. He also didn't smell the greatest and suddenly grew self-conscious of his appearance in front of the general.

"Gods, I need a bath," Rider mumbled.

Gael laughed again. "You're fine. But you're welcome to use the one in here and change into some of my clothes. Did you lose your bag?"

Rider felt a fresh wave of panic as he realized it. His entire bag was gone. Which would be fine, as it was just clothes and some equipment, but the picture of Alida. He had been carrying it in the pocket of his soldier's clothes and now it was gone. He didn't realize someone had changed him into these clothes.

"I guess I did," Rider said, trying to keep the tremor out of his voice. "I'll have to head back to the infirmary tent and see what they did with it."

"Be my guest. And afterwards, you're welcome to come back here and use the bath, change into a fresh set of clothes. I have a meeting with all of my captains about our next move and that will take me awhile, so you'll have the place to yourself," Gael said.

Rider still felt somewhat sick to his stomach, both from the shadow and the thought of losing the picture. He thanked Gael and walked back towards the exit of the tent. He hurried back through the camp again, not exactly knowing where he was going. He briefly asked one of the passing soldiers to point him back towards the infirmary. The soldier did and he found himself back in the giant tent full of the slightly battered soldiers. He tracked down the nurse who had helped him.

She saw him and rolled her eyes. "You again," she said as she wrapped a bandage around a man's ankle. She was sweating and looked as if she hadn't slept in several days. The battle had taken a toll on more than just the soldiers.

"I'm sorry. I hate to bother you again, but I was wondering where my personal effects would have gone after they changed my clothes."

She looked annoyed. "They would be in the storage room. Because you didn't have any identification, yours probably ended up in the general pile of lost things."

"Where is that?" Rider asked, fighting hard to keep the impatience out of his voice. This woman was a hero, a nurse who had left her home to come help the war effort of Orinth. She had probably saved countless lives and he refused to get irritated with her.

She pointed towards a flap at the back of the tent. "In there. You're welcome to go look yourself."

"Thank you very much," Rider said, trying to be genuine. "I truly appreciate everything you're doing to help."

The nurse's gaze softened a bit. "Run along," she said, returning to the soldier's ankle.

Rider hurried towards the tent flap and entered. It was a small room, with tables piled with junk that smelled rancid. He didn't care as he started to dig through the pile. It was mostly clothes, all the same Orinthian soldiers' uniforms and small trinkets. It appeared more than one man brought someone's jewelry. He found necklaces, bracelets, single earrings and more and he felt bad for any men who had lost them. They carried a piece of the people who they had left behind, a way to keep them beside them, if it was going to be the end.

He was making a mess. He threw dirty clothes and trinkets onto the ground as he searched for the picture. The room was starting to reek from the dirty uniforms and from Rider himself.

By the grace of the gods above, the picture fell out from the pocket of a uniform. Rider almost started to cry as he stared at it. Alida's smiling face stared back at him. The picture was more beat up than it had been days ago but gods, at least he had it. If they ever saw each other again, he knew Alida would comment on the quality of the picture. He was sure hers would be in perfect condition somehow, without a wrinkle or a rip, and that she would tease him mercilessly for it.

He wouldn't care though. He would just be lucky if he ever saw her again.

When she left the castle, the girl who had been like the little sister, he was worried and concerned for her. There were a lot of reasons but the fact that the Auntican king was searching for her, believing her to be the Last Heir? That topped the list. Regardless of whether Alida was the sacrifice he needed or not, he was going after her.

But Alida was safe. She was going somewhere far away, from the war, from the Shadow Wall, and from the king who wanted to sacrifice her. Thank the gods for that. If he could choose one person to survive the war, it would be the princess.

Rider looked around the tent for his gear bag, but it was nowhere to be seen. It didn't matter. He had the picture and could borrow the rest. He exited the storage and the infirmary tent and found his way back to Gael's, gripping the picture in his hand, as if it were about to spontaneously float away. The general was gone from the tent, presumably going to go to the meeting with the captains.

He stripped out of his clothes and stepped into the small, mobile bathtub the general had somehow acquired. He washed his hair and his body as quickly as he could before borrowing some of Gael's less fancy general-like clothes, which happened to be black pants, a white shirt, and a black jacket. Rider realized his sword had also gotten lost during the battle, but that he didn't care about that. He wasn't actually very good at sword-fighting and had never had to rely on it before. Regardless, he had to be carrying some sort of weapon. He decided on strapping one of the general's extra throwing knives to his belt.

He shaved his face for the first time in weeks and then sat down on one of the cots and stretched out. The pain in his head had dulled significantly but was still present. The soreness in his muscles had dwindled and his body felt almost normal. Physically, he had recovered from his use of the shadow, but mentally, he was lacking. But he could feel the shadow beneath his skin, not a single part of it diminished whatsoever. If need be, he could use it this very second.

Rider took a deep breath and exhaled out his mouth.

He often wondered what his life would be like without his power. He wanted to be rid of it desperately but there were times like he felt that it was the only thing he had. There were times where he felt he was getting high off the capability of his power. He knew it wasn't him that felt this way, but the shadow making him feel that. Still, when he felt the most alone, the shadow had been there, a calming presence that always ensured him that if things went wrong, he could protect himself.

Of course, someone would eventually try to destroy the wall. Although undoubtedly evil, the temptation of releasing a shadow realm on their world would overcome someone. He was surprised it had taken this long. Arca had been born almost a thousand years ago. The truth that the blood of her heir could destroy the wall had existed since the construction of it. The knowledge was protected and very few people knew it, but it was there.

The fate of the world rested on the True King's shoulders, whoever they may be. If Grafph found them and took them, he need only to slit their throat and let their blood run fall onto the wall. What would happen to the life they had created for themselves? What would happen to all of them?

He didn't want to find out.

These thoughts plagued his mind and he decided to ignore them and find something to eat in the general's tent. There wasn't much but he selected a piece of bread and some venison jerky. He ate it quickly and got more. He couldn't remember the last time he had eaten, and his body suddenly felt overwhelmingly undernourished. But then again, he did run away from the infirmary and the nurse, who probably would have given him the nutrients he needed after being out for days and days. It didn't matter now. Plus, he had emptied the bed at the infirmary for someone who actually needed it. Not him. The soldier next to him had informed him that they had won the battle.

Now, the king was sending for them in Lou. Rider wondered why but didn't question it. He trusted Tieran and was eager to see his old friend, to see how he was holding up. He was grateful to know that his king was alive and well. Hearing news of him only increased his relief. He wished he could have some sort of way to know how he was doing. But no news was good news, he told himself. Rider ate some more of the general's food and drank another glass of water. He tried to turn off his thoughts, but it was difficult. He leaned back into his pillow and closed his eyes.

About an hour later, he awoke to the sound of Gael coming into the tent.

Rider sat up. "How was it?"

Gael looked simultaneously distressed and happy. "Good and bad, I suppose you could say."

"Oh?"

"The good is we're set to leave tomorrow for Lou. If the path is clear, we'll reach it in a matter of days and be reunited with the rest of the army. I don't know the reason the king has sent for us but I'm sure it will be revealed once we reach it. I'll be happy to give the command to someone else, one of the higher generals."

"Don't sell yourself short," Rider said. "I know when I give my report to the king, I'll mention the fact that you're one of the best generals I've ever seen."

Gael grinned. "I'll throw in some money if you butter me up a little more to him. But it's okay. I'm one of the younger ones. I'll still have a position of command, just not the leader of all of it. It'll be nice to give up some of the responsibility."

Rider could tell he wasn't telling the truth. Gael desperately wanted to lead the entire army and felt confident he could do so. He didn't say anything, though. Gael had just won an important battle as a leader and Rider had no doubt that he would have many more victorious moments in his military career. There was no need to rush it right now.

"I know whatever position you're put in, you'll do your best," was all Rider replied.

Gael nodded. "That's a given. I also got the final number of our losses. There are casualties but very few deaths. It could have been a lot worse, but any death is bad. Still. The rest of the men, according to my captains, are healthy, happy, and eager for the next part of the battle. I don't think it could've gone much better."

"Thanks to you," Rider said.

"Thanks to the men," Gael corrected and Rider, once again, was amazed that someone so young could be such a skilled, yet humble leader.

"Maybe," Rider said.

Gael started towards his desk and he stopped just before it. His eyes locked onto something and he reached for a small piece of paper. Rider realized he was staring at the picture of Alida, which he had forgotten to return to his pocket. He cursed himself inwardly. He was not being responsible with his one possession on this trip.

"This is the princess, isn't it?" Gael asked.

Rider nodded. "Yes, it is. She's like a little sister to me and we split a picture of us before we left. Something to remember each other by," he said.

"She's beautiful," Gael muttered. "It really is a shame."

Rider felt his heart stop. "What's a shame?"

Gael looked up at him from the picture. "Well, that's the bad news, you see. A messenger arrived this morning, with news from some of the Orinthian spies. It seems that the Aunticans have taken Princess Alida. Just a few days ago.

He found it difficult to breathe. All of his muscles froze up at once and he suddenly felt dizzy. Rider hoped to the gods he didn't just hear what he thought he did. "What?"

"We know he's been trying to find her. Some of our men reported pamphlets with her picture on them that were being distributed by some Aunticans or something."

Rider tried to control his rising anger. "Why wouldn't you tell me that?" he asked softly.

"I didn't find out until today," Gael replied. "All I know is what was in the report they gave me. Princess Alida was fleeing to Nagaye on Sahar Bow's boat, the smuggler on the Dela River, who works with one of the Vacci's. They betrayed her to the king, in Tilda. We're not sure what his play is, with the princess. We can't think of a reason he would want her, besides a ransom. It's confusing."

The shadow was terrifyingly close to exploding. His senses shut down as the reality of the news hit him. Grafph had Alida. She hadn't gotten away to Nagaye. She had made it onto a ship and had set sail, but someone had betrayed her and given her to the king. The king had her and was going to kill her in the Wilds because he thought it would be her blood to open the wall.

Slowly, Rider stood up and took the picture from the general's hands. "He's going to kill her."

Gael's head snapped towards him. "How do you know that?"

Rider took deep breaths to try and numb the shadow, that was coming dangerously close to erupting. His heart pounded and he was suddenly alert again. They were going to kill Alida, and it was for nothing. "I have to go," was all he said.

"Rider?" Gael said, stepping closer to the man. "What's going on?"

"Grafph thinks killing Alida is going to amount to something that it won't. I have to go."

"Rider, you don't even know where they are. What are you going to do, ride around until you find her?"

He wanted to destroy something, anything to release the mixed emotions of fear, panic, confusion, but mostly anger. Every time he blinked he could see the picture in his mind as clear as day; Grafph standing over the corpse of Alida, holding the knife that he had used to slit her throat, him spreading her blood on the wall, and whatever would come afterwards. Alida, strong, courageous, bossy Alida. The girl who he had saved from the caves by killing seven people, given her a second chance at life and she was about to lose it. He stared down at the picture of her, at her sixteenth birthday party, the surprise he had thrown. It had only been two years since then, but she still looked the same as she did in the picture.

And now the king had her.

He would kill the king first, when he found her. He would make it long and painful and let the shadow do whatever it wanted to him. He would then track down the person who betrayed her. He didn't know who it was, but he would find out and they would meet the same fate as Grafph would. And if anything had happened to Alida, a single scratch or anything more, he would make every person responsible suffer until it was made right. The more he thought of it, the more he could feel the shadow, coursing through his veins, eager to enact the revenge at that moment.

"I'm going," Rider said, tucking the picture into his pocket and looking back up at Gael.

Gael looked distressed. "Rider, I need you here-"

"-No, you don't," Rider said impatiently. "You know what you're doing, and you will be fine. March to Lou, join the king's army, and keep fighting for Orinth. I'm going to find the princess."

"The king won't like this. This is against his orders. You're supposed to be advising me throughout this. I don't know if I can do it on my own."

"You just did it on your own, Gael. You don't need me right now, but the princess does," Rider said, clenching his teeth.

Gael shook his head once more. "The king won't like this, Rider. Not at all. He wouldn't want you going off by yourself in the midst of a war when who knows what will happen? He won't like it."

"He won't like me going to save his daughter?"

"Rider," Gael pleaded. He ran a hand through his hair and made a sound of frustration. The two men stared at each other.

"What can I say to make you reconsider? And if you find Grafph, if you find the princess, she will be heavily guarded. There will be no way to save her with only you. It's a suicide mission," Gael said, taking a breath.

Rider laughed under his breath, no joy in the sound. "Trust me, Gael, I will be fine. Take care of yourself." He turned around and began walking out of the tent, ignoring the general calling after him.

He found his horse in a pen with some of the other captain's horses. Starlight, the name that Alida had given him. Rider climbed onto his horse's back and led him out of the pen. He pulled the picture out of his pocket, not to look at it, but to use it to track her. It did technically belong to Alida, it was her birthday present two years ago. The shadow moved within him, feeling the picture, before he knew where she was, the mental scent. She was still in Tilda, at the moment. She was still alive. If she wasn't, he wouldn't have been able to sense her with the shadow.

Rider left the camp within a matter of moments and began the long trek up to Tilda, to save the princess of Orinth.

Chapter 17

Tilda, Orinth

She sat on the bed inside a small room of some inn in Tilda. She took long and deep breaths trying to calm herself from hysterically crying but it was growing hard not to. When she looked under her door, she could see the shoes of some guard standing outside of it. The window was too small to climb out of. They had taken everything from her, her weapons, her gear, her extra clothes, her money and had left her with the clothes on her back and the picture of Rider tucked into her pocket.

Alida was going to die.

She realized it the moment Sahar called her a princess, only hours ago on the ship.

"I don't know what you're talking about," Alida had managed to mutter after Sahar had spoken, gripping the back of the ship. They were getting closer and closer to the shore, to the harbor. They were almost three hundred yards away, close enough to where she could see people on the docks.

"Yes, you do," Sahar said, once again adopting a tone of indifference. "You're Alida Goulding, princess of Orinth, heir to the throne."

"No, I'm not," Alida said slowly. "I'm Nova Grey."

"Stop it, Princess," Roman said, wearing a stony expression. She barely recognized him compared to the boy who had shown her around Aram only a week ago. "We know who you are."

She stopped. "How?" was all she said, putting her hands behind her back so they didn't see them trembling.

Sahar sighed. "Eria Elliot is based out of Abdul. She's grown up there. She knew who you were the second you stepped through the door of Alfie's."

"That doesn't explain why you're holding a crossbow at me, Sahar." The fear had disappeared, replaced by complete and utter rage.

"Eria went on to explain that the king was offering an immense reward for Princess Alida. We contacted him in Aram, through some Auntican spies, and were told to meet in Tilda to hand you over." There wasn't a trace of emotion in her voice. Gone was the girl who for the last three weeks had become Alida's best friend. The girl who painted her fingernails and toenails and did her hair and dared her to chug an ale. The girl who was going to take her shopping in Aram and show her the sites. That girl had disappeared, replaced by the captain of the Valley who wanted a reward.

"You're supposed to be my friend," Alida said, her voice low.

"You knew the king was coming after you." Sahar glowered at her. "You knew, and you still boarded my boat and put every single member of this crew in danger. If he had found you on his own, he would've destroyed everything I've worked hard to build."

"I did what I had to do to protect MY country. Because I'm Orinthian. If the king takes me, it will be devastating to the war effort, so I left. Your boat just happened to be the one I took, Sahar. And now what? You turn me over to the king of Auntica, our enemy country. You're disgusting."

Roman shook his head. "I told you, princess. We do things for profit. We don't care about this war. We don't care about if you win or Auntica wins. We care about our business and our crew."

"I hate you both," Alida said, a tear slipping out of her eye. "Betraying your country for a profit. I guess I couldn't expect much from a whore," she spat.

Sahar flinched as if she had been struck. Roman glared at her. "That's enough," he said firmly.

"Is it? You know what?" she said, reaching into her pocket and taking out the picture of Rider. "I think I ought to get out of your hair." She gripped the picture in her hand, holding on tight, took a step back, and dove off the boat.

She didn't consciously make the decision to jump off the boat, it just kind of happened. Alida gasped as her body met the surface of the water. It was absolutely ice cold. She knew it would be, Tilda was way farther north than Abdul, but it was still a shock. She had tried to take a deep breath before her plunge, but she didn't know if she did. She opened her eyes. The current was strong but luckily, she was a good swimmer and could hold her breath for a long time. Years and years of competitions with Rider had ensured that. Who could hold their breath longer? Rider always won but sometimes they would be under for three or four minutes before she had to come up for a breath. Although, those times she was prepared to swim. In her cotton skirt and blouse, she was far from ready for the plunge.

She started swimming, slowly to conserve energy, towards the shore but away from the harbor. The boat couldn't follow her into shallow waters. She had to move fast though. She swam deeper, trying to remain out of sight. Her brain had gone into survival mode, ignoring the absolute pain of their betrayal, and focusing on getting away. If they caught her, and handed her over to the king, it was a death sentence. There was no other choice but to do everything in her power to get away. She had left her bag on the ship. She had nothing but it was far preferable to being turned over for a profit.

After five minutes, she came up for air and turned around. The Valley was far from her, sailing towards the harbor. She could just barely see the figures on top of it. Alida took a couple deep breaths and turned back towards the shore. There, almost two hundred yards from her, she could see a small cove. It would be too difficult for the ship to sail into it. That was where she had to swim to. She panted. Already, she was drained but she had to keep going. Drowning wouldn't do her any good either. She took a couple more breaths and then started.

The water was so cold it numbed her body, but she kept going. She wouldn't stop until she reached the shore. She had no choice but to keep going. Dying was not an option. The picture of Rider stayed clutched in her hand. She couldn't lose it, no matter what. It might be waterlogged and wrinkled after this, but she didn't care. It had gotten her through this journey, and she wouldn't lose it.

It took her ten minutes before she made it to the shore. Alida dragged herself onto the sand and fell onto her stomach. She was both freezing cold and sweating at the same time as she laid there, breathing hard. Her soaked clothes made it worse, but she had nothing else. She had to move. She couldn't sit and lie here because they would find her. They weren't far from the harbor and they would figure out she would be on the shore.

Every muscle in her body quaked as she got to her feet and stumbled forward.

The city was close to the cove and she could already see people walking around and going about their own business, not noticing the soaking wet girl who had emerged from the water. She had to find someone to help her but who? She knew no one in Tilda and she wasn't sure mentioning that she was the princess of their country would do anything. The king was offering an immense reward for her capture and return to him. Sahar and Roman were both Orinthian and they hadn't thought twice about giving her to the king for that reward.

The reality of their decision hit her like a ton of bricks. Sahar. She had spent more time with Sahar than she had spent with any other girl her age in the last 18 years. She finally thought she had it, a best friend. Of course, she always had Rider and knew he would always be in her life, but he was more of an older brother than a best friend. Rider wouldn't stay up late with her and gossip about stupid, silly stuff. Well, maybe if she begged him to, he would. But Sahar had become something different, even though she had only known her for a few weeks.

And Roman. She was starting to like him. Really like him.

When he told her about how they felt about profit, she didn't like that. But she never thought that she would be affected by it. The pair had decided to turn her in to their enemy king for money. Didn't they have enough? Roman was a Vacci for gods sake.

She felt a tear slip out of her eye as she started walking towards the city. She would find an inn. She would tell them who she was and pray to the gods that they would give her a place to stay instead of reporting her to some Auntican or gods forbid, Sahar. Hopefully, they would give her some new clothes and some materials and then she was getting out of Tilda. She wouldn't sleep until she was miles away from the cursed place. Then, she would look for Rider. She wasn't going to get to Nagaye, she had accepted that. Sahar was the queen of Orinthian sailors and Alida was no longer safe. Eria had recognized her; anyone could be next. But if she found Rider, she would stay with him. His soul sucking shadow power or whatever it was would protect her. Maybe she should've stayed with him in the first place, but it was too late now. The seed had been sown and now she had to deal with the consequences.

She regretted calling Sahar a whore. The look on her face had been worth it, but she shouldn't have said it.

Alida laughed at herself as she stepped onto one of the stone streets. Sahar had sold her out to the Auntican king and here she was defending her.

In her wet, cold clothes, gripping the picture with white knuckles, Alida stepped into the first inn she saw, an old, almost falling apart building with a cracked sign that read Sylvia's Stay and Play. She hated the sound of the title and had a feeling it was a brothel, not even a hotel, but she had to try.

She tried not to gag at the smell as she stepped into the place. The overwhelming scent of human sweat and alcohol mixed together, and some sort of drug in there too. There was a bar and empty round tables scattered unorganized around a small room, with one woman, dressed in a shirt that barely covered her bosom, leaning bored against the counter.

Alida walked towards her, trying not to breathe. It was a pigsty, but it was her only option. She couldn't risk walking around Tilda, looking for a better place than this one. It wasn't a large city, and with such a large crew, they could be able to cover all the streets in their search for her. It had taken her twenty minutes to walk from the shore into town, stumbling and tripping several times as she shivered. In that time, it was possible the Valley was docked, and they were already looking.

The woman who was scantily dressed looked up at Alida, her brown curls bouncing. "Can I help you?" she said, clearly annoyed.

"I need a room to stay in," Alida said through clenched teeth.

The woman looked her up and down. "What happened to you?" she asked, suddenly taking an interest.

"Long story," Alida said. "I really, really need a place to stay."

"Fine. You got money?"

"No. I don't."

The woman snorted. "I hate to break it to you, sister, but these rooms cost money. They're cheap but not free."

"My name is Alida Goulding," she said to the woman, praying to the gods for a miracle. "I'm the princess of Orinth and I was captured by people who are going to turn me over to the Auntican king. They took all my money and the clothes on my back are all I have left. If you give me a room, some food, a fresh set of clothes, and maybe a weapon of some sort, I'll be out of your hair in three hours. I just need to rest a little and then I'm getting out of this town. Please. I have access to more money than you've ever seen before. If you let me have this for free, I'll pay you twenty-fold of whatever you would charge me to begin with."

The woman stared. "Princess Alida Goulding," she repeated. "THE princess. Of Orinth."

Alida nodded impatiently. "My father is King Tieran, my mother was the late Queen Natasha. I live in the palace in Abdul. I'm eighteen years old and I am very, very cold and tired and hungry. I am begging you. Please."

The woman didn't look convinced. "How do I know this isn't some ploy to get a free room and food and gear. I haven't seen the princess before but I don't know she's you."

Alida swallowed back a sob that wanted to come out of her mouth. "Please. I give you my word. If you want it in writing, then fine. If there's some way I can prove I am who I say I am, then I will. But there are people coming after me and if they find me, they will kill me."

The woman looked her up and down before reaching below the counter and pulling out a piece of paper and a pencil. "I want it in writing," was all she said back.

Alida almost cried as she took the pencil and wrote: *I, Alida Goulding, will reimburse Sylvia's Stay and Play twenty-fold their regular charging price.* She didn't know what that was, but she had much bigger concerns than paying her back at the moment.

Alida slid the note back to the woman, who read it and gave her a brisk nod. "Follow me," she said, walking out from behind the counter and towards a set of stairs in the corner.

Moments later, she deposited Alida into a small, cramped, and frankly smelly room. "I'll bring you an extra set of clothes and some supplies," she said, about to close the door.

"Thank you," Alida said, putting her hand on the pane. She looked into the woman's heavily made-up eyes that were slightly on the bloodshot side. "But please, please don't tell anyone I'm here. I'll be out of your hair in three hours. Please."

The woman stared at her again and nodded, before closing the door all the way.

Alida started crying the moment it closed. Not because of the room, though it was dismal at best. A small bed in the corner and a single candle on the nightstand. The bed wasn't made and there was broken glass covering the nightstand. There were a few puddles on the floor from what, Alida did not want to know. She sighed though. The quality of the room didn't matter. She had escaped from them. She would rest now, change into clothes that weren't soaking wet, and then get out of Tilda.

She couldn't force her heart to rejoice, though. She still had to get out of the city. She still had to somehow find Rider. She still had to come to terms with the fact that two people who were close to her betrayed her and their country. Her country.

They didn't even know about the Shadow Wall, Alida suddenly thought. They thought they were giving her up to the king for a ransom or to hold her over her father's head. They had no idea that the king was going to kill her to try and open the Shadow Realm. They had no idea that it might not be her and he would do it for nothing.

She fell onto the bed and buried her face into her hands, taking deep breaths to stop the tears. No, she wasn't going to cry about it. Just like she had in the sea, she would keep going and not look back. If she stopped now and let all her thoughts and fears and problems crush her, they would eventually find her. Instead, she took her hair out of the knot it had been in and shook it out. It was cold but had started to dry. She unbuttoned the green blouse she had started the day in and took it off, standing there in only an undergarment and white cotton skirt.

The day had definitely not gone to plan. This morning, she thought she would be in an embassy, seeing some of her acquaintances from Nagaye. She thought, by now, she would be in a safehouse, far from Grafph's reach. She was still in Orinth. Normally, she hated leaving her home country. But now she begged to be anywhere else.

There was a quick knock on the door and the woman had returned. She set down a pile of clothes in front of Alida, a bowl of stew and a piece of bread, a package of some kind of crackers and a small dagger. "It's the best I could do," she said, closing the door before Alida had a chance to thank her. She would eventually, the payment in twenty-fold.

Alida reached for the stew first and consumed it in under a minute, letting it burn her throat but make her warmer. She used the bread to mop up the rest of the stew and was just as hungry afterward. She didn't touch the crackers though; she had to save them for her journey. She picked up the clothes the woman had brought her which consisted of white pants and a grey top. She had also included a pair of fresh socks, which Alida was glad for. Her shoes were sopping wet but the only ones she had. The dry socks would at least help that.

Her undergarments were wet, but she put on the new clothes. The pants were loose fitting, and the top was designed to only reach the navel, but it was far superior to the soaking wet skirt and blouse. She threw her wet clothes over the headboard of the bed to let them dry, so she would at least have a pair to change into. Then, she fell on top of the blankets and closed her eyes.

It was impossible to fall asleep between her racing thoughts and incredibly sore muscles. But she had to get rest. She wasn't going to sleep, after this, until Tilda was far from her. Eventually, sleep claimed her.

When she awoke, it was still light out. She wasn't sure how long she had slept but she stood immediately. Alida felt her clothes were slightly less damp and tied the pair of pants around her waist. She put the dagger in between the pants and her waist so it wouldn't fall. She threw her shirt over her shoulder and gripped the crackers in her hands. She took a few deep breaths and once again, tied her now dry hair into a knot on top of her head. She was ready. She wasn't going to look back.

She left the room and returned down the stairs, back into the main room of the inn. Alida headed straight for the door when a voice piped up from behind her.

"I didn't think I would see such a respectable person in a place like this."

It was unmistakably Roman's but she didn't stop to look. She took off running towards the door of the establishment, but his body crashed into hers before she even made it to the door.

She landed on the ground with a hard splat but wriggled out of his grip and rolled over. She grabbed the dagger from her hip, jumped to her feet and turned around.

Roman was already standing, staring at her in the same clothes he had been wearing this morning. He wasn't in any sort of position to attack but Alida knew better. He was always ready and alert because he was a damned Vacci. She was right to hate the family and she should've known better than to trust one of them.

"What are you going to do, Alida? Stab me?" he asked, nonchalantly.

"I will if I have to," she breathed. He was between her and the door and she would stab him if it meant getting away.

"You don't think there's more people waiting outside?"

"If there was, they would've come in here. Not just send you."

Roman shook his head and laughed bitterly. "It's such a shame, isn't it? I was really starting to like Nova Grey. The girl from Tenir with four older brothers who was smart and educated and beautiful. She seemed perfect."

"How did you find me?" she yelled. The woman who had brought her the clothes and food was nowhere in sight.

"I told you, I have people everywhere."

"I never should've trusted a Vacci. You're just like your father, aren't you? You'll hurt anyone if it means getting what you want," Alida spat, still holding the dagger in front of her. Surprisingly, it felt natural to her. The days of swinging her sword at nothing had paid off, apparently.

Roman shrugged but there was anger behind his eyes. "Your mistake. Like you said, I'm a Vacci."

"Do you know what the king is going to do to me?" Alida asked him. His face stayed the same, but she could tell she caught him off guard,

"He's going to use you as a ransom."

Alida laughed, shaking her head. "No. He's going to kill me. He thinks a blood sacrifice of an Orinthian firstborn will open the Shadow Wall. He's going to slit my throat and let it flow and he doesn't even know if it will work." Roman said nothing but she kept talking, "Do you really want my blood on your hands, Roman? Because if you turn me over to him, not only are you betraying your country but you're killing me. I know you hate me because I lied about my identity but are you really ready to send me to my death?" She was babbling and she knew it, but it was the only way she might stand a chance of getting away from him.

"You're bluffing," Roman replied, but she could see he was concerned and almost frightened at her words.

"I know you're not a murderer," Alida pleaded with him, her voice cracking. "You're a lot of things, but not that."

He shook his head. "I'm sorry, Nova. There's no other way."

"I can pay you much more than his reward. Two, three, four times as much," she said to him.

In the blink of an eye, he charged at her. She stabbed at him with the dagger, but he dove to the side and rolled into a standing position, using his hand to knock the dagger out of her grasp. She swung her fist at him, but he grabbed it, yanking her to the ground and holding her there with both hands.

"I don't want to have to hurt you," he breathed heavily, pinning her down. "But I will if you keep fighting."

She spat at him, a glob of her saliva landing on his cheek. "You're a bastard," she said, swallowing back a sob. It was over. There was no getting out of this. She tried to use her head to slam into his, but she couldn't move, and he wasn't anywhere close to her range.

"I'm sorry, Nova," Roman said, his blue eyes searching hers. The anger and the fear were gone replaced by something else that she could hardly read. It looked like regret.

"My name is Alida Goulding," she said, starting to lose breath from how tight he was gripping her.

"I guess it is."

And now, she sat inside the inn, wearing the same clothes the woman had lent her, holding Rider's picture.

Roman hadn't been lying; there were other men waiting outside. Once he had gotten her up, he had marched her to an inn streets away from the one she was staying at. It was much nicer, but the quality didn't matter because she was a prisoner. She had tried running as they were marching and had been tackled only seconds after. She tried climbing out the window, but it wasn't large enough. She tried luring the guard into her room and then attacking him to break free. None of it had worked. She had been in the room for almost three hours. It was getting dark out and she hadn't seen another person. She was hungry.

Alida had never contemplated her death before.

She didn't want to start now but there seemed to be no other choice, with death staring her in the face.

She knew she wasn't the Last Heir or the True King. Having Sahar and Roman betray her should have set off her powers. She hadn't ever been angrier than seeing the captain hold the crossbow at her heart and nothing had happened. No magical power had choked them out. Nothing had saved her. The king had it wrong and she would beg with him and plead with him and hopefully make him realize that she wasn't the person he needed.

Rider was.

She suspected it almost from the moment he told her about the True King. Rider knew, or at least strongly believed, that it was he himself whose blood would open the wall. He let her leave because either way, it would be safer to be away from Orinth. If she would've stayed by his side, it would have launched her into even more danger. By letting her think she might possibly be the Last Heir, he ensured she would leave Orinth. She had tried her best, but alas.

Rider was the True King.

Somehow, his family line had gotten the curse, gotten the evil power that came from the other side of the wall. One of Rider's ancestors was the bastard child that Rider himself had told her about. And it was his blood, Arca's blood, that would open the Shadow Wall.

If she had to die to prevent Grafph from finding out, then so be it. If she had to die to save a person she loved, it would be a worthy sacrifice.

If only she could say goodbye though. She wouldn't know how to put it into words, but she wanted to see her old friend, the brother she never had, one last time. She wanted to see her father and tell him how much she loved him and thought the world of him. She wanted to hug them both and wish that it weren't like this.

But it was.

There would be no goodbye. Tonight, maybe tomorrow, she would be handed over to Grafph. They would travel to the Wilds and he would kill her. She could try to escape on the journey to the wall, but she had a feeling the king would be well warned of her tendency to try to run. It was over.

"I haven't done everything I wanted to," Alida laughed to herself. "But I had a good run, didn't I?"

She had a wonderful friend and a wonderful father. She had danced with a boy in Rein who showed her what it was like to be young and free. She had made friends and lived while sailing on the Valley. She had really learned the true meaning of pain, after it all went away. But there was still so much left. There was so much she hadn't said. There were so many wrongs she needed to make right. Her country was in danger and she had to fight for it but now she wouldn't have the chance.

The door opened and one of the crewmembers, one whom she couldn't remember the name of, entered. He gave her a nod and set a plate of food on the ground and exited all before she could say a word or try to charge out the door. But she wouldn't say no to some food. If she were going to try and make a run for it at some point, she needed as much energy as she could possibly get. And rest assured, she would try to make another run for it. The dinner consisted of chicken, noodles, and carrots, along with a glass of water.

She snorted. They could've at least given her something stronger to get her through the next couple of days.

Alida ate the food and left an empty plate and glass by the door. She laid back down on the bed and tried to think of happy things. The smell of the garden in the morning. She would go on walks before breakfast and admire the incredible work of their gardeners. The smell of gardenias would always overtake the rest of the flowers, but she loved it. Occasionally, Rider would skip his typical morning run and join her. She closed her eyes and pictured it all so clearly.

Her thoughts were interrupted by the door opening. She sat up abruptly and opened her eyes.

Roman was back, standing with his hands in his pockets as if nothing had changed.

Alida laid back down. "Yes?"

He snorted, "I'm sorry to interrupt you in your chamber, your majesty- " he said mockingly, "-but we have to go."

Alida crossed her arms. "No. And it's your highness, by the way. I'm not the queen yet."

"Why do you have to be so damned difficult?"

Alida laughed out loud. "You're sending me to my death. Am I supposed to not be?"

Roman bit his lip. "The king isn't going to kill you. Sahar made the Aunticans promise."

She laughed even harder at that. "And the word of our- oh I'm sorry, my enemy king is valid? I thought you and Sahar were smart, but I guess I was wrong."

Roman threw his hands in the air. "You're impossible," he exclaimed angrily.

"Don't worry, Mr. Vacci. You'll be rid of me soon," Alida said.

He opened his mouth to respond but was interrupted as Sahar stomped in. "We have to go now," she ordered.

Alida didn't look at Roman at all as she stood up. Sahar stared at her, eyes narrowed, but she said nothing as Alida checked her pocket for the picture of Rider, just to make sure, and stepped into the inn hallway.

Two of the crewmembers stood outside, once again dashing her chances of running. Sahar stepped in front of her and the two men fell beside her as they began to walk down the hall. She heard the door close and Roman start after them.

"Where are we going?" Alida asked Sahar, trying to escape her thoughts as they walked back into the street.

"They're here to pick you up," Sahar said, as if it was her friends picking her up for a night on the town, and not her enemies about to kill her.

"Who is they?"

"The Aunticans," Sahar replied.

"Where?"

Sahar didn't answer and they continued to walk down the street. Alida thought about screaming and shouting for passersby to help her but that thought was shut down when she felt a crewmember behind her press a dagger onto the skin of her back.

"Don't get any ideas," Sahar warned under her breath as they continued to walk down the street.

She wasn't afraid, surprisingly. There was some sort of release when you accepted there was nothing else you could do. The fear was replaced by a mix of apathy and regret and despair.

Sahar made an abrupt turn into an alley and up a staircase to the second floor of a stone building. The guard behind her dropped the dagger as Sahar opened the door. She turned back to look at Alida.

"This is where I leave you," she said, eyes flashing.

"Leave me for dead," Alida laughed, no happiness in the sound.

"They told me they wouldn't kill you," Sahar responded. "I made them promise. You're a pawn in a political game, Alida. Nothing is going to happen to you." It sounded genuine but it was hard to trust the person who was handing her over.

"I truly, truly feel sorry for you if you believe that, Sahar."

She said nothing but opened the door and gestured at Alida to enter. Alida turned to take one more look at Roman, who stood in the alley, eyes on her. There was no more anger in his gaze, but fear. Genuine and real fear. At what, she wasn't sure. She tore herself away before she lost it.

She took a step into the building and Sahar closed the door behind her. It took a minute for her eyes to adjust but she was in a small apartment building, in the living room portion. There were a few couches scattered around and a dining set behind them. In the corner she could see a kitchenette and a hallway that she assumed led to rooms. There was no one in here and she wondered if this would be another prison for the day. The windows were barred somehow, and she had come through the only entrance. She tried the doorknob, but it was locked. Yes, this was her new prison. And she assumed that King Grafph himself was her captor, though he was nowhere in sight.

She remembered what Grafph looked like as clear as if she had seen him yesterday. He was a few years younger than her father and hadn't aged as much. He still had the black, shoulder-length hair he had when she was just a child. He always wore a slight smile on his face, with his chocolate brown eyes and smooth skin. Before the tension between their two countries had happened, Grafph had been like a second father to her. One of his daughters was the same age as Alida and she remembered vividly when they used to sneak down to the kitchens and steal treats, both in Orinth and Auntica.

She recalled her father mentioning something about Grafph not being himself and suddenly wondered what he had meant.

"You've made yourself at home, haven't you?"

The voice came from the dining room table, in some accent she had never heard. It sounded young but with a heaviness that came from age.

Alida turned around.

The woman standing by the table had long, golden blonde hair that reached her navel. She was utterly beautiful, with the smoothest, pale white skin and blue eyes. Her lips were perfectly red, and she wore a dazzling gown, for some reason. Alida wondered if she were in a dream as she observed the red, sparkly dress that Alida herself would've only worn for a ball. She wore a diamond necklace that Alida wagered was worth more than most people's homes. She stood tall and proud and elegant.

"Who are you?" was all Alida managed to say as she took the woman in. It wasn't Grafph nor his wife, that was for certain.

The woman frowned, still managing to stay gorgeous. "I'm surprised you don't recognize me, Alida. Given that we share the same blood."

"Who?"

The woman clapped her hands together. "Well, I suppose I shall introduce myself anyways. My name is Cassia Messina."

Chapter 18

Outside of Tenir, Orinth

S he had tracked them down before the sun came up. Sawny had ridden around the city, looking for any sign of the men who took Adriel. She didn't go into any buildings but looked in windows and looked for a large group. There were none. So she left the walls, passing through the other side of Tenir and towards the North of Orinth. It was all grassy plains from Tenir to the River Dela.

She emerged from the wall after hours of searching the city without a sign of him. Perhaps they had left. The thought of it terrified her. All of her emotions had disappeared. Replacing it instead, the feeling she had the first year after her parents were gone. Instincts. The need to survive. The desperation to save herself. Except it wasn't her life at risk; it was Adriel's and somehow it seemed even more important. But she knew if she started thinking about him dying, she would lose her focus. She wouldn't let him die, it was just that simple.

She began systematically searching for tracks. It wasn't easy, given that Tenir was a hub of activity day and night. There were still guards at the wall who gave Sawny a nod as she rode out of the city. The sun had not yet come up, but the sky was light. She jumped off Indira and knelt down on the ground, looking for any signs of a large group on horseback, according to what Jare had told her. It was almost impossible, with the number of tracks leading out of the city. Sawny bit her lip to hold back frustrated tears. She needed to find him. He could already be dead.

She followed the path outside of the city. They wouldn't have kept him within its borders, she had to believe, with a group that large. Beating someone and kidnapping them was illegal, regardless of whether the victim was from the Wilds or not. They would've taken him some place. Sawny was one person. She could travel faster than a group of Orinthians with a captive could. She would keep riding outside of the city until she found some sign of him.

By luck of the gods, she saw a flash of something on the ground. Sawny jumped off of Indira and picked up a piece of navy-blue fabric that had caught on something. She had no way of knowing if it was the men who had taken Adriel, but something in her gut told her it was. Listen to your instincts. She had lived by that alone for the last four years. She mounted Indira and started towards the tracks where the piece of fabric had been found. The tracks indicated by crushed grass and scuff marks in the dirt that it was indeed a massive group that had been through here rather recently. Something told her that if she followed them, she would find Adriel, alive.

He might already be dead. A voice in her head chimed but she ignored it.

She rode for less than twenty minutes when she saw them. There was a faint trace of smoke beyond a hill. It could be anyone, Sawny thought. There was no telling that this apparent small fire would lead her to Adriel. But there were no other signs of him. She had to at least check. If it wasn't him, then she didn't know what she would do. How was she supposed to find someone with no leads? The panic that had been coursing through her veins threatened to overcome her. No, she said to herself. No, she couldn't panic yet.

She rode Indira to the top of a hill before dismounting her and tying her to a small tree. Then, she crept on her stomach, positioning herself so she could just see over it. There was a fire, a small one, and a camp with several tents. Sawny clamped a hand over her mouth to keep from screaming. Because on the outside of the camp was a large tree. And tied to that tree was Adriel.

She counted seven men sitting around the fire and could hear their laughter and talking from where she laid. There could possibly be more in the tents but it was impossible to tell. These men had taken Adriel. He was still alive. If he wasn't, they wouldn't have tied him to a tree. He was alive but he couldn't be in good shape. She needed to get to him as fast as she could.

Sawny was a distance from them, and it was too open for her to sneak up on them on horseback. They would see her from a mile away. She could possibly take on seven men with her bow and arrow, but the problem was she had no idea what she was up against. She didn't know who the men were or how many there were or why they had taken Adriel or what skill set they had with weapons. She inferred they were skilled enough to jump a man from the Wilds, who had extensive training. But multiple men against one, it would always be easy to attack someone. It didn't necessarily mean they were skilled.

One of the most important lessons she had learned from her father, or her adopted one at least, was how to shoot on horseback. He had started teaching her at the age of twelve and she didn't successfully do it until she was fourteen. But it was invaluable. To be able to gallop on horseback while aiming at your enemy could prove to save your life in a battle. Her bow and her quiver were both strapped to her back. She could take them out in an instant, but they would see her coming, if she rode Indira. That was the problem. Who knew what they would do if they saw an unknown masked figure approaching their camp? They may kill Adriel and run away. She couldn't risk that. No, Indira would have to be left behind. She hated to do it. But it was either her or Adriel and at that moment in time, her sole purpose was saving him.

Sawny returned to Indira on the tree and petted her nose. "I'll be back soon," she whispered. Indira snuggled her head into Sawny's chest, not as skittish as she normally was when she was left behind. Maybe Indira had grown to like Adriel and knew he was in danger. Sawny kissed her nose and started towards the fire.

The sun was just beginning to rise above the sea. She could see the blue waves and on any other day, would be enjoying the orange and pink light dancing across it. Instead, she wished it would go away. It was dark, but with those rays, they might see her coming. She had put on a dark cloak to mask her, but it might not be enough. She couldn't afford to make mistakes with this.

She trusted herself. She trusted her instincts. As she pulled out her bow and arrow, she made a promise to Adriel. "I won't let you die," Sawny whispered, hoping he could hear her.

Sawny moved quickly and stealthily towards it, stopping periodically and laying in the grass. If any of the men had seen her, and she disappeared, they might believe it was an illusion, a shadow, their eyes playing tricks on them. She would creep forward on her stomach for a while before rising to her feet and continuing to walk. There were no sentries, which she took as a good sign. A well-trained group would have guards patrolling the perimeter. Maybe she had a shot.

It was taking ages to get closer. She had been trekking for almost thirty minutes and yet, the fire looked like a distance. But as Sawny looked back at Tenir and the sea, they were farther away. She could still see the outline of Indira by the tree. She had made progress but not enough. Every minute was a minute they could've killed Adriel.

She was surprised Jare hadn't sent his men.

She had known him since her early days as an investigator. Jare was a person drawn to sadness, and the moment he had met Sawny, he took her under his wing. At the time, Sawny was okay with it but he wasn't a normal person. He, like her, had lost most of his family and his life had become his job. Smuggling and the records room. Jare was a storyteller. He was attracted to anyone and everyone who had a story, one he could write down and add to his collection. Jare was extremely Orinthian. Almost too much because his bias against people of the Wilds was strong. Yet Sawny thought they were friends. She thought their friendship would outweigh his hatred of the Wilds.

But as she walked towards the fire alone, she guessed it wasn't enough. She wouldn't tell Jare about the story of her real father. He would be interested, but for the wrong reasons. A story about young love that turned into disaster and resulted in a love child would be addicting to Jare. He would want to see the letter, to copy it, turn it into a story and keep it in his records room. No, she wasn't sure she would share the story with anyone. She wasn't even sure how she felt about it. Her confusion about her past, her real father, and the lies her mother had been telling her whole life had taken a backseat. All she needed to focus on was Adriel.

She was drawing closer to the fire, and she narrowed her eyes to see Adriel better.

Sawny was still far away so she couldn't see him clearly, but he was alive.

The several men who took him were sitting around the giant bonfire, laughing. They were drinking out of bottles and cooking something. They were speaking Orinthian, that much she could tell. It was hard to hear from where she was at what they were saying, but she recognized words here and there. She was back on her stomach, slowly crawling closer, her bow and arrows remaining on her back.

Adriel himself was tied to a tree, sitting down. He was tied extremely tight, she could tell from here, and knew right away he had probably tried to escape more than once. If he was anything, he was a fighter. There were no injuries as far as she could tell.

Why had these Orinthians taken him? Who were they?

It didn't matter at this point. They were a threat to Adriel. They had taken him for some reason and were going to hurt him.

It was impossible to fight off the seven men by herself. Even if she began to shoot from afar, they would eventually realize it and either kill her or Adriel before she could get to them. No, an attack would never work. She was skilled but she wasn't a one-woman army.

She would have to sneak him out. It was the only way.

Slowly, Sawny retreated and began to circle around so that Adriel would be in front of her. The men continued to laugh and drink, not noticing the Auntican crawling through the grass outside of their fire. Not a single one of them had their eyes on Adriel. He was far enough away from them that she might be able to sneak him away without them noticing. They would have to remain distracted though. She prayed to the gods that they would.

She took a deep breath, returning her bow to her back, and began to crawl towards the tree that he was tied to. She could feel the heat coming off the fire as they got closer. It almost made her more confident. No one in their right mind would build a fire so large, without knowing how much attention it would attract. They had to be drunk or just plain stupid. She hoped it was both the former and the latter. It would make her job much easier.

She approached the tree gradually, stopping every minute or so to see what the men would do. Finally, only a foot or so away from the tree, she pulled out the small hunting dagger and observed what was in front of her.

Adriel was tied to the tree with so much rope she was surprised he hadn't suffocated from it. She could see the blood dripping through it, and she flinched. They had hurt him. She was able to see it from afar but up close it was entirely different. He was wounded but she didn't have time to observe how bad. She just had to free him and get him out of here. He was clearly unconscious; she could even tell from behind him. His head was slumped against the tree.

An unconscious man who probably weighed twice as much as she. A group of drunk Orinthians only feet from her, who had beaten up a warrior from the Wilds, and it was up to her to save him.

Gods, the odds were stacked against her.

Sawny began to cut the rope from behind. There was so much of it, wrapped around and around the tree. They had tied him with his arms pressed against his body, so she didn't have to worry about possibly cutting his arms or hands. The rope was thick and coarse and soaked in his blood. She held her breath as she cut. The first priority was freeing him and getting him out of here. And then, she would immediately have to deal with his wounds. She wasn't sure the exact manner of them yet but from the amount of blood covering these ropes, she knew they were bad.

Each rope took a minute or more to cut through. She cursed inwardly. She should've brought something better to cut with. The small dagger was not doing the trick. Every so often, she looked up to ensure that the men hadn't noticed yet. They continued to drink, ignoring the prisoner they had tied to the tree. It disgusted her. This was a human being and what they had done to him was evil.

She was halfway done when the cold blade of a dagger pressed up against her throat from behind.

Sawny hadn't even heard anyone. She had been so focused on cutting him loose, getting this man from the Wilds out of this situation without dying, that she had completely lost all of her senses to outside dangers.

"Well, well, well, what do we have here?" It was a man's voice, raspy and deep, and she felt every single bone in her body freeze in fear. No. This couldn't be happening. She had been so close to cutting him free. It wasn't possible that she herself was about to be captured.

"Drop the dagger and stand up."

Her body had begun to shake as her fingers released the dagger. With the blade still pressed to her throat, she managed to stand. Halfway. The ropes had already started falling off the tree. She had been so close but now they were probably both going to die.

"Walk," the voice commanded, the blade shifting from her neck to her back. She knew several maneuvers to get out of this. Her father had trained her extensively. As she was about to try one, the voice said, "If you try anything, I will not hesitate to kill the man."

Sawny closed her eyes and took a step. It was done. She was done. She had tried and she had failed. She took another step and was shoved towards the men sitting around the fireplace.

All their heads snapped up, eyes widened, faces of shock and surprise. She stumbled and fell onto the ground a little ways from them as the man who had pushed her spoke. "What's this, boys? I go to take a piss and this little rat tries to free our prisoner. And none of you even saw her. Shame, shame. She would've freed the man who killed our boys, and you would have just let her. Shame. It was a good thing I took that piss now, wasn't it?"

There was mostly laughter from them as Sawny looked up and saw that Adriel was now partly conscious. The fear disappeared and was replaced by worry instead.

Adriel...he was not in good shape. Her eyes met his and she saw something in them that she had never seen before. Resignation. She could see why. He had no shirt on, and his chest was covered in blood, from what she assumed was a flogging. There was a piece of cloth stuffed in his mouth to prevent him from talking. One of his eyes was swollen shut and a long, bleeding scar ran down the side of his face, still dripping. His arms were covered in cuts and bruises of all shapes and sizes. His pants were still intact but barely. Through the rips, she could see much the same, bruises and cuts. How were they able to do this in the hours that she had been searching for him in the city?

They had tortured him. Her Adriel. They had beaten him and whipped him and cut him and tortured him.

She was numb.

"Who are you?" the Orinthian demanded, the obvious leader. He was a younger man, with dirty blonde stringy long hair. He didn't wear a soldier's uniform but something about his manner made Sawny wonder if he had also deserted.

"Let him go," was all Sawny replied, getting to her feet. She didn't have her dagger anymore. But she still had the bow. If she drew it quickly enough, she could take out the man who had caught her and the man closest to Adriel. It would be impossible to take out eight men all at once, but she had to try. She wouldn't give up and let them both die.

The man smiled, an evil, wicked smile with not all of his teeth. "Do the honors, Grayson," he said.

The man leaning against the tree suddenly punched Adriel in the side of the face, hard enough to make him groan, a whimper that hurt Sawny to her core. She cried out, reaching towards Adriel, but couldn't get closer to him.

"Don't talk to me that way, bitch," the man snapped at Sawny, walking towards Adriel. "Let's try this again. And if you give me the wrong answer, Grayson will hit him harder next time. Now, you've snuck all the way out here to free this Wilds bastard, so I assume he's important to you. He killed three of our men. Three of them and we punished him for it. I would hate to hurt him even more than we already have-" he paused to pat Adriel's head, a movement that caused him to wince, "-so give me the right answer and we'll be okay."

Sawny choked through clenched teeth, "My name is Sawny."

The leader walked towards her, taking small and lazy steps with his hands in his pockets. "Sawny who?"

"Lois. Sawny Lois."

He pondered on this, then shook his head. "It doesn't sound Wilds. But you don't sound Orinthian either. Where are you from?"

"I'm Auntican," she didn't hesitate to say, keeping an eye on Adriel and the man who had the knife next to his throat. Adriel watched her, trying to say something with his eyes, probably to run, but she wasn't going to leave him.

There was a low chuckle throughout the remaining men as they all glanced at one another. The leader turned back to her. "Auntican, you say?"

Sawny nodded, slowly starting to feel something blossom in her chest. It was anger, so deep and powerful that she could almost hear it.

"And this man. From the Wilds. He's your lover?"

Sawny shook her head. "He's my friend," she growled, "and if you don't let him go, I swear I will kill every single one of you."

They laughed out loud at this, and she felt the anger grow slightly more in her chest. She clenched and unclenched her fists. She didn't know how she would get out of this one. Her bow was on her back but the moment she went for it, the man would slit Adriel's throat. He was already in such bad shape that another blow to the head would kill him if she gave a wrong answer. She was stuck and she would do anything to save him, and they were eight Orinthian men. She knew where this was going.

The man howled, "She has a temper, this one." He stepped so he was face to face with her, running one finger down her cheek. "I like it though, it's okay," he whispered.

Sawny shuddered but didn't touch him as he moved his hand and put it on her shoulder.

"Well, you see, sweetheart. Me and my friends here. We HATE people from the Wilds. And we were just coming out of a bar when we saw YOUR friend talking to an Innkeeper about getting a room. His fake Orinthian accent was terrible, and it was clear to us he was from the Wilds. And what business does a bastard from the Wilds have in Orinth. We kicked them out of here twenty years ago, sweetie. Didn't we? Auntica helped too, remember? So, we decided to have a little fun, a little brawl with the man. And what did he do? He killed three of our men. Took his sword and stabbed them with it. Three of our own men. We managed to knock him out and get him out here for a little-" He pondered it for a moment, "-payback. And we had a little fun while we did it."

The anger in her felt as if it were about to explode. They didn't know Adriel, then. They were a group of random Orinthians who had tried to start a fight with Adriel. He had defended himself and they had punished him for it, by beating the living shit out of him. Her Adriel. They were going to kill Sawny, she knew that much. After they had used her, they would kill her in front of Adriel and then kill him.

"Bastards," Sawny whispered, feeling the tears drip down her face as the man continued to stroke her shoulders.

"Oh no. No, no, no, no, no Sawny, my dear. All of us are Orinthians. Purebloods. The bastards are anyone from the Wilds."

"I hate you all," she whispered.

"What was that?"

"I HATE YOU!" she screamed at him, before punching him in the face. The leader fell to the ground with a yell as soon as she made contact.

Everything seemed to slow down. The man sat up, eyes glowing with anger, holding where she had struck him with one hand. He was bleeding, she could see, the blood dripping down his face. Then, he said two words that ended it all.

"Kill him."

The anger exploded within her.

She wanted him, needed him to feel pain. The pain that he had put Adriel through and something in her snapped. She closed her eyes and her hand shot out, almost instinctively.

He started screaming.

She had never felt like this before.

He was foaming at the mouth, quivering and shaking as he screamed, the anger pouring out of her faster than she could control. His screams echoed across the field before he froze, collapsed, and was dead.

Sawny threw her head back, letting the anger course through her as the two men closest to Adriel began screaming just as loud.

All the anger she had been carrying with her for ages seemed to rise to the surface in a matter of seconds. Anger at the people who murdered her parents. Anger at her parents for leaving her. Anger at her mother for telling her lies. Anger at the war, anger at her king, anger at the forest witch for using her. The rage boiled through her, and she felt as if she weren't even a person anymore.

The two men crumbled.

The remaining men were gone when she opened her eyes. The fire was still roaring, and three corpses now lay on the ground. From where she had killed them.

With her mind.

Sawny fell onto her knees. She had just killed them with her mind. She could still feel the power coursing through her, wanting more, wanting to consume the five men who she could still see, running. Wobbling, she got to her feet and let it, extending a shaking hand towards them. She watched as one of them stopped, fell to his knees, and shook. She could hear his screams from where she was, though he had already gained so much distance. The power consumed him faster than the others and she felt the rush once again.

It caught up to the others before they had a chance to even breathe. She lifted both of her hands this time. The power twisted around their bodies, toying with them, playing with them, before diving in and destroying them. This time, there were no screams. They just fell and laid there, dead.

She had never felt this way before. But it felt so right.

Sawny looked around for another Orinthian to kill, but saw only a man, tied to a tree, with one eye swollen shut.

Adriel.

She got to her feet and stumbled towards him, having a hard time controlling her body with the rush of power. It wanted more. It wanted to kill the man in front of her. It wanted her to lift her hands once again and allow it to finish him.

But no, it was Adriel, and he was hurt, and she had to save him because he was all she had left.

She collapsed to her knees in front of him, not meeting his eyes, drawing her knife. She started to cut the rope, being careful not to hurt him anymore. Already, her hands were covered in his blood and he was breathing too softly. The rope fell to the ground and he slumped into her arms.

"I've got to get you help," Sawny said to him, trying to hold him off the ground but it was hard. He was heavy and couldn't hold himself up whatsoever. "We need to find a healer in Tenir-"

"No!" Adriel cried through clenched teeth. "We're not going back there," he whispered, the pain apparent in his voice.

"I don't know how to help you," Sawny said, panicked. "We have to find someone who can or you're going to lose too much blood."

"I'm fine," Adriel insisted. "The wounds are mostly closed."

"Adriel, you are the farthest thing from fine." Sawny ripped the bottom of her shirt off and gently, started to dab the blood away from his chest, where the biggest cuts were. He winced and swore loudly in his language but didn't stop her.

"Sawny!" a voice yelled from behind them.

She whipped around to see Jare on horseback, accompanied by ten or so other men. He jumped off and ran towards where they were leaning on the tree.

"He's lost a lot of blood," Sawny told Jare, trying to keep her voice steady but wanting to panic. Adriel might die and she just killed a group of men with her mind.

"Ashar!" Jare shouted at his men. One of them jumped off the horse and came running towards them. Sawny's vision was starting to falter, and she could almost see three of him, with a large satchel. He knelt beside him and asked Sawny to move aside but she couldn't control her body anymore. The rush was still there but it was choking her.

"Sawny?" Jare asked hesitantly. "You have to move away from him so Ashar can start cleaning the blood away. He's a healer, you can trust him."

She had always felt that she had her anger under control but right now it was controlling her. Or was it her anger? It was moving beneath her skin, aching for more, making her dizzy. She could barely crawl away from Adriel as she moved to make room for the healer. She watched as he knelt by her companion, pulled a cloth out of his bag, and started mopping the blood. Adriel was moaning softly, drifting in and out of consciousness. But she couldn't focus on him. All she could see, hear, feel was the power that had come to life in her.

She had killed men with her mind. What was happening to her?

She stumbled a few steps away from the group that was now surrounding Adriel and collapsed. She stared up at the sky, panting, trying to control whatever it was that was taking over her body.

She didn't see Jare approach but felt as he helped her to sit up and lean against him.

"Are you okay?" he asked her. "Are you hurt?"

She managed to shake her head. "No. I'm fine."

Jare looked around at the scene, at the bodies that lay, without any signs of blood or wounds or anything. They were dead, with no signs of weapons. The fire was roaring and most of Jare's men sat on their horses, shocked by all they saw.

"What happened, Sawny? I tried to find you as quick as I could after you left, and I tracked the man as well. It wasn't until dawn we saw the fire. We came as quick as we could, but I think you took care of it."

Her head was still spinning but she tried to explain. "It was a group of Orinthians, drunk. They picked a fight with Adriel, just because he was from the Wilds. He killed three of their men in self-defense. They struck him down and took him out here and beat him before I arrived. They were just sitting around drinking. I tried to free Adriel without them seeing but one of them discovered me."

Jare's eyes fell onto the number of bodies that laid scattered around. "How many were there?"

"A lot."

"You killed them all with the bow, then?"

Sawny shook her head, tears starting to run down her face. "I don't want to talk right now, Jare. Please, I'm so tired."

He said nothing but put an arm around her shoulders. She let her head fall onto his and she closed her eyes.

The shadow. She had read about it all only hours ago. A power that came from behind the wall, one that could be used to kill, like the person in the caves had used. What other explanation was there? How else could she fathom the immense power she had just used to take out the men who were holding Adriel captive?

She had no way to tell, no way to confirm or deny this theory. She could ask Jare but then she would have to explain to him how she devoured the lives of the men without even thinking about it. She could've let the ones running go free, but she didn't. Her power followed them and consumed them without any regrets. How could she explain that to Jare and expect him to look at her in the same way?

He would be curious, she knew that. Jare would let her have a few minutes to breathe and then he would be begging her for the story. A nineteen-year- old Auntican killing several men to save her client, who happened to be a man from the Wilds. Jare had probably guessed by now that the nature of their relationship was no longer strictly about business. It would be too much for him to just let go. He needed the story and part of that story included what she had just done.

Sawny tried not to think about it as she gently settled into a subconscious state on Jare's shoulder. She couldn't worry about what just happened until they were out of danger. She only had to be concerned with Adriel's well-being.

That's all that mattered to her, now. Forget everything else, just make Adriel be okay.

Sawny wasn't sure at what point she fell asleep, with everything running circles through her brain. But somehow, the power had exhausted her. She awoke with Jare shaking her shoulders, attempting to rouse her.

She was on the ground now, her head on someone's bag, covered in a burlap blanket. The sun was fully risen. They had let her sleep for hours, thank the gods. She needed it. She also saw that most of the men had left, leaving only Jare, a guard, and the healer, attending to Adriel. Indira and Adriel's horse had also arrived at the scene somehow, tied to another tree, munching on grass contently.

"He's awake and he wants to see you," Jare told her, his eyes searching hers with desperate curiosity.

The bodies were all gone, and the fire had been put out. Sawny was unsure of where they had been taken but she felt eternally grateful she didn't have to see them again.

She could still feel it. The power that was within her. She could feel its mass and its hunger. She knew if she dipped into it, it would respond in kind. If she wanted right now, she could kill someone without ever having to touch her weapon. The thought of it terrified her but at the same time reassured her.

No one would touch Adriel as long as she was around.

Jare helped her to her feet.

Adriel leaned up against the same tree. His shirt was off, and his entire torso wrapped in bandages. His forearms also had them. There was dressing strapped to his swollen eye and the other eye stared at Sawny as she approached him.

She knelt down in front of him. "You look awful," she said.

Despite the injuries, the ripped clothing, the dirt and the grime and the blood, Adriel smiled at her, the same beautiful smile that always managed to crawl under her skin. "Thank you," he replied.

She sat down in front of him, slowly grasping one of his hands in her own. He squeezed her hand, in reassurance or something, she didn't know.

"How are you feeling?" she asked.

"I've had better days than this one."

"I'm sorry, Adriel," she said, dropping her hand from his.

He picked it back up again. "What do you have to be sorry for?"

She shook her head. "I shouldn't have let you be in the city alone."

"Sawny, I'm not a child. I'm a grown man, and you didn't do anything wrong. I was just in the wrong place at the wrong time. You, on the contrary, saved my life."

"I was the reason you were in trouble in the first place."

"Hey," Adriel said, softly gripping her chin and forcing her to meet his eyes. "I'm the one who came to you. I'm the one who's paying you. I'm the reason I was in trouble. You're the reason I'm still alive. And speaking of that, I think you have a little explaining to do."

Sawny tried to look away but she couldn't. "I-Adriel-"

Adriel dropped his hand and let it rest on her knee. "Not now, if you're not ready. But there were eleven men who captured me. I killed three of them, and eight took me out here and did this to me. Now, eight of them are dead. No wounds, no blood, no weapons anywhere. Which begs the question: how did they die?"

Sawny glanced back at Jare, who was standing just far enough to give them privacy, but close enough to hear their conversation. She looked back to Adriel. "It was poison."

It was an obvious lie. Adriel knew it and anyone with half of a brain knew it, but she prayed to the gods Jare believed it. "I had darts that were laced with poison. Once I got close enough, I shot them, and they died immediately. I'm not surprised it didn't leave a wound. They're very small and almost impossible to see."

Adriel's eyes were narrowed but he played along. "I'm lucky you're such a good mark, Sawny Lois."

She nodded slowly. "I guess you are."

"I mean eight men with your bow and the poison darts is extremely impressive."

"Do you remember anything?" Sawny asked him, suddenly very very frightened. How would Adriel react upon finding out that she had some sort of powers. In fact, she had the same powers that most likely had killed his brother. It made sense. Seven bodies found with no wounds, dead, killed with some sort of power. She had just killed eight, with no wounds. It had to be the same thing. What if Adriel hated her for it? What if he ran away and cast her out of his life?

"I was going back to the library. I had just gotten into the alley, leading my horse by the reins. I remember them coming up to me, clearly drunk. They were aggressive, shouting out slurs and such. Not unusual but then they started getting physical. I pulled out my sword and I told them to back off. They didn't. One charged with his fists and I stabbed him. And then the two closest to me. I was about to run, go as fast as I could away because even I can't take out eight men on my own. Something hit me in the back of the head. Everything went black."

"When I woke up, I remember this huge fire in front of me. I stared at it the whole time the leader flogged me. It was all hazy after that." He held up his arms, where the cuts and the bruises were. "I think these are from being dragged here and tied up. The black eye is from when one of them punched me in the face. I can't remember you showing up. I don't remember anything until I woke up and one of Jare's healers was helping me."

As if on cue, Jare approached them. "I talked to my healer. You're going to be okay, Adriel. Just got to switch the bandages every couple of days. You lost a lot of blood so next time you get the chance, eat a lot."

Adriel nodded. "Thank you. I wish I had the words to express what this means to me, you helping me and all."

Jare gave a small smile. "Yeah, well. If you would've told me a few days ago that I helped a Wildsman, I don't think I would've believed you."

Adriel chuckled. "It's been a strange past couple of hours."

Sawny couldn't agree more with that. The action and excitement had distracted her from one revelation to another. She knew the name of her real father and her mother had lied about her identity. She also possessed an evil power, the same one that killed Adriel's brother, and most likely came from behind the Shadow Wall. Great. Adriel was right. Strange past couple of hours. "You're welcome to come back with us to the library. We can give you a room to recuperate and recover in, meals and all," Jare offered.

Sawny opened her mouth to speak but Adriel shook his head. "I'm not going back into Tenir anytime soon," he said quietly.

Jare frowned and reached a hand towards him. Adriel took it as Jare pulled him to his feet. Adriel grunted softly, shifting so the pain wouldn't be as bad from the wounds. "I'm sorry for what happened to you here, Adriel. I'm ashamed that these were my countrymen who did this. I hope my men and I were able to help in some way."

Adriel nodded. "You did. Thank you."

Jare returned the nod and said, "We have to get back to the library. There's some business going on today I can't miss. Did you get everything you need, Sawny?"

Sawny replied, "I think I did. All of my notes are in Indira's bag anyways."

"Where are you two going next?"

Adriel looked at Sawny. "Well?"

Sawny looked back at him. "I don't think you should be going anywhere," she said, straightforwardly.

He was clearly taken aback. "What do you mean? I'm fine, I told you."

"You almost died last night, Adriel."

He opened his mouth to protest but Jare stepped in, "I left a lot of gear on Indira for you. Replenished your food and supplies, as well as some extra money. You can pay me back later. And I found a sword in the alley, covered in blood. I assumed it was Adriel's so I left it with his horse."

Sawny stood up and embraced her old friend. "Thank you," she whispered into his ear, "for everything."

He patted her on the top of her head and rustled her hair. "You're welcome." He pulled back and said quietly, "You owe me the truth. Next time I see you."

Sawny nodded. "I can do that."

Jare turned away from her and towards Adriel. "It was great to meet you and I hope you start healing soon." He extended a hand towards him, which Adriel shook.

With that Jare, his guard and healer, jumped back onto their horses. The other two men started galloping back towards Tenir as Jare turned around one last time. "Be careful out there. There's a war going on and neither of you want to be caught in the crossfire."

Sawny nodded and waved as he turned around, following his men. When they were a long distance away, she turned back to Adriel, who was staring at her.

"What did you mean when you said I shouldn't be going anywhere?" he asked her. For the first time since she had met him, she could detect traces of anger in his voice.

"Adriel, it's common sense. You're wounded. You don't need to be galloping off with me and putting your life at risk again. You almost died."

Adriel shook his head. "That's not your choice to make, Sawny. I'm a warrior from the Wilds. I can make my own choices."

Sawny snorted, "Well, you didn't make the best choices last night, did you?" She regretted saying it almost instantaneously. What had happened had not been his fault. It was the fault of the hatred that had existed between Orinthians and people of the Wilds for decades. But she was angry with him. Angry with herself. Angry at everything and the words just slipped out.

His face darkened. "I get it. You saved my life. And I'm grateful, Sawny, I really am. But I started this journey with you and I'm going to finish it. You have to tell me what you found out in Tenir and what our next move is, all of it."

"No," was all she replied.

He looked as if she had slapped him. "What do you mean 'no'?" he asked quietly.

"I'm not going to tell you what I found out because if I do, you'll follow me to where I'm going next. And that will put your life in danger. So, no."

Adriel yelled something in his language as Sawny turned to walk towards Indira. "What will you have me do then, Sawny? Go back to the Wilds? Without fulfilling the oath and get exiled for the rest of my life? Is that much safer than me being in Orinth?"

"You'll take your horse, and you'll go back to the Wilds. You'll stay away from major towns and cities. Once I find the answers, I'll give them to you, and you'll give me the money. Then you'll never have to see me again. It's best for the both of us."

"Is that what you want?"

She didn't respond, her heart pounding.

"How did you kill those men, Sawny?" he asked her.

She stopped.

"It wasn't poison darts. It wasn't with your bow or arrows or dagger. There were eight of them. How did they die?" She turned around. He was bracing the tree for support and had taken the gauze off his face. He stared at her, shoulders moving up and down with his panting.

"I—I-" Sawny stuttered, trying to find the words to tell him but struggling.

"Neither of us should be alive right now," he said, all anger in his voice gone. "Eight against two. Not even. Eight drunk Orinthian men against one Auntican girl. Granted, a stellar shot with a bow and arrow, but still. How did you walk away alive?"

"I shouldn't be."

"But you are."

"Aren't you glad?"

"Of course I'm glad. Tell me why."

"After I tell you, it'll make you want to leave without me forcing you too."

"Then I guess neither of us will have to fight about it."

Sawny fell to her knees, overtaken by the sudden waves of emotion that flooded her. It was too much. "I killed them with my mind!" she screamed at him. "I lifted my hands and I killed them with my mind. I didn't have to; I could've let them go but I didn't because they didn't deserve to live after what they put you through. I killed them with the same power I think someone used to kill your brother all those years ago. Yes, I have it and I didn't know until I saw you bloody and beaten to death, tied to a tree and I felt so angry, livid that the one person that I still care about in this gods damned world was about to die. I thought that and then I exploded, and I felt a power unlike anything in this world and I used it to kill eight men. And you know what? I don't even regret killing them. I don't regret it at all. The only thing I regret is that I didn't get to them fast enough to spare you the pain. You're leaving, Adriel. You can't be around me anymore because there's a part of me that's so dark that I don't regret sucking the souls from eight men. I can't be responsible for letting you die and if anyone even tried to touch you again, I would kill them. I wouldn't even have to think about it, I would kill them. That's why you have to leave," she choked on a sob and finished, breathing heavily, staring at the ground. She couldn't look him in the eyes.

He was shocked into silence.

It all made sense, though. Ever since her parents had died, there had been a darkness there. It was partly from the grief of it. But it never left. It felt at place. She flourished in the darkness and now she knew why. The darkness was a part of her soul. It always had been.

Her parents had been killed by men who were after her real father. Her real father was a man named Auden Frae.

Somehow, she had the power of the shadow. Somehow, it didn't scare her as much as it should've.

She buried her head into her hands, trying to fade away from the world. It had been only her and then Adriel had snuck into her world and her heart and now he was going to leave too because how couldn't he, after hearing that? How couldn't your first reaction be to run, run as far away as you can because the girl who you thought was normal has a part of the demon world within her.

He fell to his knees in front of her. She looked up at him.

There were tears in his eyes as he picked up her hands and grasped them in his own. "You know how Zelos was killed?" he managed to say, his whole entire body starting to tremble.

Sawny nodded. "Yes."

"And you have the same power that he was killed with?"

Sawny closed her eyes. "Yes."

She waited for him to run and leave and get as far away as possible but still, his hands remained in hers.

"Sawny," he whispered, her name a breath on his lips.

"Yes?" she asked, her voice cracking.

"I'm not going to leave you."

She opened her eyes and stared into his. They were puffy and bloodshot and the one was still swollen, but he looked at her with an intensity that made her want to hide.

"Why?"

"Because my brother is gone. He's dead. He was killed for trying to destroy Orinth, and maybe rightly so. For most of my life I've had to cope with the consequences of his actions. He destroyed my family and he destroyed me. Gods, if I don't kill his killer, I'll get exiled from my home. Where will I go? Orinth? I just had a dozen men beat me to death. I have nothing anymore, Sawny."

"I'm so sorry," she breathed.

Adriel let his forehead fall onto hers. "Don't you dare apologize, Sawny Lois. I don't care who you are. I don't care what powers you do or don't have. I don't care that you could kill me with your thoughts if you wanted to. I don't care about any of it. I'm not going to leave you. So much shit has happened to us on this journey and somehow, we've made it through. There's no way I'm going to leave you."

She was shaking. "Promise me," she whispered. "Promise me you aren't going to leave me." After all the reason she wanted to send him away was because her fear he would run away from her and her darkness. If she sent him away, she wouldn't have to face that.

Adriel gently cupped her face in his hands. "I promise."

"Adriel, I can feel it in me right now. I can feel it waiting and wanting. It's like this giant ocean of anger that I can wield whenever I want. There's no bottom to it. When I killed those men, I looked up at you and it wanted to kill you too. I had to stop it and realize who you were but even then, a part of me wanted to."

Adriel said nothing and then nudged her playfully. "I tell you I won't leave you and then you tell me how you wanted to kill me."

Sawny, despite herself, laughed. "I'm just warning you ahead of time."

"You stopped yourself, didn't you?"

"Yes, I did."

"Did you stop yourself from killing the other men?"

She bit her lip, hard enough to draw blood. "No. I didn't. But they deserved it."

"I'm not saying they didn't. But you didn't kill me. Somehow, you were able to hold back. I'm not worried about you killing me."

Sawny leaned back, releasing his hands and standing up. "Just make sure not to test me," she warned him.

He smiled at her. "I doubt you having a magical soul sucking power would put me in any more danger than you with your bow."

She returned his smile. "That's true."

He stood up alongside her and grabbed her hand, wrapping his arms around her waist and pulling her close, close enough for his lips to meet hers, but they didn't. "Nothing has changed, Sawny. Okay? You're the same girl I threatened with a crossbow a couple weeks ago."

Sawny snorted. "You had to bring that up, did you? I still don't understand why you did that." But she looped her arms around his waist and pulled him closer, closing the space between their bodies.

He laughed. "We do things different in the Wilds, what can I tell you?"

"Speaking of being the same girl, there's more about me you need to know other than the fact I can-you know."

"I get it. What else is there?"

She took a deep breath. "I know who my real father is."

Adriel looked taken aback. He pulled his face away from hers, much to her dismay. "How?"

Sawny looked around. They were still in the field, still in the place where all of the death had happened, where Adriel had gotten hurt and where she had exploded in anger. She wanted to get out of here. There was a bad feeling from it. Plus, Adriel needed to rest.

She pointed the opposite direction of Tenir. "There's a village that way. Twenty or so miles. It's small but I know there's an inn there. I'll get us a room and we're going to spend the next few days resting."

Adriel opened his mouth to protest but Sawny covered it with her hand. "No arguments. You're hurt and you need to rest. I feel like my brain is about to explode if I don't get some more sleep. We have to get moving. Who knows what other people could come after us in Tenir. I'm not sure if the secret that a nineteen-year-old Auntican girl killed eight men by herself will stay secret for long."

Begrudgingly, Adriel nodded. "You're right."

She grinned at him. "Aren't I always?"

He rolled his eyes but didn't let go of her. "Not always. But right now, you are."

"Let's get to the inn and then I'll tell you everything. Not just about me."

"What do you mean?"

"I know who murdered your brother. I know where to find him. And I'm going to help you kill him."

Acknowledgments

First, I would like to thank my family for supporting me throughout this entire process. Thank you to my dad for helping me get this dream off the ground. Thank you LeMay and Rem for being the first people to ever read and like my work. Thank you, Savannah and Mom, for always being there for me.

I would like to thank my group of editors who gave up a lot of their time to help me. Thank you to Grandma Sullivan, Lorelei Bond, Meghan Roznowski, Brooke Stevens, and Tami Estes.

Thank you also to Rose Cruz for helping me out with illustration ideas and being such an amazing help.

Thank you to all of the people in my life who inspired me to write.

Finally, thank you, reader, for giving this book a try. If you liked it, please consider leaving a positive review on Amazon or tell me all about it at falltodarknessseries@gmail.com

Please check out our website falltodarkness.com for updates on upcoming books, release dates, merchandise, and more!

The True King

Book #2 of the Fall to Darkness Series

Coming 2022…

About the Author

Summer Sullivan is a college student who grew up in rural Northern Michigan and attended a small high school. She enjoys biking, golfing, writing, and spending time with friends and family. Currently, Summer spends her time between her hometown and Northern Florida, working and writing as much as she can.

THE LAST HEIR

Book 1 of Fall to Darkness

to Gabby -
enjoy the book!

Summer Sullivan

SUMMER SULLIVAN

SUMMER SULLIVAN
Published by AuSable Publishing
Ausablepublishing.com

Printed in the United States of America
First Printing 2021
First Edition 2021

ISBN: 978-1-7373611-1-4

10 9 8 7 6 5 4 3 2 1